Mister Lawson – Book 2
Mister Dixon – Book 3
Mister Stark – Book 4
Mister Lane – Book 5
Mister Marshal – Book 6
Mister Steel – Book 7
Mister Reed – Book 8
Mister Stitch – Book 9
Mister Lyric – Book 10
Mister Riggs – Book 11

BREANNE BERGIE

Editing: EJL Editing

ONE

New Beginning

"He'll make it on time," I whispered to myself.

I spun the shiny silver-gold band on my ring finger and waited for my husband to arrive. I repeated the words in my head and tried to remain calm. My hand clenched my purse strap draped over my shoulder and my luggage bag was beside my feet. He'd be here on time. He promised me. We made a promise to each other.

This vacation was our only chance. We lastly hoped to make this work. Our marriage needed this to survive.

So where was he?

Maybe he got held up with airport security and he was having a hard time. He was always unorganized, and that was one of our problems. I stayed organized and arrived on time. But he was the complete opposite.

I got through airport security with no issue, but a man behind me had a problem. He kept walking through the X-ray machine and the device made a loud sound. The man was annoyed and would throw his hands up in the air in defeat. He hadn't followed the rules and removed all the belongings he needed to in order to pass. I brushed it off as not my problem, but now it could be.

My husband wasn't here, and I looked through the crowd of people. There were families gathered with their children and it made me want what they had. Couples held hands or huddled close and waited to board their flight.

Then there were people like me, alone and on their cellphones or checking the time. But they didn't have a marriage looming over their heads.

I did.

I had so much to lose. My marriage was falling apart. I had to make it work, and that's why I was here.

But where was James?

I sighed and peered out at the airplanes on the tarmac to clear my head. The white planes with their flight company plastered on the sides. Different colors of blue, pink, and orange text. Some got ready for takeoff, and others packed with luggage. Cleaned for the next round of passengers to take them where they needed to travel.

It was a bright and sunny day. Perfect for air travel and a smooth takeoff. One I eagerly waited to do.

I tore my eyes from the tarmac and gazed up at the time on the screen. Bright numbers caught my attention, and I breathed some relief. He wasn't late. It was half past ten. James still had twenty minutes until we boarded our flight for Hawaii.

He'd be here.

But what if my husband didn't make it?

I shook my head and brushed off the negative. I had to remain positive and keep a level head. Falling apart wasn't an option. My marriage depended on it.

I spun around, but my leg hit my luggage and it fell to the ground with a loud thud. The sound echoed through the airport and I blushed with embarrassment. I hadn't checked in my bag and now I regret it. I wanted to wait for my husband, and we could check our bags together. We were flying together, after all. My choice only made sense.

Now the decision made little sense. Because James wasn't here. I was alone with a crowd of people looking in my direction because of my own mistakes.

"Here..." a husky voice said, "Let me help you with that."

A pleasantly dressed man stepped out of the crowd with a dashingly handsome smile on his face. He wore ripped blue jeans and a black shirt. He bent down to retrieve my fallen luggage, and I couldn't help but admire his hand. The way he gripped the luggage handle and veins popped out of the skin. They travelled up his forearm and got lost underneath his shirt.

He stood up and his smile changed into a half smirk. One that was way too good on him. His brown hair fell in his face, and he brushed it away to reveal eyes that took my breath away. A pure blue gaze shone back at me with tease and my heart hammered in my chest.

He held the luggage handle and breathed, "I believe this is yours."

"Thank you," I sighed out in a whisper.

This man was gorgeous.

But I had to quit my ogle of this stranger who made me forget about my husband for a moment.

"Are you lost, darling?" he asked as he raised an eyebrow and a strand of hair fell above of it.

I scrunched up my face. "Um, no, I'm just looking for..."

And a female voice boomed over the speaker, "Flight 310 for Hawaii will take the last call for baggage check-in."

I blinked several times and glanced over at the flight desk. The luggage claim was too soon. James still wasn't here. I needed more time. We needed more time.

I gazed down at my luggage in the stranger's hand and up into his curious blue eyes. They sparkled when the hues hit the light and butterflies flew inside my stomach, but I shooed them away. I grabbed the handle from his grasp and our fingers brushed. An electric current sparked between us and abruptly made me pull back.

"Are you okay?" he asked as he brushed the hair from his eyes and his gaze lingered on my face.

"I'm fine, but I need to check-in my luggage." I smiled with reassurance, but my stomach was a mess.

A giant disarray of tension, uncertainty, and attraction. All of which I shouldn't have felt at this moment. I should be happy and ready to board a flight with my husband. Instead, here I was lusting after some stranger because my husband wasn't here.

He looked down at my bulky luggage and nodded towards it. "Hopefully, your bag passes the weight check."

I wrinkled my nose. "Why do you say that?"

"Because you packed your suitcase tight, and it was pretty loud when it fell," he replied with a small smile. "I'd hate to see you not make your flight, darling."

"Well, I appreciate the concern, but I'll be fine," I convinced him and tried to do the same for myself. "Everything will all work out and thank you for your help."

"Anytime, darling." He nodded with a small wave. "I'll see you on the flight."

I simply smiled and turned my back towards him, but I could sense his eyes on my backside. The burn from them lingered there until I got to the flight desk and presented my passport to the attendant. She took it with a smile and typed something on her desktop screen. I watched and glanced around the airport.

There was still no sign of James.

"All right, ma'am, I will take your luggage," she said, and I handed her the handle. She struggled with it slightly and placed it on the scale. Her smile turned into a frown, and she shook her head. "This is just over the weight limit. You will need to take some items out."

Damn that stranger...

He went and cursed me. I checked and rechecked my baggage at home. The scale had read it was just at the weight requirement, but now it wasn't. Either I broke my scale or that incredibly hot man brought me bad luck.

"Just great..." I mumbled under my breath.

I placed the oversized luggage on the floor and unzipped the bag. The sound of the zipper was loud enough, and my ears buzzed with embarrassment once again. I'd drawn attention at the airport for a second time.

"Ma'am, there's a table over here for you..." The attendant mentioned.

"I'll just be one moment," I grumbled, and I bent down at my luggage.

I opened the suitcase up and quickly got to work. The sooner this nightmare was over, the better. I pulled out my hair straightener, my designer high heels, and my makeup bag. I put those belongings inside of my large purse.

I closed the lid and sat on top of my luggage. I was sure others thought I was off my rocker, but I didn't care. All I cared about was boarding the flight to save my marriage. Nothing else mattered right now.

My gaze avoided the crowd as my body weight pressed the zipper together and I did it up with a bit of force. I was sure others noticed my struggle, but I kept going.

Once the drama had passed, I got off of my luggage and handed the handle to the kind attendant. She took it and weighed the bag on the scale once again, but with a pleased look this time.

I smiled with relief and whispered, "Thank god..."

She took my luggage, and I was glad that part of the process was over. Hopefully, my husband had better sense than me and already checked in his baggage. This was a process I didn't want to have to repeat. I just wanted to get on this airplane and fly away to mend my relationship. To fix this mess of a marriage and live happily ever after.

But all I needed was my husband to show up.

"Flight 310 will begin boarding with groups A to D," a female voice said over the speaker.

My heart dropped, and I looked up. Twenty minutes had flown by, and our flight was on time. But James wasn't.

I stood on my tippy toes and peered over the crowd for my husband. His black hair would glisten with the overhead lighting, and his brown eyes would sparkle at me with adoration. I looked for him one last time, but never saw him anywhere.

He could be caught up and had to use the restroom. Maybe he stopped to get his morning coffee to help him wake up. He could still be hung up with dreadful airport security and afraid he would miss our flight. He could be...

But my cell phone rang.

I hurriedly rummaged through my purse to find the shrilling device and peered down at the caller ID. It was him. James was calling to let me know he was here.

I gratefully smiled and answered on the fourth ring, "Oh, thank god, I was getting worried you wouldn't show."

The line was silent as I held the cellphone to my ear and listened to nothing. I frowned and down at the caller ID for reassurance it was him. And it was.

"James? What's going on?" I asked, and my heart hammered in my chest.

The beats were so loud I could hear the sound in my ears. My blood pulsated along with the rhythm and raced through my body with anticipation. The very second I had waited for. The moment my husband would explain where he was. James would comfort me and tell me everything would be okay.

"I'm not coming," James answered with certainty.

"What? You're not coming?" I asked and clenched the phone. "Do we need to reschedule? Did you forget to set your alarm? Were you so tired you—"

James let out a long sigh and interrupted me, "The only thing I'm tired of is our marriage. It's over, Brielle. We're done."

My hand shook at his harsh words. I was here ready to work on us, and he wanted to call it quits. How dare he.

My anger bubbled, and I blurted out, "But we promised to give this one last try. You promised me—"

"You wanted to try, but I was already done. I'm in love with someone else and I want a divorce," He interrupted with a bitterness to his tone.

My world shattered.

The man I thought I loved with all my heart had betrayed me. He stepped out of our marriage and threw it away. I made it on time for our flight, but he had already checked out.

And our vows were over.

My teeth chattered with rage, and my blood boiled over. Tears bit my eyes and clouded my sight, but I didn't let them fall. He didn't earn it and he never deserved me.

I slowly lowered the phone from my ear and his voice rang through, "Brielle? Did you hear me? Are you there? Answer me, damnit!"

But I disconnected from his call.

I peered down at my wedding band and engagement ring as they shone with the light. I pulled the rings off with a shaky hand and held them up in front of me. We made a vow to each other till death do us part, but he disrespected his promise to me. Our love was dead and so was everything these rings promised me.

I peered past their shine at the small line left to board flight 310 for Hawaii and back at the two very expensive bands. I could leave and try to save my marriage, but I knew it was over long ago. It just took me this long to see we were through.

My vision cleared, and I made my mind up. I took those bands of broken promise and laid them on a table in front of me. Our marriage was through, and it was time for me to move on.

I got into the small lineup, left my marriage behind, and boarded the flight. I did it without him. This vacation was now meant for me.

TWO
Take Flight

My purse weighed heavily on my shoulder as I made my way through the tunnel and onto the plane. Flight attendants greeted me, as well as other passengers. The females dressed in dark blue dresses with heels and dark blue suits with pants for the males. A woman took my boarding pass and glanced at it as she directed me to my seat. James surprised me with a flight in first-class and it was a complete first for me.

I never expected the notion from James, but I never expected a lot of things from him. He made a ton of money, but never usually spent a cent on me. James was cheap, and he shocked me when he bought us first-class tickets.

But maybe this was the plan all along.

James must've known he was going to leave me high and dry. He had this planned, and he hoped a first-class ticket would help soften the blow. His slap in the face of cheating on me with someone else. This was his way of trying to slither his way out of being the bad guy. And I bet this had everything to do with our upcoming divorce.

I dreaded signing divorce papers because the document was final. The seal of approval for our marriage, but it had to be done. The only thing I hated hanging over my head was a failed marriage. I now saw our love wasn't real as soon as he touched another woman and made his bed with her. I just did not know the end was coming.

James completely blindsided me, and I just assumed we were going through a rocky patch. No relationship was perfect, and every marriage had its problems. But I never imagined stepping out of our vows was one of them.

I guess the red flags were there and screamed in my face, but I refused to see. He worked late hours, and he wasn't coming home. New unusual appointments popped up. We were never a couple who used each other's cell phones, and I liked that about us. But now I hate it.

If I could've seen what he was doing behind my back, I wouldn't even be here right now. I wouldn't have suffered this humiliation alone. The embarrassment of having someone I thought loved me use me like a piece of trash. Toss me to the curb for his next new shiny piece of ass.

God, I wish I could get my hands on him.

And her.

Who was she?

I bet she was some pampered princess wishing upon a star for her hero to come and save her. Well, honey, James was nothing but a two-timing loser who doesn't want to spend his money on his women. He may seem all charming and brand-new, but it would wear off. James would reveal his true colours, eventually.

Once a cheater, always a cheater.

I groaned with frustration as I found my seat and sat down in the comfortable fabric. It cushioned my behind, but I still fumed with thoughts of James and his mistress. I should enjoy this vacation and focus on myself, but it was off to a terrible start. James's cheating on me left an unpleasant taste in my mouth. Not to mention the thoughts running through my mind.

I placed my purse on the floor and the seatbelt sign came on with a ding. My hands fumbled with the belt, but I got it on and fastened it tight. I felt enclosed in this tight space, and I clasped my hands together in my lap.

I hated flying.

It was a nightmare for me, and I always envisioned the plane crashing. It never did, but the worst thought drove into my mind every time I boarded a flight. If I had the option to drive, I would, but in this case, there wasn't that alternative. An airplane would have to do.

I wanted to focus on myself and get away from my everyday normal in the sunshine. A sandy beach at every turn and being pampered every day. But I'd be far away from James, the cheating bastard.

"Attendants, please take your seats and prepare for takeoff," the pilot announced over the speaker.

I must've boarded the flight later than the rest of my group because take off came quicker than I expected. My nerves kicked up a notch, and I tried to calm them. I rubbed my fingers against my sweaty palms and wished I wasn't such a wuss with airplanes.

Even though I hated James's guts, I wanted him to be here for a selfish reason. I needed him to be here for one reason and one reason only. To calm me for the flight.

But he had to bang some other woman.

James wasn't around to comfort me, and I had to get used to it. Damn him for leaving me and not wanting to give our marriage another shot. I was mad at his choice and disappointed in myself.

I fell for his lies. I believed in him when he spoke his vows. And I should've paid better attention to his betrayal.

The truth stared me right in the face this entire time. I just carried on like everything would work out. And now I was here alone.

In a panic. On a plane. And it was about to take off.

This was a terrible idea. My decision was a huge mistake. James destroyed our marriage, despite me trying to save it with this vacation.

My breath became erratic, and I laid the back of my head back against the seat. My heart beat loudly in my ears and my pulse raced. I put my forearm up to my forehead, and it was wet. I was a fool to think I could get on this plane without him.

What the hell was I thinking?

I moved my head from side to side in a cold sweat and said, "I can't do this, I can't do this..."

Gas fumes filled the vents, and the engine roared to life. The nasty stench blew in my face and made me sick to my stomach. The plane was almost ready to leave the tarmac, but I was unsure I was prepared to take flight.

Was I ready?

All systems go to fly away from my marriage and move on with my life. Lift off from my normal and step out into the uncertain. Take off into the clouds in a different direction than I had planned for myself.

I had to be because he left me no choice. James left me and I was about to leave him. I'd drift off into another country without him because I didn't know what else to do. I had my bags packed and boarded, about to leave that part of my life behind.

All alone. Screw him. I had to get out of here.

I went to get up and tell the flight attendant to stop the plane, but a hand touched my arm on the armrest. An electric current cut through my nerves and left me with tingles. Goosebumps crawled over my skin and up my arm from the touch. It was the smallest and simplest gesture, but the gesture calmed my anxiety.

I looked over beside me and the man who helped me earlier was there. His eyes were kind and not at all amused. They held genuine concern and the blue tones spoke to me. He didn't need to say anything, and I knew he was there to assist. He touched me in the sweetest way, and it was what I needed right now.

He passed me a brown paper bag and instructed, "Breathe into the bag. Trust me, darling."

I don't know if it was his eyes or the way he spoke to me that made me believe him, but I wanted to believe in something. I wanted to have faith in a man again after another man broke my trust. After he shattered everything I thought I knew.

So, I took the bag and trusted him. A complete stranger, but one who already helped me when he didn't have to. One who clearly attracted me.

I opened the brown bag and held it up to my mouth. My body leaned forward slightly as I watched him take a deep breath, and I did the same. The bag crinkled as it opened and closed with each breath I took. I noticed his eyes squinted as he gave instructions and he gestured with his hands.

My focus became solely on him as the plane picked up speed and bumped slightly on the tarmac. I watched his broad chest rise and fall as the aircraft took off. The plane set for the sky and the gravitational pull fought us with each climb. But he kept me grounded.

He continued to dictate to me and I remained zoned in on him. He was the only one I saw, and I was his main focal point. In some way, we both helped each other.

"I hate flying too," he admitted as the push of gravity subsided and the seatbelt light turned off.

I nodded my head in response because I was afraid to speak. He was gorgeous, and I just had a freakout in front of him. I also had an embarrassing moment with my luggage situation and I was sure he saw everything. But I had been on a mission to save my marriage.

My wedding vows committed me. I was with someone. But now I wasn't.

Everything changed in the blink of an eye and he got to witness the change in me firsthand. My dedication to save something broken and my sham of a marriage. But he didn't need to know that.

I'd just keep it to myself. What he didn't know wouldn't hurt him. But it would certainly be another embarrassment for me.

A failed marriage to everyone else was a huge thing. Word would eventually get out, but I didn't want it to right now. I wanted to live my life for myself. It was time for me to shine. Instead of living with someone who never respected me enough to stay.

Everything inside me was now calm, and it was all thanks to this man. I didn't even know his name or where he was from. Hell, I knew nothing about him other than he was compassionate. Kind enough to help a stranger. Not once, but twice.

I lowered the paper bag and tucked it into the elastic compartment in front of me, but my eyes never left him. He made me curious, and I wanted to know more, but I was unsure if he would reciprocate.

So, I whispered with a small smile, "Thank you."

The one side of his mouth formed a small grin. "You're welcome, darling."

He tore his gaze away from me and opened up a menu. I watched as his eyes glanced over the contents and he stroked his brown beard. He took great care to groom and comb his whiskers perfectly into place. Everything about him was professional and flawless. But he appeared powerful. Very influential indeed, and someone nobody wanted to mess with.

We flew in first-class and I knew he had the funds for it. Well, I assume he does because he was alone. But so was I and I couldn't afford first-class. James could.

He had me perplexed, and I studied him further. He dressed casually, but he wore a shiny watch. An expensive one I recognized from the store. Not just any store, but the one James would shop at. He always had extravagant taste, but only for himself.

So, it was a toss-up if this guy came from wealth. His appearance fit the part, but then his dress didn't. We headed for a vacation destination and maybe he wanted to appear as ordinary as everyone else. Not stand out like a gold thumb.

"You're staring, darling. Do you like what you see?" he asked in a smooth tone and didn't gaze up from his menu.

I turned crimson and blinked several times. I immediately turned away and grabbed my purse from the floor to distract myself. Gawking was never my intention, but he caught me and I was self-conscious once again around him.

What the hell has gotten into me?

This person who I don't even know had me strung out. Mixed with the stress from everything I had just experienced within the last several hours. I was off my game and a mess. I had to pull myself together and come out of this funk at some point.

He probably thought I was some nut job just released from the crazy house. A person who lost her way and couldn't escape the madness. A woman who resorted to keeping everything inside until one day she had a mental breakdown and checked herself into an asylum. I felt a tad bit crazy and why wouldn't he assume the same?

I unzipped my purse and opened it up, but there sat the reminder of my mistakes. My belongings I had to pack quickly into my oversized purse instead of my baggage. I wanted to find something, anything, to distract myself from this shit show.

I pulled out my hair straightener, designer high heels and makeup bag. I placed them on the floor in the aisle and looked for the airline catering trolley. The cart was nowhere in sight, with food and beverages to serve. All I needed was another disaster created by me and leading to another humiliating moment.

I was having a bad day. The worst time of my life in a long time. But it was all because of a dirtbag who was soon to be my ex-husband.

"So, I see your luggage didn't meet the weight requirement after all?" he stated with amusement and cleared his throat but pointed at my belongings in the aisle. "Those are too big to carry in your purse."

I plastered on an annoyed smile and bit my tongue. His sarcasm made me think twice about checking him out the way I had. He was compassionate, but a wise ass. I sure knew how to pick them.

"Do you always play so hard to get?" he asked.

He caught my attention, and I blinked repeatedly at him, "Excuse me?"

He turned in his seat, and his broad chest puffed out. It wasn't on purpose, but a natural form for him. His shirt was much too tight, but revealed sculpted abs underneath it. His muscles screamed at me and begged me to reach out to touch them, but I refrained.

"I've been trying to form some sort of conversation with you since we met and you constantly give me the silent treatment," he explained and raised an eyebrow. "Most women don't, but I'm drawn to a challenge every once in a while."

"Well, I'll have you know I'm not like most women," I admitted and meant it.

Most women would curl up in a ball and sleep away their failed marriage. Some women even stuff their face with ice cream for comfort after being betrayed. Others result to revenge sex and an escape.

I got on a freaking plane and flew away on a vacation. A trip meant for me and my cheating husband. A way for us to reconnect, but now for me to move on with my life.

He looked down at my fingers and I was glad I got rid of my wedding bands. The rings would show I was spoken for and completely off-limits. His eyes searched my hands and darted back up to my face.

He formed a handsomely dashing smile, and it triggered my insides. The butterflies were back and my heart pounded in my chest. Heat rose throughout me and I was sure my cheeks admitted my truth. He turned me on; he attracted me and I couldn't deny it anymore.

"Have a drink with me?" he asked with a daring challenge in his ocean blue eyes.

"I don't even know your name?" I admitted with doe eyes.

He reached out his hand and said in a low, husky tone, "My name is Baxter. Baxter Lane."

My hand fell into his like a moth to a flame. "Nice to meet you, Mr. Lane."

His eyes locked with mine and I had an instantaneous impression everything would be okay. I didn't need to chase after a man who didn't love me and never put me first. Something in his sea-blue eyes made me safe, and he confirmed it when he kissed my knuckles. His soft, pillow-like lips caressed each one and made my cunt wet. I instantly soaked my panties. He did a number on me and he only kissed my hand.

"And what is your name, darling?" Baxter asked as his warm breath tingled my skin.

I was so surprised by him. So, lost in the moment, I almost gave him my married name. But I realized before it was too late.

"My name is Brielle. Brielle McKinsey," I introduced my half-truth.

He lingered there for a moment before he released my hand and looked down at my belongings in the aisle. "You should move your stuff before the trolley comes down the aisle, darling Brielle."

I gazed down the aisle, but no catering trolley was in sight. "But why? No one is coming?"

He grinned at me with wittiness and let out a slight chuckle. "Because I'm going to buy you a drink before this flight lands in thirty minutes."

And he pressed the call button for service.

THREE
Hawaii

Our flight landed without delay. The pilot announced it was a bright and sunny day here in Hawaii and to enjoy our stay. Everyone clapped for a safe landing. I never quite understood the meaning, but for me, it was a thank you for letting me live to see another day.

I stood at the baggage terminal and waited for my luggage. Everyone did the same once they got through security. Passengers of flight 310 all appeared like they had just been on an airplane for hours and I was sure I appeared the same. Jet lag was a struggle, and a well-known fact.

I gazed around and my eye caught Mr. Lane as he stood a few feet away from me and watched the baggage belt bring around luggage. The next step should transfix me, but he drew me in. He rubbed his whiskers and lost himself in deep thought. His expensive shiny shoes tapped, and the sound echoed against the floor tile. The way he rested his hand on his hip and popped out his perfectly tight ass. A rump I'd love to get my hands on and squeeze. I wondered if he had a bare ass or if it would be coated with hair. It wouldn't matter to me because the shape of Mr. Lane's ass in those tight jeans was all I...

A throat cleared. "Are you looking for this or has something else caught your attention?"

Mr. Baxter Lane stood in front of me, and he held my luggage by the handle. I blinked repeatedly as he broke me from my sensual thought of his nicely shaped rear and took my luggage from him. My cheeks blazed at his comment, and it was hard to look him in the eye. There was no doubt the attraction was there, but I didn't need to be an ogling idiot.

"Yes, of course, my luggage. Thank you, Mr. Lane." I breathed as I looked down at my suitcase and willed my flustered self to calm down.

He reached out and tilted my chin until I met his eyes. "I think we're on a first name basis by now, darling Brielle. Please call me, Baxter."

I sucked in a breath at his touch and his blue hues sparkled back at me. His thumb gently caressed my chin before his hand fell. His touch had me lost for words and he had me captivated.

Our constant run-ins were electric, and the attraction sparked life between us. Flickered brightly and rushed through our bodies. The interest was there, and the spark had me lost on what to do about it.

I was going through a divorce and a possibly messy one if James got his way. Another man consumed me after my life was completely tossed upside down in the matter of hours. One I barely knew, and he was about to leave. We both came here to get away from our lives, but we'd go our separate ways. He'd go one way, and I'd go mine.

Why was this goodbye so hard?

"Um, well, my car is waiting." Baxter hesitated but bit his tongue. "I should go."

Baxter turned his back to me and I panicked. He was about to leave, and I just stood here unable to speak. If this was the way I was going to be single, I'd never find true love. I had to learn to take a chance, a leap of faith.

So, why not start now?

"Baxter, wait..." I cried out.

Mr. Lane peered over his shoulder and a grin lit up his face. "Yes, darling?"

His constant nickname for me made me smile. His blue eyes pierced into mine and my womanly parts sung. Mr. Baxter Lane was a heartthrob.

"Do you believe in fate?" I asked.

Baxter brushed the hair from his eyes and responded, "Yes, why?"

"Well, I didn't. But with the day I had, it made me change my mind," I admitted.

"Really?" Baxter breathed as he stared at me with sincerity. "Maybe fate will strike twice, my darling Brielle, and we'll meet again."

I walked up to him and flashed him my best smile. "I doubt it."

I could hear his deep chuckle from behind me as I kept walking and felt his eyes roam over my body. They burned into my backside and caused me to quiver with need, but my confidence conquered. My quick wit had won, and I left him with something to think about. I didn't stand there like a fumbled fool and flirted my way to the top.

I was about to be single and it felt good to have my first real interaction with a man in my favor. He wasn't just any man, either. Mr. Baxter Lane was breathtakingly handsome. He may have the charm, but I had my sanity. I still got it. I could do this dating thing with my eyes closed.

The doors for the departure of the airport automatically opened, and I walked out into the bright light. The glare of the sun was too intense, and I needed my sunglasses. I pushed them up my nose and hailed down a cab. The vehicle stopped at the curb and the driver got out to help me with my bags. He put them into the trunk and behind him I could see Mr. Lane. But his ride wasn't a car, it was a limousine.

Mr. Lane gave his suitcase to the chauffeur and had a quick word with him. Baxter took out a pair of sunglasses from his pocket and put them over his eyes. He never glanced my way and got inside the vehicle.

"What the hell?" I muttered under my breath.

I knew Mr. Baxter Lane had money, but I didn't think it was that much. He had expensive taste and rode first-class. I never thought fate would land me in a seat next to a wealthy man. Let alone flirt with one.

I shook my head and got into the cab. "Unbelievable."

"Pardon me, ma'am?" the driver asked as he looked back at me through the rearview mirror.

"Oh, I'm sorry, I'm just having a crazy day," I replied with a small smile.

"Don't we all..." He sighed and put on a smile. "Where to, ma'am?"

"I'm going to Grand Bay Spa. It's a resort right near the ocean," I replied.

"Oh, it's a beautiful choice. Is this trip for business or pleasure?" He asked.

"Neither," I responded as I gazed out the window at the beautiful view of palm trees and blue sky.

"Then why are you taking this trip, ma'am?" he pondered with curiosity.

I watched the planes take off from the airport. The same place I had once been and dreaded. But a complete stranger had made me feel secure when my husband was supposed to.

Mr. Baxter Lane had opened my eyes to new possibilities. I didn't have to be some love sick woman lost without her cheating husband. I could be me and find myself again. Baxter made me see that.

I smiled with enthusiasm. "For a fresh start and to see where fate takes me."

***

The cab ride to my resort was a long one. This vacation destination may come highly rated, but it was further away from the airport. The long distance was rather inconvenient. But my thoughts were on Mr. Lane the entire way there.

I got lost in thought about how we met and the smell of him. A slight aftershave scent and aroma could make any single woman swoon. Baxter could have any chick he wanted, but I seemed of interest to him.

To what extent?

I wasn't sure.

He was probably like any other rich bachelor and just wanted a quick fuck. But at this crossroads in my life, I wasn't sure if I should be.

I had an impending divorce looming over my head. I should focus on a signature to sign. Not meaningless sex with Mr. Baxter Lane. Very hot, no strings attached sex with an extremely attractive man.

The bourbon he bought me made everything tingle. The alcoholic beverage was strong and clouded my judgement, but his deep ocean blues were sensational. My brain was fogged and his tender touch still lingered on my skin. I couldn't forget him and wasn't sure I wanted to. But I had to move on.

We may have travelled to the same place, but it didn't mean we'd have a second chance encounter. Fate may be on my mind, but I was still level-headed. There was no way I'd ever see Mr. Baxter Lane again.

My cab driver made it through security set up for Grand Bay Spa. He drove up to a circular driveway right out in front of the resort. The retreat was extravagant right from the main gate. The high brickwork tunneled through to a beautiful view of the oceanfront. People who worked at the resort came towards the cab as we pulled up and the vehicle came to a stop.

I exited the cab with a smile of wonder at the beauty of my vacation spot. The driver brought my luggage to me, but a bellhop stepped forward in a pure white outfit. The clean, pressed appearance was professional.

He took my luggage handle with a smile and said, "Welcome to Grand Bay Spa. Right this way, ma'am."

"Thank you, sir." I nodded with openness and followed his lead.

The kind bellhop brought me through the tunnel shaped brickwork and there was a main entrance into the building with a desk set up beforehand. He walked towards the desk, but I admired the fabulous landscape.

There were flower beds and dark rocks created the outline of each one with beautiful flowers inside. White Hawaiian Gardenia, Blue Ginger, orange and yellow Hibiscus. All a decorative and peaceful touch. At the center of the masterpiece was a mini waterfall. The calm sound of the water trickled down over the top of the rock bed. But the prime view was the ocean.

Behind all the man-made sights laid the scene of mother nature's true creation. The ocean with clear blue tones throughout the water. The waves crashed up to shore and mixed with the sandy beach. Vacationers splashed in the water or laid on the beach in the blazing tropical sun.

"You will need to check-in at the front desk, ma'am," the bellhop instructed as he wheeled my suitcase along the floor and up to the desk. "I will take your luggage to your room."

I nodded my head at his instruction and a front desk clerk asked for my passport. She had black wavy hair pulled back in a neat ponytail and long black nails. She also maintained a clean and professional appearance.

I gave her the information she wanted, and she got my reservation sorted out. Everything went smoothly with no hiccups, but the only problem was my husband wasn't present. He should be here, and he wasn't. James was back home screwing his mistress.

"This is your keycard to suite number 314. Take the elevators after the main doors and up to the third floor." She smiled with delight. "We hope you enjoy your stay at Grand Bay Spa."

I returned her enthusiasm and headed through the doors, but I knew I wanted to get into a bikini to enjoy the afternoon on the beach. My clothes had a stench to them after being on a flight for so long, and I could really use a new outfit. A sexy bikini would do the trick.

The elevators were right where she implied, and I pressed the button to take me up. No one was around and I heard a ding right away. Everyone was too busy enjoying the sand and sunshine. I couldn't wait to be one of them. This vacation was perfect for me and turned out to be what I needed.

No one would bother me. No work to keep me busy. Complete and utter relaxation.

Not to mention, nobody here knew me.

I stepped foot onto a spotless elevator with mirrors all around. I peer at my reflection and see myself from head to toe. Not a fingerprint in sight on the clear glass.

But boy, was I a mess.

I had wrinkled my dress from sitting for so long and my brown hair with blonde streaks fell out of its ponytail. My makeup needed to be touched up and my lip gloss had faded. The skin on my lips was dry, and I looked tired. But I never felt more alive.

I was ready to tackle my newly single life and move on. Despite being married, my relationship with my husband had ended. I freed myself and could live the way I chose. No more rules, vows, or an ungrateful man leading me on.

The elevator stopped on the third floor. Right where I needed to be, and I got off. My heels clicked along the sparkly black tile, and I didn't find anyone in the hallway. Except for the staff, of course. Busy doing their duty and making their daily rounds. A maid's cart with cleaning supplies was up ahead and she was busy getting the supplies she needed. A broom and spray bottle in hand with a towel over her shoulder. Another cart stood close by with fresh white laundry folded and ready to clean each suite.

I beamed at the thought of not having to lift a finger. No cooking or cleaning and total tranquility. A calm before I go back to the storm. I'd regret leaving this place once the time came. But for now, I was in paradise.

I took out my keycard and pressed it up against the screener for suite 314. A green light flashed and signaled me to step through the door to my home for three days. I opened the door to the smell of a fresh room with a hint of an aftershave scent. A man must've stayed here last. Maybe by himself or with a lover.

The door softly closed behind me and it surprised me to see my luggage had made it there before my arrival. The bellhop was right on schedule and everything was ready for me to enjoy. I discarded my heels and felt like royalty.

I gazed around at my room with a king-sized bed for me to enjoy all by myself and clean white sheets. A silver throw blanket laid overtop at the end of the bed with silver pillow shams. The room had colored tones of silver and grey throughout. There was a big screen television across from the bed for entertainment and a mini fridge stocked up with drinks.

I wandered towards the large patio door and the blinds were open. I opened the door, and it led to a balcony with a hot tub. The jacuzzi was on and the warm water bubbled. A perfect view of the ocean was just over the terrace and there were two lounge chairs overlooking the beach scene.

The warm breeze blew my wispy strands of hair as I took in the sight and felt happy to be here. This was going to be a vacation I'd never forget. My getaway was off to a wonderful start.

I walked back inside and closed the patio door behind me. I missed the fresh ocean air already and I couldn't wait to throw on my bikini. But I needed to touch up my makeup first.

The bathroom was to my right and the only area left to see, but I knew it would be just as fabulous as the rest. My eyes fell on a closed door, and I repeatedly blinked with surprise. I would assume they would leave the door open, and I didn't understand why it was closed.

I ignored the thought and walked across the black tile in my bare feet. First, I had to get my makeup bag out of my purse and my sexy black sequined bikini out of my luggage. Nobody else was there, and I took off my dress without another thought. But my beige undergarments stayed on.

My purse was on the bed where I left it and I went over to it. I opened it up and was just about to grab my makeup when I heard a door open from behind me. I spun around, startled, and couldn't believe my eyes.

There was a man who stood outside of the bathroom and a small white towel hung loosely from his hips. Steam misted at his bare feet as my eyes travelled up his sculpted torso and over his chest. But my eyes locked with his deep ocean blues.

"Well, fancy meeting you here, darling." Mr. Baxter Lane grinned.

FOUR
Mix-up

"What the hell are you doing here?" I shouted in shock.

I startled Baxter and caused him to jump. My eyes watched as his towel fell from his hips and landed at his feet. I stared, stunned, at his thick dick and heat instantly rose to my cheeks. I was a flustered mess, and I couldn't stop gawking at his massive cock.

I hadn't seen a man's dick in months. His girth stood in front of me and became fully erect. The decent thing to do would be to turn away, but here I gawked and grew hornier by the minute.

"And your beauty is a pleasant surprise," Baxter announced with wit as his eyes roamed over my body and I had forgotten I was half naked.

"Oh, my god..." I groaned with embarrassment and grabbed my large purse to hide my body.

Mr. Lane stood there naked and not afraid. He was sure of himself and he even put a hand on his hip. He encouraged me to enjoy the view. Baxter threw me completely for a loop, and I motioned for him to cover up his junk.

But did I really want him to?

"Fine..." He groaned and rolled his eyes.

He did the gentleman thing to do and covered his dick with his hand. He bent down and retrieved his small towel. The white cloth went back into place and tied around his hips. But I have to admit, I missed the ravishing sight.

Mr. Baxter Lane was hot with clothes on.

But underneath, he was on fire.

Once my brain could function, I cleared my throat and asked, "Why are you in my suite?"

He walked forward, and I had to avert my eyes from his cock. His erection moved with each step he took from underneath the towel. Instead, I caught his eyes and the hint of amusement played within them.

"Do you think this is funny, Mr. Lane?" I asked.

He licked his lips, and my mouth watered. "No, I find this very distracting, darling Brielle."

"Stop calling me that," I muttered with frustration.

"Why? Do you like it?" He asked as he came closer to me and I couldn't move.

"No, I-I..." I fumbled and couldn't think straight.

"Does it turn you on?" Baxter asked with a thick huskiness in his voice, and it made my knees shake.

I held my composure as he reached out and touched my lower lip. His thumb caressed it and my breath sucked in. The electric flames he ignited erupted between us and he captured me in his world. Consumed by him and only him. A man I barely knew.

But I needed it to stop.

I swat his hand away and glared into his eyes. He let out a light chuckle and bit his lower lip. A gesture I found all too amazing.

He brushed his wet hair from his face and breathed. "Playing hard to get, darling?"

"No..." I huffed with annoyance and pointed towards the bathroom. "Now, please go get some clothes on, Mr. Lane."

He smirked at me as he stepped backward with a cocky attitude, and his gaze never wavered from my body. My heavily turned-on body. Halfway through the room, he turned around and went towards the bathroom.

Baxter grabbed the door handle and glanced over his shoulder at me. "We're on a first name basis now. Remember, Brielle?"

I sighed. "I remember, Baxter. Now, go get dressed!"

He chuckled as he closed the bathroom door behind him and I let myself slump down onto the bed. Relief came over me and the embarrassment wore off. My worked-up body calmed down and I could use a cold shower. The vision of him still lingered in my mind, but I had an additional problem.

What was Baxter doing in my room?

I sighed with annoyance at the situation I had to deal with as I found a sundress and quickly tossed it over my head. This mix-up I never saw coming and never would've expected. I thought the airport would be the last place I'd see Baxter and here he was in my suite.

There was one explanation for all of this. Mr. Lane had the wrong room. This was my room and there was no way he was taking it. I wouldn't let him. I was a new woman, and I would not let another man walk all over me.

The sound of running water came from the bathroom and I knew he should be out soon. It didn't take long for a man to get ready. Unless this man took his time getting ready. He was dashingly handsome and groomed, so it wouldn't surprise me. But that was beside the point. This suite was mine, and I'd be damned if I let him take it.

I was prepared for war as soon as the bathroom door opened. Baxter stepped out dressed in clean cut shorts and a tight muscle shirt. The appearance suited him more than I wanted to admit, and his toned muscles distracted me. He swiped his hair from his eyes and grinned my way. He was far too dashing handsome and tried my patience with his charm. I had to stay focused and get him out of here.

"Now, I have one simple solution..." I snapped with determination and pointed at him. "You need to find another room."

"Me?" he asked as he raised an eyebrow and pointed at himself. "Why do I have to find another room?"

"Because you're a man and supposedly a gentleman," I added with hope.

Baxter stepped closer towards me, and I stepped back. My ass bumped into the end of the bed and he didn't stop until he was right in front of me. His much too gorgeous face was only inches from mine as his eyes roamed down my body and came back up to meet my eyes.

"Who said I was a gentleman?" Baxter asked with tease.

And my wishful thinking was shot to hell.

I shook my head and broke myself from his unwanted distraction. My index finger pointed right against his firm chest and I hardened my stare at him. I wanted him to see I wasn't backing down, and he'd be the one to leave.

"Well, I had hoped so, but now you will be the one leaving," I said firmly and pushed him out of my way. "Pack your bags and get out."

He backed up and put his hands on his hips. "This is my room. They gave me a keycard, and it worked for this suite. I'm staying."

His face reflected the same determination I felt coursing through me, and I knew the battle had begun. He wanted a fight, and I was going to give him one. Two could go to war, but only one would win this war.

"We shall see about that." I breathed with frustration and went to the bathroom.

I found his luggage and grabbed it. I struggled to remove the handle from the awkward bag. The damn thing was stuck, and I resorted to picking it up instead. The suitcase's weight caught me off guard; I hadn't expected it. The suitcase fell to the floor, and I grabbed the fabric to pull it towards the door.

"What the hell are you doing?" he asked from behind me.

"If you won't leave..." I puffed as my hair fell further out of the ponytail and covered my face. "Then your luggage will."

Suddenly, his brawny arm wrapped around my waist and he lifted me off of my feet. I had no choice but to let go of his bag as my hands clawed at the air, and I felt shocked. Baxter wasted no time and took me out of the bathroom.

"Hey!" I shouted as he tossed me onto the bed and faced me once again.

"I paid for this suite and it's mine," He growled at me.

Baxter leaned over me on the bed with his finger pointed at me in stern warning, but he didn't scare me. It was quite the opposite, actually. Baxter Lane oozed dominance within this moment. A take charge move and I had to admit, he turned me on.

His warm breath lingered on my face with each puff he took. His eyebrows knitted together with annoyance, and his hair fell in front of his eyes. I could tell I got on his nerves and that was good. I was getting to him and in no time, he would leave.

"Fine." I huffed.

Baxter let out a long sigh and stood up. He brushed his brown hair back with both hands and appeared more relaxed. But not for long.

He breathed with a grin. "Good. You've come to your senses."

I got off the bed and moved past him. "I'll just call security and have them kick you out."

His groan of irritation brought a smile to my face. I got better with each passing minute of how to push Mr. Lane's buttons and any moment now, he should crack. I had him right where I wanted him.

I walked over to the landline in the room with a mission in mind. I could hear his feet move from behind me, and I was ready this time. He wasn't about to sidetrack me, and I'd fight him till the bitter end.

I placed my hand on the phone, but he stopped me. His hand covered mine, and it was much larger. I couldn't help but notice a sexy vein crawling up his arm. The way his hand fit over top of mine so perfectly and the electrified current rushing over my flesh. His touch was tender and not forceful. A plea for understanding and a will for a truce.

Baxter whispered into my ear, "Now, just wait a minute..."

A moment passed.

I blinked several times and wet my lips. "Okay, I'm waiting. What is it?"

His thumb caressed my hand, and he breathed. "There's a better way to go about this."

I bit my lower lip in thought. "Oh, ya? What is it?"

He brushed my hair behind my ear and whispered, "Why don't we call management and have them sort out this issue?"

My being quivered at his touch, and my mind raced. Baxter captured me. Caught up in the moment created between us and our strange situation. Another chance encounter that was completely unexpected and out of our hands. We didn't create this mess. The resort did. Management should figure out the problem and give us a solution.

Not us.

Baxter was right.

I nodded and he must've felt the fight leave me. He pulled my hand off the phone and I willingly let him hold my hand in his own. I turned around to face him with fire burning between us. The flames flickered and dared us to get closer. But I had to maintain my focus.

I picked up the landline from behind me and passed it to him. "Okay, make the call."

I walked away from him as soon as he took the phone and exhaled a sigh of relief. I needed some distance from him so I could think straight. Baxter made my head spin. He had me engrossed in him and these sensations needed to stop.

We'd gotten too close for comfort and I let him consume me. This was a high-stake situation between us and our sexual tension was out of this world. I couldn't hole up here in this suite with him by myself. There was no way in hell.

His powerful voice followed me as he talked with someone on the other line. I didn't stick around to see how the situation turned out and needed some air. I opened the patio door and went outside.

The warm air hit my face, and I closed my eyes. My head tilted up towards the sunshine as the rays of light beamed down and the sun felt great. A distraction from what I had just been through.

I could hear the waves crash in the ocean and the sound of chatter from the beach. The noise of an airplane in the distance caught my attention, and I pondered when my divorce papers would arrive. I imagined they'd deliver them as soon as possible and James wouldn't want to waste any time. He'd want this over with as much as I did now that the truth was finally out.

James was nothing but a liar, a cheat, and a part of my life I wanted to forget. I couldn't wait to sign my name on the dotted line and become a free woman. A person who wanted to find true love.

Baxter cleared his throat from behind me and said, "Management is here to talk with us."

He broke me from my clarity, and I opened my eyes. I turned around and nodded in his direction. My feet moved below me and I went back inside the room. This mix-up needed to be straightened out once and for all.

An older gentleman in a blue suit stood by the front door in the room. He seemed overdressed to me, and I figured he'd be sweating underneath his outfit. But he had to maintain a professional appearance, and it came with his profession.

"So, we investigated the situation and it would appear there was a slight mix-up," he explained as he looked from me and towards Baxter. "Mr. Lane reserved his room, and you reserved yours, but somehow we booked them on the same date and for the same room."

"How could this happen?" Baxter asked, with frustration.

"Sir, I'm unsure at this point," the manager explained with sincerity. "I apologize for any inconvenience this has caused."

"Inconvenience? We're two strangers stuck in the same room!" Baxter shouted as he grew impatient.

I reached out and touched his arm. He blinked and looked over at me. His body relaxed, and he apologized for being short-tempered.

I breathed. "Okay, so just give him a new room."

Baxter shot me a glance, and I shrugged my shoulders. He knew I wasn't leaving, and I had made it fairly clear. He didn't put up an argument, and his eyes softened.

Baxter sighed with defeat. "I'll go get my belongings and you can direct me to my new suite."

The man sighed and shook his head. "I'm afraid I can't do that, Mr. Lane."

"And why not?" Baxter asked.

"Because I don't have any more available and we're booked up for your stay," the manager explained with a pained face and looked at our shocked faces. "Again, I'm sorry for any..."

"You've already said that, but your apology doesn't fix the situation." I sighed with defeat and gazed right into my newest roommate's eyes. "I'm stuck with you for the rest of my vacation."

Baxter sighed with regret. "And so am I."

"Gah..." I breathed as I rolled my eyes and hated everything about this.

I was in deep. Buried in a profound mess. But there was no way out.

James booked this vacation. He left me for another woman, and fate led me to Baxter. A smoking hot single man.

I was in trouble.

FIVE

Truce

Baxter escorted the manager of the resort out of our suite and all he could offer us for the inconvenience was a percentage off our next stay. The percentage was a small amount and would only cover the taxes. This resort was a popular one and definitely wasn't hard up for the money.

Like hell I'd stay here ever again.

This vacation was a complete disaster, but it made sense for the way my life was going. No sex for months, a crumbling relationship, a cheater for a husband, an impending divorce, and a vacation in shambles. This was supposed to be a time to find an alternative path for myself, for me to grasp the feeling of being single again, but now fate ruined my plan.

All thanks to a booking mix-up.

Baxter let the door close and turned to look at me. He put on a smile, but I knew deep down it was fake. He did not express excitement about this situation and there was nothing we could do about it. We were stuck together in this suite with only one bed, one shower, and an incredible view. We'd simply have to set some boundaries and hope for the best.

I could get through this. I had dealt with much worse. He was just another man I'd have to live with. It's not like I hadn't done that before.

I plastered a smile on my face and breathed. "Neither one of us expected this to happen, but I think we should set up some ground rules."

Baxter raised an eyebrow and crossed his arms across his chest. "Okay, I'm intrigued. What did you have in mind?"

"I'll use the bathroom first thing in the morning, since women take longer than most men," I instructed and pointed towards the bathroom with certainty.

"Oh, I'm not like most men, darling," Baxter teased, as he shook his head and smirked at me. "You think it took ten minutes to look this good?"

I sighed with frustration at his ego and ignored him. "Keep the toilet seat down. I have a vagina and need to sit to use the bathroom."

"Do I look like an asshole to you?" he added in defense.

"Well, you are a single bachelor. I take it you don't live with a woman?" I explained, as I patted his shoulder and batted my eyelashes. "Just a friendly reminder for my sanity."

"Okay, anything else there, sweetheart?" he asked.

"No smoking, no parties and for the love of god don't bring a lover here," I added as I sat down on the edge of the bed and cringed at the thought. "I want to keep the sheets clean if I'm going to sleep here."

"I wouldn't dream of it..." Baxter admitted as he stepped towards me and the room felt compact with him so close. "My darling Brielle, you're more than enough woman for me to handle on this vacation."

My heart hammered wildly in my chest at his comment, and my stomach flipped with a somersault. My breath hitched and my pulse pounded against my neck. I wouldn't be surprised if he noticed my throbbing flesh on my neck because of his intense stare. His greedy eyes fixed on me like I was his and only his.

My chest rose and fell as everything closed in. It was just him and I. I felt like I had just run for the Olympics, but I just sat here on the bed. His eyes glued on me and my mind transfixed on his every move.

I cleared my throat with flustered frustration. "Good. I'm glad we both agree."

I needed some distance from him. A moment to breathe and think without him clouding my judgement. An immediate necessity to gain some space and I got off the bed.

My feet stepped away from him and I wandered over towards the bright window. I wanted the sunny day to distract me from everything inside of me. I needed this beautiful scenery to deflect my body's natural hum whenever he was so nearby.

Baxter's voice rambled from behind me and the vibration of it crawled up my spine. "I want you to join me for dinner, Brielle."

His unexpected invitation threw me off, and my heart leaped with excitement. I peered out at the vivid, clear blue sky and repeatedly blinked my eyes. I just demanded a checklist from him and he was asking me to dinner. This man threw me for a loop, but I didn't want him to know how much his request meant to me. My life was a mess, and he wanted my company at dinner.

Me?

A woman on the verge of divorce. My world turned upside down, all within twenty-four hours. He wanted me to join him, but he didn't even know what he was getting himself into.

"Why on earth would you want to have dinner with me?" I asked and didn't dare turn around.

I didn't want him to see the hope I had in my eyes that another man could want me. A man as sexy as him would even want to spend time with me. I didn't need him to see how desperate I was to know I still had what it took to be single.

"So, we can call a truce between us," he admitted. "You know, smooth things over and get to know each other better."

"A truce?" I breathed and felt like a silly fool.

"Yes," he simply whispered.

Of course, Baxter would do something like that. It should be the natural thing to do in a strange situation like the one we found ourselves stuck in. I didn't know why I didn't think of it. We were stuck in this together and we might as well get to know each other better.

I turned around, and he remained right where I had last left him. His gaze bore into mine with question and I could tell he wanted this unwanted arrangement to work out. He didn't want to argue, and wanted to enjoy his vacation just as much as I did. In order to do that, we had to learn to co-exist. To share what we had and survive through this together.

I smiled at him. "Okay, I can do that."

He grinned the most stunning smile, and my heart picked up its pace. "Perfect. I'll get everything arranged and wear something comfortable."

I watched him head for the bathroom as he turned his back to me and I couldn't help but stare at his ass. His rear end tempted me and called out my name. His rump should have a sign that reads 'Smack my cheeks.' An ass that firm shouldn't be legal.

The door closed behind him and broke me from my dirty thoughts of Baxter. It was just dinner, and I had to pull myself together. I had to learn to live with this hot hunk of a man for the rest of my trip.

So much for rest and relaxation...

SIX

Reservation for Two

"I'll be out in one minute!" Baxter announced from behind the bathroom door.

I heard some rummaging around and the door opened. He came out, and he looked way too good. He was a sight I could eat up and not regret a single taste. Baxter Lane was delicious till the last bite.

He wore stylish beige shorts, and of course, the material hugged his ass. His toned legs were long and anyone could tell he worked out. He had on a fresh white buttoned up dress shirt with the sleeves rolled up. His brawny forearms made my mouth water.

The collar of his shirt was up, and he fixed it with his masculine hands. The veins within them made me shiver. He had an expensive black watch clasped around his wrist and displayed his extensive taste.

"The bathroom is all yours, darling," Baxter declared and left the door open for me with a grin. "I even put the toilet seat down."

His remembrance of my rule shocked me. Deep inside, it pleased me and his need to satisfy me intrigued me. I tore my eyes away from him as I grabbed my clothes and belongings I needed to get freshened up. Nothing too fancy and just casu-al. This dinner was to form a truce, and that was all. I didn't need to get dolled up for him. This wasn't a date.

"Thank you, Baxter." I breathed as I walked past him and made brief eye contact.

"The pleasure is all mine," he said in a soft tone.

I shivered as his blue ocean eyes sparkled at me and he brushed his hair back. His slight smirk had my heart pounding a mile a minute, and I didn't know how he did it. He was so perfect, but I had to withstand his charm.

When I entered the bathroom, I hadn't even seen yet, it amazed me. A massive dark tiled shower with a glass frame and a steam glass door. Beside it was a toilet with a fancy design and a bathroom sink. I noticed the black waterfall faucet and the shiny black vanity around it. The mirror behind the sink was large, and the lighting matched the atmosphere of the bathroom, along with the open space overhead. The view displayed the clear blue Hawaiian sky with not a cloud in sight.

I was in heaven.

I smiled at the toilet with the seat down and remembered Baxter's words. Thoughts of him flooded my mind as I got undressed and discarded my clothes to the floor. I stepped into the luxurious shower and turned on the rainfall shower above. Water beads fell down and the warmth of the water caressed my skin. I washed away the smell of my chaotic flight and was ready to start anew.

I kept the shower brief because I knew Baxter waited for me and I had no idea what he had planned. He didn't hint at where we were going and the suspense built inside of me. I wasn't a fan of surprises, but I had a feeling Baxter was full of them.

I dried my hair and pulled it up high into a ponytail. The tail of my ponytail hung down my backside and undried appeared brown. The appearance of my hair strands was misleading because the blonde streaks remained hidden. Lost within the wet locks of my hair.

I touched my makeup with a smokey eye and black waterproof mascara. The cosmetics suited my eyes. The brown depths stared back at me in the mirror and I added one last touch. Clear lip gloss and it shimmered in the light.

I puckered my lips together and flung my ponytail over my shoulder. My fingers ran through the hair strands as I admired my dress of choice. Tight black shorts and a long buttoned up purple blouse. It was perfect, but casual for the occasion.

"Perfection." I smiled at myself.

I tidied up the space and exited the bathroom, only to find Baxter by the door. He was engaged by his cellphone and I pondered what was on there. The things he searched, who he talked to, and what he did. There was so much about him I didn't know. But that was the thrill of meeting interesting people.

I cleared my throat and announced, "I'm ready whenever you are."

Baxter glanced up from his phone, and his eyes roamed over me. He drank in the sight of me and his stare was a laser beam. His blue hues flared against my flesh and made the hairs on my body stand up straight. Goosebumps crawled over me, and I felt naked in front of him. Nude only for him, but fully clothed for everyone else.

"You clean up rather nice, darling Brielle," Baxter murmured as his eyes caught mine and wouldn't let me go.

I simply smiled and couldn't bear to speak. My heart hammered rapidly against my chest and the sound of it travelled up into my ears. But my body heated and the sizzle of it turned my cheeks crimson.

His eyes searched my face, but he smirked. "Are you alright?"

Mr. Lane knew he affected me. He knew he got under my skin. And my burning cheeks were a dead giveaway.

"Shall we get going?" I asked and assumed he knew the answer.

"Yes, we shall..." He murmured as he held open the door and escorted me out. "After you, my darling."

I walked past him and led the way towards the elevator. He followed behind me and his gaze burned into my backside. His eyes followed the curve up my back and landed on the back of my head. The torture of his stare made my thoughts turn sexual. I wondered if he was a hair puller. If he wound a lover's hair around his fist and fucked her senseless from behind. My pussy quivered at the sensual notion, and I had to stop.

I was stuck with this man and had to quit viewing him as a sexual god. I wasn't his goddess and never would be. He wasn't mine to devour, even though my body told me otherwise.

Yes, he drew me in, but I had to keep a level head. I had to stop this torture with myself. In the end, I only tormented my raging hormones.

We took the elevator down to the main floor in silence. It wasn't awkward, but the sexual tension loomed in the air. I tried my best to ignore it as we walked past the main desk and I wished I could see his eyes. I couldn't tell if he peered my way because of the sunglasses resting on the bridge of his nose. Maybe it was for the best.

His deep ocean blues did a number on me, anyway.

Baxter took the lead because I had no idea where I was going. No clue where he had reserved this dinner. I felt like I walked into this situation blindfolded. But I let him and I had no one to blame but myself.

I had to place trust in him. Into a complete stranger and let him lead the way. But my nerves worked overtime.

My palms grew clammy as the afternoon sun beat down on my skin. The waves crashed against a docking station and I noticed we were going in the same direction. Away from the resort and onto the sandy beach.

"Where are we going?" I asked with curiosity.

Baxter glanced over his shoulder at me and smiled. "You'll have to wait and see."

I reached out and grabbed his arm. "Where are you taking me, Baxter?"

He rested his hand over mine. The warmth of his touch fell over my skin, and Baxter made me feel safe. Protected in his hands.

He whispered, "You'll have to trust me. Can you do that?"

I blinked several times and looked from him towards the dock. The waves rocked against it and my stomach turned. The view was beautiful and I shouldn't be on edge, but I was.

And Baxter knew it.

"I can learn to try," I admitted in a small voice.

He squeezed my hand and flashed me a brief smile. "It will be alright. I made sure we're in excellent hands."

I nodded my head and returned a smile. He released me and we walked up towards the wooden dock. I noticed a small speedboat on the other side and a man stepped up onto the dock.

Baxter gave him a slight nod, and I followed him up onto the landing. A wave splashed and water wet my feet within my sandals. The beads of wetness washed away the sand that got stuck to them from our short walk here.

"Is everything set?" Baxter asked.

The man nodded and answered, "Yes, Mr. Lane. We are ready to go."

The man from the boat got in the driver's seat. He held the tiller in his hand, and Baxter held out a hand for me. I took a deep breath and let it out as I grabbed his hand. He escorted me safely onto the boat as it moved with the waves. Everything about this had me on the edge of my seat because I had never been on a boat.

I was from the city. The hustle and loud streets were a joy for me. I never thought about going on a boat. Until now.

The ocean rocked the small boat, and I held onto the side of it in my seat. The driver made the speed boat move with the handle and we went forward. Slow at first and I was happy about that.

Baxter must've felt my unease and took my hand in his. I gazed over at him and he gave me a smile. The perfect view of his face always made me think dirty thoughts, but not this time. I was on a freaking boat and I had a feeling, things were about to get rocky.

"A tad bit anxious, are we?" Baxter asked as his thumb caressed my skin.

"Try a lot..." I replied.

"I take it you've never been on a boat before?" Baxter questioned me.

"No," I responded firmly.

"Well, hang onto me, darling," he instructed as he wrapped an arm around me and pulled me in closer.

"You'd like that wouldn't..." I said as the speed boat launched forward and he caught me in his arms.

Wind whipped into my face, and my ponytail blew backwards with the breeze. The speed boat crashed against the waves and right over top of them. Our bodies collided with one another because of the swift speed and the bumpy ride. The momentum was unlike anything I had ever felt before, and this ride was completely out of my comfort zone.

We flew past other boaters, and the speed kept up at a high pace. Our resort became smaller and smaller until it was out of sight. Baxter held me close and never let go. He wanted me to trust him, and I had no choice. No other option but to let him lead the way towards a dinner that was much further away.

My stomach turned, and sudden nausea took over me. The middle of my stomach swam with nausea with each wave we rocked against. The turbulence did something to my insides, and it wasn't a good thing. It was bad, and I was going to be sick.

The unforeseen motion sickness took my breath away and my head spun. I laid a hand against my belly and prayed I could hold it back. But I couldn't hold off the queasiness.

"See?" Baxter said as he bounced in his seat and looked down at me. "It's not so bad."

"I'm going to be sick," I muttered in panic.

"Oh, no..." he said with concern and focused towards the front of the boat. "We're almost there. Can you hold it?"

The nausea crept upward and threatened to erupt. I was sure my face was pale, and I was a dreadful sight. Everything spun and Baxter's unsettled face turned into three.

"Does it seem I can?" I exclaimed in panic.

"Stop the boat immediately!" Baxter yelled against the loud wind.

"What?" The man at the front yelled in return.

"Stop the boat now!" Baxter ordered in a powerful tone.

Suddenly, the boat slowed, and Baxter didn't waste a second. He picked me up from my seat and faced me towards the water. The craft came to a standstill, and I threw my head over the side of it.

Baxter held my ponytail as I let the contents of my last meal spill out into the ocean. Motion sickness had won, and embarrassment ran through me as the world stopped spinning. Everything calmed down, including my once wild stomach.

"Oh, god, this is mortifying..." I mumbled over the side of the speedboat and didn't dare face Baxter.

I just threw up in front of him. Mr. Baxter Lane was getting to see the good, bad and ugly of me. And I didn't like it one bit.

Color came back to my face and my cheeks blazed bright red with embarrassment. I wasn't used to being this awkward in front of a man. Let alone one this handsome, affectionate, and attentive. If there was any chance with him, I had completely blown it all to hell.

I spit the last bit of bile into the water and risked a look back at Baxter. His eyes narrowed together and his hair was windblown. But he was the most gorgeous man alive.

"I'm so sorry..." I groaned in defeat.

"Do you feel better?" Baxter asked as his eyes searched my face and he still held my hair.

"My stomach does, but I'm a mess," I admitted with a sulk and looked down.

He reached out and tilted my face until I met his eyes. "Mess and all, I wouldn't change a damn thing about you, my darling Brielle."

His unshakable forwardness shocked me. I just threw up, and he held my hair back for me. He took care of me and respected me. I thought for sure he'd express his disgust and order the boat to turn around. His genuine behavior gave me a pleasant surprise and showed how much he cared.

But how, in such little time, could he care this much?

The question spun around in my mind as he helped me back to my seat and the boat went forward with ease. The driver was aware of my motion sickness and the ride was much smoother. Never in a million years would I have guessed I'd get seasick.

I gazed out at the clear blue ocean and all I could see was water from all angles. Except for straight ahead where a yacht sailed on the water. Our tiny speed boat came closer, and the yacht became bigger. It wasn't just any yacht, but a massive and fancy one.

The tiny boat pulled up to the side of the yacht and a landing was there for us to step on board. It appeared this was our destination. But it wouldn't surprise me if there was a helicopter on the way.

A waitress with a lovely black dress stepped down onto the landing. She gaped at the driver of the boat, but I knew her primary concern was us. We were the passengers she had waited for and we were of utmost importance.

"Flying first-class and now a fancy yacht?" I teased him, "Are you made of money?"

Baxter chuckled. "More like independently wealthy through a family-oriented business."

So, Mr. Baxter Lane was rich, and I was right about him. His casual appearance must be a cover up for his true self. He was on vacation and probably wanted to keep up the appearance. But I bet back at the office he was all about business.

He got up from his seat and carefully stepped onto the landing. His hand reached out for mine and his eyes shimmered. They gleamed just as blue as the wild waters we'd just travelled across. His blue oceans glistened at me to trust him and I knew deep down I could.

"Dinner is waiting, darling," Baxter announced, and he escorted me safely onto the yacht deck.

"Welcome aboard, Mr. Lane," the server declared. "Please follow me to your table."

We followed her up a couple of steps and down a skinny hallway. The sound of the speed boat filled my ears as the craft left and I was happy the ride was over. The driver could take the boat and ride it where the sun didn't shine.

The hallway had a white railing and the beautiful scenery of the ocean. An array of blue filled the sky, and the sun shone from the sky above, but dark clouds were visible in the distance. The sight caught my attention as the darkness appeared to eat up the blue sky and I pondered if a storm was just on the horizon.

"Is there a storm coming?" I asked the server.

She glanced back over her shoulder. "The captain has assured me we are in no danger of any storm in the forecast."

I smiled and relaxed more with her answer as we came to a set of stairs. The staircase led up towards the blue sky and the top level of the yacht. And the sight was the prettiest.

There was a table for two set up right beside a clear glass railing and all I could see was the water. The blue stretched out as far as the eye could see and it amazed me. But most of all, I was in awe of Baxter.

He planned all of this. A truce between us with dinner and an incredible view. But this probably cost him a fortune.

"This is too much, Baxter," I admitted in astonishment.

The server went away, and we were alone. I turned to look at Baxter and he gave me the most dashingly handsome smile. One I could gaze at for an eternity and never get used to.

"This isn't enough for you," Baxter confessed as he took my hand in his and kissed it. "Your beauty captivated me from the moment we first met. There is something about you and I can't deny it, darling Brielle."

The moment was intense. Baxter was sincere, and he was sure. I knew there was something there, but I still didn't understand it. I still had to be cautious with someone that felt so sure. He may be certain, but I wasn't. Our chance encounters could be fate, but I still had to keep a level head. This was just who I was.

I avoided his certainty and pulled my hand from his. "Well, I don't know about you, but I'm starving."

Baxter grinned. "You can play hard to get, Brielle, but I will win. I always do."

The certainty glowed in his eyes, and my stomach flipped. My heart hammered into my throat, and it was hard to breathe. He made me weak in the knees and I had to find my seat. Mr. Baxter Lane's confidence scared the crap out of me.

He pulled out my chair for me, and I found my seat. The server came back with a lightly dressed tossed salad to start. She placed the green leaves in front of me, and Baxter found his chair. She poured us two glasses of red wine and left the bottle on the table on top of the white covering.

"Our chef will serve baked salmon with rice and vegetables for this evening," the server said with a smile.

I returned her kind gesture and gazed out at the view again. I overlooked the glass railing and held the landscape of the water. But my eyes looked up and became more aware of the clouds overhead.

The darkness was closer and almost loomed over the top of the yacht. Despite the sun still being in the sky, it was about to disappear. The view made the clouds appear more frightening than they should have. But then, thunder clapped.

"Ah!" I cried out and jumped from my seat.

Baxter stood up and checked behind him just as the wind picked up. The draft blew his hair into a tousled mess and my ponytail went right with it. I was happy I hadn't chosen a dress because I'd have another embarrassing disaster on my hands.

Raindrops fell from the sky and lightly wet Baxter's white shirt. The wetness touched my face, and I knew this storm would not hold off. The sky was opening up and revealing its true nature. Mother Nature was about to show us her strength.

Bolts of lightning lit up the clouds and the storm quickly covered up the sunlight. The sun was gone, and the rainfall picked up. Baxter and I looked at one another with fright.

He turned to question the stunned server. "I thought you said the storm would hold off?"

"The captain assured me it would. I-I didn't know..." She stammered as the wind blew stronger and the red wine tumbled.

The red stained the white tablecloth, and the raindrops soaked into the fabric. The glasses fell from the table and shattered on the wooden deck. The yacht rocked with the waves and the server ran for it.

She stumbled with each sway of the massive craft, but made it inside. Out of the rain and behind the glass door. I went to follow, but lost track of my footing with the rocky yacht.

And sent me straight into Baxter's arms.

He held me up as the thunder clapped and sounded closer. The lightning bolts struck the water below and my eyes grew wide with fright. The darkened sky finally unfolded and the rain poured down.

"Come on! We have to get inside!" Baxter shouted from behind me.

He held me close as we swayed towards the glass door and the wind blew harder. The yacht rocked with each gust and I felt panicked. Baxter pushed me forward as my breath picked up pace and the thunder boomed in the sky.

I reached the glass door and pulled it open. We stumbled inside, but the rain had soaked our clothes. Rain water fell from us and we peered at one another with shock.

"What the hell just happened?" Baxter puffed heavily.

"We just got caught in the middle of a tropical storm," I responded.

The yacht continued to rock, and our footing had to match its rhythm. If I stumbled, Baxter was there to hold me up. He was my anchor and if it wasn't for him; I don't know how I'd get through this.

The storm continued to rage outside, and we had to bear its wrathful environment. We had no choice but to stick this out until the weather calmed down. And yet again, we had to do it together.

"I want to speak with the captain immediately," Baxter demanded with power as he looked at the server and she nodded her head.

"You can use the phone on the wall. It will connect you to his cabin," she informed him.

Baxter brought me towards the phone where there was a railing I could hang onto. The turbulence rocked my body one way and the other, but I held on tight. He picked up the phone and waited for an answer.

"Captain," I heard Baxter speak. "How long until this storm passes?"

I watched as his face changed and he asked. "Are you certain?"

Baxter peered over at me and something about the look in his eyes spoke to me. Something was wrong. I had a terrible feeling about this.

I should've turned down his invitation to dinner and just kept to myself. I could be on the sandy beach in a bikini right now. I was sure the weather was perfect there. Everything about this trip was one disaster after the other. Fate played some cruel joke, and it always happened when I was with Baxter.

Baxter hung up the phone and he shook his head. "I have bad news, darling."

"Oh, what the hell is it this time?" I muttered with annoyance.

"The captain said we're stranded here until the storm passes," Baxter confessed as he locked eyes with me, and I knew we were screwed.

SEVEN
Turbulence

"Stranded?" I cried out in disbelief.

"Yes, we can't dock with such turbulent waters," Baxter explained with certainty.

"This is great! Just great!" I exclaimed with frustration and let go of the railing with my arms up in the air. "First, I got left at the airport, then stuck with you at the resort, and now this. I don't know..."

Suddenly, the boat swayed with another gust of wind and threw me in Baxter's direction. He caught me in his embrace with my head back against his shoulders and his protective arms surrounded me. His blue eyes stared down at me and searched my face. I swooned in his hold and butterflies flew in my stomach. He looked down at me with concern, questions, and something I couldn't describe. But he intoxicated me and wrapped around me like a tender caress.

"At the airport, you got left there?" Baxter asked in a whisper.

His question swirled around in his eyes. The unanswered thought clouded his mind, and I knew he wanted an answer. But I simply couldn't give him one.

Baxter couldn't think less of me. I couldn't risk him knowing I had a husband back home and we were on the brink of a divorce. I had a failed marriage under my belt and my husband cheated on me.

Why?

I don't know, but he did. James could've cheated because he lost interest in me. He could've broken our vows because we weren't getting along anymore. Maybe I became a nag and he couldn't stand it anymore. Maybe he fell out of love with me and in love with another woman. Whatever led James to disrespect his wife, I didn't want this man in front of me to find out.

Because Baxter might toss me aside, too.

I broke the moment and pushed away from him. My hand grabbed the railing for support and I was on my own. I couldn't afford for Baxter to think any less of me. I just couldn't take it.

"It doesn't matter right now," I mumbled from beside him and changed the subject. "We have a much bigger problem to deal with."

Baxter simply nodded and knew not to press the issue. I was grateful for his understanding and relief fell over me. Now, I just had to learn to keep my mouth shut about personal details.

"I assume chances of this situation are highly unlikely, but what is your protocol for an unexpected overnight stay on this yacht?" Baxter asked as he looked over at the server and demanded a solution, "I mean, you must have a plan, right?"

"We've actually had nothing like this happen before, Mr. Lane," she explained with a bewildered expression. "But we have room for the both of you to stay."

"Oh, that's good news, at least." I sighed with slight ease.

"But you'd have to share a bed," she said as she shrugged her shoulders and continued, "The captain has his own cabin; the chef and I have our own rooms for times with these occurrences."

"Well, that's comforting..." I mumbled with disappointment.

Baxter sighed and looked at me. I knew he thought the same thing as me. How the hell does this keep happening?

"The winds have died down now that the storm has moved in. I can take you to your room if you'd like?" she asked with raised eyebrows.

"Sure, why not?" I confessed as I peered outside at the pouring rain and down at my drenched clothes. "What else is there to do?"

"Okay, right this way," she instructed as she walked forward, but wandered in the direction the yacht swayed. "Just watch your step."

"No kidding..." I muttered under my breath.

Baxter held out his hand and demanded, "Take my hand."

"And why would I want to do that?" I asked with a huff.

"Because I'm the one who got us into this mess," Baxter admitted with concern. "I'll be damned if it gets worse."

Baxter's genuine worry brought out his protective side. The need to keep me safe and no more harm comes to me. His compassionate behavior made my heart swoon. I knew if I took his hand, I'd let my guard down. But I couldn't do that.

I needed to shield myself and him from me. I was a woman about to have her world turned upside down, and I didn't need to bring anyone down with me. Baxter should remain at a distance. But he was hard to deny.

"And that's exactly why I'm better on my own," I snapped, but didn't want to.

Baxter's face remained unreadable at my harsh comment. If he felt anything by the rash comment, he certainly didn't show it. I felt the slap. The sting pained me deep inside because I didn't want to do it, but I had to.

I didn't waste another glance at him and followed the server's lead. We drifted forward as the craft swayed this way and that. The inside of the yacht was extraordinary, just like the outside. They painted the walls light grey with hardwood floors throughout. White furniture set the tone, and they lightly decorated the inside, creating a polished appearance. Well, I imagined it would be much cleaner if the craft wasn't rocking through a storm.

We wandered past a lobby, and there was a kitchen with a bar. The storm threw stools across the floor and I imagined the kitchen was a disaster. But I didn't see the chef anywhere in sight.

We continued on and the sway of the yacht became a slight nudge every couple of minutes. Barely enough to move my footing. The winds must be dying down, but that didn't mean we weren't still stuck here. No one would risk coming to get us with such uncertainty. We were stuck here till daylight.

The server stopped and pointed down a hallway. "Your room is just right around the corner. Follow this hallway down."

I shivered inside of my rain-soaked clothes and asked, "What about our clothes?"

"Hold on one moment..." She instructed as she went into another room and came out with two robes. "You can change into these in the adjoining bathroom next to your room."

She handed us each a warm and fluffy black robe. I wanted to strip down right there and change out of my cold clothes. The fabric was heavy and my teeth chattered.

"What about food?" Baxter asked as he took the black fabric and flung it over his forearm. "We didn't even start dinner before the storm hit."

"Right, food..." she mumbled, deep in thought, and tapped her chin. "We passed the kitchen on the way here. So, just make your way back and see what the chef has left."

She tried to give her best smile and keep professional, but anyone in this situation would struggle. She was doing the best with what she had. No one should fault her for that. At least the crew had a room for us to sleep in such an unexpected circumstance. We were lucky in some weird, twisted way.

"Thank you so much for your help," I expressed my gratitude.

The server simply nodded her head and was off. She went back the way we came, and I watched her until she was out of sight. We headed down the hallway towards our room for the night.

The passage was long, but brightly lit and no other rooms connected to it except ours. There was no way to get lost, and everything was pretty straightforward. Our room was off to the right and I pushed the door open.

"Oh, great..." I muttered under my breath.

The size of the bed caught my attention. The mattress was small. Meant for one other crew member and probably a double bed. Not doable for two people of the opposite sex. Two humans who had needs and found each other attractive. The odds of me sleeping through the night with this hot hunk of a man beside me were slim. Extremely slight indeed.

Baxter's eyes caught sight of the bed and amusement played in his eyes. "Okay, I guess I'll be sleeping on the floor."

My gaze caught his with surprise. "There's no way you'll be able to sleep on the floor."

"So, I won't get much sleep, but you will, darling," Baxter admitted with a shrug.

He was right, but that didn't make it okay. I couldn't let Baxter do this. There had to be some way we could make this work.

"Don't be ridiculous," I argued. "I won't be able to sleep knowing you're on the floor."

His eyes locked with mine, and a hint of desire flickered through them. "I don't think I'll be able to sleep next to you."

My heartbeat picked up pace at his admission and I couldn't deny I thought the same. The attraction between us was overwhelming and had been since the beginning. The spark was always there, but only one of us needed to ignite the flame.

I could imagine us giving in to temptation and falling into desire. Our arms entangled around one another and caught up in the moment. Lost in the sexual chemistry and bond between lovers. Never to escape.

But we could never give into temptation.

I couldn't.

I brushed off his comment and explained. "We can sleep on our sides facing away from each other. It will work, you will see."

"Okay..." Baxter sighed.

But my eyes widened when he pulled down his shorts.

I blushed and turned around. "Um, what are you doing?"

"I'm getting changed. I'm freezing in these clothes," Baxter explained.

"But I'm standing right here?" I stated with flustered frustration.

Baxter lightly chuckled. "Oh, I know, darling, but it's nothing you haven't seen already."

I sucked in a breath and held it. My cheeks burned even brighter, and he made me remember his hot, naked body. An extremely firm, muscular and tempting nude man.

But now, he stripped himself down behind me.

Baxter enticed me to turn around. The option raged through me and I so badly wanted to give my body what it screamed for. Baxter taunted me with a decision, and he knew how to tease me. But I had to remain on course.

I wouldn't be the one to give into impulse.

So, I nibbled on my lower lip and kept my back turned. I tapped my foot to distract myself from his tempting move, but a door ahead of me caught my attention. I knew it must be the bathroom. His distraction made me forget there was a bathroom connected to this room. I had somewhere to escape.

I heard him call out from behind me, "Where are you going?"

"I'm going to get changed!" I shouted back in a hurry and slammed the bathroom door behind me.

My backside hit the door, and I let out a deep sigh. The long exhale of sexual desperation. I was safe in here until he was decent.

My eyes wandered around the bathroom, and it was a suitable size. Wooden floors decorated the restroom, which featured a spacious porcelain bathtub and a toilet. The sink was small with a mirror overtop. The bathroom wasn't spectacular, but it would do for one night.

I discarded my wet clothes, and each piece fell to the floor with a wet slap. The soft black robe wrapped around my cold flesh and I tied the knot snug. I was naked underneath and I couldn't chance the robe unfastening. I picked up my wet clothes and laid them over the side of the bathtub to dry. They should be ready by morning light.

"Oh, god..." I muttered at my reflection in the mirror.

My ponytail had loosened, and I pulled my hair free. I let my brown hair down and the wet strands framed my shoulders. My hands ran through my hair to give it a nicer look, and it would have to do for the rest of this chaos.

I pressed my lips together and held my breath. My ear pressed against the bathroom door, but I couldn't hear anything on the other side. I couldn't risk opening the door and there he was, naked in all his delicious glory.

I asked, "Are you dressed, Baxter?"

"Possibly," he answered from the other side.

"Cut it out, Baxter!" I snapped with desperation, "Are you naked or not?"

"No, I'm not naked," he responded.

I let out a sigh of relief and opened the door. Baxter put on the black robe they gave him and my god he was incredible. His hair tousled to the side, with a few strands hanging over his eye and a devilish smirk was on his face. He was up to no good in that brilliant mind of his. I just knew it.

His eyes danced over me, and he teased. "But I can disrobe for you, my darling Brielle?"

I giggled and rolled my eyes. "Come on, let's go get some food. I'm starving."

I walked past him and heard him grumble from behind me, "So am I."

We made our way back down the lengthy hallway and away from our room. Time had passed since we last saw the server and I hoped someone still salvaged some food for us. My tummy grumbled, but if I waited until morning to eat, I could.

The yacht didn't rock anymore, and the winds had calmed, but the storm still banged outside. Our bare feet didn't make a sound on the floor as we came closer towards the bar. I knew the kitchen was located right behind it and delicious food waited for us. A marvelous piece of steak with roasted potatoes sounded good, but I could go for a can of beer right about now.

Suddenly, I heard a voice, "Oh, chef..."

I halted and glanced over my shoulder at Baxter. "Did you hear that?"

Baxter narrowed his eyes at me and whispered, "No."

I followed the direction of the voice. My feet moved one right after the other, but at a slow pace. I needed to hear it again.

"Chef, I have something for you..."

I whispered, "There it is again..."

I went to move further, but Baxter reached out and touched my shoulder. The warmth of his contact spread up my spine and made me quiver. His touch made me aware of his nearness and his need to protect me. He held me back and took the lead.

Baxter crept forward, and he whispered over his shoulder, "Follow me."

We entered the room with the bar and went in behind it. The crew cleaned nothing up from earlier and were still in disarray. Baxter glanced around, and I watched his every move.

"Why do you get to take the lead? Why can't I..."

I observed as Baxter's eyes widened and he looked towards a window viewing the kitchen. "Well, I'll be damned..."

"What?" I blurted out as I turned my head to look in the same direction and couldn't believe my eyes.

There was the server from earlier with her head tossed back. She sat on the kitchen countertop with her legs spread and a man who had to be the chef pounded her brains out. Her plump tits bounced with each thrust he gave and sent her straight to fuck town.

"Oh, shit..." I gasped with surprise.

Baxter grabbed my arm and pulled me down. We sat down on the floor and were out of sight. The sexual escapade in the kitchen had caught our attention, but hopefully, we didn't catch theirs.

We both breathed heavily and looked at each other as we heard, "Oh, you are a naughty chef!"

And from her cry of pleasure, I knew nobody had seen us.

EIGHT
Closed Desire

Our eyes locked, and our minds were in shock. Baxter's eyes swirled with a hint of amusement, and I expected it. Leave it to a man to think this was entertaining. But I knew we had the same thought in our head.

How do we get out of this without getting caught?

Never in a million years did I picture myself stuck behind a bar and hidden from a couple. Trapped with a man I was extremely attracted to while we listened to the twosome screw. The sound of their skin smacked together and her juicy cunt lubricated the ride. Her moans of delight filled the air and his grunt of pure euphoria followed along.

We walked here because our grumbling stomachs were hungry, but apparently these two were starving. The pair craved something different from what we sought. Now we were stuck.

"Is it over yet?" I whispered and tugged on his robe, "Please, look."

Baxter shook his head and mumbled, "I'm not doing it. You look."

"Fine..." I huffed and rolled my eyes. "Do I have to do everything?"

"Yes, you do, because you were the hungry one." Baxter breathed in a low tone and smirked. "But from the looks of it, they were famished."

I gently swatted his arm and made a face. I couldn't believe him. In a way, he was right. But I would not give him the satisfaction of knowing that.

I knelt on my knees and slowly peeked my head over the window frame. My eyes caught sight of the woman now bent over the counter and she was facing our direction. Her mouth was open as he banged into her from behind, and she held onto the table for a good time. He stood behind her and ran his hands down the arch of her back. His hands squeezed her plump ass cheeks, and she squealed for him.

I couldn't help myself and bit my lower lip. The sound and sight of their sex made me wet when it shouldn't. But this risky sexual encounter was like a porno.

Who doesn't like a good filthy film?

She didn't see me and I had watched for much longer than I should've. I ducked back down, but I labored my breath. I had to gain control of my aroused self because I didn't want Baxter to notice. That was all I needed right now.

"Well, what are they doing?" he asked with curiosity.

"They haven't finished yet," I replied quickly and cut to the chase.

"They haven't finished getting it on, or they have moved onto foreplay?" he asked with amusement and raised an eyebrow.

I sighed with frustration. "He's screwing her from behind over the kitchen counter."

"Really?" he asked in surprise and went to look.

I pulled him back down and breathed. "Don't you dare."

And we heard, "Oh, yes, chef, yes!"

Some dishes crashed to the floor, and I was sure she had climaxed. The man's grunt of pleasure followed, and more moans escaped her mouth. The sex went on and the noises made me hot.

Baxter's gaze joined mine, but this time, our faces were only inches apart. His breath fused with mine and I swallowed hard. I wet my lips and his eyes caught the flick of my tongue. I swore I had a groan rumble deep inside his throat, but I couldn't be sure. My ears were so transfixed on the sexual escapade and I couldn't focus right. Nothing worked properly except my raging sexual energy.

Baxter's eyes travelled back up to mine and glinted with a hint of desire. Passion soared through me, and it didn't help with him this close. His eyes danced with something new and a light bulb turned on.

"Wait, a minute..." He whispered as his mouth grew into a small smirk. "Is this making your kitten purr, darling?"

Baxter caught me.

"No, I am..." I whispered as I blinked repeatedly and tried to hide my desire, but had a hard time.

"You are what?" he asked as his hand flicked open the hem of my robe and his eyes never left mine.

"I am... I am..." I breathed heavily as his hand travelled lower and rested on the knot of my robe.

"You're turned-on like the bad little cunt you are..." Baxter whispered in a hoarse tone, "And I'm going to see if you're hungry for something other than food."

He gestured towards the knot, and my body deceived me. I bit my lower lip, and he took the flirty motion as an invitation. A warm welcome to devour me.

It had been months since I felt a male's touch, and this was doing me in. The sound of pure bliss and the thought of Baxter. And now Mr. Lane's hands were on me.

He slowly undid my robe as he listened to my breath pick up its pace. His eyes stayed on my face and he watched my reaction to his touch. He wanted to feast on me when I came undone.

"My darling Brielle, you're quivering with need." He breathed against my cheek as his lips brushed against me.

"Yes..." I purred as my legs fell open and urged him to come to play.

To tease me. Taunt me. And consume me.

His feather-like lips caressed my cheekbone and tickled my neck. A small giggle escaped me from his whiskers, but his tongue wet my skin. He travelled lower as his breath blew along the wetness he left and I shook for more. The want was so strong my pussy throbbed underneath the robe. A fiery need sizzled inside of me and I begged him to light the match. I wanted him to set me on fire.

Baxter's teeth grazed along my flesh and goosebumps rose in his wake. His fingers toyed with the front of my robe. I knew he taunted me and I wanted him so badly. His manly hands needed to squeeze me, pinch me, and set me aflame.

I brought my hand up to cover his as he grabbed the fabric, and I helped him pull it open. The frisky invite made him gaze up at me and grin wickedly. I looked down at him as his eyes fell upon my tits and my perky nipples pointed in his direction. My chest rose and fell with an urgency I had never felt before. This man intoxicated me in every way and I had never wanted someone so much in my life.

"Please..." I begged in a raspy tone.

"Please what, my dirty darling?" Baxter asked as his warm breath teased my nipple and my tits ached.

"Please, Baxter..." I repeated with an urgency.

"Mm, yes, say my name when I make your kitten come." He groaned as his tongue flicked my nipple.

I gasped at his pleasurable torment. "Oh, yes..."

He ran his tongue up my plumpness and took my nipple into his mouth. Wetness surrounded my bud, and a moan escaped me. His tongue stroked my perky mound between his moist lips. He suckled me and toyed with me. His hand found my other breast and cupped it in his grasp. He stopped his play with my one tit and gave the other one some attention. Baxter repeated this elation until my hands were in his hair and I moaned for more.

He gave me more as his lips left my tits and travelled down my belly. His whiskers teased my skin and his teeth nibbled at my belly button. His tongue dipped inside the center of my abdomen and the sensation steered straight to my clit. It was an uproar I had never experienced before, but I liked it. I liked his foreplay a lot.

Baxter let his hand wander over my belly, and his mouth played with me in the middle of my universe. His fingers grazed me until he landed right over my bare cunt. The one place he wanted to go and the exact location I craved him to be.

He whispered against my abdomen, "Now, let's see if my kitten is ready for me."

His fingers touched the top of my hairless mound, and he drifted his fingers down. He went in between my wet folds and pressed his fingers against my clit. He circled the nub and my hips rolled with his motion.

I could still hear intimacy from the kitchen, and it aroused me even more. The plead from her to fuck her harder and his thrusts grew louder. The smack of bare flesh and Baxter's touch on my body was too much. My world would open up and expose the true dirty cunt I was.

Baxter's mouth sucked at my flesh, and my hands moved from his hair. My fingers crawled down his face and fisted the fabric of his robe at his shoulders. My hands balled up as his rhythm grew faster against my clit, and his fingers swirled around the nub.

But his movement changed.

Baxter rubbed. He swayed from side to side and circled. The sweet intoxicating pattern built me closer and closer towards a release. A moment I had waited for and had craved for months. The deliverance of an orgasm given by a glorious man. Not just any man. A billionaire named Mr. Baxter Lane.

And Baxter sure as hell knew how to do his thing.

His mouth left my belly, and Baxter peered up at me in my sensual delight. His fingers against my clit stopped their play and my pussy throbbed for him. But two fingers dove into my entrance.

Baxter grinned wickedly and breathed, "My darling's kitten is all wet."

"Oh, yes..." I moaned with pleasurable surprise.

His fingers worked and moved in and out of me. He created a smooth pattern through my wet, tight folds. Baxter finger banged me with such ease and added a third one to the mix. The rhythm was slow at first, but picked up pace.

Baxter kissed my tits, and his tongue flicked each nipple. I couldn't take my eyes off of him as he toyed with me and I enjoyed every minute. He wanted me aroused, alive, and pampered. I was the luckiest woman on the planet.

But the woman in the next room could have second place.

"Oh, Bax..." I purred.

Baxter gazed up at me, and his eyes fastened on mine. He wasn't hungry for food any longer. He had a thirst to please me, and I wasn't about to complain.

"Yes, my good darling girl." Baxter breathed in a hoarse voice. "I want to hear my name from your sweet, muffled lips."

His pace picked up even more as his fingers pounded deep into my juicy folds. The sound of the fluid filled my ears and I couldn't hold back much longer. I was about to come.

Baxter knew I was on the top of release and he let out a low growl. The sound of his desire made my release imminent. His teeth nipped my nipple as his fingers worked overtime and he locked eyes with me. But his hand covered my mouth.

"Eyes on me, darling," he ordered. "You're mine."

And my climax took over.

"Oh, Baxter!" I cried out my muffled call of pleasure.

Wave after wave of release went through me from head to toe. My sweet juices broke free and spilled onto his fingers as they still played inside of me. Black beads of light shone before his turned-on face.

I quieted down, and Baxter uncovered my mouth. He kept his fingers inside of me until I was done and we both breathed heavily. His forehead touched mine, and I thought he would kiss me. But his lips never once touched mine.

I looked down at his soft lips and touched my fingertips against them. I craved the touch of his mouth against mine and wanted his lips more than anything. But Baxter never kissed me.

Not even once.

Baxter simply breathed. "You've enraptured me, my darling Brielle."

His lips met my nose. A tender kiss as my fingertips fell from his lips and his fingers left my wetness. I couldn't speak and didn't want to ruin this moment. A moment I had long waited for, but never imagined would happen.

A quick release in the shadows of another couple's ecstasy.

My cheeks turned crimson at the thought of what we had just done and how much I enjoyed it. The thrill of Baxter pleasuring me to someone else's desires. The feel of him against my skin and his skillful way of making me his. Lost with him in a couple of moments in time.

Baxter closed my robe as I watched him care for me like he always did within the little time I knew him. A man I barely understood, and I let him have his way with me. I let him give me the best orgasm of my life.

Baxter stood up and held his hand out to me. "Shall we get some food?"

I could see I had aroused him because of the pointed bulge under his robe, but he didn't care. He knew they turned me on and he took the time to take care of me. Baxter wanted to please me and show me what kind of man he truly was.

Boy, did he ever.

"But they are—" I argued.

"They are gone," he interrupted with a slow, gorgeous smile.

I knelt and peered through the window, but the horny twosome was nowhere in sight. Thanks to Baxter, I had been otherwise engaged. I shyly peered up at him and he still extended his hand for me to take. My hand fell into his and he helped me stand up.

I pulled the neck of my robe together and knew I was hungry. I had come here for food, but ran into a problem. We had created an even bigger complication, and I didn't need Baxter to think this meant anything. I was still a woman with a divorce over her head and he was still a man I barely knew. We had to keep our distance or at least try.

I flashed a glare at him and snapped, "Don't you dare think this meant anything?"

Baxter gave a slight chuckle. "Oh, darling, it meant everything."

NINE
One Bed

There wasn't much choice for food selection. The storm had done its worst and most of the food had been spoiled. We found an untouched double chocolate cake in the fridge, along with some premade sandwiches. I imagined the chef had made these for another occasion, but plans had changed. A wild thunderstorm shook up the yacht and caused disruptions in our lives.

Mine was one of them.

Now, here I was eating in awkward silence with a billionaire bachelor I barely knew. We calmed our hungry stomachs after he claimed my pussy. My life had taken a drastic turn.

I never let a man consume me the way Baxter Lane had. Under no circumstance let any man please me when we hardly knew each other. I had never lost all control with a man to another couple's erotic sex.

What had gotten into me?

Mr. Baxter Lane had.

I glanced over at him seated beside me at the bar while we ate in silence. He took slow bites of his sandwich and looked down at the alcoholic beverage he had poured himself. A whiskey, but not on the rocks because there was no ice.

He swirled the drink inside the glass and took a swig. I could envision him after -hours in his office lost in thought while he drank away a long day of work. Seated in a comfortable leather chair as he leaned back in it and let the alcohol hit the spot.

Baxter looked over at me and raised an eyebrow. "Are you going to stare at me all evening?"

"Not true. I wasn't staring." I blushed.

"Then have some cake because you need to keep your energy up," Baxter ordered, as he held out a fork and put the cake between us.

"My energy level is fine, thank you very much," I announced matter-of-factly as I took the fork and took a bite of the chocolate cake.

He touched the tip of his fork against my nose and locked eyes with me. "Well, my darling Brielle, it's probably depleted from the orgasm I gave you."

I choked on the cake and couldn't fathom the words that came out of his mouth. My cheeks blushed brighter, and I had a drink of my bottled water. The liquid helped soothe my throat and free it of cake crumbs.

I gained my composure, breathed my comeback, "Do you tell that to all your hookups?"

Baxter took the fork from my hand, placed the tines of the fork into the dark cake to grab a piece, and raised it to my mouth. He leaned into me and his ocean blue eyes stared into mine. He lost me in his trance. A daze of only him and that gorgeous face. He pulled me in and entrapped me, but I let him without another thought.

He let the tines touch my lips. "No, only you."

I opened my mouth for him and he fed me some cake. Caught up in his magic and he cast a spell over me. Lost in the depths of his eyes as they told me a tale of all the things he'd do to me, but it was probably all in my head.

I swallowed hard. "Why only me?"

The way he looked at me gave me his answer. His certainty of what he knew was true. But he spoke the words, anyway.

"Because you're mine, darling." Baxter breathed as he reached out and tucked a strand of hair behind my ear.

My heart pounded in my chest and I felt the vibration of it come up my throat. The organ pumped blood through me and made me boil over. Baxter made me hot and the certainty of his affection was real. His eyes showed me the truth.

But he didn't know me.

Baxter knew a small part of me. The fragile and disorganized part. I flew away on this trip without a husband. James left me so I could find myself again before I found my true love. But he couldn't be the one.

Could he?

I fake yawned and broke myself from his spellbind. "I don't know about you, but I'm exhausted."

"I'm not in the slightest." Baxter admitted.

His unquestionable eyes watched me as I stood up and stretched my arms over my head. I couldn't look at him because I knew if I did, he'd bewitch me again. Instead, I turned my back to him and felt his stare burn into my backside.

His gaze was a laser beam through the black robe and I knew he viewed my bare skin. He remembered every inch and curve I had let him touch. The naked sight of me seared into his memory, and he couldn't ever forget.

I sighed. "I'm going to head back."

"I'll be right behind you," Baxter said as his fork hit the plate and his bar stool scraped the floor.

I didn't peer back and kept my gaze straight ahead. Baxter followed behind me as he had promised, but I knew his eyes observed the sway of my ass. His attention made me feel sexy and wanted, but I knew this couldn't last.

This vacation was temporary, and I had to keep my heart safe. Baxter Lane was a temptation I couldn't afford to get entangled with. I had too much on my chest and I didn't need to bring his certain stare back home with me.

The entire way back to the room was quiet, except for the storm outside. The thunder clapped and lightning strikes lit up the empty hallways. I wasn't sure if I could even sleep because the thunderstorm was so loud. But I had to at least try.

Morning was just around the corner and this would all be over. We could get back to our suite at the resort and go our separate ways. Never to think about one another again. We could enjoy our individual vacations, soak up the sun and rest in relaxation. This high-stress situation was about to come to an end.

But in order to get there, I had to sleep.

I rounded the corner and found our room. The door to our room appeared sooner than I expected and I let out a sigh as I opened the door. I remembered the compact space when my eyes caught sight of the bed and I knew I had to sleep next to Baxter. An extremely handsome man who I let fingerbang me not even an hour ago.

"Okay..." I announced as I clapped my hands together and turned to look at Baxter, "Some ground rules for sleeping arrangements."

"More rules?" Baxter sighed.

"Yes, more rules," I added and went towards the bed.

"This will be my side..." I explained as I pointed to my side of the bed and his with an invisible line right down the center, "And this will be yours."

"And what happens if I cross the line, darling?" Baxter asked with tease, "Because I think you might want me to."

My heart fluttered at his flirty tease, but I ignored it. "You don't want to find out."

I shot him a warning glare, and he surrendered with his hands out in front of him. "I'll only cross the line if you want me to."

I nodded and commanded, "No touching, kissing, and your dick doesn't go near my ass."

He returned my nod. "I will try my best."

"Good, I'm glad we can agree." I sighed as I went to my side of the bed and pulled back the sheets.

Baxter headed for the bathroom without another word, and I was grateful for the space. The separation gave me some time to clear my head and think without him so near. Baxter was a man who left my brain foggy with only images of him. This was the time to get my thoughts straight and let my body rest.

I laid down on the firm mattress and the memory foam shaped to the outline of my body. My hands fluffed the pillow behind my head and I ran my fingers through my hair. I tried desperately to fix it. I didn't understand why I even tried because there was no need. It wasn't like I felt the desire to impress Baxter. He was the last thing on my mind, and sleep was the main priority.

I let out a sigh and turned on my side just as Baxter opened the bathroom door. My ears listened to him walk across the floor and to his side of the bed. I heard the rustle of fabric and something fell to the floor. My eyes narrowed at the sound he made as he got into bed and pulled the sheets over his body.

"Sweet dreams, darling." Baxter breathed.

"Goodnight, Baxter." I sighed and squeezed my eyelids tight.

His steady breaths transfixed me as I closed my eyes and willed sleep to come. Baxter didn't move a muscle, and I found myself fidgeting with the sheet. My toes rubbed against my foot as I tried to relax myself and let the world fall into slumber. But sleep never came.

The thunderstorm had died down, and the sound from outside wasn't a threat. This was my prime opportunity to drift off into Lala land. But I couldn't.

Not with Baxter so nearby.

I squeezed my eyes tighter and begged myself to rest. I tried to think of anything other than this fine hunk of a man beside me, but his breathing reminded me. The thought of Baxter brought me back to our arrangement and the rules I had set in place. So far, he upheld his end, and I crumbled to break. I fumbled with reminders of him when all I should do was go the fuck to sleep.

But a loud clap of thunder shook the yacht.

"Ah!" I cried out and sprung from my side of the bed.

Straight into Baxter Lane's arms.

TEN
Meant to be Broken

I had crossed the line. My rule broken. Well, almost all of my rules.

I clung to Baxter as if he was the last man on the earth. Scared of the storm and I couldn't think straight. But I was safe in his arms.

He had wrapped his arm around me and caressed the back of my head with his large hand. My cheek laid on his bare chest and his upper body rose with each breath. The smooth skin heated my cheek and my hand was up near my mouth. Each staggered breath I exhaled warmed my palm. I was afraid to look up at him towards what I might see and if he would tempt me. But I glanced without one more thought.

My hand rested on his muscular chest, and my eyes met his with a heated flurry. Baxter peered down at me with intensity and the storm flashed in his deep blue eyes. Bolts of lightning beamed in his eyes along with a pure longing. A hunger so profound I too felt temptation throughout me.

His breath fanned my cheek, and he cradled my head against his brawny arm. A strand of my hair moved with each puff of air, my mouth exhaled and his gaze caught sight of the movement. He reached out his hand and his fingertips tenderly brushed the hair from my lips. Mr. Baxter Lane was a passionate and sweet man.

But a heat throbbed against my thigh.

Something swelled against my skin and formed a strong girth. The growth moved against me as his heated gaze never left mine and gave me an answer. Baxter was bare naked underneath the bed sheets.

"What the hell, Baxter?" I exclaimed in disbelief.

The tenderized moment broke. Replaced by the realization, I laid with him and he was nude. But his cock came to life against me.

I sat up in bed to create some distance from him with my cheeks on fire. The thought of Baxter undressed beside me flustered me and I was angry with him all at the same time. He must've taken off his robe before he crawled in beside me. At this point, I had no idea why heat blazed inside of me.

"What?" Baxter said as if it was no big deal and raised his arms. "I love to sleep in the nude."

I exclaimed with an attitude, "But we're sleeping in the same bed!"

He covered himself with a thin white sheet and said, "Your regulation was me on my side of the bed and you on your own."

"Not naked!" I exclaimed.

"You never said that," Baxter pointed out as his eyes teased me and he breathed. "I didn't break any rules here. You did, darling."

Humiliation filled me as I stared at him and groaned with frustration. I was the one who did it and broke my rule. I ended up on his side of the bed and should've been clearer about the situation with a gorgeous man like him. Baxter loved to push my boundaries, but he was right.

I was the one out of line.

Suddenly, another harsh roar of thunder shook the bed, and I cried out with fright. Out of pure instinct, I jumped back into his arms and right onto Baxter's lap. He wasted no time and wrapped his shielded embrace around me and hugged me close.

His breath tickled my ear, and I was afraid to move a muscle. Scared to leave his arms in case the thunderstorm would strike again. Petrified to breathe until Baxter's hand drew small circles on my back. The motion soothed me and made me focus on it. Zoned in on his touch as the soft fabric of the robe tickled my skin and made me forget what was happening outside. My senses heightened to his every move and my body was in tune with his.

"It's okay, darling, I got you." Baxter whispered huskily.

I slowly drew back my head, and my nose dragged along his cheek. His warm breath caressed my full lips and our faces were inches apart. The moment was heavy with passion and a need that never seemed to fade. A desire for me to be his and him to be mine.

My blonde streaked hair fell into my face, but he brushed it behind my ears. His hands cupped my face with his eyes locked on mine. He told me a tale of all the things he wanted to do to me as lust swirled through their very captivating depths. His lips touched my forehead, pecked the tip of my nose, and he looked at me one last time.

But I knew this time Baxter would kiss me.

And he did just that.

Baxter captured my mouth in a sweet kiss. I yearned for his lips all this time and craved to have them upon my own. His kiss was soft and his lips smooth as velvet. A pleasant surprise. I got lost in him as his hands went into my hair and he deepened the desire.

Now all my rules were shot to hell.

My hands held onto the nape of his neck and played with his hair there. The smooth strands touched my fingers, and I wanted to grab them, but I dug into his skin instead. Baxter groaned at the hot gesture and his tongue parted my lips. He made his way inside my mouth and I welcomed him with a nibble of my teeth. Just enough to pick up the heat and send me over the edge. Right where I wanted him.

I pulled back and touched my index finger against his lips. My eyes locked on his and he gazed at me with confusion. I straddled his lap and made my intention clearer as my legs wrapped around his torso.

I wanted him close, so he couldn't escape. Temptation had turned into undeniable lust and he had made me fall into passion. Baxter was mine, and I was his, but only for tonight.

I admitted. "I don't need to know you, Baxter, but please make me forget who I am."

"We can just feel." Baxter breathed and kissed my finger. "I want you to understand the woman you truly are inside. A very tempting, vibrant and sensual being, my darling Brielle."

Baxter continued his lingering kiss up my finger and into the palm of my hand. He took my arm and moved the sleeve of the black robe out of his way. His lips trailed tender kisses up my wrist and towards my elbow. The kisses made my flesh crawl with goosebumps and he did as I asked. Baxter Lane made me forget everything I used to be. But he made me see the true feverish flame in the core of me.

"Please, Baxter..." I moaned with desire.

Baxter's lips left my skin, and his eyes locked on me. "All this pleading from such a delicious dame."

He let go of my arm, and my limb fell out of his way. His fingers untied my robe, and he opened the black fabric to reveal what his eyes sought. My naked being all ready for him.

Baxter reached out and his fingers grazed my perky nipples. I gasped at his touch and craved for more. He responded with a slight pinch to each round bud and I sucked in a breath.

"But can my knob unlock a scream from my delightful darling?" Baxter asked with a husky tone and yanked on the robe's fabric belt.

I cried out in surprise, "What are you doing?"

The fabric piece whipped from my robe and he held it in his hands. His eyes never wavered from mine as he stroked the fabric piece from one end to the other. His play with the robe's tie made me ponder what he would do with it.

My body shivered at his tease, and I knew Baxter felt my need because he looked down at the belt. I peered down at it and my breath hitched. I watched him wrap one end of the cloth around his hand and he did the same with the other. He yanked the fabric belt tight and gave me the most devious grin.

But he was so sexy doing it.

"I'm going to tie you up," Baxter taunted me and his eyes met mine.

"What?" I gasped.

"You heard me, darling," Baxter said with tease as he placed the fabric belt behind my neck and pulled me closer. "I'm going to bind you and screw you into ecstasy."

My pussy pulsated at his every word and got wet just for him. Baxter Lane had a sweet side, but a dirty mouth. I liked it. I had a spot for his filthy mouth right on my cunt.

His mouth was one breath away, and I teased, "Well, what are you waiting for?"

"Permission to make your sweet slit all mine," Baxter replied in a hoarse tone.

My eyes locked on his lips and I smirked. "Consent granted."

Baxter let out a growl, and his lips crashed onto mine. He kissed me in a frenzy and my mouth opened for him. He didn't waste a moment and dove right in. His tongue swirled with mine and we made a rhythm within my wetness.

The fabric belt from my robe fell from my neck as his hands went into my hair and I moaned into him. My teeth nibbled at his tongue and he caught my lower lip between his. He held onto my hair and pulled my head back as my lip slowly flicked from between his teeth. He yanked my hair to the side and I let out a squeal of delight. I exposed my bare neck to him and he ran a finger down the skin on the nape of my neck.

His tongue ran up my neck, and he whispered in my ear, "Say you're mine."

"I'm yours to have, but just for tonight," I breathed as my voice quivered with lust.

"We'll see about that." Baxter growled and he kissed my flesh.

His mouth moved down my neck as he laid me back on the bed and my robe fell open. I exposed my entire body to him and he could do as he pleased. I didn't care and wanted to get lost in him. Captured in his lustful way and never to return.

His lips toyed with my tits, and he grabbed each breast within his grasp. Baxter's tongue came out to play, his teeth nibbled and his breath puffed. His fingers pinched my nipples, and he made it better by stroking the buds. He was powerful as he loomed over top of me and I was a goddess in his grace. Baxter was my god, and I was ready to give myself to the eternal, almighty king.

"Oh, god, yes, Baxter..." I moaned with pleasure.

I arched my back off the bed and made my chest more available to him. My hands reached out and grabbed his hair. The smooth strands fell between my fingers and I held on tight. He continued his taunt with my tits and my legs unwrapped from him. I wanted him to move and do as he pleased with me. I needed him to devour me.

My legs were on either side of Baxter as his hands ran down my hips and down my legs. His mouth travelled lower over my stomach and his masculine hands still covered my tits. The pads of his thumbs caressed each nipple and tingles spread down to my pussy. His mouth kissed, bit and sucked. His tongue licked at my skin and his mouth blew over the wetness. I shuddered underneath him and pleaded with him for more. He did as he was told as my hands pushed him down and straight towards my pulsating pussy.

Baxter paused over the top of my cunt, and my hands fell from his hair. I peered down at him, and he looked up at me.

He draped my legs over his forearms as his hands ran up my thighs and cupped my buttocks. My breath picked up pace at the excitement and he squeezed my plump cheeks. He knelt over my entrance with the stare of a man hungry and ready for his next meal.

"Say you're mine." Baxter growled once again.

His deep ocean blues never left mine as Baxter dipped lower and flicked his tongue over my nub. I sucked in a breath and watched with flustered anticipation. He halted and waited for an answer, but I didn't dare give him the satisfaction.

Baxter puckered his lips together and blew out slowly onto my cunt. The warm air mixed with my wet juices already flowing from me and made me tremble. He noticed and repeated the action, but this time with another lick. A quick flick of my clit and he made me want more.

He demanded with a raspy breath, "Say you're mine, darling."

I held my stance with a shaky breath, and my nostrils flared with desire. I watched him linger on the edge of giving in, but his eyes narrowed and he lifted an eyebrow. Baxter wanted me to give in to him, but I couldn't. I wasn't his and I could only be for tonight.

"No, I can't do that," I voiced with defiance.

Baxter straightened his back, and his cock bobbed in the air. His firmness throbbed, and it was massive. A sight I remembered from the view of him nude in the suite we shared. Bolts of lightning flashed outside and lit up his brawny body. Baxter Lane held all the power, and I was to bend to his will. But he'd have to make me.

"Fine." Baxter growled as he held onto my ass and flipped me onto my stomach.

"Oh!" I cried out with surprise and a pillow muffled the sound.

"I'll make you say it," Baxter ordered from behind me and gathered my hands behind my back.

Baxter was behind my legs and kept me from budging. He secured a gentle cloth around my wrists. I wanted to turn around, but I couldn't from the position he had me in. He should frighten me, but it was the complete opposite. The forcible action he displayed turned me on.

I turned my head to the side and laid my cheek on the pillow. Hair covered my face, but I didn't care. All I could think about was his dick inside of me. I needed him to fuck me, and I wanted him to leave his mark. His cock was what I truly craved, and he knew I'd give in, but I could still put up a hard front.

Baxter's firm length pressed into my leg, and he whispered in my ear. "Are you ready to tell me you're mine?"

"No. It wouldn't be the truth," I argued.

"Fuck the truth, because I'm going to make it a reality." Baxter growled from behind me.

He tugged at my bound hands and my face dragged along the soft bed sheets. My knees were bent with my ass up against his cock. His shaft throbbed and my cunt dripped with juice for him.

Baxter towered over me and panted with his other hand running over my butt cheek. He gave my cheek a good slap and squeezed it immediately afterwards. The flesh on my behind jiggled in response, and I let out a soft moan of desire.

"Give in to me, Brielle..." Baxter breathed huskily. "Say you're mine."

I didn't speak as he smacked me again and turned up the heat between us. His fingertips bit into my skin and I bit at the bed sheet. The cloth concealed my cry of pleasured torment.

"Come on, say it..." He murmured as his cock rubbed at the entrance of my cunt and he demanded I speak the words he wanted for release.

His dick stroked me and my body begged me to give in. My pussy quivered with an achy need and I breathed rapidly into the bed sheet. I held off with temptation at an all-time high as the head of his cock was right at the opening of my pussy and begging to come inside.

"Please, I need you, Baxter..." I pleaded with him.

"But I need you to speak the words." Baxter breathed as he twitched the firm head of his dick against my pussy lips. "Tell me you're mine."

"I can't..." I moaned in pleasurable agony. "I..."

The thick tip of his shaft entered me, and my mouth opened. The bed sheet fell from my lips and a whimper full of pleasure escaped me. He gripped my bound hands in his grasp, but his other hand found my hair.

"Let me have you..." Baxter groaned with lust. "Just say it, my darling Brielle."

I held back no longer and sighed with passion. "I'm yours."

"Yes..." He growled in pleasure and filled my pussy with his cock.

"Oh, yes!" I cried out as his dick hit the hilt and he pounded into me from behind, "I'm all yours, Bax!"

He yanked at my hair and my upper body rose off the bed. Passion exploded through me as he hammered into me and never stopped. The built-up sexual tension had made for a fuck I would never forget.

Baxter tugged at my tied hands with each thrust in sync with it. His massive cock pumped me full and my tight pussy folded around him. The warmth of my wet walls was a lubricated journey neither one of us would soon forget.

My tits bounced, and he let go of my hair. He set me free to circle my ass against him so his dick could dive in deeper. I bit my lower lip, and I heard him grunt from behind me. Our spark had ignited, and the flame was lit, but I never wanted it to burn out.

"Oh, fuck me, Bax!" I panted for him with pleasure.

The storm picked up outside, but our own cyclone spun out of control. Our sexual frenzy was at its peak and ready to burst. My climax grew higher, and I knew it was only a matter of time before my release would strike.

Baxter banged into me harder to the point I didn't think he could anymore, but he proved me wrong. His cock hammered me and I let him. I gave myself to him and let him screw the shit out of me. I needed this after months of no sexual interest and a husband who disrespected me.

It felt good to be respected and desired. He made me want everything my husband could never give me. Baxter made me want to live again.

His dick continued to pump as he drove into me like I was his world and stars came to my eyes. Bright lights entered my vision, and I was ready to burst. Baxter grabbed my chin and turned me so I could see him. His eyes were full of hunger and something else I couldn't describe.

Baxter commanded with urgency, "Keep your eyes on me while you fall into ecstasy."

Baxter knew I was at my peak, and he banged into me while my release took over me. My pussy clamped down around his massive cock as strikes of passion struck me. Flashes of release seared through me, but I kept my eyes locked on him.

"I'm yours, Bax! I'm yours!" I cried out in pleasure.

Baxter's climax surged through him. "Oh, yes, Brielle!"

Baxter pumped into me as his cock released his seed, and he filled me full. He didn't stop until we were done and the last sparks of release left our eyes. His gaze was on mine the entire time, and I had a glimpse into his life. A world I could get lost in if I wasn't careful and he would welcome me with open arms.

But Baxter didn't know the real me.

I had kept my reality from him and that was the way it would stay. Baxter Lane would never find out my truths. He couldn't know my biggest failure in life.

My marriage.

As for right now, I let Baxter untie me and take me into his protective arms. The arms I had grown to trust and hated to admit it. But once tomorrow came, everything had to change.

ELEVEN
Resist

The sun rose in the distance on the rim of the ocean. The colors of yellow and orange beamed into the sky. A pretty reflection of the sun shone into the water below. Clouds hung in the sky from the storm, but moved into the distance. The skies were clearing and it would be a beautiful day.

But my stomach was in knots.

I had the best sex of my life with a man I barely knew, but I had begged for it. I had pleaded to be fucked till the break of dawn and I should bask in joy. Instead, I was a wreck.

I enjoyed the intimacy so much. The closeness, the pent-up sexual tension and Baxter's sensual skill. But I was guilty as hell.

I was a married woman.

My divorce was just a flight away. I have a failed marriage under my belt and one I was not proud of. My husband cheated on me with another woman and left me for her. But the worst part was, I kept it all from Baxter.

Baxter did not know I was going through this. He had no clue I had divorce papers waiting for me at home. I hadn't wanted him to find out because of my pride.

How selfish of me?

This new life I began was turning out to be a sham and one I wasn't proud of. It was far too late to turn back now and fix my mistake. Too late to clean up the mess I had created. I just needed to ride this out, and I couldn't let Mr. Baxter

Lane get under my skin. I had to keep him at a distance. This was just a one-time deal and just a hookup to escape everything.

No more sex.

Baxter sat beside me in the speedboat. He had instructed the driver to take it easy because of my seasickness, and my heart swooned at his kindness. Mr. Lane was not only great in bed, but extremely affectionate. He had me thrown for a loop because I wasn't used to a man being so attentive to my needs. Baxter was the complete opposite of James.

"I don't know about you, darling..." Baxter whispered into my ear as the boat lightly bounced over the waves. "But I had a great time."

He referred to our dinner that unexpectedly turned into a one-night stay on a yacht. Not just any regular stay, but an unpredictable one. One with two people extremely attracted to one another who had hot, sweaty sex together. The only problem was he was single, and I was married.

Baxter reached out and touched my thigh. His contact felt amazing and my skin zinged with electricity. My heart hammered behind my ribcage, and my body craved more. I pressed my lips together, but I so badly wanted to bite my lower lip. To show him how much I still wanted him and to display my growing affections.

But I couldn't do any of it.

I sat here with thoughts of him I shouldn't even have. Baxter shouldn't touch me like this and I shouldn't let him. It was wrong, and I led him into this concealing the truth.

I didn't even understand what this was between us, but it doesn't matter. This attraction between us would end. I would put a stop to it.

I pushed his hand away and snapped, "It was a one-time deal."

Baxter brushed wispy hair behind my ear that caught in the wind. My ponytail had let some loose, and I needed proper hair care. My hair was a mess, just like my upside-down life.

Baxter whispered in my ear, "Deals can fall through."

My flesh crawled with tingles at his words. I knew he meant business because he was all about it. He was good at his profession and anyone could see that with his expensive taste. But Baxter has met his match.

I came here with a promise to myself. I was here for a fresh start. A vacation to get away and focus on me. Not finding a man to distract me from my failure of a marriage. Mr. Lane was an interruption I didn't need, and I had to be clear. This one-time hookup would go nowhere, but us going our separate ways.

"This deal won't," I voiced with determination.

Baxter ran his fingers down my jawline and I held back my body's response. He grabbed my chin between his index finger and thumb. My face turned with his guidance to meet his ocean blue eyes as they blazed into mine with promise. And my heart flip-flopped at the sight of him.

"Are you sure about that, my darling Brielle?" Baxter breathed, as his fingers left my chin and ran down my neckline. "Because your pulse beats otherwise."

My breath puffed at a rapid pace to the caress of his fingertips on my skin. I watched as his eyes left mine and danced down the nape of my neck. His intent burned into me and made me doubt myself. He was a powerful man, and I knew he could bend me to his every will. But I would let him in a heartbeat if I wasn't careful.

"I'm sure." I voiced when I could get the words out.

Baxter brought his nose close to my neck and sniffed in my scent. I could hear him inhale me and it made my insides quiver. His never-ending need to make me his, excited me. But I knew I had to resist his advances.

Baxter let me go and pulled away, but his eyes locked on mine. "Time will tell."

The speedboat pulled up towards land and I recognized the docking station from yesterday. I exhaled a sigh of relief, but didn't know if it was because we made it back or Baxter had given me space. It was probably a bit of both, and now we could go our separate ways for the rest of our vacations. It should overwhelm me with joy, but for some strange reason, it made me miss him already.

Baxter had lent me his hand to help me get off the speedboat, but I refused. I didn't need his help and could do it on my own. I was a strong and capable woman. Plus, I had to get used to not having his help. We'd be going in opposite directions once this vacation was over and I had to get used to that reality.

I lived without his help before and my life was a crazy mess. I could do it again and I would have to. But this time as a divorced woman.

I got off the speedboat as the waves crashed into the side of it and the craft gave an unwanted wobble. My balance was unsteady, and I felt Baxter's eyes on me, but I would not give in. I reached for a wooden post attached to the dock and placed a foot on the landing. I was half on the unsteady boat and half on balanced land. The push and pull of both made the task harder, but I willed myself to pull through.

And I did.

I shook off the worry and didn't wait for Baxter. I walked ahead of him and didn't bother to turn back. Ready to break free of last night and our one-night stand together. I needed to let go of our raunchy, mind-blowing sex we had together.

"Lord help me..." I mumbled under my breath.

I could hear Baxter's footfalls behind me and chatter surrounded me from the busy morning at the resort. Beach goers were out basking in the daylight's sunshine and the humidity was about to pick up. I could really use some time to sunbathe like everyone else and unwind. I felt like my panties were in a bunch and this was supposed to be my time for relaxation. Not sit around and stress about a man who would remain off-limits to me.

A nice soothing shower was what I needed and time to clear my head. The tranquility could be done, and I had to have space for myself. But there was only one problem.

Baxter.

I halted at our suite door and spun around to face him. He stopped directly behind me and peered down at me with confusion. His blue eyes teased me and reminded me of all the dirty things he could do to a desperate woman like me.

But I had to remain strong and keep my independent composure.

I cleared my throat and said firmly, "I think it's time for us to go our separate ways for the remainder of our vacations, Mr. Lane."

"And why is that?" Baxter asked as his warm breath touched my cheek and he leaned in closer. "As far as I could tell, you took pleasure in my company last night."

Baxter grinned with wicked tease at me, and I moved backwards. My backside bumped into the door for our suite, and Baxter closed the gap between us. His firm body pressed up against mine and took my breath away. I couldn't budge, even if I wanted to.

I wanted to move, but I couldn't and my mind was a hot mess with reminders of him. His lips on my skin, his mouth and its wicked taunt, but his massive cock. Oh, his thick dick with thrusts of passion. His rock-hard length did a number on me and sent me straight into oblivion.

"I... I... Did not, Mr. Lane," I stammered with some resistance.

He reached out and touched my lips. "These plump pillows of beauty would love being wrapped around my cock."

I inhaled a quick breath, and my mind wandered to the thought of Baxter receiving a blowjob from me. The smooth skin of his massive dick on my lips as I wrapped him in warmth and he groaned from above me. The power I'd have over him and the control he'd let me own. He'd be all mine as I'd take him fully into my mouth and his world would explode wide open. His seed would gush from him and leave a salty wanted taste between my lips.

Baxter's eyes studied me, and I knew he took notice. He knew he affected me and his strong advances had me dying to give in. To let him take me and give me what I so desperately wanted.

But I had to withstand his tempting dirty talk.

"Enough of the foreplay, Mr. Lane," I snapped firmly and raised an eyebrow at him. "You have your own arrangements to oversee."

Baxter dropped his fingers from my lips and glared back with challenge. "My plans have taken an unexpected turn."

I snapped back, "Well, you can take them far away from here."

"I don't plan on it, darling," Baxter declared with determination and swiped his keycard to open the door.

Suddenly, the door opened behind me, and I stumbled backwards into our suite. The change of atmosphere threw me for a quick spin, but I regained my footing. Baxter followed me inside with a huge grin of accomplishment on his face. But the only thing he had accomplished was to piss me off.

His reluctance to take a hint got on my last nerve and he wasn't about to win the game he set into motion. The bold-faced move made me give into our attraction once again. But little did he know he'd be the horny loser.

"I'd like you to go now, Mr. Lane," I admitted, but was unsure of how much I meant it.

"But this is my room, too," Baxter argued with a reluctant huff. "We came to that conclusion yesterday, along with other things."

"If you're referring to our one-time romp, well, that was a mistake," I lied and headed for the bathroom. "Now, if you'll just see yourself out..."

"Where are you going?" Baxter asked with frustration.

"I'm going to take a shower," I admitted as I kept going and walked into the bathroom.

Baxter stepped towards me, but I held up a hand. I spun around to lock eyes with him and knew I needed to make myself clear. My heart beat wildly in my chest and I knew what I craved. I wanted him. My mind screamed at me to stop being such a stubborn ass and let him make me forget. But I had to stop this before the situation got worse.

"Care for some company?" Baxter teased and wouldn't give up.

"No, I'd rather use the shower head," I lied through my teeth and hated myself for it as the door slammed shut.

I leaned back against the door with a long sigh and regretted everything I said. I had to do it, though, to push him away. He knew what he wanted, and he wanted me. At least he wanted the fake me. Not the real me he doesn't even know.

A silly woman who let her husband cheat on her when all the red flags were there. A wife whose marriage was on the brink of a divorce. Baxter only knew a desperate woman who wanted to forget her past. He only knew this woman who tried so hard to move on and create a better person who could find true love. He never would and never could understand the real me.

His footsteps echoed as he walked, and I could envision the look of bewilderment on his stunning face. I wanted to open the door and tell him the truth of all my faults, but knew he could never understand. I couldn't even understand it.

"The thought of you naked behind this door is killing me, darling," Baxter admitted with a groan from the other side of the door. "Just open the door and we can forget this even happened."

I turned around and touched the door. My hand ran over it and I felt his energy through the door. The attraction sizzled even with this wooden structure between us. The need to give in was strong, and I wanted to be back inside his affectionate embrace, but I couldn't bear the thought of telling him the truth.

"No, please go, Mr. Lane." I whispered in defeat.

"Fine, I'll respect your wish, but I'm coming back. This isn't over, Brielle," Baxter said with certainty, and his footsteps followed.

I let out a breath as I heard the suite door close and I stood up from the door. I wandered over towards the mirror and gazed at my reflection. The face of remorse stared back at me from a woman I didn't recognize.

I hated myself for keeping the truth from Baxter, but I was in too deep. I feared he wouldn't understand my faults, and I didn't want to start off my life as a new woman with his judgement under my belt. This excursion was the start of my process and gaining freedom from the things James had done to me.

A phone ringing caught my attention, and I went out into the main room. I recognized the chime and knew it was my cell phone. The familiar ring tone made me follow the phone's direction, and I answered it on the fourth ring.

"Hello?" I answered.

"Brielle?" My best friend said on the other line.

"Oh, Evelyn, is it ever good to hear your voice." I sighed with happiness.

My best friend, for as long as I could remember, was on the other end. She was not only a great friend, but my business partner. We owned Match My Heart, a dating service to help clients find their soulmate.

"It's so good to hear yours too, but I've been trying to reach you," Evelyn admitted.

"You have?" I asked as I gazed down at my cell phone and saw the missed calls. "I'm so sorry. I left for dinner and thought I had taken my phone."

"Dinner? But it's got to be morning in Hawaii by now," Evelyn questioned.

"It is, but someone invited me to dinner and we ran into some trouble," I admitted and nervously bit my lip. "I mean... I went to dinner alone and—"

"Wait a minute..." Evelyn interrupted.

"It's not what you think, Evelyn. I..."

"I know about James," Evelyn blurted out.

"What?" I whispered in disbelief.

"I know that bastard left you for another woman," Evelyn admitted with anger. "And I know you took the vacation all alone and I've been trying to reach you since I found out."

"Oh, god..." I sighed and ran a hand over my face as I slumped down onto the bed. "I'm sorry you had to find out like this. I just never thought it would get out so soon."

"Well, somehow it did and I've been worried sick about you!" Evelyn exclaimed with concern in her voice.

I hadn't even stopped to think about my best friend. I had felt all alone and through all this, I still had the one person I could always count on. My mind was a mess, and I hadn't even considered reaching out to my best friend. Thoughts of James cheating and my impending divorce took over. But now I had one other problem.

My attraction to a man I couldn't have.

"I'm in such a mess, Evelyn..." I groaned with frustration.

"I could kill James," Evelyn admitted, and it made me smile. "No, better yet, I'll cut off his dick so he can never screw around on another woman again."

We laughed until tears fell from my eyes and it felt so good to have a piece of home with me. Evelyn was always the one person I could trust through every obstacle in life, and she always knew how to make me feel better. We'd always get through everything together and my divorce was next on the list. I knew coming home would be hard, but she would help make it right.

"Oh, I miss you so much," I admitted with a smile.

"I miss you too and can't wait to have you back. The business needs you right now," Evelyn said with dread. "The bills are continuing to pile up."

I knew exactly what she meant. Match My Heart was in debt. Every day that passed by was another day closer to us, having to close our doors on love. We were experts at finding the perfect fit, but we couldn't do it without paying our bills.

The business couldn't hold up much longer. We needed a miracle to save it. Fate needed to step in and help us keep Match My Heart afloat.

"Well, I'll be home before you know it. I just needed this time to refresh and start out as a new woman," I confessed with a smile.

"It sounds to me like you started out as a fresh woman with a dinner date last night," Evelyn teased.

"It was not a date. He was simply a man calling a truce," I explained as my cheeks blushed and I felt flustered inside at the thought of Baxter.

"A truce for what?" Evelyn asked with curiosity.

"A truce to be civil because we have to share a suite together," I added.

"What?" Evelyn exclaimed with shock. "You're sharing a room with another man after your husband left you at the airport?"

"Yes," I admitted.

"Is he hot?" she asked.

"Evelyn!" I exclaimed with flustered surprise and my cheeks burned hotter.

"I'll take that as a yes..." She giggled and teased. "Try not to sleep with him, okay?"

A silence fell over the line and my eyes widened with my hand clamped over my mouth. She spoke the words I didn't want to hear out loud. The truth of what I had done, and the attraction burned like an out-of-control flame between us. A man I couldn't have and wanted so desperately to give myself to just one more time.

"Brielle? Are you there?" Evelyn asked.

"Yes, I'm here." I sighed and knew right then she knew the truth.

She was my best friend, after all. Best friends had a sort of six sense. And Evelyn knew me better than anyone else.

"So, the sex was good?" Evelyn asked.

"Okay, that's enough prying into my life for today," I declared and wanted to reach through the phone line.

"Okay, okay, at least your vacation got off to a good start," Evelyn said, as I heard a phone ring in the background. "Well, business calls and I better go get that. I will see you when you get back."

"Okay, sounds good!" I sighed with relief and was glad my sex life wasn't a discussion any longer. "Go get us a new client!"

"Lord knows we need it..." Evelyn grumbled.

"Agreed, bye." I breathed and hung up the phone.

The conversation could've gone better, but at least I informed Evelyn of everything from my point of view. Not the gossip from the city. Now, she knew I'd be coming home from a hot one-time fling and at least the news was behind us.

When I got home, we needed to focus on our company. Match My Heart was top priority, and signing my name on the dotted line. I was determined not to let our business sink, and I'd do anything to keep it going.

Right now, I need to unwind and relax. There was a lot waiting for me at home and I needed to be prepared for it. This vacation had me pent-up with tension and not the good kind. But now it was time to decompress.

Forget the shower. I had a nice hot tub to enjoy with no one else around. The hot jet would help soothe the tension and get me to relax. Just the thought of it had me excited and ready to indulge.

I went over to my luggage with an extra spring in my step and opened up the zipper. My hands fumbled through my belongings in search of my black string bikini. But my eyes landed on something else.

Lingerie.

The black see-through lingerie I had purchased for the trip to help save my marriage. My last big ditch effort for us to be intimate again after months of him pushing me aside. Months of him pushing my affection to the sideline while he screwed another woman.

I had bought it on a whim and never even tried the piece on. I had wanted to save the surprise not only for James, but for myself. To see me in this see thru black flowered lace and feel sexy. I wanted to remember what it felt like to be admired, even if it was by myself.

"Fuck it..." I mumbled and grabbed the fabric.

I discarded my clothing on the floor right where I stood and changed into the lingerie I had chosen for this trip. James wasn't here to appreciate it, but I was. I wanted to feel sexy again. I had bought the intimate garment on a whim and I'd wear it on impulse.

The black garment fit me just right and hugged every curve of my body. I wandered over towards the full-length mirror by the window to admire the invested purchase for this vacation. But my reflection stunned me.

My desirable self stared back at me with wide eyes and my voluptuous ass stuck out to the side. Black lace followed the curve of the piece with stripes down the sides attached to my thigh high black stocking. I let my brown streaked hair out of its ponytail and my locks tumbled down my shoulders. My hands ran through my hair with a motion that made me feel attractive and the afternoon light shone against the hair strands.

The lingerie was a perfect fit for me, and I didn't even have anyone to share it with. James had left me and I was alone. This desirable garment was only a reminder of that. I shouldn't have even put it on.

What the hell was I thinking?

Again, I wasn't.

This new me was doing everything impulsively. I was supposed to find myself, not act like someone who I didn't even recognize. This was a bad idea and I should get changed.

But before I could, the door to the suite opened.

And in walked a surprised Baxter Lane.

TWELVE

Give Into Me

"Darling Brielle..." Baxter breathed as the door clicked closed behind him and he admired the view.

Baxter should have horrified me. I should run and hide, but something in his ocean blue eyes made me stay. I was stuck on the spot like a deer caught in the headlights.

Too drained to speak. Too shocked to move. But completely and utterly lost in his enchantment on me.

Baxter took one step at a time towards me with a slow movement, but his eyes never wavered from my body. He caught sight of the sunlight glistening on my tanned skin. His eyes spoke to me and told the tale of how much he admired my beauty within the seductive garment. The way my smooth skin looked in the lingerie and the way the black lacy fabric hugged my voluptuous figure.

I broke my gaze from Baxter, and unease crept over me. I was a stupid woman for even putting on something that symbolized my failure of a marriage. This piece of fabric was a memory of a desperate woman who wanted to save a marriage that was over. A woman who couldn't clearly see the wedding vows were broken and didn't want to admit to a doomed relationship.

I was a hopeless, dumb, and a betrayed woman.

"Baxter, I..." I gasped with embarrassment and held my hands over my intimate areas.

"No, don't..." Baxter breathed with certainty as his gaze roamed up my body and he met my eyes. "The piece is made for you. You're pure fucking perfection."

Baxter's index finger rubbed over his lips and his blue hues drifted back down my body. His gaze was electric, and I was under his spell. I slowly removed my hands and exposed myself to him. A move I knew I shouldn't make, but his eyes made me weak. They made me vulnerable and once again I was his.

He was inches away from me and at my backside. Baxter's deep gaze stared at my figure in the mirror's reflection. He removed his fingers from his lips and traced the outline of my body, but he wouldn't touch me. He wandered in a world I had never experienced with him before and I watched, holding my breath.

Baxter bit his lower lip with restraint and breathed huskily. "You fit the garment perfectly. The black lace embraces your womanly figure. The piece is destined to touch every inch..."

He touched my shoulder, and his warm breath caressed the flesh. "Every curve..."

He trailed his fingers down towards my cleavage and cupped my breast in his large hand. "Every shape..."

My breath left my lungs and exited my body. Excitement at his passionate touch coursed through me and made me shudder under his magic. The pad of his thumb caressed my nipple and the rosy bud came to life. My perky nipples were on full display from the natural light, and Baxter took it all in. He replaced his warm breath with his lips brushing my shoulder, and his eyes caught mine in the mirror.

His blue eyes were ablaze and on fire for me. I was the match, and he was the spark. We connected and our attraction blazed to life.

"You're more than just the perfection of beauty." Baxter breathed with coarse lust. "You're mine, my darling Brielle."

Baxter pinched my nipple, and my breath shuddered. I couldn't hold back because he did me in. My pussy was wet from his tender and affectionate touch. But his words made me completely his.

And I wanted nothing more within this moment.

"Yes..." I sighed with desire.

Baxter fondled my tit while his eyes left mine and his mouth kissed my shoulder. He ran his tongue where he kissed and went right up to the black strap on my lingerie. He took the strap between his teeth and pulled it over my shoulder blade. The fabric piece became loose and fell down on my arm. The move gave him full access to my exposed neck, and I quivered at the thought. I watched with an agape mouth lost in pure lust as he ran his tongue up the side of my neck. But I titled my head to give him more access.

"You smell like sun kissed rain, my darling," Baxter murmured along my skin.

I shivered when his warm breath caressed my flesh and he brushed my hair out of my way. Baxter flicked his tongue at my earlobe and the sensation of it quivered straight down to my cunt. My pussy ached for him as he took my lobe into his mouth and suckled on it.

Baxter wrapped his arm around my body and played with my other nipple. I leaned back against his rock-solid form and let him do his worst. I couldn't deny this and gave right in. He caught me at my lowest, but now lifted me up and showed me I was worthy. Worthy of passion, desired and full of life.

"Oh, Baxter..." I moaned as the back of my head leaned back onto his brawny chest.

Baxter's tongue continued its wanted taunt, and his hands squeezed my full breasts. The pads of his thumbs caressed circles around the rosy buds and the sensation made me ache for more. Under his sorcery, my hand fell over my navel and travelled towards my clit. My nub throbbed for attention, and Baxter's hands were busy. His mouth transfixed on other things, but I didn't have my hands tied up.

"Oh, yes..." I sighed with hunger.

My fingers found my nub and rubbed the wet flesh. Sweet juices leaked through the see-through fabric and coated my fingers. I circled my clit as he toyed with me, and I moaned for more.

A groan crept up his throat and vibrated against my ear. I knew he caught me playing with myself and the sight turned Baxter on. His cock throbbed against my behind and I circled my hips with the heated passion growing inside of me. The friction of my ass rotated against his dick and his hands left my nipples. They travelled down the curve of my body and rested on my hips. He made them sway and my ass pressed firmer up against his shaft.

"Fuck me, Brielle," Baxter groaned in my ear.

"Oh, I plan to," I teased with taunt.

Suddenly, Baxter let out a growl and spun me around to face him. I gasped at the quick change, of course and his eyes burned into mine with heated intensity. He breathed heavily into my face and my heart beat rapidly inside my chest. The sound roared and beat up into my throat as I maintained his stare with my hands at my side. His gaze travelled down to my lips that puffed out unsteady breaths and he reached out to touch them.

The tip of his index finger gently tugged down my bottom lip, and he breathed. "I want your pretty pink tightness wrapped around my cock."

I heard him pull down the zipper for his shorts and my eyes stayed fixated on his face. The way he gazed at my mouth and the way he bit at the inside of his lip with want. His nostrils flared with desire and my scent filled his lungs. Mr. Baxter Lane was a wild animal in heat and ready to pounce.

His shorts fell to the floor, and I knew his briefs went right with them. I couldn't turn away from his intense attention on me, even if I wanted to. His energy was on fire and dominated the room. He trapped me and completely intoxicated me.

Baxter's fingertip left my lips and his hands travelled down into my soft hair. His fingertips grazed down the nap of my neck and he rested them on my shoulders. He looped his fingers through the straps and pulled at the elasticity of them.

"But first, I want to see those beautiful tits while you suck on my dick." Baxter breathed with need and pulled the front of my lingerie down.

"Oh!" I gasped with surprise.

My tits spilled free and their plumpness bounced with his sudden movement. Baxter growled at the sight and grabbed my busty breasts. He didn't waste any time and bowed his head to lick my nipples.

His tongue wildly flicked over each one as they shared the lustful sensation he gave them. I moaned with desire and grabbed his hair. The strands of brown hair fisted into my hands and I watched him devour my tits. He took each mound and toyed with it. He pinched the nipples between his fingers, nibbled at the plump flesh, and suckled each breast into his ravishing mouth. I couldn't get enough of him and my pussy quivered with a longing I couldn't tame.

He was a savage, and I was his untamed temptress.

I tugged at his velvet smooth strands and he let himself breathe in the air. My chest rose and fell as his head rose. I looked him straight in the eyes and a wicked smirk crawled across my lips. I bent my knees and my face slowly fell away from his.

My tongue ran across my upper lip and I breathed. "It's your turn now."

Baxter watched me with his mouth slightly agape as air left his lungs and the anticipation grew within him. My eyes never left his and my hand found his solid shaft. I wrapped my hand around his massive cock and stroked him. Up and down while I watched his eyes swirl with lust. I pumped slowly as his smooth skin made the journey easy and I picked up the pace. His upper lip gave a slight twitch, and a groan escaped his gorgeous lips. He loved to watch me and I got off on observing him come undone.

"Oh, yes, Brielle..." He growled with desired encouragement.

Baxter's grunts of pleasure filled the room, and I bit my lower lip in desire. His eyes caught the motion like a bear hungry for meat and my pussy pulsated. Mr. Lane was incredibly sexy when pleasured.

"Oh, fuck, yes, pump me, darling..." Baxter groaned as he took off his shirt and exposed his spectacular chest.

I knelt on my knees and admired the view. Baxter stripped down with natural light gleaming off his magnificent body. His brawny abs tightened with gratification and his arms flexed as he reached out for my hair. He gathered my locks into pigtails and fisted the strands within his hands. He oozed power and Baxter made my mouth water. I wanted to delight him and please him the way any temptress should.

I switched my wicked taunt up and stretched out my tongue to flick the head of his dick. His stiff shaft bobbed in the air and he groaned with excitement. I repeated the action and a hint of pre-cum hit my tastebuds. The taste of his seed excited me, and I let my tongue glide down the sides of his shaft. One side and then the other, but I licked my way back to the tip. Once there, I swirled my tongue around his mushroom head dick and he groaned from above. My eyes were still on him as I brought him into my mouth and he clung onto my pigtails.

"Oh, yes, darling..." Baxter moaned with pleasure. "Fill that pretty wet hole full."

I wrapped my lips around his massive shaft and bobbed my head up and down at a slow pace. His cock reached the back of my throat and I'd pull back. I repeated this motion and picked up the pace. Baxter grunted in ecstasy and I watched him give in to me. I felt in control and I knew I held the power. The ability to bring him to his knees and kneel before his temptress.

I moaned against him, and his dick twitched at the vibrations. He enjoyed it so much I tasted another hint of precum as the man juice swirled with my spit and lubricated his dick for even more suction. My tits bounced with each bob of my head and made my pussy soaked. I craved his firm length inside of me and wanted him to fuck me senseless.

My tongue swirled around his cock when I pulled back, and I gave him a nibble of tease. He panted heavily as his hand moved my head to a rhythm of his own and he thrust his hips. His climax built, and he grunted from above. Baxter was close.

But I wanted to be screwed.

I pulled his dick out of my mouth with a pop and licked the head. "Fuck me like you mean it, Baxter."

"It would be my pleasure, darling." Baxter breathed with need. "One last nibble for me, sweetheart."

I did as instructed and swirled my tongue around his firm shaft. Twirled my tongue until he pressed my head forward and I took him whole. Filled my mouth full of him until the tip of his dick hit the back of my throat and I gagged. He pulled my pigtails back, and my head followed. But I gave him his desired nibble on the way out.

"Oh, yes, darling, you're so good to me, sweet thing," Baxter growled, and he let go of my hair.

"Oh!" I cried out as he lifted me up into his arms and carried me through the patio door.

I faced Baxter with my legs wrapped around his firm torso and his hips swayed with each step. My hands clung to his neck as he walked us straight towards the hot tub and I saw the jets bubble water inside. I quivered with desire in Baxter's arms and knew he intended for us to get into the warm water.

A gust of afternoon air brushed against my warm skin and cooled it. The humidity hadn't set in and the wind was a pleasant touch on my skin. The sunshine beamed off of us as Baxter stepped into the water and carried me with him. He sat us down inside, and I let out a slight gasp at the warmth surrounding me.

The bubbles from the water jet tickled my backside, and my legs unwound themselves from him. I kept my arms around his neck because I craved him this close to me. He protected me, made me feel secure and desired with him so nearby. There in his ocean blue depths was the sheer passion he had for me and his need to be buried deep inside me.

Baxter leaned in close, and his breath caressed my lips. "Be a good girl and spread those pretty little legs for me, darling."

I did as I was told, and he leaned me back into the water. My tits floated on top of the warm beads and he took each perky nipple into his mouth. He teased them again as I moaned with pleasure for him and his tongue swirled around each rosy bud.

The desired motion kept on and he put his hand under the water. He found my clit and circled it with his fingers. My hips rocked with his taunt and the warm jet from the hot tub caressed my spine. I shuddered with pleasure as he moved the lingerie's fabric aside and his mouth left my tits.

But his lips crashed onto mine.

Baxter took me into an earth-shattering kiss, and my head spun lost in desire. My lips parted for him and welcomed him inside. Our tongues twisted with each other and his finger moved on my nub. My climax grew, and he knew I was as close as he was. But I needed him inside of me.

I disobeyed his order and wrapped my legs around him once again. This time, his gigantic dick was right at my pussy's entrance and I enticed him to dive inside. He kissed me with such passion I thought I was going to explode, but he eased back and caught my lower lip between his teeth.

He let my lip go, and his gaze burned into my hungry eyes. "You are so fucking bad and I'm going to punish you, darling."

And his thick dick dove inside of me.

Baxter claimed my pretty lips and concealed my cry of desire. We trapped my moans inside his throat as he thrust to the hilt and never stopped. Waves of water gushed out the sides of the hot tub with each pound as he pumped me full of him and my pussy walls clamped down. Baxter grunted deep within his chest and let his need for me escape onto my lips. Our heavy breaths mingled as one and our waves of passion moved in unison.

Baxter broke our kiss and groaned a command, "Look at me, darling."

I did as he ordered as our release built higher and higher. The waves of water crashed, but his lust for me was strong. A force no one could break, not even me. Baxter Lane wanted me more than anyone else in this world, and I couldn't deny him any longer.

"Oh, yes, Bax!" I cried out with my release.

Baxter thrust deep into the hilt of me and exploded. "Oh, fuck!"

Wave after wave of pure frantic frenzy zinged through our bodies as we came together and reached our peak. Baxter's dick spasmed inside of me and let his seed free. The warm liquid gushed into me and mixed with my own. The water calmed as Baxter's thrusts of pleasure subsided and he tenderly kissed my forehead. Next came a peck on my nose and then he captured my mouth once more.

Baxter lifted me back into the safety of his arms and carried me to the bed we had to share within the suite. A room I was supposed to share with my soon-to-be ex-husband, but fate flew in. James left me and Baxter was here. I was in another man's affectionate arms and I never wanted to leave.

I had tried to push away from him, but his certainty of me was too strong. Baxter wanted me and he wanted all of me, but I knew I couldn't give him that. I had too much to deal with at home and he had no clue what he got himself into.

So, as he held me close in his arms, I listened to his heartbeat. The sound of his heart against my ear as he held me close and never wanted to let me go. I'd miss the attentiveness from him and my soul ached.

If I had fallen for Baxter Lane, it was too late. I couldn't let him discover the real me in fear he'd hate me. Baxter gave me no choice but to leave him once the early morning sun rose.

THIRTEEN
Back to Reality

I took the earliest flight I could. The plane was on time and everything went smoothly. Even my fear of flying.

Why?

Because I couldn't stop thinking about Baxter.

The man I left behind in our shared resort suite. In a bed meant for us because fate had brought us together against all odds. A wonderful man who made me see I could trust again. A passionate man, both in and out of the sack. Baxter was a man who wanted me.

But I couldn't commit.

I was untruthful and kept my reality from him. I headed back to my real life and had to face it head on. This mess I couldn't bear bringing Baxter into.

An impending divorce. A failed marriage. My broken life.

Baxter was an exceptional man, and he deserved more. He was a billionaire with his own company and his own life. Baxter should have a woman ready for all of it. My disaster of a life wouldn't fit into his world. I wasn't ready for more heartbreak. My focus was on my company and myself. I had to find myself again.

My cell phone chimed as I made it back to the condo and I gazed down at multiple text messages from my best friend. She kept me up to date on everything business related and I had sent her a quick text before I left Hawaii. I let her know I was coming home early, but that was all she needed to know.

For now, at least.

I knew a billion questions would come out of her mouth and she'd want the inside scoop. She'd want to know why I left vacation so soon, and I wasn't sure I was ready to reveal the truth. I wasn't even sure I was ready to admit the truth to myself.

I shook my head and opened the door. The still air greeted me from inside the condo I used to share with James. A loneliness crept over me and I sighed.

I missed being wanted. I craved to be touched. But not by James and someone else.

"You need to forget about him..." I sighed out loud to myself and left my luggage by the front door.

I left vacation prematurely simply because I had more important matters to attend to at home and that would be the last. No more missing a man who was never mine to begin with. Mr. Baxter Lane would stay in Hawaii and become a mere memory. Our lives had to move on.

A small pile of mail was in my hand, and I had gathered envelopes at the mailbox. An oversized envelope stuck out from all the rest, and I knew what was inside. I didn't have to open the package to know it was what I had been waiting for since I left the city and flew away on vacation.

I put the rest of the mail down and zoned in on the large beige envelope. A million thoughts entered my mind, but I knew this was coming all along. The moment was here, and I had to face it head on. I had to face my new reality.

I was about to sign for a divorce.

My key ripped away at the sticky opening of the envelope and I sat down on the bar stool. The island was spotless, just the way I had left it. I had wanted a clean home to come back to with my husband and our second chance at love. Everything was to be polished and a fresh start for the both of us. But here I sat with divorce papers.

I peered down at the dotted line I was supposed to sign right near James's signature. For him, this was a done deal. He was ready to move on with another woman and leave our vows behind. James had made that clear when he stepped outside of our marriage and into bed with someone else.

But was I ready?

Inside my mind, I was. James was a cheater and an asshole. He never understood me and never wanted to try. It was easier for him to find someone else.

Deep down inside myself, I wasn't ready to give up because I didn't want to admit defeat. I didn't want a failed marriage. Our unsuccessful marriage had nothing to do with James and more to do with me.

I wasn't a person to give up. I was a woman who fought for what I believed in and I believed in marriage. Divorce was never something I wanted. But life doesn't always go according to plan.

I picked up a pen and stared down at the spot I was supposed to sign. My chest rose and fell with a heavy weight I couldn't shake. The pen tapped anxiously on the island and I bit my lower lip.

Once I signed on the dotted line, my marriage was over. All we had would be gone. I got this condo, but that was it.

James had me sign a prenup, and I was more than willing to prove my trust to him.

But James shattered his word into pieces.

James was a wealthy enough man to afford whatever he wanted. He never needed me, and he certainly proved his point. He never loved me the way a real man should, and I wasn't even sure he loved himself.

Bitterness boiled inside of me at a man I thought I knew. A person I wanted to spend the rest of my days with. An individual I once pictured myself having children with. But he never existed, and I lied to myself.

I made up a version of my husband, who wasn't even real.

And I needed to move on.

"Fuck you, fake husband." I breathed with resentment and signed on the dotted line. "Now ex-husband."

The deal was done. I sealed my fate. Our marriage was over.

A calm washed over me, but the hatred for James continued to loom. I hoped one day the bitterness would fade. Little by little, I could let go and learn to love again. But I knew I could trust.

All because of dashingly handsome Baxter Lane.

I groaned and tossed the pen aside. My brain needed to forget Mr. Lane. I had to get his touch, the sound of his voice and the hot images of his body seared into my mind out of my head. The remembrance of him needed to leave me alone. Just for a little while.

I got the divorce papers ready and my next stop was to hand them into my lawyer. The firm would take care of the rest and I'd be a free woman. Ready to take on the world with a failed marriage. I was nowhere near ready for the dating scene, but I could dive into my clients' love matched worlds.

At least I had my business to look forward to.

Match My Heart was now my entire world and its very existence was a top priority. The company Evelyn and I created was the baby I never got to have. I was determined to see our hard work thrive.

The business needed me now more than ever, and I desperately wanted to make it a success. I had to succeed at something now that my marriage bit the dust. I couldn't have Match My Heart follow right along with it.

I quickly checked my reflection in the bathroom mirror and touched up my bright red lipstick. I still wore the dress I had worn for the plane ride home, but it would do the trick. A simple stop to my lawyer was overdue and a brief stop for groceries was in order. I was back in business and work demanded my prompt return.

I had a business crumbling at the seams and Match My Heart needed to be saved. There was no time to waste because my career depended on it. My entire existence needed this to work. Without my job, I had nothing left, but this condo which was written in my name.

I neatly tucked the divorce papers into my oversized purse and I put on my high heels. I straightened my back and fixed my dress. My mission was clear, and I was not only going to save my company. But I was determined to rescue myself.

FOURTEEN
New Client

A few days had passed since I handed in my divorce papers. The lawyer promised to inform me when he would finalize the divorce, but in my eyes, our marriage was over long ago. There was no need to hold on to the past when James had disrespected me the way he had. But according to the law, it would take up to six long months.

The time was meaningless compared to everything else. I had my broken heart to mend. Along with memories of a man I had vacationed with in Hawaii and I must get Baxter out of my head. But Match My Heart had to come first because it was worse than I expected.

My return to work had been a chaotic one. We had no new clients while I was away, which meant no money to pay the bills. Not only were bill payments piling up, but we soon faced foreclosure. We weren't able to make loan payments anymore with our savings drained. Our own savings were the only payments keeping this place afloat. But now the money was gone.

Our business required funding, and in order to get the money, we needed a client. Preferably a wealthy customer. Match My Heart needed a miracle.

Hell, my business demanded fate to step up to the plate.

I gazed down at my wristwatch and knew it was almost time to leave for work. Evelyn expected me and needed my help today with getting bill payments in order. She wanted everything organized so we could pay the bills off once we had the funds for each one. The process would take time and it all depended on how quickly we could gain new clientele. I had my fingers crossed that help would come soon.

My reflection gazed back at me as I pulled my blonde streaks back and secured the hair tightly with an elastic band. The ponytail was high just the way I liked it, and my professional appearance suited me for the day. I always maintained a professional look even if the workday wasn't too busy. We had no customers, which meant very little to do except get everything prepared for when we did.

My black knee-length dress tightly hugged my curves and my shiny lip gloss shimmered with the light. I pucker my lips together and fluff my ponytail. My cell phone rang out with an alarm for my last wake up call, but I had been up early enough and didn't need it. I switched the device off and reset it for tomorrow. A brand-new start and another day.

Hopefully, a day with a new client.

I smiled to myself with positivity and headed for the kitchen. My favorite coffee mug was all set to go, and I pressed start to get the machine running. The appliance started right up and gave me a gentle good morning. The machine hummed, and I got out the creamer. A few minutes later, my coffee was ready, and I prepared it in my favorite mug. I stirred the hot liquid and blew over the top. The coffee cooled down slightly, and I took a quick sip.

Just right.

My black heels clicked along the floor, and I swung my purse over my shoulder. I grabbed my keys and locked the door behind me. I was careful not to spill my beloved morning brew and made my way towards the car.

This coffee was my only boost of energy for an early morning start, and I didn't care if I carried around my butterfly coffee mug from home. My favorite mug was a normal routine for me and one I had got used to after all these years. I wouldn't stop now. Plus, butterflies were beautiful and my preferred choice. There was no reason to be ashamed of an insect with such elegance and the image always uplifted my day.

I found my black Bentley convertible parked right where I left it and clicked my key fob until it chirped. As I opened the door, the warm sun shone on my exposed shoulders and I warmly accepted the greeting. I took another sip of my coffee and placed the hot mug in the cup holder. I had to be sure I drank enough and the brew wouldn't spill. This car was expensive and I couldn't afford parts for it right now.

James had helped me pay for the most luxurious car I had ever owned, but I got to sign my name on the dotted line for it. This car was all mine, and I didn't owe him another dime. Especially since he stuck his dick inside someone else.

My convertible purred to life, and I opened up the top. It was a beautiful day, and I wanted to bask in the sunshine. I put on my sunglasses as my foot hit the gas and I was off into the busy city.

Street after light passed, and the breeze blew my ponytail behind me. The wind felt good against my heated flesh from the sun and the car moved faster. My workplace wasn't far away from the condo, but I hit a slight traffic jam. I distracted myself with some tunes and my favorite song came on. My fingers drummed on the steering wheel as the beat filled the air and put me in a perky mood.

I peered to my right at the red light and a gorgeous gentleman was in a fancy car beside mine. He flashed me a charming smile and pulled down his shades to get a better view. His black hair shone in the daylight and he had green eyes. I flashed him a flirtatious smile, and he eyed me at the light. The flirty gesture made me feel sexy and his engine revved. I knew he flirted with me, but I gazed back towards the green light and took off. I left him in the dust and took off down the street.

Match My Heart was just up ahead, and I didn't have time to waste it on a man I'd never see again. I had more important matters to deal with and my company required my full attention. I would have to put my dating life on hold and my love life would suffer. But so would my sex life.

I frowned at the thought as I pulled into work and parked the convertible in my regular spot. My only parking spot with my name plated on a sign in front of me. Our very own parking space had been Evelyn's brilliant idea, and I loved it. The thought of my space made the job feel rewarding, and the idea was unique.

The car turned off, and I put my sunglasses back where they belonged. I swung my purse over my shoulder and grabbed my cooled coffee. The liquid went down nicely and a zig of energy went through me. I carried the mug with me and glanced up at the sign with a banner overhead.

Match My Heart.

I walked through the doors of my business and pride fell over me as I took in the surroundings. We picked pink and black tones of furnishing, but kept the walls white. The colorless paint made the pink and black colors throughout come to life. We wanted Match My Heart to be elegant with a splash of love.

Up ahead, I saw my best friend seated behind the front desk with our slogan across the front of it, 'Where two hearts become one.' We didn't have a secretary because we couldn't afford one and Evelyn volunteered to do the job. She was the best choice for managing incoming clientele and answering the phone line. She would have to do it until we could hire the perfect fit.

Behind the front desk was a large closed off office and the workroom held two desks. One for myself with my nameplate and the same on the other for my business partner. A bunch of paperwork was on top of mine and the area needed some organization.

We had some large filing cabinets along the wall to place information on each client, old and new. Along with potential matches. I didn't rely on technology to help a lost soul find its match. Technology was too unpredictable and was bound to fuck up at some point. I printed out each client's information, their matches, and everyone who joined our dating service hoping to find their missing piece. Match My Heart had a ton of potential, but we were missing one important factor.

Word of mouth.

Our business had enough people hoping to bring matches together, but we just needed the right clients to spread the word about our business. Match My Heart just required an extra push to throw it into the spotlight. Our company demanded a wealthy customer to take us from a small business to a thriving success.

Don't get me wrong. We have had plenty of clients come through, but unfortunately, we needed someone who made a ton of money. We desperately needed luck on our side this time.

A couple of clients would do the trick for the time being and help us pay the bills, but I was tired of just getting by. Just making ends meet had eaten into our personal funds, and those investments were gone. I was driven to find something more and set us on track for the finer things in life.

"Good morning, beautiful." Evelyn announced as she greeted me with a morning peck on the cheek and smiled with upbeat spunk.

I returned her smile and knew something was up. Evelyn was far too chipper for this early in the morning. She either had big news or got laid last night.

My best friend's deep brown eyes sparkled with excitement, and she clasped her hands together. I knew the gears spun inside her brown headed mind and I wanted to find out what information she held. Evelyn was up to something.

"Something has you in bright spirits this morning..." I mumbled with curiosity, "So, spill the beans."

"I thought you'd never ask..." She grinned with excitement and clapped her hands together in front of her pretty red lips. "Luck is finally on our side."

"Okay..." I asked and urged her to continue, "And..."

"And we've landed a new client!" Evelyn answered, "But not just any client. One that's guaranteed to pay the bills."

"What? Who?" I questioned her with shocked surprise and placed my coffee mug on the desk before I made a mess.

"He called a few days ago and he wouldn't give his name," she mumbled with uncertainty and thrust a piece of paper in front of my face. "But this was just the down payment."

I gazed at the transaction with a bunch of zeros in black ink, and it blew me away. We only required fifty percent for a down payment before services began, but this was far beyond that. This number was more than any of the services we required.

The deposit was far too generous, but it would be the boost we needed to pay off some of the foreclosure payment. The amount didn't cover it all, but once the job was done, we'd be free. There was no way I would let this client slide, and he'd be our ticket out of this mess.

"So, it's a man I will have to find the perfect match for." I breathed with determination and headed towards my desk in the office.

"Yes." Evelyn sighed with relief and followed behind me. "But this is our big break and we can't afford to screw it up."

Male clientele didn't come around often. Customers of the opposite gender usually came through the doors of Match My Heart in desperate need of love. Females wanting to find their soulmates and happy ever afters.

"There's no way in hell we can fuck this up." I laughed with comfort at the thought of our prayers being answered.

I grew more curious by the minute about this male client we knew absolutely nothing about except he was filthy rich. He wanted a small dating service to find him a match when he could go with a well-known company. I didn't quite understand why he'd pick us, but at this point I couldn't care less. The man was about to save our company from destruction and he didn't even know it.

Evelyn grabbed my wrist and peered down at my wristwatch. "He should call at any moment."

"Well, I can take the call and..." I said.

"No, I'll do it," Evelyn argued and released my wrist from her grasp. "I'm the receptionist until we can afford to hire one. We agreed on that, remember?"

"I do," I agreed with a smile. "I should stay focused on not screwing this up for the both of us."

"Right." Evelyn nodded. "Besides, I'm better at taking phone calls."

I worked best at finding the right match. Evelyn helped, but in the end, the responsibilities all landed on me. She was counting on me to come through and the pressure was on. I was determined to tackle this new project with a rational mind and leave all my emotions on the doorstep. Nothing could mess this opportunity up and I wouldn't let anyone stand in my way.

Not even myself.

Suddenly, the phone rang from the front desk, and Evelyn sprang into action. She knew it had to be our mystery man who would save us from foreclosure. She glanced back at me with a smile and I returned my excitement.

Evelyn picked up the phone and breathed. "This is Match My Heart, where two hearts become one. How can I help you?"

My being beamed because we were back in business. Everything was on track for success and nothing could break down the journey. Our newest customer wanted to find his perfect equal, and I had a job to do.

Nothing could go wrong.

I heard Evelyn wrap up the call with welcomed words. "Okay, we will see you in ten minutes."

She hung up the phone with a squeal of energy and clapped her hands to a beat. She swayed her hips and made her own rhythm. The excitement grew within Match My Heart, and I loved this sudden turn of events. The victory was just the boost we needed and a necessary distraction from my undesirable love life.

"This calls for a victory dance!" Evelyn shouted from the main room.

"Damn right it does!" I shouted in return.

We giggled and basked in the joy of the successful moment in time. A moment our business needed to move forward and not crumble into dust. We danced a happy dance and got ourselves pumped for what was to come.

I danced around the office to Evelyn's beat and cleaned up. The paperwork I had to organize would have to wait, and I stuffed papers inside the filing cabinet. That work wasn't a priority anymore and the arrangement would come later. I hummed a tune to her tempo and rearranged items that really didn't need it, but I was pleased to do it for our unnamed client.

Evelyn stayed at the front desk and prepared for his arrival. She would greet him professionally and lead him towards our office. We knew exactly what to do and everything had to run smoothly. We terribly required this to all work out. If not, we were doomed.

The seconds ticked by and they turned into minutes. The clock on my wristwatch clicked and the arm moved forward. Time moved at a slow speed as I tidied up and got everything prepared. But around the ten-minute mark, the front doorbell chimed.

He was a man of his word. Our mysterious man wasn't late. He was right on time.

The sweet sound of his welcomed presence made me purr with excitement and I took my seat at my desk. The dance left me and I turned into a businesswoman. A pure professional matchmaker ready to make a match in heaven.

My ponytail tossed over my shoulder and I pressed down on my black dress. I was a woman who knew exactly what to do and could achieve any requirement he set for me. I was ready for this. We were born for this. Our business was ready to take on the world.

Bring it on, Mr. Mysterious.

The chair swiveled forward, and my knees hid underneath the desk. I clicked a button on my laptop and our logo lit up the screen. Pen and paper were ready for note taking and questions. My brain went into matchmaker mode and I set myself up.

I heard footsteps lead towards the office, and the moment was here. Evelyn stepped into our office with a bright smile on her face, but she meant one hundred percent business. She set her deep brown focus on the prize and she knew how much we needed this to work. She understood the risk and we could lose everything. Our dreams could be gone, but destiny was about to step through the door and save us.

Evelyn turned back to the man who came here for his soulmate and announced, "Brielle, I'd like you to meet our new client, Mr. Baxter Lane."

Everything slowed down as Baxter walked through the doors of my office with a handsome grin on his face. His brown hair fell into his eyes and he brushed the strands away like he always did. He was a stud in a suit with a tie and not in any vacation attire. His expensive black shoes clicked along the tile and matched the blink of my eyes. His ocean blue eyes seared into mine and he searched my face for an answer I wasn't sure of.

"It's a pleasure seeing you again, Brielle." Baxter breathed with certainty. "But I need Match My Heart to find me a wife."

FIFTEEN
Blindsided

Fate just burst in through the front door, and I had no idea how to react. I couldn't move anything except my wide eyes full of surprise as they took him in and fluttered his way. Baxter Lane was here in my office and he wanted a wife.

Mr. Lane wanted me to find him a wife.

Baxter was the man I met on vacation and no matter what happened, I couldn't escape him. A man I fell into bed with and he made me come alive. He had respected me and my emotions. He was a lover I couldn't forget, but now I had to because he sought his perfect match.

Our worlds kept colliding, no matter what we did. Fate unexpectedly trampled in one more time and our lives were on a collision course of epic proportions. Baxter hired me to find him love. He wanted the woman he slept with multiple times to obtain him dates. He needed me in a way I never would've dreamed of and I wasn't sure how I felt about it.

Evelyn looked between both of us and scrunched up her face. "Wait, you know each other?"

I didn't answer her because I couldn't form the right words. I was stunned and I couldn't wrap my brain around my terrible situation. We could save Match My Heart if everything went right.

But how could it?

Baxter was an ex-lover. He was a hot hunk who I fell into bed with not even a week ago. But worst of all, he was a billionaire bachelor who extremely attracted me.

Damn him.

Baxter's gaze never left mine, and his ocean blue hues searched my face for understanding. I didn't know how to give it to him because I wasn't ready for any of this. We'd have to work closely, and I'd have to know everything there was to know about him. I'd have to be alone with him and stuck within close proximity. Forced to be near him when I should be anything but because he was everything I couldn't forget.

Baxter answered Evelyn with honesty, "Yes, we do."

Evelyn turned towards me with her mouth open and asked, "How do you know one another?"

I just shook my head in defeat and looked away from Baxter. My eyes fell to my hands, and they shook in my lap. I clasped them together and made them stop. This was too much, and I did not know how to deal with this unpredictable situation. Everything was out of my control and destined to fall apart.

But I couldn't let it.

I had to push through, no matter what. My world depended on it. He already made a deposit of great value. I couldn't turn away and had a job to do. A project I couldn't fail at even though my heart felt like it would burst out of my chest.

Baxter cleared his throat and replied, "We met on vacation."

Baxter didn't lie and was truthful. He just left out the most important part, and I didn't want to fill in any blanks. I just wanted to run into his arms and forget this ever happened. I wanted him to make me forget.

Unfortunately, it was too late because Baxter required a wife. Not me, and I wanted this to all be a bad dream. One I'd awake from and he would be anyone other than him. A complete stranger and not a man who fascinated me.

I blew out a shaky breath and knew I had to pull it together at some point. All eyes were on me as Evelyn raised her eyebrows and opened her mouth, only to clamp it shut again. Baxter simply stood there with his hands in his pockets like he just didn't come in here and burst my world wide open.

The more I let this situation process, the more I grew enraged. Baxter came here and expected me to do this after we spent days together. He must have known I'd be here, and this was completely insane. Frustration grew inside me and bubbled to the surface. I wouldn't let him off easily, and I deserved answers.

I stood from my seat with a fuse of annoyance and stalked over to him. My finger pointed at him and I held my stance as I confronted him. There had to be an explanation for this. Fate couldn't be this cruel.

"Are you stalking me, Mr. Lane?" I asked and demanded an answer.

Baxter's eyes blazed into mine, and they swirled with amusement. He enjoyed himself and it only rattled me more. His behavior reminded me of my vacation and when I found him in my suite. A room we shared and slept together in.

His mouth curved up into a grin, and he crossed his arms in front of him. "No, this is all pure coincidence."

My eyes blinked at him with his response and I couldn't believe life would throw me this curveball. No wonder I never believed in fate before. Destiny was a cold, hard bitch.

I dropped my finger and knew from this point forward I had to forget. I had to treat Baxter like any other client and push whatever was between us down into a hole. Deep down and far past my heart. I had to bury this attraction in darkness and never let it see the light.

I plastered a professional smile on my face and peered up into his sapphire eyes. "In that case, welcome to Match My Heart, Mr. Lane. How can we help you?"

"I need you to play matchmaker," Baxter responded.

"And why is that?" I asked with curiosity and crossed my arms.

"I work for a family-owned lingerie company. I need a wife because it will be good for my business," Baxter stated with little detail.

I eyed him with uncertainty in his answer, but I had no choice in the matter. It was my job to believe every word he spoke. Baxter was my client and he could give me any explanation he wanted. He was the one in charge and called the shots. I was the target and just had to learn when to dodge the gunfire or let him hit me with the next bullet.

Mr. Lane was my boss and whatever he wanted went. I had a job to serve. Match My Heart depended on him, and there wasn't anything else to it. I had to remain professional, qualified, and I had a task to complete. I'd find Mr. Baxter Lane his perfect match.

I turned my back to him and walked back to my desk. I tapped the enter button on my laptop and got ready to take down his basic information. We required the details of contact and it was standard protocol.

"Okay, I will just need some personal information if you have time?" I requested with a smile.

Baxter peered down at his high-priced wristwatch and met my eyes. "Unfortunately, today won't work. I have a business meeting to get to."

"Okay, not a problem, Mr. Lane." I breathed and got ready to type in an appointment time. "How does tomorrow at noon sound?"

Baxter smoothed his tie with his hand and replied, "Tomorrow at noon sounds perfect, but we will meet at my office."

We don't normally meet anywhere else except Match My Heart. This was a rule, so we could remain professional and get the job done efficiently. But this project differed from any I had before.

Baxter wasn't any normal task, and I couldn't afford to mess up the job. I'd do anything to please him. He was just a customer, after all. A very high paying one.

"Okay, we will meet there." I breathed with certainty, and Evelyn peered towards me with the opposite. "Can I get your company name?"

"It's Lane's Lingerie," Baxter replied.

I searched for it on my laptop and retrieved the address. "Got it. We're all set for tomorrow."

"Perfect..." Baxter said, and he fastened his eyes on me. "I look forward to seeing you again, Brielle."

"Yes, we will see you tomorrow," I said with a nod of my head and kept it brief.

"Evelyn, it was a pleasure meeting with you..." He breathed in a hoarse tone and the sound was far too sexy. "I look forward to this, ladies."

"We're pleased to have you, Mr. Lane." Evelyn beamed with excitement. "We will find you the woman of your dreams."

Baxter's eyes roamed over me, and my skin crawled with heat. The familiar tingle fell over me and he awakened the flame. But I had no choice and had to let the attraction fizzle out.

We were in a commitment of business. A strict professional manner had to be upheld, and it was up to me to do it. I couldn't cross the line or this could all go up in smoke.

Baxter's blue oceans met mine, and he bedazzled me. "I'm sure you will."

He broke eye contact and left the room with confidence. Something I lacked at this point and I had to fake it till I crossed the finish line. Evelyn peered at me all the way out of the office as she followed behind him and saw him out.

I blew out a breath of relief and fell back into my chair. His dominant presence no longer held me back. I didn't have to continue to fake what I truly held inside. Pure fear mixed with doom. Undeniable terror. This was all a huge mistake. I dreaded tomorrow already, and it hadn't even begun yet.

What the hell was I going to do?

Evelyn wandered back into the room with her arms crossed and stood in front of my desk. Her brown eyes seared into me with a million questions, and I knew she demanded answers. But I understood she deserved the truth.

"Will you please tell me what the hell that was all about?" Evelyn insisted, and wouldn't back down, "Mr. Lane is officially our client and I want the truth right now."

"What do you want to know?" I asked and rested my arms on the chair.

"Did you sleep with our client, Brielle?" Evelyn asked.

I sighed my truth. "I did, but he wasn't our client at the time."

"Oh, my god..." Evelyn groaned with fright. "How does this even happen?"

"You're asking the wrong person here." I sighed with frustration.

"Did you tell him this was your job?" Evelyn asked.

"No, we never exchanged personal details. He only knew my first name, and that was it," I explained and shook my head. "I do not know how this could happen."

"Well, fate must have it out for you," Evelyn teased.

I shot her a look and muttered, "Luck isn't on my side."

"But success is on the horizon." Evelyn beamed with positivity. "Your billionaire fling is going to save us from ruin."

Evelyn was right. She was always the voice of reason. I had to believe in something great while the rest of my life headed for destruction.

"You're right." I sighed. "Now I just have to forget I had amazing sex with my client not once, but twice. It should be a piece of cake, right?"

Evelyn leaned down and placed her hands on my shoulders. Her deep brown eyes peered into mine with uncertainty, but her face remained without doubt. Certain I could do this, but her eyes didn't agree.

"You can do this, Brielle..." She breathed and shrugged. "But you need a drink to go with that piece of cake."

I frowned and gave her a troubled look. "No, I'm going to need a full bottle of wine."

SIXTEEN
Strictly Business

I awoke with a foggy brain. My mind was a mess from a troubled evening and not much sleep. Little bits were a blur, and I knew I enjoyed a few glasses of red wine. But now my head hurt and I regretfully wished I hadn't.

"Oh, god..." I groaned with anguish.

I shouldn't have taken my best friend's advice and just indulged in my normal routine, but nothing about this was ordinary. My life was a mess and headed for destruction. My career hung by a thread and Baxter Lane could cut it apart.

My blurry vision adjusted to the light, and I covered my hand over my eyes to block it. I must have passed out on the couch, and my back ached in response. My morning would follow in the course of my evening. Completely out of the ordinary.

My alarm never sounded because there was no need to set it. Evelyn didn't need me and wanted me to prepare for an afternoon with Baxter. She wanted me to be ready for him, but all I felt was hungover.

I painfully rolled off the couch and my feet hit the floor. I stood there with wobbly legs while the world spun, and I wished I could go back to bed. To curl up into the fetal position and leave this grim day behind. Let the world fade away and I drift off into slumber. A place where reality doesn't matter and my imagination took over. But the dream wasn't an option.

The clock ticked by and made my head throb. I needed a strong coffee. The powerful brew would do the trick and I needed a wakeup call.

The time on my wristwatch read I had an hour. I slept in far too late. Our brand-new client couldn't wait and I had to get it together.

Evelyn would meet me at Lane's Lingerie and we agreed on that before I left work, but plans had changed. I was in no shape to drive and sent her a quick text. She responded right back, 'I'll swing by on my way. Be there in twenty.'

Twenty whole minutes. I had very little time to get my shit together and get ready. I needed to get the stench of a boozy night off of me, prepare an intense brew and gather my thoughts.

I got my coffee going and headed straight for the shower. There was no time to be clean, and I'd organize my mess later. My clothes from yesterday fell all over the bathroom floor and I didn't wait for the water to warm up.

I let out a sharp gasp as the cool beads covered my skin, and I cleansed my body. The dirty smell turned into a fresh scent and I moved onto my fruity shampoo. I scrubbed my hair in a quick motion and rinsed the fruitiness out. Everything fell down the drain and I turned off the faucet. I dried up the wetness and got dressed in a red dress.

There was no time to brush my teeth, and a breath mint would have to do. Makeup could wait until the car ride over to my scheduled appointment and a quick bun for my wet hair would be enough. I fastened my locks in place and grabbed a new butterfly mug for my powerful coffee. The warm liquid would help clear my hungover head and I'd be ready.

At least, I hoped so.

There was no time to dwell on it and I grabbed my purse along with the laptop I needed for the job. My legs sped me out the door in a flash just as Evelyn pulled up in the parking lot. Everything was back on track.

But why did my mind scream at me otherwise?

"Morning sunshine." Evelyn beamed as I opened the door to her little blue car and she smiled brightly. "Someone looks hungover."

"Don't remind me..." I mumbled as I got into the passenger seat and my head throbbed.

I took a much-needed sip of my coffee and the warm liquid felt good on the way down. My head continued to ache from the bright morning light and I put my shades on. The sunglasses blocked the rays and helped, but I just had to wait for the warm brew to kick in.

"So, are you ready for this?" Evelyn asked as she pulled out onto the street and headed for Lane's Lingerie.

"Nope, but do I have a choice?" I responded with question.

"It's not too late and I could go for you," Evelyn added with concern. "You could play hooky and pretend you're sick."

I wanted nothing more at this point than to be ill. I'd take on a cold and tackle the sickness in bed instead of having to face this. Time spent with Baxter Lane. A billionaire bachelor hunk who wanted me, his latest fling, to find him a wife.

"No, we both need to be there and present as a united front for our business," I responded with a regretful sigh. "For the first meeting, anyway."

"Well, this is out of the norm for a meeting with a client. We don't go where the customer chooses. They come to us," Evelyn added.

"Everything about this is out of the ordinary." I sighed and looked over at Evelyn. "But Baxter is the luck we've been waiting for, and I will not let him get away."

"You mean Mr. Lane, right, Brielle?" Evelyn questioned with a raised eyebrow.

"Right, Mr. Lane," I agreed with a shake of my head.

"We need to keep this strictly business and we do as our client wishes," Evelyn said in a matter-of-fact tone.

My best friend meant business, and I did, too. We had too much at stake and we both knew it. Unfortunately, Evelyn didn't understand. It was harder for me when I knew Baxter in a different light. I spent personal time with him and none of it would've happened. But it had.

I knew what our client looked like in his own time and away from his business. I had seen Baxter in his natural environment. Him with his expensive things and his unique taste. I experienced the affectionate side of him and his touch.

Plus, I had seen Baxter Lane completely naked and what a sight he was.

All toned, powerful, and dominant. Baxter was a man who knew what he wanted and went for it. And for my vacation he had made it extremely clear he had wanted me.

Now, we weren't at a resort anymore. We were back in our normal environment. This time, Baxter was within mine and I never even knew he wasn't far away.

Lane's Lingerie was in the downtown core of our upbeat city. Not even a half an hour away. He owned a billionaire dollar lingerie franchise and from my brief search online; the company was popular.

I never paid much attention to lingerie and barely wore it. James had never taken much interest in it. Well, he had taken little notice of me after we got married. Especially the last few months leading up to him leaving me at the airport without a husband.

I peered out the window as tall buildings went by and horns honked on the streets. Evelyn had the windows cracked and the cool breeze was nice. I needed it to calm my unease.

"I know." I breathed and laid my head back on the seat.

"You're the best for the job and I just know you will find Mr. Lane the perfect match," Evelyn reassured me with positivity.

Evelyn was a great friend, and she meant well. She wanted the best for me and Match My Heart, but doubt lingered. My mind thought positive words of encouragement, but something nagged inside me. Negativity and confidence were at war. A battle I wasn't sure would end until this was all over and Baxter Lane claimed his wife.

I had to distract myself and remember my unmade face. I desperately needed makeup on my bare skin. The visor pulled down easily, and a light popped on. I applied my favorite smokey eye and some ruby red lipstick to match my dress.

Just as I smacked my full lips together, we pulled up in front of an enormous building. Enormous windows crept up the tall structure, and the sunlight beamed off of the windows. A large sign was on the front of the property and read 'Lane's Lingerie' in big bold letters.

Evelyn parked across the street from Mr. Lane's big corporation and my stomach tied in knots. I took the last big gulp of my coffee and wished it was a shot. But I had to pull myself together and get this meeting over with.

We headed through the front doors, and the constant chatter was everywhere. This wasn't only his business headquarters, but he had a lingerie boutique on the main floor. A place for customers to shop and buy his product where he worked. It was quite impressive and a great idea.

The process brought money straight to him and would be a reward for him to see. Every time he strode into his workplace, he could see what he had created. People bought firsthand the product he worked so hard to please customers with. That would be encouragement enough to keep going.

Chandeliers hung overhead with glass mirrored ceilings. The light beamed off of them and showed my reflection from above. The mirrored effect gave off a luxurious touch, with mannequins set up out front of the store and the company's latest pieces. Sexy garments were all lined up in a pretty row, but in an elegant, tasty fashion.

We didn't visit the boutique because it wasn't necessary, but the layout attracted me. The setup had me curious to know more about what made this man tick. Baxter Lane had to be the one to call all the shots, and his store had me intrigued.

"We might stop sometime," I announced with curiosity. "You know, for business purposes."

"Uh huh..." Evelyn breathed with a slight smile.

"What?" I added with a shoulder shrug.

"You mean get to know Baxter better?" Evelyn teased.

"It's Mr. Lane, remember?" I added with sass.

"Not to you it's not..." She muttered under her breath.

"Hey!" I giggled as we walked towards the elevators and I read Mr. Lane was on the top floor. "We remain professional, right?"

"Keep telling yourself that because I think you're going to need it," Evelyn said as she stepped onto an elevator and pressed a button for the highest floor.

I blew out a long sigh and knew she was right as the elevator climbed upward. The elevator was a typical one, with clean steel walls and mirrors over top. The red number lit up as we moved up each floor with no stops. Everyone headed to their assigned floor, which surprised me, but I remembered it was a workday. No one would leave except us in hopefully a short period.

The less time spent in Baxter Lane's closed circle, the better. That man did something to me when I was within his presence and I had to push the attraction towards him aside. I had a job to do and I would see this, though.

I'd collect his basic personal information, and we were out of here. The task was as easy as that. No need to bring anything else to the plate. Just get the facts and get out. Easy as pie.

But the elevator jerked to a stop.

"Is Mr. Lane expecting you?" A female voice called out inside the lift.

The voice startled us, and I jumped slightly. We gazed up and saw a camera staring directly at us. I was so lost in my thoughts; I hadn't even realized we were being watched. Let alone there would be a woman ready to speak to us on the other side.

"Um, yes..." Evelyn replied, and looked over at me.

"Your names, please?" she asked.

"Evelyn and Brielle," Evelyn replied.

"Mr. Lane will see you now," she said.

The elevator dinged for the top floor and I heaved out a sigh. "Let's get this over with."

Evelyn followed my lead as soon as the doors opened and my eyes took in the sight. Baxter Lane had no secretary present, and the elevator led straight to his office. The change pleasantly pleased me and I loved the personal touch. The secretary must be off in her own space and should learn to announce her presence sooner when riding the elevator.

Crystal chandeliers hung overhead like the ones on the main floor, but these had red within them. A taste not only elegant, but sexy. Mr. Lane's office had a darker tone. The furnishings were plush red with black leather and the floor sparkled black. The lighting from above shimmered off of the tile and gave it a unique beam. Baxter's desk was massive with darkened cherry wood, and his armchair had black leather.

There was a circular stage set up across from his desk and a red carpet surrounded the platform. Deep red curtains cast out the daylight behind the stage and I knew windows were behind them. I imagined they were floor to ceiling windows from the size of the drapes and they would show off the city landscape.

Baxter made the platform of smooth black wood for models to stand upon and display each garment for its master. Around the stage were mannequins set up with different lingerie pieces on them. I bet they were his bestsellers, and he'd want to surround himself with his best work.

I had to admit; they were stunning.

I noticed a black and red lace corset first. The red velvet for the background color and the black for the seams with lace flowers throughout. The next was a shimmering velvet red piece set up with a matching bra and panties, but a seductive style. A black plush robe hung over top, but it was on the smaller side.

I noticed the last garment was a bra and panties attached together. The piece screamed BDSM and had a whip. The lingerie was one I'd choose to wear if I was daring enough. Deep red velvet cupped under each breast with black lace over the hem of the cleavage. Thin black straps over each tit to connect them in the center of the chest and thin spaghetti straps over each shoulder. The bottom half had deep red velvet underneath a black see-through lace. Baxter designed shapely cuts to show off a woman's smooth skin underneath and would beg to be touched.

"Welcome to Lane's Lingerie, ladies." Mr. Baxter Lane announced as he rounded a corner and greeted us.

My mouth fell open at the sight of him.

Baxter wore a mouthwatering suit with a black dress shirt and velvet black tie. His hand smoothed over the tie, and my eyes followed his masculine hands with noticeable veins. A red suit jacket hung over with a red blazer underneath and black buttons. He neatly folded a black handkerchief in the square pocket over the left breast of the jacket. Baxter neatly pressed his red dress pants to match, and he wore high end black dress shoes. Mr. Baxter Lane had it all and my attraction towards him sparked to life.

But I had to tame myself and keep the flame unlit.

I tore my eyes away from him and looked over at Evelyn. I needed something to distract me from my body that hummed for him. Anything to take my mind off the sensual thoughts that could follow. She gazed back at me with her brown eyes and down at my agape mouth.

She gave me a stern look and asked, "Do you have something you'd like to say, Brielle?"

His greatness left me so astounded that I couldn't open my mouth. I prayed I hadn't made a fool of myself when the job had just begun. I had better get it together and for the sake of everything.

Baxter chimed in, "Yes, Brielle, do you need a moment?"

I looked back at Baxter, and he met my eyes with amusement. He knew his striking appearance had gotten to me and he loved to enjoy my squirm. Baxter played a game he wouldn't win this time because I was about to resist my sexual awareness and get down to business.

"No, let's find you a bride." I beamed in a business-like manner and walked over towards his desk. "Shall we get started, Mr. Lane?"

Baxter cleared his throat and took a seat in his armchair. "Yes, we should. Have a seat, ladies."

Baxter pointed towards the plush couch set up on the other side of his desk and we each found our seats. His dominant existence beamed from him on the other side of his workspace and he impressed me. His work environment was booming, and he was at his best. This was the real Baxter Lane, and he was unstoppable.

I opened up my laptop and clicked the enter key. The screen took me straight to the document I needed to gather his personal information. I started with all the basics. His personal number, his work number, home address and work address. Then we moved onto other things like his email and when would be the best time to reach him.

"And what would be the best form of contact?" I asked him and awaited his response.

"I want you to reach me on my personal cell," Baxter replied.

I typed in his request and asked, "Would you prefer a phone call or a text message?"

"Well, I love the sound of your voice..." Baxter replied, and his ocean blues caught mine. "But I want to reach you immediately. Do you always carry your cell on you, Brielle?"

My cheeks heated, and I breathed out my best professional response. "You would be required to call the office, Mr. Lane."

"But I want to speak with you personally," Baxter requested in a stern tone.

I swallowed hard, and his eyes left mine. Baxter locked in on the slight bob of my throat and I stopped breathing.

I pulled my gaze away from him and looked over at Evelyn. My eyes pleaded at her for help, and she turned her attention to Mr. Lane.

"We can have that arranged for you, Mr. Lane." Evelyn smiled in agreement and looked back at me. "Isn't that right, Brielle?"

Professionalism went right out the window. Whatever Mr. Baxter Lane wanted, he got. He wanted to deal straight with me. But I didn't like it, not one bit.

They trapped me in a corner all on my own. Evelyn took his side, and I had no choice but to cave. First, he wanted to meet here and now he wanted my personal number. Baxter got his demand once again.

Anything to please the client, I repeated over and over in my head. This was the new norm, and I had to get used to the reality. Baxter was the one with the money and willing to pay top dollar. Everything had to go his way in order to find what he sought.

I plastered on a smile and breathed. "This isn't the way we normally run our business, Mr. Lane, but we can change it for you."

Baxter grinned with satisfaction at my answer. "Good. Please put your personal number in my cell, Brielle."

"Of course." I smiled with fakeness and took his phone from across the table.

I punched in my first name with my cell number and regretted it to the highest extent. I didn't want to have any personal ties to a client. Especially this billionaire stud who I had to find a wife for. All of this was out of my comfort zone and I had a bad feeling about it. But my best friend had insisted and Baxter had given a command.

I handed back his cell, and he gazed down at the screen with a pleased smile. He had claimed what he wanted and a small part of me liked it. I took pleasure in pleasing him while on vacation, but we fell into business. This had nothing to do with pleasure, and I had to remind myself of that.

"And to answer your question..." Baxter added, "I wish to speak with you directly through a phone call or a text message."

Baxter locked eyes with me. And he meant business. He gave an order, and I was to follow it. His stare blazed at me and burned into my core. I was to act accordingly and do as asked.

"Anything for you, Mr. Lane." I breathed and resented the words I spoke.

They would come back to bite me in the ass.

"I love your dedication, darling," Baxter said in a husky tone.

"My name is Brielle, for business reasons, Mr. Lane," I argued and shot him a look.

The remembrance of his nickname sparked a fuse. The flicker of heat blazed between us and wanted to ignite. Baxter demanded the flame with the intense burn of his stare.

The blue hues darkened and lust shone through. Baxter entrapped me and begged me to give in to him. I wouldn't and I couldn't because I wasn't his anymore. A woman had to be sought to be his. I had to obtain Baxter a wife.

"I will call you what I see fit, my darling Brielle," Baxter shot back with determination.

Suddenly, the sound of notifications chimed from a cell phone. The noises didn't come from mine, but I was thankful for them. The constant ding distracted Baxter as he checked his cellphone and he frowned down at it. His eyes shot back up and he looked from me towards Evelyn. The notifications didn't come from my cell phone or his, and I peered over at my best friend.

Evelyn gave us a shy look as she gazed down at the screen, and she apologized, "I'm sorry for the disruption, Mr. Lane."

"No need to apologize, Evelyn." Baxter shook his head.

The phone kept going off and wouldn't stop. The noise was a distraction no one needed, and it caused us to be here longer than warranted. It was the end of the meeting and the end of the tunnel was in sight. I could see the beams of the finish line, but Evelyn's stupid cellphone interrupted everything.

I gave a nervous laugh and mumbled under my breath, "Now isn't the time, Evelyn. Time to shut it off or put it on vibrate."

I looked over at my best friend and she peered down at the screen in a state of shock. Evelyn glanced at me and hid the screen from view. I knew her better than anyone, and I could recognize that look from anywhere.

Something was very wrong.

"Give me the phone, Evelyn," I demanded and shot her a warning. "Don't make me ask again."

"No, I'll just turn it off and—" Evelyn said as she kept the phone out of my reach and her fingers worked to shut the device down.

The moment of interruption had passed. Curiosity and urgency took over me. I needed to see what was on her phone, and I wanted to see it now.

"No, you won't," I interrupted her and held out my hand. "Give it to me."

Evelyn looked up at me, and her eyes pleaded with mine. "You don't want to see this, Brielle."

The cat was out of the bag and I really wanted to know what the hell was going on. I didn't waste another second and grabbed the phone. I held it in my grasp and tugged, but Evelyn yanked right back. We wrestled for the device in a tug of war and got up off the couch.

Baxter stood with the commotion and tried to break us apart. This was a battle to the finish and I wouldn't let my best friend keep something from me. Even if it was for my own good.

We both cried out, and the phone fell from our grasp. Evelyn's cellphone landed at Baxter's feet and he reached down for it. He peered at the screen and the light from Evelyn's cell lit up his face.

"Don't read it!" Evelyn exclaimed out loud.

Baxter Lane wouldn't have a clue what any of this was about. We were both on the same side for once, and the suspense of what was on the phone was on our minds. He doesn't heed Evelyn's warning out of pure curiosity.

"Who is Abbey?" Baxter asked with confusion, and he peered straight at me with jealousy. "And when did you plan on disclosing you have a husband?"

SEVENTEEN
Friendly Mistress

I stared at Baxter with an expression of guilt. I was guilty to the core and kept him in the dark about my failed marriage. Shame crawled over my skin and buried itself within my bones. I wanted to die on the spot and I knew heaven wouldn't have a place for me. I was a scorned woman caught in an untruth and Baxter had just received the icy sting.

I was married when we were together. He had slept with a married woman and his eyes shone with hurt from the fact. Baxter may be a man in need of a wife, but he wasn't blind. He saw the truth radiate from me and didn't need an explanation. But I felt he deserved one.

Some of it, at least.

"I didn't realize I had to reveal my marriage status," I snapped and upheld a business front.

I grabbed the phone from him, and he didn't put up a fight. Jealousy and hurt shone throughout him. Baxter showed me a side of him I never expected to see. Undeniable anguish.

But it was all because of me.

Baxter lowered his tone and harshly whispered, "You should when you find pleasure with an unexpected business partner."

"It's not what it looks like..." I mumbled as I changed the subject and tried to ease his pain.

"It's exactly what it looks like, Brielle," Baxter shot back with a fuse of anger. "You have a husband."

I glared back. "Soon-to-be ex-husband in a matter of months. He cheated on me."

The truth flew out of me. I had locked the fact away from him, but honesty wanted to be set free. The secret I had kept from Baxter outweighed the shame. The guilt of my failed marriage was out on full display. I couldn't keep it inside, no matter how hard I tried, because Baxter deserved the truth.

I owed Baxter that much, at least.

Baxter stared at me, stunned, as if I had pushed him to his limit and he didn't know how to respond. His sapphire eyes searched my face for a reason for all of this, but I couldn't give him one. I didn't even understand any of this myself. My marriage was over and my husband cheated on me. I still didn't even know why or who the other woman could be.

But that was all about to change.

My eyes focused on Evelyn's cell phone screen and not on a shocked Baxter. Time stood still as I looked at text messages from our dear friend Abbey to Evelyn. The multiple messages shook me to my core and I couldn't believe the words before me. The truth unraveled and everything happened in front of my unforgettable fling.

Abbey: 'Evelyn, are you there?'

Abbey: 'I need to discuss something with you...'

Abbey: 'Goddamnit, I can't wait because it's eating away at me. I slept with Brielle's husband and it was a terrible decision, but he loves me.'

Abbey: 'Are you there? Please don't be mad. It was a mistake. But then it happened again and has been happening for months.'

Abbey: 'I'm sorry, but I had to tell someone...'

And I couldn't read anymore.

Abbey was the other woman.

She was more so Evelyn's friend and I met Abbey through her. We weren't extremely close, and now I understood why. Abbey waited for the right time to pounce.

Right on my husband.

Abbey had blonde hair and blue eyes with a big busty chest. I bet James just loved that. She was now the blonde bimbo who was sloppy seconds and a relationship I couldn't wait to forget.

"That lying bitch!" I exclaimed with hatred and I saw red. "She's been sleeping with my husband for months?"

How could I have been so blind?

So... Naïve?

How could I get past this?

Evelyn looked at me with worry in her eyes. "I'm so sorry, Brielle. I did not know until now, and I didn't want you to find out like this."

Evelyn glanced from me to our client, and regret filled through me. I was regretful about what I had done to Baxter. My faith in the vows I made to James was misguided, as he didn't treat them seriously. I was ashamed of befriending a woman who only wanted my husband and wanted nothing to do with me.

I held Baxter's stare and breathed. "Neither did I..."

Evelyn looked at Baxter with her hands out in front of her and apologized, "I'm so sorry for all of this, Mr. Lane. This is extremely unprofessional and we can understand if you don't want to continue with our company."

My eyes blinked with shame and I regretfully added, "My so-called friend and my husband were sneaking around behind my back. I can understand if you feel I'm not the right one for this job anymore, Mr. Lane."

The words tumbled out even though my mind screamed not to speak them. This was the client we had waited for. Our big break to save Match My Heart from ruin. But my failed marriage was out, and it was too late to turn back.

Baxter deserved to know what he had gotten himself into. He earned the right to decide if all this was worth it. Mr. Baxter Lane needed to find a wife, and he would pay a hefty price for her. He held merit to understand I had doubts about my ability. I didn't before, but I do now.

Baxter looked at Evelyn and crossed his arms. "Can Brielle and I have a moment in private, Evelyn?"

Evelyn's eyes shot towards mine and I begged her not to leave me alone with him. I pleaded with narrowed eyes, and uncertainty swirled within them. This was my mess and I should deal with it, but when I was by myself with him, there was no way I could deny Mr. Baxter Lane.

Evelyn gave me an apologetic face and responded, "Yes, I can do that, Mr. Lane."

I shot my best friend a look of betrayal and watched her turn her back. She left the room and headed straight for the elevator. I wondered how long Mr. Lane would make her wait or if this departure would be brief. But I had much bigger problems to worry about.

And his overbearing stance stood right in front of me.

Baxter's ocean blue eyes swirled with questions and my doubt in myself reflected at me. He uncrossed his arms and stepped towards me. The distance between us no longer remained as he touched my cheek and trailed his hand gently up my skin. To my ear, where he ran a fingertip along the sensitive flesh and back down again.

I wanted to close my eyes and give into him, but I knew if I did there would be no turning back. We'd be back in Hawaii and in our shared suite once again. Back to where it all began with our mouths finding each other in a frenzy and he'd consume me. He'd make my messed-up reality burst into a heated one-time sex and we'd be naked in no time.

Baxter was my client. I had to uphold my end until he called it off. Until he said the deal was off.

I waited for those words to come. This deal should've been over as soon as he stepped into Match My Heart. I couldn't do it.

But the agreement to terminate never came.

Instead, Baxter ran his fingers back over my cheek and left goosebumps in his wake. He grazed the pad of his thumb over my lips and my mouth slightly parted at his touch. My warm breath caressed his thumb as he made his way over the plumpness and down my chin. But his attentive touch left me all too soon and my being quivered for more.

"Your personal relationships hold no power over what you can achieve within your profession, my darling Brielle." Baxter breathed, as his eyes held strength and wisdom. "It may not thrill me that you kept this from me on a personal level, but that doesn't mean I wish to go elsewhere."

"Trust me, I'm not too happy with myself either..." I breathed with truth and looked down towards the floor. "My husband left me at the airport and I found out he had been unfaithful to me. But then you came along and we..."

Baxter reached out and tilted my chin until I met his eyes. I thought I'd see pity for me within their rich blue depths. I figured he'd view me as a shattered, scorned woman who had lost her place in the world. But I didn't see that at all.

I saw empowerment. The strength to move on and take charge of my life. All with a gorgeous grin just for me.

"We had the best time of our lives," Baxter admitted.

"My soon-to-be ex-husband wouldn't agree." I sighed.

"He doesn't get a vote. He stepped outside of what was sacred and it may not feel like it right now, but..." Baxter stated as his thumb caressed my chin, "You are worthy of love, my darling Brielle."

I blushed and shyly smiled at his affection. "And so are you Baxter Lane."

Baxter's eyes met my lips, and I felt the pull between us. The undeniable attraction was on fire, and I wanted his mouth on mine. But I still had a job to do and a duty to uphold.

His reaction confused me, and I asked him, "Do you wish to continue with Match My Heart and for me to find you a wife?"

Baxter licked his lips, and he bit his lower lip, lost in deep thought. There was something there I couldn't place. A longing I couldn't quite place. He gazed down at me and searched my face, but let go of my chin.

Baxter's face got back to business and whatever he longed for; he pushed deep inside. Buried within the walls of his heart and sealed away until he set the need free.

Baxter cleared his throat and gave a throaty response, "I wish to continue with your service, Brielle."

Relief fell over me, and I sighed. "I'm happy to hear that, Mr. Lane."

"Are we done for today?" he asked in a rushed manner.

I reached for my laptop and peered over the information. "Yes, I think I got everything we need."

"Very well then." Baxter breathed and met my eyes. "What happens next?"

"Well, I'll need to go over a questionnaire with you and have you answer questions. It's standard and all of our clients do it, including online applicants looking for love," I explained with a smile.

My professionalism was back and front center. The worry and shame I could put behind me for now. Baxter wanted me to do this. He needed me to find him his perfect match. No matter what my disaster of a love life looked like. None of my past mattered to him and we could move past it.

"How long will the next session take?" Baxter asked.

"Well, that all depends on how you answer the questions regarding what you're looking for in your match. Along with personal details about yourself," I answered with certainty.

"So, you need to know everything about me in order to find me a wife?" Baxter asked with a raised eyebrow and sighed. "What did I get myself into?"

I giggled at him and touched his shoulder. "You got yourself on the right path to love, Mr. Lane."

His eyes locked with mine at the friendly contact I gave him, and my skin tingled. The sensation went all the way to my toes and my heart pounded in my ears. There was nothing friendly about it, but I had to make it appear that way. Baxter was only a contract and one I had to complete. I had to view him as such and not a hot hunk of meat ready to be devoured.

No matter what, I had to maintain a business-like manner with him. A friendly one until this was all over. Baxter needed a romantic relationship, and not with me.

"I hope you're right because that's exactly why I came to you," Baxter whispered as his eyes burned into mine and he placed his hand over top of my own. "Destiny brought me here and you will guide me to love."

There was that look again. A longing I couldn't place danced around in his gorgeous ocean of blue. He focused on me and rippled right into my soul. The look wasn't for me and it would be for his bride. But it sure as hell felt intended for me.

My hand fell from the comfort of his shoulder, and I shook my head. A shy grin laid on my face and I turned away from him. I focused on my belongings and getting out of here. Before I brought myself to do something, I knew I'd regret. Especially since he was now a job I needed to complete. Another task on my list of to dos and a forbidden client.

I cleared my throat. "We can start on it tomorrow in my office."

"No..." Baxter ordered, as he crossed his arms in front of his muscular chest and looked around. "I want you to come here."

"Oh, but—" I argued.

"And I want you to come alone," Baxter interrupted.

Alone?

The thought of enduring this all over again weighed heavily on my mind. Half of this appointment wasn't even solo, and I still had a hard time. Baxter was difficult to maintain a professional relationship with when I knew exactly what he looked like, with no clothes on.

"I'm not so sure that is the best idea, Mr. Lane," I disapproved with my head held high.

But I felt the quiver inside.

Baxter stepped closer, and he asked in a husky tone, "Why is that, Brielle?"

"We don't normally do business outside of the office," I replied and took a step back.

Baxter continued to walk towards me and raised an eyebrow. "But you're here now. What could be the harm?"

Baxter was right. I was being cautious. He had proven his point.

"Very well then, Mr. Lane," I responded with a tilt of my head and prayed he kept his distance. "We will meet tomorrow at the same time?"

"You read my mind, darling," Baxter admitted with a wicked smirk.

"Perfect." I breathed and turned my back towards him.

"Just one last thing before you go," Baxter said from behind me.

My ponytail flicked through the air as I glanced over my shoulder and met his eyes. "What is that, Mr. Lane?"

"You are to call me by my first name from now on, and that's an order," Baxter growled his demand.

My cheeks burned crimson, and I turned away from him. I felt his eyes burn into my backside, just like they had when we were at the resort. I couldn't be certain, but my skin crawled with remembrance. Maybe my mind just played tricks on me.

Either way, I knew a command when I heard one and his was final. Baxter was the boss and called the shots. Whatever Mr. Baxter Lane wanted, he got.

"Very well, Baxter." I said and set foot for the elevator. "I will see you tomorrow."

EIGHTEEN

Questionnaire

I rode in the elevator and waited for the secretary to announce her presence. Her invisible existence was no longer creepy once she had made herself known. She watched and waited for the right moment to speak, but I knew it would be soon.

My hands pressed against my black skirt and purple buttoned blouse. I clenched my laptop against my chest and had my purse strap rested on my shoulder. I left my hair down because I didn't have time to put it up. This session was an important one, and I didn't have time to be behind.

The elevator climbed higher, and I got lost in my thoughts. My attention drew towards my forthcoming divorce and Baxter's reaction had thrown me for a loop. I expected bitterness and backlash, but it never came. Of course, he wasn't happy I had kept a husband hidden from him. But his response was respectful.

Baxter was on my side. He had crossed the boundary and didn't sit on the opposed side. He didn't linger between borders and was certain of where he stood. I was worthy, and he took my side.

Something James could never do. James was the complete opposite of Baxter, and he held me back. Baxter wanted me to fly, and he was the wind beneath my wings.

But Baxter Lane was a client.

A well-known fact I had to remember. Baxter was in search of a wife and not of me. He didn't come here for me and our close encounters while on vacation would have to stay there. Mr. Baxter Lane was soon to be taken, and I'd get him there.

The elevator came to a halt, and I gazed up at the floor number. I had reached the top floor of Lane's Lingerie, but the door wouldn't open. No voice came through the speaker, and I narrowed my eyebrows. I had to stay there until those doors opened, confused. I had no control over them.

Maybe Baxter wasn't quite ready for our meeting. I was on time and he was late. But that didn't appear to be his style.

"Um... Hello?" I announced with a slight wave, "Is anyone there?"

The speaker gave a slight crackle and a low hum. The sound hurt my ears for a slight second, but subsided. I just wanted to get off this damn elevator and get this over with.

"Yes, I'm sorry about that..." The female voice responded in the elevator, "I had a technical issue."

"Don't we all from time to time?" I muttered with relief, "I'm here for my session with Mr. Lane for Match My Heart."

"Yes, of course. He's expecting you, Brielle," the voice hummed with recognition and the doors opened.

"Um, thank you," I said as I looked at the security camera and gave a slight wave.

I was on a first name basis with the secretary and had become familiar around here. The recognition was nice. Not that I wanted to make a habit of this or anything. I'd prefer to do this at my office on my terms, but this was his journey to love and Baxter wanted this.

Baxter was in charge, and I was just along for the ride. A process towards a happily ever after and not my own. This was my job, and he was the perfect catch I'd find for one lucky woman.

Knots tied in my belly as I stepped out of the elevator and remembered his environment. Everything was the same, from the desk to the drawn curtains and the circular platform. Even the mannequins wore the same lingerie outfits, but one thing was different.

There was soft music in the background. The sweet beat filled the entire atmosphere and hummed in my ears. The rhythm wasn't upbeat, but sensational. A sensual tune, and I found my toes tapping along to the beat.

"There you are..." Baxter announced as he stood from his desk and his eyes found mine. "I was afraid you weren't coming."

"Why would you think that?" I asked with curiosity.

"Well, there's a slight possibility you could change your mind and back out of our arrangement," Baxter explained as he came around the desk and greeted me, "Our partnership is unique, don't you think?"

Baxter referred to our shared suite while on vacation. The time we spent together was out of our control. The temptation we endured and fought to resist until we couldn't anymore. His kisses had caressed me and his touch made me wild. A getaway of a lifetime lost in each other's arms until we had to come back to reality. A conventional fact: I had to find him his soulmate, and it wasn't me.

I cleared my throat. "Yes, I agree."

"So, you can understand my unease?" he asked with a raised eyebrow as he brushed back his hair and pulled at his suit jacket.

"Yes, I can..." I breathed and plastered on my most professional smile. "But you need not worry because I have our unique situation under control."

At least, I hoped I did.

Baxter didn't need to know my deepest thoughts, and he certainly didn't need to know my being hummed at his easy on the eye's appearance. He wore a much different suit than yesterday, and my mouth watered at the sight of him. His bright blue eyes stood right out with the light grey suit jacket and dress pants.

Baxter decided on a tie and draped it over his plain pressed white dress shirt. He appeared much more relaxed and at ease with the jacket open to reveal a black leather belt strapped around his waist. Baxter Lane was a man no woman could ignore, and if his fashion trends didn't find him a wife, I don't know what could. Mr. Lane was a dashingly handsome hunk with charm for days.

"Right then..." Baxter breathed, and he grinned. "We should get started."

"Yes, you read my mind." I beamed and opened my laptop.

I found a seat on the plush couch near his desk, and Baxter sat down beside me. The laptop sat in my lap and I tapped some keys to distract myself from his unexpected nearness. I had expected he'd sit in his designated armchair and my brain wasn't ready for this close contact. But his close proximity woke up every fiber of my being.

"Alright, so..." I sighed with unease and tugged at my skirt, which felt much too short with him so close. "I guess we should start with the qualities you will bring to a committed relationship."

"Okay, well, I'm compassionate and a great listener," Baxter admitted with a half-smile. "I have a successful business and money is not a problem. I'm family-oriented, but it's on the smaller side."

"Speaking of family..." I asked with curiosity, "Do you have any brothers or sisters?"

Baxter frowned. "I have a step-brother."

"I sense a but in there?" I questioned him and stopped typing.

My eyes met his, and his blue depths didn't shine. They darkened, and he went somewhere else. Towards memories, he locked inside and threw away the key. A place buried deep in the past and never to see the light of day.

Until now.

"But we don't get along." Baxter snapped harshly. "Maybe scratch the family-oriented part."

"No, we will still keep it because you want a family of your own." I breathed with reassurance and typed in a fresh response. "This is all for a first impression. The more personal issues you can decide when to bring them up with your life partner."

I hoped my smile would do justice because inside I couldn't help the need for more. To dive further into the subject of what happened between him and his step-brother.

The pain and anger seared into their relationship so long ago. I had so many questions within myself for him, but I wasn't his perfect match and I had no right to push. Baxter was my client and we couldn't venture into personal territory.

I had to just let personal history go. I had to let Baxter tell me as much as he wanted to. But right now, it wasn't much.

"Alright, we will move on..." I muttered as I sensed his uneasiness and tucked a strand of hair behind my ear. "What are your must-haves for a future partner?"

Baxter was silent and lost in thought. I peered up at him as he looked at me and I wondered what reeled around in his beautiful mind. The thoughts he had and his deepest desire. His blue eyes searched my face and heat rose inside of me when it shouldn't.

I shifted in my seat and couldn't break away from his intense stare. He looked at me like I was supposed to give him the answers. He peered into my soul, and it was like he wanted me to be his answer.

I cleared my throat and whispered, "Baxter?"

"Ya..." He breathed in a raspy tone.

"What are your preferences in a match?" I asked.

"Right... My match... Um, she would have to be reliable, trustworthy, compassionate with a sense of adventure, but most of all, a breath of fresh air," Baxter admitted, as his gaze never wavered from mine and my heart beat a hundred miles per hour in my chest. "I'd want her to breathe life into me with her by my side for the rest of my life."

Baxter's answer was like a dream, but it wasn't mine to have. He meant for someone else to live his vision. His destiny was a match made in heaven and something I'd give to live.

Suddenly, the phone rang on the desk. Baxter tore his eyes away from me and reached for the phone. The old-style landline chimed from its black cradle and I pondered who it could be. The caller would be all about business, and I wondered how long the unwanted call would take.

Baxter grabbed the phone off the cradle, brought the device to his ear and barked an order. "What is it?"

His behavior was clear, and the distraction annoyed him. Mr. Lane told the undesired caller not to disturb him while he was in a meeting, but the voice on the other end wouldn't give up. The call was of utmost importance, and Baxter's face changed from angry to serious in a matter of seconds.

"I see..." Baxter said as his eyebrows narrowed together and he rubbed the whiskers on his chin, lost in thought. "Send only the garment up and have no one disrupt me again for the rest of my meeting."

Baxter hung up the phone with no goodbye, and his mood changed. He was no longer annoyed, angry, or perplexed. His handsome face shone with wicked delight, and he directed it all at me.

What was that all about?

"What's wrong?" I asked with curiosity, and tilted my head at him.

"Stand up for me..." Baxter ordered from above as he stood up and his eyes pierced into mine. "I want to have a better look at you."

"What?" I huffed with annoyance. "I don't have time for you to gawk at me. I have a job to do and..."

"This is part of your job," Baxter barked and he closed my laptop. "Do as I say when I say, and you get to keep the job."

My eyes glared at him with displeasure, but he was right. I had no choice. Baxter was my customer, and I was to do as he wanted. And right now, he commanded me to stand.

I huffed out a frustrated breath and put my laptop on his desk. I stood in front of him as his sapphire eyes roamed over me and my being heated with something far darker than anger. The passion he brought me sparked to life and threatened to ignite a flame. One I wasn't sure I could put out if he tempted me too much.

I patted my hands on either side of me and muttered with flustered frustration. "There. Are you happy now?"

"Not just yet, my darling," Baxter admitted as his eyes flowed back up my body and he touched the air around my shapely form.

"Well, what's taking so long?" I huffed.

"I'm seeing if you're the perfect fit for my latest creation." Baxter breathed with a devious smirk. "And it turns out, you're perfection, my darling Brielle."

"Perfect fit for what?" I asked with confusion.

Baxter stroked his chin and gave a command. "Follow me."

I stomped my foot down and argued with him. "We haven't finished the questionnaire yet."

"Forget about the questionnaire," he snapped at me. "I will send the rest of my answers to you later."

"I don't understand you one bit, Baxter." I sighed with defeat.

"You don't have to, darling," Baxter whispered as he brushed a strand of hair behind my ear and he licked his lips. "You just have to do as you're told."

Suddenly, the elevator dinged, and Baxter strode towards it like a man on a mission. Operation: Confuse the fuck out of the matchmaker and give me an assignment I had no choice but to do. Mr. Baxter Lane was full of surprises, and I was his prime target.

The elevator doors opened and there was no one inside. I watched as Baxter bent down and picked up a single parcel from the floor. The flaps of the box were open, and he looked down inside as his long-toned legs strut back in the direction he came.

Right towards me.

"There's no model coming in today for the latest fitting," Baxter explained as he placed the box on his desk and pulled out a piece of pricey fabric. "She fell ill overnight and I need a replacement."

Baxter Lane peered right at me. The question of who would wear this latest lingerie piece lingered between us in the still air and the answer came without another thought. He wanted me to model his current creation, and I stood no chance of refusal, but I would sure try.

"I'm not a model," I snapped with an argument. "You hired me to be your matchmaker, not strut around in your lingerie."

The garment was a black teddy with dark leather at the front of the corset. Black string crisscrossed in the front to help display cleavage and show off bare skin all the way down to the belly. The piece had a burlesque taste with black flowered lace on either side to give a see-through touch.

Underneath was a single black G-string thong and a black masquerade mask to cover the face. The entire outfit screamed incredibly sexy, and the garment wasn't on the comfort radar. This piece was strictly for mind-blowing seduction, and my boss wanted me to bring the intimate apparel to life.

"I want you to put it on for me, Brielle," Baxter demanded with a wicked glow in his eyes. "I need to inspect the product on your beautiful body."

The mention of him referring to my figure as beauty made me blush. The notion was hard to ignore, and the temperature in his office turned up a notch. I was front and center in his world. Baxter's pushy behavior flattered me and left me wanting more when I shouldn't succumb to temptation. I was the only option he saw, and he scared the hell out of me.

"No way!" I exclaimed, with refusal to quit.

Baxter stepped forward and grabbed my chin in his grasp. A surprised gasp escaped me and he took notice of my agape mouth. My lips pushed in from his force and his need to be in control. Baxter Lane oozed dominance and my pussy quivered to his powerful torment.

Baxter growled. "No argument. You work for me, my darling Brielle. You will put on the piece and walk your beautiful ass up onto my stage."

"But I—" I squeak out.

"That's an order," Baxter interrupted and shushed me with a finger over my lips. "Now be a good girl and go get dressed, darling."

NINETEEN
Inspect Me

I had no choice. No decision in the matter, because Baxter was the boss. He gave a command, and I had to suffer the consequences. I had to do whatever he pleased and there was no way around the fact. No matter how unprofessional his matchmaker getting dressed up in lingerie just for him was, it didn't matter.

Whatever Mr. Baxter Lane wanted, he got.

I snatched the garment from his grasp and turned on my heels. Anger fumed from me, but there was nothing I could do about it. So, I did the only thing I could. Stomped my feet to show him I was upset with his demand. But I had no idea where I was going.

"Go around the corner and get dressed in the bedroom," Baxter ordered from behind me.

Bedroom?

But I thought this was his office?

I followed his instructions and entered the only room around the corner. The door clicked closed behind me and my surroundings shocked me. The room was indeed a bedroom and, from the smell of the cologne in the air, the bachelor pad was his.

Everything was dark. Dim lighting, dark grey paint and a black king-sized bed. Baxter drew the curtains shut just like his office, and there was a master bathroom with a walk-in closet.

There was a swing in his bedroom, and it made me giggle. Mr. Baxter Lane was a man full of surprises and must be a big kid at heart. The swing had a black cushioned seat and hung from the ceiling. But I pondered why it was there.

This was his private space and he could have whatever he wanted in here. I just couldn't wrap my head around the swing. There must be an explanation for it.

Baxter had lovers come here, and the fact was clear from the dance pole across from his bed. I could imagine he'd love to watch his lover give a sensual dance from the comfort of his bed. I bet he had many women come here.

My nostrils flared at the thought of another woman in this room. My body temperature rose at the thought of manicured hands on his gorgeous body and giving him pleasure. I had no right to be envious, because Baxter Lane was a single man. He was a very wealthy one and could have any woman he pleased. This spiteful behavior seething through me had to go, and I had no place to hold such emotion towards my boss.

I let out a bitter breath and shook my head at my unwanted convictions. Frustration still boiled through me from this ridiculous request he demanded me to do, but it was time to get the show over with. We had a partnership and a professional relationship to uphold. This was a one-time deal and wouldn't leave this office.

The clothing I wore fell onto the neatly made bed and I shuffled down the business side of me. I had a job to do and Baxter needed an odd favor. I had to view the situation as something different to even go along with this preposterous notion. Match My Heart was on the line, and Baxter could back out whenever he wanted. I didn't want to be the one to make him.

Besides, I wasn't naked, and this had to do with his business. He needed to view the product on a woman to ensure the garment was perfect. Baxter had no one else to do the job, and I was here. At least, I tried to convince myself this was the right thing to do.

Get dressed up in lingerie for my boss. My billionaire boss who I slept with multiple times while on vacation. This crazy situation was no big deal.

Right?

The black teddy was the right size and hugged the curves of my body. I tied up the black lace for the leather corset until my cleavage hung over the hem. I gazed down at my busty chest and was in awe of how the garment made them appear enticing. My tits were eye-catching and the black lace gave me a sexy look as I put on the G-string. The underwear wasn't uncomfortable, and the thin fabric surprised me. I had never worn one in my life because of the string piece and the thought of it trapped between my butt cheeks. But this was smooth and I couldn't even notice it was there.

My ass hung out in its shapely form and I ran my hand over the top of it as I admired the view. This lingerie wasn't my taste, but the piece suited me well. I felt sexy and in charge. The sensual garment made me invincible.

But in reality, I wasn't.

Baxter Lane had me wrapped around his cock, and I was at his command. He barked orders at me and he got his every wish. He was the man in charge and I was just a woman set out to obey.

"Let's get this over with..." I grumbled to myself.

The air nipped at my bare legs, and my high heels clicked along the floor. I left the comfort of my isolation in Baxter Lane's bedroom and walked out the door. I blew out a deep, unsteady breath as I rounded the corner to his office and peered down at the floor. My eyes couldn't bring themselves to look at him out of fear of what I might see. Baxter may be a charmer, but he was dominant, and I knew this all too well.

I heard a low groan come from the direction of his desk, and I pondered what he thought. If his sky-blue eyes turned as dark as the bottom of the ocean with lust. Not a hint of a professional streak within them.

Or if he would continue with a business minded attitude and only view the lingerie piece and not my body. The only way I'd find out is if I meant his gaze, but I couldn't bring myself to see it through.

I stopped in the middle of the floor across from his desk. The music from earlier still played, and I tapped my toes within my heels to the beat. I tried to forget I stood in front of my boss practically naked and my hair flowed over my shoulders. I pretended I was anywhere else other than here with his eyes all over me. We had to get this over with.

"There..." I grumbled with frustration. "Are you happy now?"

"Not in the slightest," Baxter answered as his voice boomed with power and he took charge. "I can't see your face."

"I didn't put this on for you to look at me," I muttered out of annoyance.

"Look at me, Brielle," Baxter commanded.

"Fine." I grumbled with a shaky breath.

I glanced up and met his eyes. First, his blue hues glowed at me with irritation from my reluctance to agree, but his indigo eyes sparked with something else right after. His eyes blazed with lust when he took in all of me before him in his creation.

"Yes, my darling." Baxter breathed with passion.

Baxter's awakened stare beamed at me and only me. He seated himself at his desk with a glass of hard liquor. I took notice of how the liquid swirled around in the glass as he admired me and raised it to his mouth for a sip. His hair had fallen over his eyes and he had taken off his grey suit jacket. The grey tie still hung from around his neck and he must've forgotten to do it up. He had other matters to deal with, like me, almost nude in the privacy of his office.

How convenient for Mr. Lane.

"I think that's all you have to see," I urged as my hands fell to cover my most intimate area and I was ready to get dressed.

I needed to get the hell out of there. Baxter's intense stare burned laser beam holes through the fabric of his masterpiece, and my body responded. My juices soaked the G-string and he could probably smell my scent from where he sat. My boss completely aroused me when he shouldn't.

This situation tempted me and I should've denied him, but I couldn't when he made a request. Baxter was in charge, and he had wanted this. His matchmaker in his lingerie for his enjoyment and on full display just for him.

Baxter was a man who had seen me in my barest form and knew my most intimate desires. He had given me the finest pleasure I had ever known, and he could make me melt on my knees. He could have me do whatever he pleased.

"Get up on the platform, darling," Baxter urged as he brushed the hair from his face, and his eyes never left my body. "Show me how desirable you feel in my design."

I wanted to tell him no. To get angry and argue this game was over. But my mouth wouldn't speak the words.

My body refused to listen to my mind and my legs strut towards the stage. I was going to give him a show and unveil how the piece made me a vibrant, beautiful, wicked goddess. His masterpiece.

Baxter was my master, and I was his puppet on a string. A thread he wound so tightly I could never escape, no matter how hard I tried. He made me dance and my pussy sang for him. I had to give him all of me for this performance and whatever he chose as his eyes watched me from his stage.

I stepped up the small set of stairs and onto the black platform. Right where Baxter wanted me with my back to him, but my legs spread. I arched my backside and lifted my arms above my head. Only to bring one down as my fingers trailed along the skin of my other arm and into my hair. My plump ass stuck out, and I swore I heard a groan escape him from across the room. The sound excited me and made me wicked for the master in charge.

"Is this good enough?" I exhaled out a flustered breath and glanced over my shoulder at him.

"No, not yet..." Baxter breathed huskily, and he rose from his desk. "I need to get a closer look."

Baxter held all the power as he stalked towards me and unbuttoned the top two buttons of his white dress shirt.

He needed some air and the loosened collar helped. The tie wrapped around his neck slowly fell and he held the grey fabric within a clenched fist.

"What are you doing?" I asked as I turned around and faced him.

"I need to ensure the product is perfect." Baxter breathed.

Baxter stood below me. I loomed over him in his creation as his eyes fucked me and made my skin crawl with desire. I craved his touch. The one I knew could set me on fire and I never wanted the flame to burn out. But I had to remember no matter how much I yearned for him, Mr. Baxter Lane was still my boss.

"This is highly inappropriate, Baxter," I protested.

"I beg to differ," Baxter argued as he caught my eyes, and his hand reached out to touch my leg. "This is part of the job because I gave the command."

"But I'm your matchmaker..." I quivered as my body shook at his caress and I wanted more.

"No, right now you are mine," Baxter growled, a hungry demand as his hand went higher and touched the black lace. "This is my latest design, and it's mine."

My breath hitched, and I blinked my eyes as the desire pooled from me. The temptation made me bend to his every wish, and he joined me on top of the platform. The stage was small and not fit for two, but he made room.

Baxter stood right in front of me, and his masculine cologne surrounded me. The same smell from within his bedroom and my body begged for him to take me to his bed. I couldn't deny how much I wanted him and I wanted him to consume me. The need for him to make me his was so powerful, and the force drew my soul closer to his.

I looked at his lips as I licked my own and his hand ran up the side of my thigh. His fingers grazed the G-string on my hip bone and pulled the elastic strap back until it snapped against bare flesh. The noise made me gasp and part my lips.

Baxter's desire filled eyes met my mouth, and he breathed. "I have to inspect every inch."

He followed the thin string back to the small of my back and hovered over my rounded buttock. I longed for him to cup my ass cheeks and squeeze them within his firm grasp, but he never did. Instead, he watched my reaction as his one fingertip travelled over the black string and stopped where the G-string disappeared between my ass cheeks.

"Every crevice..." Baxter hissed with passion.

Baxter dropped his hand from my behind, but brought his grey tie around the small of my back and held it within both of his hands. The silk cloth touched my skin, and he moved it up my back. Each time he brought the tie higher, he pulled me in closer. I didn't think we could get any closer, but he proved me wrong. The tie came up to my neck and his warm breath fanned my lips. Our mouths were closer than they should be and his nose brushed mine.

Baxter let the tie fall to the ground and his hands framed my face, but he never touched me. My chest rose and fell with staggered breaths and he knew exactly how turned-on I was. He could have me if he wanted to, and he knew it. I could tell by the wicked dance of amusement within his eyes as the passion swirled with red feverish need. Baxter

Lane wanted me too, and I bet his cock was rock-hard within those neatly pressed grey dress pants.

Baxter's hands moved down towards my shoulders, and his eyes dropped to my spectacular cleavage. His eyes gobbled up the sight and a hungry groan escaped his lips. He brought his hands over the top of my tits, but he never touched them.

"Every curve..." Baxter growled with starvation.

My nipples ached for his caress, and the need was so strong I almost gave into temptation. I could push my aroused mounds right into his eager hands and leave him no choice. But for once, my body refrained.

Baxter was my boss, after all. He was the man I fell into bed with. But I had to find him a wife.

"Are you satisfied with your latest design, Baxter?" I whispered as my breath touched his lips and I met his heated stare.

"I'm extremely pleased with it," Baxter replied in a hoarse tone. "But one last thing, Brielle."

"What is it?" I whispered, lost in his trance.

"Could you turn around and pick up my tie for me?" Baxter asked.

I let out a deep breath through my nose and replied, "Anything for you, sir."

Baxter smirked at me as I turned around and bent over. He desired this and begged for a tease from me. I gave him what he wanted and stuck my ass directly into his junk.

Mr. Lane's very hard shaft.

I plucked Baxter's tie up off the landing and stood up quickly. The moment of contact was brief and could be mistaken as an accident in any normal situation, but this was far from that. Baxter had purposely set this whole ridiculous situation into motion, and he knew exactly what he was doing. I didn't understand why because he wanted me to find him a wife. But the reason didn't matter as long as Baxter remained our client and the bills for Match My Heart were being paid.

I turned around and flung the tie back around his neck. The silky cloth hung in my grasp and I pulled him towards me. Baxter's deep blue eyes met mine, and I knew the task was complete. His erect dick was a clear sign.

I pulled Baxter's face in close with his tie and whispered, "I think we're done here."

The tie fell from my hands, and an amused smirk played across his lips. His eyes danced with need, but he wouldn't give into the desire he felt. Baxter withstood the attraction between us and left us both incredibly aroused.

"We shall call it a day," Baxter said as he backed down from the stage and returned to his desk.

I breathed an unsteady sigh. "I'll get dressed and see myself out."

Baxter sat down at his desk and wouldn't look my way. I knew if he did, we may succumb to temptation and give into our desires. He knew that as much as I did.

"Please keep the lingerie. It fits you to perfection," Baxter added as he got to work at his desk and went back into business mode. "Send me the rest of the questionnaire and I will return it by tomorrow."

Baxter's complete brush off stunned me as I went back to his bedroom to get dressed and leave this performance all behind me. His behavior and his drive to show me who was boss confused me, but now his complete drawback. I almost hated to admit the notion to myself, but his behavior stung.

Maybe his pleasing demeanor was simply what I wanted. For him to desire me, even though I was to find him a bride. Or maybe he felt the passion too and had to hide it for the sake of his company.

Either way, as I got dressed and found my belongings, I knew we couldn't give into any sort of temptation. There was too much at risk and the stakes were too high. We had to remain in a professional partnership no matter how much our bodies disagreed.

Baxter needed a soulmate, and I wasn't it. I had to keep my business from foreclosure and move on from a divorce. We were both at different crossroads and our lanes didn't meet up. Our roads were miles apart.

TWENTY
Match Made in Heaven

I sat at my desk and peered at my laptop screen. My face scrunched up at the potential matches for Baxter Lane, and it had been days since our last meeting. Our session was anything but professional.

The closeness we shared shouldn't have happened and had been on my mind since. The attraction between us interfered with me doing my job. Yes, I followed every word and demand he made, but his charm shouldn't tempt me. I simply should handle the orders he gave and not give them a second thought. But my mind wouldn't give me a break.

Thoughts of everything between us won't leave my brain. Encounters with Baxter frazzled my memory, and my body was flustered. I was a hot and bothered mess.

"Too blonde..." I muttered at the profile of a pretty and intelligent woman.

But she wasn't for him.

"Too tall..." I grumbled at a young woman with glasses.

She was gorgeous and had all the qualities he matched with. Her height was the only issue. I pictured her as she stood in front of him and their mouths closed in for a kiss. I hated the thought of Baxter lip locked in passion, and it made me bitter.

So, I imagined her as a tall animal instead.

She'd loom over the top of him like a giraffe and her long tongue would flick out of her mouth. She'd lick the side of his face and leave a long trail of wetness there. Baxter would remain a gentleman and pull out the napkin from his pocket to wipe at the saliva.

"Next." I giggled and closed her profile from sight.

But my eyes fell upon a woman perfect for Mr. Lane.

The business-like side of me buzzed at the match made in heaven. My eyes looked through her profile with the hope of a love match. But the thought tied my stomach into knots.

I didn't want this match to be true.

She was wonderful and met all the characteristics he could want in a future wife. The ideal woman was career driven, but would put being a mother first. She was highly intelligent, with a long list of educational backgrounds. Baxter's match loved long walks on the beach like he did, an expensive bottle of wine to share wrapped in one another's arms, and she loved to travel just like him. They even shared the same movie interests and music taste for god's sake.

Baxter had a perfect fit. His missing puzzle piece. A soulmate.

But I hated it.

"No, no, no..." I mumbled with anguish and hit my forehead against the keyboard with each word.

"Well, this doesn't look too promising," Evelyn said as she entered the room and scrunched up her face. "Do you need help finding Mr. Lane his ideal fit?"

I shot my head up and glanced at her concerned face. She couldn't know I loathed every minute of this. I held a pure hatred for this woman, who was a splendid match for Baxter. My head spun with jealousy, but I had to let it go. I couldn't let my friend see this bothered me to no end, and I wanted nothing more than to throw my laptop across the room.

This was the worst job ever!

"No, I got this," I answered with a fake smile plastered on my face.

"Then why the glum face?" Evelyn asked with curiosity.

"There's no doom and gloom here," I lied and pointed towards the laptop screen. "We have a match."

"Good. I was worried we had a problem," Evelyn admitted.

"A problem?" I sighed with a hint of sarcasm to hide my fright. "Why would you possibly think that?"

"Well, you've been at this for days and you usually have a match on the first day..." Evelyn replied with concern in her eyes. "It's just that..."

Evelyn's voice faded away, and an awkwardness hung in the air. She could drop a pin and anyone could hear it within the silence. My best friend had an admission. But she hesitated to speak, and I grew worried.

"What is it, Evelyn?" I asked with my eyebrows narrowed together.

"Well, ever since you've come back from your last meeting with Mr. Lane, you've been quiet," Evelyn explained as she looked at me from over the top of my laptop screen and gestured with her hands. "You're normally upbeat and enthusiastic about finding a perfect love match."

Evelyn was right.

I had been distant and withdrawn. Time has gone too fast and I have otherwise preoccupied my thoughts with Baxter. I wanted everything to slow down, and I didn't want to do this. The passion wasn't there for this task. I despised every woman's existence on this planet who was a match for Baxter Lane and wasn't me.

But I had to keep the truth to myself.

I had a promise to uphold, and it was my job to see it through. Baxter wanted a wife. My thoughts on the subject didn't matter. He was my boss, and I was his matchmaker.

The business arrangement was as simple as that.

"I've just distracted myself with finding Baxter the perfect female companion." I smiled, and it was a complete sham.

Everything about this was bogus. A disaster waited in the wings and the devil would wrap me inside the darkness. I not only lied to myself, but to everyone around me. I was headed straight for hell.

I grabbed my coffee beside me and took a big sip. I wished I had put some alcohol in it this morning, but no such luck. Good fortune wasn't on my side and it hadn't been for a long time.

"Okay, I'm just going to come right out and say it since you won't admit it..." Evelyn breathed with frustration as her hands hit her sides and she crossed her arms. "You have feelings for our client. Don't you, Brielle?"

I choked on my morning brew and laid the mug on the desk. The warm liquid would've spit out of my mouth, but I stopped myself. My hand covered my mouth, and I wiped the bit of coffee onto a blank piece of paper.

"No, I do not." I argued, but knew deep down I only hurt myself.

Evelyn came around my desk with a look of determination on her face. I knew my friend, and she had a plan up her sleeve. Evelyn set herself on calling my bluff. She was hell bent on the truth.

"Alright then. Let's get Mr. Lane set up with his love match," Evelyn announced as she looked at the profile of Baxter's perfect fit and picked up my cell phone. "Do you want to tell Baxter, or should I?"

I swallowed hard and shot her a phony grin. "It would be my pleasure to call him."

Evelyn raised an eyebrow and breathed. "I'm sure it would."

My best friend was on to me. I stood no chance in hell of upholding this job if I didn't go through with this. A date had to be scheduled for Baxter and his match. A gorgeous woman named Beverly who owned her own company, just like Baxter. She wanted kids just like him. And they would get married on their beach destination wedding under the ocean sun.

But I heated with red-hot envy at the very thought.

Evelyn glanced over her shoulder as she left my office and I held up my sham of a smile. I let the grin fade as soon as she left and peered down at Baxter Lane's number. But I typed in the regrettable words and hated every moment.

'I've found your perfect match. Are you ready for the first date?'

TWENTY-ONE
Date Night

Tonight was the night. We had set the date. I ordered flower arrangements for the centerpiece and reserved a table for two. The fancy restaurant was accommodating and the mood for the evening would be perfect.

Everything was just right.

I should bask in joy with a job well-done. My task was complete, and I was sure this was Baxter Lane's exact fit. This called for a victory dance, but I didn't want to celebrate because they knotted my stomach in a bunch. My nerves were in overdrive, and I knew the cause. But I had a job to do and nothing else mattered.

It was time for the next step.

Normally, when a potential love match had a date, I'd wait in the wings. I'd book a table for one and watch to see how the arrangement played out. If the date headed for disaster, I'd intervene and professionally call it quits, but if everything went well, I enjoyed my meal in peace. But nothing about this meeting of matches was tranquil.

Not for me, at least.

I was a basket case and a hot mess. I didn't want to go, but this was my job and I had to see it through. Evelyn wasn't an option because I couldn't bring myself to ask. She was already up my ass and knew something was up. I didn't need to prove her right.

So, I was going to break a rule and invite a man. A date for myself to help distract me from the inevitable and save me from myself. But deep down, I hoped Baxter Lane hated it just as much as I loathed him going out with Beverly.

I searched through the directory of potential men in the long list of contacts on my cell phone. It has been quite some time since I had to look for potential dates. Half of these gentlemen were taken, as far as I knew.

The dating scene had never been my thing. I loved doing it as a career, but not in my personal life. The thrill I got from the job was everything. The excitement in bringing two hearts together for a happy ever after made my heart happy. But going out with the opposite sex had never been my thing.

"David Bane..." I whispered to myself.

I remembered David as a fit man with blonde hair and emerald eyes. He was hot as heck, but totally lame. He was a successful bodybuilder and he was all about his career. Conversation with him was difficult because all he did was talk about himself. I don't even remember why I kept him on my list of potentials.

Delete...

"Brock Stevens..." I purred with remembrance.

Great in bed and a total heartthrob. Dark hair and hazel eyes with a mix of color. Brock was a doctor and knew his way around the anatomy. But he took things way too fast and became obsessive. Huge red flag.

Next...

"Garrett Grant..." I sighed with a tap on my chin.

I couldn't quite place him until I remembered the amazing sex in his laboratory. Mr. Grant had been a professor with black-rimmed glasses and an excellent upper body. He was great around the test tubes, but he couldn't hold up a conversation for the life of him. Great in the sack, but he was too geeky.

Removed...

But my eyes landed on a man who had been hard to forget. Hopefully, no woman had taken him yet. Jack Wade was a model, and everyone knew him for looking fabulous in only expensive underwear. Mr. Wade could look good in anything, but we were never intimate. Our quick conversations never got too far because I had been married to James and they were friends.

Jack was definitely an option, but I had to gain the guts to call him. I couldn't imagine him being single. He had always appeared to be a straight up gentleman and he was a fine specimen. He couldn't possibly still be waiting in the wings for his match.

"Just dial his number, Brielle..." I mumbled to myself.

I could do this.

I was a confident woman who was on the verge of being single. I needed a date to get through this evening in one piece. The bonus on top was Jack probably knew I wasn't with James anymore. He would know my marriage had sunk.

I blew out a deep breath and hit call on his number. The phone rang in my ear as I paced and wondered if this was even the number to reach him at. I never called him, yet he gave me his details in passing. Probably from James, in case

I ever had to get a hold of him when he went out with the guys.

Oh, God... This was a huge mistake. But before I could end the call, a manly voice answered the phone.

"Hi, beautiful." Jack said with confidence, "I've been waiting for you to call."

My eyes went wide and my cheeks grew hot. I didn't expect a response like this, and his admission stunned me. His voice was smooth and made me tingle to my toes. I dug his assertiveness and charm right away.

"Hi, Jack," I said with a smile.

"I heard about James..." He breathed through the phone line.

I knew my failed marriage would find its way to nip me in the ass at some point in my life, but never this soon. This call was a lapse in judgement and I shouldn't even have bothered. I should end it before this gets even more embarrassing.

"I'm sorry to have bothered you—" I mumbled.

"You could never bother me, beautiful." Jack interrupted, "James is a jerk for what he did to you, Brielle. He never deserved you."

"So, I take it you two aren't on speaking terms?" I asked and held my breath.

"No, not since I found out." Jack answered with certainty.

I blew out a breath of relief and mouthed, 'thank you, lord.' All I needed was word to get back to James that I was dating again. What I did and who I did it with was no longer his concern. We were over and James had no place in my life any longer.

"So, listen..." I breathed with nervousness. "I know this is last minute, but I really need a date for this evening. Would you be up for it?"

"I thought you'd never ask." His voice came through with a smile and not a moment of hesitation.

I giggled. "Great. Thank you."

"You name the place and I'll be there." Jack added.

I smiled with delight, like a woman bedazzled by his straightforwardness, and gave him the directions. The time and how to dress came next. I made the reservation under my name, but he told me he'd wait by the front door and guide me in.

"Beauty deserves an escort." Jack said with appeal.

I blushed even brighter and was thankful he couldn't see me. Something about Jack made me pick him and I was glad I had. He was the perfect gentleman to help me through the evening. But Jack had no idea what he had signed up for, and I wasn't about to let him in on the secret mission.

Jack was my distraction. He was my date. But Jack was a man I hoped would lead Baxter into jealousy.

This would be interesting.

"Okay, I'll see you then." I sighed with a smile.

"Till later, beautiful." Jack said his goodbye.

I hung up the phone without another thought. My feet glided me towards my closet and I picked out a brown dress. The tight fabric was perfect for my shapely behind and made my rack look fabulous. The dress would cut off at my thighs and I'd wear my black knee-high boots.

Maybe this would work out after all?

Right.

Who was I kidding?

I was ready to get this evening over with. At least I had Jack to share it with. Baxter didn't know what he was in for and Jack had no clue what he had got himself into. This could only end in catastrophe. But deep down, I wanted Baxter Lane to wish he was the one with me.

***

In the city center, there was an extravagant restaurant known as the Golden Gate. The rich colored sign stood out in the evening dim-lit street and my heart skipped a beat. The clock struck the right time, and the show was about to begin. But I had second thoughts.

I knew I should turn around and call the whole thing off. Jack Wade appeared to be a straight up gentleman and I walked into this date with false pretenses. He was nothing more than a distraction from a man I couldn't have.

I was here to spy on a love match I had set into motion. Baxter and his date didn't need me snooping around in their blossoming relationship. I had no right and should stop this immediately.

But I couldn't.

I couldn't bring myself to do it because I still had my job to do. I still had to ensure the date went off with no problems, even though I felt like I was the issue. This entire mess I had created.

Unfortunately, there was only one way out. To get through it. Jack Wade would be the one to help me. But he didn't have to know.

I walked through the shiny gold doors of the restaurant and into a flashy entryway. The tiles were bright with the hint of gold throughout and the lighting was just right. The dining area was dimly lit and the perfect romantic setting.

This was the fanciest restaurant in the city and one of my personal favorites. The food was top-notch and left customers' mouths watering for more, but their stomachs full. The staff were highly accommodating and never missed a beat.

I had picked the right place for Baxter's first date and I took pride in the fact. The rest was up to the couple to achieve. They would either ignite with passion or fizzle out the fire. But I secretly wished the date went up in flames.

"Brielle..." Jack called out from in front of me.

"Jack..." I smiled and walked to his side. "I'm surprised you remember me."

"I could never forget a face as beautiful as yours." Jack answered with charisma.

I blushed at his remark and noticed his gaze as it roamed over me. He drank me in like a full bottle of wine, simply his for the taking. His eyes stopped on my cleavage and I knew I had picked the right dress for the occasion. I took Jack Wade, and I felt sexy under his intense stare.

But Jack sure knew how to impress.

Jack was gorgeous in a flashy white tux anyone would notice. He dressed to awaken the ladies and make their pussy's ache. His dark hair glistened with the light and his deep brown eyes seared with passion. But his affection pointed directly at me.

His attention flattered me, but my eyes wandered around for someone else. My thoughts wandered to Baxter with his date. A woman who was perfect for him and nothing like me. My date should have my full attention, but I couldn't help but stray.

I had a job to do.

I cleared my throat. "Our table should be ready."

Jack's eyes left my chest and darted towards my eyes. "It is. Shall I lead the way?"

Jack held up his arm, and I looked from his noble gesture towards his handsome face. He was like a prince and I could be his princess. Instead, I was a wicked woman out to cause havoc with my creation.

I plastered on a fake smile and looped my arm through his. "Yes."

My black boots clicked along the tile as he led us into the dining area. I swung my blonde streaks over my shoulder and followed his lead. Jack was a true gentleman, and I knew eyes fell on us with our entrance.

Light music played in the background, and the romance of the evening was everywhere. The scent of candles burning filled the air. The smell of wax, perfume, and cologne mixed. But the delicious aroma of food outweighed it all.

Jack led me in further, but I lost track of everything when my eyes caught Baxter. Time slowed down as his blue eyes twinkled back at me with surprise and my breath caught in my lungs. The man on my arm didn't matter anymore, and this moment became ours alone.

Baxter sat at the table I had chosen just for him with the flowers I ordered for a romantic touch. His hair had fallen down into his face and I wanted to brush it back. I craved touching the locks of his hair I knew were soft like silk. But I couldn't because his date had just arrived.

My eyes moved from Baxter in his dark grey tuxedo to the woman seated across from him. Beverly, a brown-haired woman in a purple dress and eyes blue just like his. She was flawless, with smooth legs for days and glossy plump lips that begged to be kissed by Baxter Lane.

And my eyes seared with envy.

I swallowed hard and tore my gaze away from the perfect pairing. My eyes fell on the reserved table I had made for two as Jack pulled out my chair and I hoped Baxter took notice. I sat down on the cushioned seat, and Jack grabbed the golden cloth napkin from the table in front of me. He opened the fabric and, to my surprise, laid the napkin out on my lap.

He gave me a slight bow and breathed. "My beauty."

I blinked repeatedly, stunned by his sweet gesture, and nodded my head towards him. Jack was quite the charmer and full of surprises. He took his seat from across the table and he placed his napkin in his lap. Jack Wade wasn't just any model, he was a man with manners.

I opened my menu and pretended to look at the meal options for the evening, but I had a bird's eye view of the love match. My eyes caught the pairing from over the top of my menu and to the right of Jack. There was a pillar with mirrored tiles and a plant of greenery right beside it. I had a great view of Baxter and Beverly seated a few tables away from ours. Baxter's date couldn't see me with her back in my direction, but Baxter Lane had a front-row seat.

"Would you care to share a bottle of champagne with me?" Jack asked from behind his menu.

"Champagne sounds good right about now," I admitted as I watched Baxter from my seat and he looked over his menu.

Beverly laughed at something Baxter spoke as she threw her head to the side and I caught a smile. She looked gorgeous when she was happy with her hair glistening in the soft light. I knew her eyes sparkled back at him, and I was sure she approved of his appearance. Baxter had charm and could swoon any woman he wanted.

"Anything on the menu to your liking, Brielle?" Jack asked.

Nothing actually.

I knew the exact food options Golden Gate offered, but I had lost my appetite. Baxter, with his date, had left a bitter taste in my mouth. I wanted to drown my sorrows in some champagne, but I knew I couldn't afford to get drunk. I still had my task at hand, and remaining sober was the best option to see this through.

"I'll just get a salad," I responded and put the menu down. "I'm not that hungry, anyway."

I watched as Baxter did the same and put down his menu, but I swore his eyes locked on mine. My skin tingles throughout my face and his laser beam vision zoned in on me. I was his target, and he was ready to hit a bullseye.

Until Beverly caught his attention.

Baxter tore his gaze away from me as his date rubbed the toe of her pointy heel against his leg. He smiled a gorgeous grin and a slight chuckle escaped his lips. My head spun with envy and I saw red. My nostrils flared and my breathing picked up pace. I was about to lose it and had to keep it together. I couldn't let my idiotic crush on my boss ruin this entire date.

I had to distract myself.

"Waiter! Waiter!" I called out as a server passed and I caught his attention. "Could you bring us a bottle of your finest champagne, please?"

"Straight away, ma'am," he responded and set off.

Jack finished with his menu and grinned at me. "Someone is ready for some bubbly."

"Anything to get this bitter taste out of my mouth," I teased and flashed him a flirtatious grin.

"Oh, I think I've got a cure for that." Jack said with certainty as he reached across the table and took my hand. "A kiss can speak many languages."

Jack let his mouth do the talking as his soft lips caressed each knuckle on my hand. I couldn't turn away from his romantic act and he drew me in. Something about the touch felt good, but dirty. Maybe because my intentions weren't truthful. But Mr. Wade was a bold man and his charm captivated me.

Jack was a great interruption for the chaos I'd created.

A heated gaze burned into me, and my eyes turned away from Jack. The stare was a burn of desire, but of sheer hate towards the affection another man gave to me. The bitter observation from a few tables away grabbed my attention and pulled me towards him. Baxter oozed with jealousy, and my world basked in accomplishment.

Jack Wade had helped me achieve what I knew could be done. Mr. Baxter Lane was envious of the man who sat across from me. He felt the same way as I did with his perfect match across from him. But this event I set in motion wasn't over yet.

"Your champagne, ma'am," the server announced and put the bottle inside a chiller with ice.

My attention broke from Baxter, and I took my hand back from Jack. The battle of both men was over. Jack's pillow-like lips still lingered on my flesh and I longed for them to be from another man. Jack had caught my attention, but hadn't won my affection. He should, since he was my date. My endearment was just somewhere else.

"Let me do the honors." Jack announced as he took the champagne bottle and peeled the wrapper off the top.

I smiled at him as he effortlessly popped the cork, and the liquid slowly fizzed. The bubbling liquid flowed into a glass and he poured it to the top. Jack passed me some liquid courage with a dashing grin and got his glass ready for a toast.

"To the surprises to come." Jack cheered as he touched his glass to mine, and they clinked together in unison.

But my eyes couldn't help locking on Baxter's.

Baxter glared our way, and he made my heart leap when it shouldn't. His ocean blues pulled me towards him and captivated me. Baxter should focus on his date and not on me. But here I sat, thrilled by the latest development.

"Cheers," I said with a guilty conscience and took a swig of champagne.

The server came back and took our orders. Jack requested a steak with potatoes and herbs, but I stuck with a fresh garden salad. We fell into small talk, but the world wouldn't fall away. It wasn't just the two of us, not for me, anyway.

Jack was wealthy. He was a pleasant distraction. A man easy on the eyes. But he wasn't enough.

He wasn't Baxter Lane.

"So, I came from a big family, but..." Jack said as his voice trailed off and my eyes fell over his shoulder.

I peered at Baxter as he finished up his meal and touched his napkin towards his lips. He stood from his seat and, to my surprise, so did Beverly. My heart grew heavy as he went to her side and his hand fell to the small of her back. A gesture I wished he'd do to me, but it was with someone new.

Baxter leaned into her as she smiled up at him, and he brushed a strand of hair behind her ear. My blood boiled at the motion and I wanted it to be me. But what came next made my heart ache deep inside my core.

Baxter kissed her on the cheek, but it wasn't just any peck. He lingered his lips against her skin for longer than I'd like. But when he pulled away, her eyes caught his.

Beverly wanted more. I felt it and I knew he could, too. She wanted him to kiss her, and I held my breath. Beverly waited with her mouth agape and I waited in agony, but his mouth never came. Instead, he brought her hand to his lips and kissed it gently.

"Oh, thank god..." I mumbled with relief.

"I know, right? It was a close call." Jack said as his voice came back to the center of my world and not the almost kiss I had just experienced.

"What was a close call?" I asked for clarity.

"The accident on set the other day." Jack responded.

"Oh, right, yes, you had mentioned that..." I mumbled with little understanding.

Jack had no clue I hadn't paid attention, and I wasn't about to tell him either. My observation of Baxter's date had been my priority. For my own selfish reason and for my business.

On a professional level, the date had gone well. There was no push back and Baxter took Beverly. But on a personal level, I hated every moment.

I loathed her touch against him. I despised the way she looked his way. But most of all, I hated him with her.

My eyes blinked several times as I watched Beverly leave Baxter's side. The date was over, and she gazed back at him with longing. But Baxter turned away and looked my way.

And I shut him out because this was all too much.

"Unfortunately, I think I'm going to have to call it a night," I announced as I placed my napkin on the table and politely smiled at Jack. "It's been a long day and it has just caught up to me now."

"You don't want dessert?" Jack asked as he took my hand in his and squeezed my hand. "I heard the double chocolate eclair is amazing."

"No, I'll have to pass," I answered with certainty, and Baxter's eyes on me made my mind spin. "I should get going."

"I'd love to do this again." Jack breathed as he kissed my hand and his eyes beamed my way. "But next time I'd love to treat you to dessert."

The way he made it sound was a hundred percent sexual. Jack Wade wanted another date with me. A woman with an impending divorce, but he didn't give a shit. But he would care if he knew I was into another man.

"I'll consider it, Jack." I answered.

Baxter's sharp, heated gaze fused with irritation right on Jack Wade's backside. I knew he hated his hands on me, but I couldn't understand why. Baxter came to me to find him his perfect match, and I found his missing piece in Beverly. She should be the only one who caught his attention, and not me. But I couldn't help my heart skipping a beat to the knowledge I held something he wanted.

I just wasn't sure what it was.

Jack let go of my hand, and I stood from my seat. I tore my gaze away from Baxter and had to maintain my focus. I had to get out of here in one piece.

"Thank you for inviting me this evening, beautiful." Jack said as he too stood from his seat and went to follow by my side.

Jack's hand found the small of my back and there should be tingles there, but there wasn't. Not like there was with Baxter. The man who I wished was by my side. The one I wanted to touch my back, but his eyes followed me as another man ushered me out of the restaurant.

TWENTY-TWO
Conference Party

"Are you ready yet?" Evelyn asked from the other side of the bathroom door.

I called back in frustration, "I need another minute!"

I brushed the comb through my hair and pulled it back into a high-rise ponytail. An elastic held my locks in place and I added a gold scrunchy over top. The ponytail hung down over my shoulder and I braided the long strands into place.

A long braid dangled as I touched up my makeup from a long day and added some gloss to my plump lips. I looked down at my gold sequined dress with a slit up to my thigh and black high heels. The fashion statement satisfied me and I was happy with what I had chosen for the party.

"The conference is going to start without us at this rate because of you," Evelyn muttered with irritation through the door.

"Oh, would you relax?" I sighed with annoyance and tossed my braid behind my back. "It doesn't start for another half hour."

The function wasn't just any normal occasion and only happened once a year. Match My Heart had to be in attendance for a conference party with matchmakers from all around. Dating agencies gathered to share ideas and trade knowledge of techniques that worked to help their clients find a love match.

Evelyn sighed. “You know I hate being late.”

“I know you do,” I admitted as I opened the bathroom door and was ready to go.

“Oh!” Evelyn gasped with surprise and fell away from the door.

“You really need to learn some patience.” I giggled at her startled face.

“I’d be far more patient if you didn’t leave things till the very last minute,” Evelyn grumbled with a slight smile. “But beauty takes time and you’re stunning. Who’s your hot date?”

“You are, gorgeous,” I teased and took my best friend’s hand.

We both laughed as we left my condo and hit the streets for the conference in the beautiful city core. The evening was bittersweet, with no wind and a clear moonlit sky. Stars spread across the darkened atmosphere above and helped light the way. But the busy city street lights brightened the route.

Evelyn drove a tad above the speed limit because I knew she was anxious about the time. My sweet friend needed to learn to loosen up, but at least one of us was on top of matters. She helped keep our business organized and on track. Without her, I couldn’t do this.

Evelyn steered the way, and I gave the directions. She was the yin, and I was the yang. We each brought something to the company and created the perfect interconnected balance.

The car pulled into a curve shaped valet parking area where attendants stood in uniform and were ready to take vehicles. We saved ourselves from the hassle of hunting for a parking spot by dropping off the vehicle. The attendant warmly welcomed us and opened our doors. We exited the car, and they gave Evelyn a ticket before her vehicle was driven away.

"A girl could get used to being treated like royalty." Evelyn sighed as she waved the ticket in front of her face and eyed the valet attendants. "Especially when they look like that."

I laughed. "You need to get laid."

We entered the front foyer through a grand revolving door as it spun around in circles and guests arrived. The fancy event greeted our eyes, with music being played in the background. Organizers of the conference were at the front and we had to name off our dating agency to be given our name tag. I stuck mine on my clutch because it wouldn't stick to my shimmering sequined dress. I had forgotten about the sticky name tags since the last event.

We wandered into the busy conference as servers walked around with silver trays of red and white wine. An excellent touch to a fine evening with like-minded guests. The conference would go by in a flash and we'd leave with new knowledge to bring to our company. Every year there was something new to learn and I couldn't wait to dive in.

But something was off.

I felt out of sorts and not like I normally do for an event such as this one. Something had changed inside of me, a shift I never expected. I had every reason to believe it had something to do with our newest client.

"This is going to be a long night..." I muttered as I noticed a middle-aged woman headed our way and she had a huge smile on her face.

I immediately drew my eyes to her name tag, where it read, 'Maggie' with hearts all around her name. I glanced back up at her gigantic smile and she was way too chipper for my liking. Her energy was too much for me and made me want to run in the opposite direction. But I plastered a smile on my face and I was sure the gesture didn't even match up to hers.

"Hi, ladies." Maggie beamed ecstatically and waved our way. "My name is Maggie and I'm with Once Upon a Romance, where you always find happiness."

My eyes went wide, and I kept a smile on my face. I looked over at Evelyn as my face gave off the vibe, 'Can you believe this chick?' Evelyn tried hard not to laugh as her smile wiggled and she turned her attention to the most eager member of the conference.

"Hi, I'm Evelyn and this is Brielle..." Evelyn introduced us professionally and pointed towards me. "And we're the proud owners of Match My Heart, where two hearts become one."

"Oh!" Maggie shouted with enthusiasm and clapped her hands. "I love the slogan!"

Maggie's fan girl behavior startled me and caused me to jump. I blinked repeatedly at her with my mouth agape. I couldn't believe this woman. She was over-the-top for such a simple task. But one had to admire her passion for her job.

"Thanks." Evelyn breathed politely.

Evelyn appeared just as off put as I was and I knew she wanted to get the hell away from this excessive woman. The short cut Maggie's hair had tons of ringlets throughout it. Her enormous brown eyes fit her big personality.

The dress she chose was of every color in the rainbow and had a sheer shine to the material. Blue heels hugged her feet and her lipstick was bright red. Her fashion sense matched her over-the-top behavior.

Good god...

"Well, Maggie, it was a pleasure—" I breathed with flabbergasted eyes.

"Oh, before you enjoy this fabulous evening..." Maggie interrupted as her big lashes moved and she looked at us. "I just need to know who your latest client is?"

I let Evelyn answer, "Our current client is Mr. Baxter Lane of Lane's Lingerie."

"On my gosh!" Maggie exclaimed with overdone excitement. "Baxter Lane is looking for love?"

I was sure she was a lovely woman, but Maggie irritated me. She made me want to boast about our company and make Match My Heart appear to be flourishing even though we faced foreclosure. But this far too curious woman didn't need to know that.

So, I breathed with pride. "Not only that, but Mr. Lane also wants Match My Heart to find him a wife."

Maggie's face went from amazed to shocked in two seconds. "What? Did I hear you right?"

"You heard me right, Maggie," I added with a proud smirk.

Maggie's eyes blinked repeatedly, and she gushed. "Mr. Lane is so dreamy... But isn't it hard for you to find a billionaire bachelor his love match? Don't you wish you could be the one he falls in love with?"

Evelyn snapped her eyes my way and raised her wine glass to her lips. "He is very dreamy. Wouldn't you agree, Brielle?"

I pressed my lips together and knew exactly where she was headed with this conversation. It didn't take an idiot to know Evelyn threw me right under the bus. And Maggie was the eager one in the driver's seat.

I ignored her comment and wouldn't give her the satisfaction. My best friend had another thing coming if she kept up this nonsense and I knew just the trick. I glared at Evelyn and stole her wine just before she took a sip.

"Hey!" Evelyn cried out in dismay.

I took a huge gulp of her red wine and walked away. Instead of putting up with Evelyn's sarcasm and Maggie's noisiness. I left the far from ordinary woman bewildered with Evelyn on my tail.

"You didn't have to be so dramatic," Evelyn muttered from behind me, and she was out of breath.

I chugged the rest of the wine and the liquid went down smoothly. Much smoother than this night turned out to be. I placed the empty glass on a tray as a server passed and didn't give up the opportunity for a fresh one.

I shot back in frustration, "And you didn't have to be so damn obvious."

I heard a huff from my friend and she shot out in front of me. The look of determination lit up her face and she stopped me in my tracks. Her strong eyes blazed at me with not one sign of anger at my unwanted outburst. But pure certainty shone from them.

I stomped my heels with irritation. “Get out of my way, Evelyn.”

But Evelyn wouldn’t budge.

She leaned in and, without a single doubt, whispered, “What’s obvious are your feelings for our boss.”

She shocked me with her words and I couldn’t believe it. My mouth opened, and I wanted to shoot back how ridiculous she sounded, but nothing came out. I stood there, too stunned to speak, and Baxter’s gorgeous face was the only thing I saw. He clouded my mind like he always did. The man just showed up when he was unwanted and claimed every inch of me.

But my friend was right.

I hated to admit the untamed emotion I felt towards Mr. Baxter Lane, but the feelings were there. I never knew how strong, but something stirred inside whenever he was around. Even the mere thought of him stirred a fire within me and it wanted to burst wide open. His inferno wanted to engulf me whole.

I shook my head and gave her a harsh whisper, “It doesn’t matter because I have to find him a wife.”

Evelyn glared with boldness. “But it does matter, Brielle.”

“No, it doesn’t, Evelyn,” I argued. “So, just let it go.”

“You know I can’t,” Evelyn urged.

“Yes, you damn well can.” I voiced with emotion clear in my stare.

A moment of silence hung between us in the tense air. A power struggle raged on and I couldn't let her in. Because she might figure out the truth. A reality I didn't even know myself, and it frightened me to my very core.

Evelyn searched my face before she said, "I can't if the matchmaker is in love with her client."

Love?

I wasn't in love with Baxter Lane.

My fondness for him was a simple crush.

Wasn't it?

Evelyn accused me of having a deep affection for my boss. The notion was a ridiculous thought and my unsettling feelings I'd have to get over. I simply had to move past all this and I could do it. There was no way in hell I was in love with Baxter Lane.

I didn't answer Evelyn and took another drink of my wine. The sweet liquid courage would get me through this evening that had turned into a nightmare. Evelyn was the demon of truth and I the slave she tormented. But the wanted buzz would help me win the fight against her.

Or at least I'd try.

The wine coated my throat and hit my stomach. A fuzziness fell over me and I realized my wine glass was empty. Before I knew it, two glasses of liquor turned into four and my world spun. Baxter filled every fiber of my being and I swayed to the rhythm. The music grew louder, but I knew the booze made the beat intense. And I couldn't care less.

"I think you've had enough, Brielle," Evelyn stated as she tried to take my drink from me.

I shook my head and refused her, "No, I haven't had enough."

She disagreed, "I think you have."

"No, I haven't, because I'm still thinking about him. He's like a pesky cat and I'm his catnip. Everywhere I go there he is, ready to take a bite with his manly whiskers and big gorgeous blue eyes." I sighed with longing and held the wineglass against my chest. "And he loves to paw at me, but his cuddles are *purrfection...*"

My feet wobbled below me, and my body fell back against the wall. My backside hit the bricks and the wine slightly splashed on my dress. Such a pretty dress to be a mess.

"Damn, t-this is my favorite dress..." I slurred and wiped my hand at the stain.

"Here, let me help..." Evelyn offered.

"N-no. You know what would help me?" I grumbled as I pointed at Evelyn and saw two of her. "Forgetting I ever met billionaire Baxter Lane."

"Well, the only way you can do that is to move on with someone else," Evelyn explained and was the voice of reason.

"That's it!" I exclaimed and passed her my empty wine glass. "Here, take this."

I touched the sides of my sequined dress and searched for my pockets. Then I realized I didn't have any because I wore a fabulous dress. I giggled at my boozy self and opened my clutch.

"Brielle, what are you doing?" Evelyn asked with a sigh.

I pulled out my cell phone and held the phone like it was a prized possession. The mobile pointed in Evelyn's direction in my wasted state of determination. I had a plan and my plastered mind thought the scheme was brilliant.

"I-I'm going to text Mr. Lane and let him know I've moved on." I refused to quit.

"Girl, that is a terrible idea, considering your state." Evelyn huffed and reached for my phone. "Give me that damn thing."

I turned out of reach and found Mr. Lane's last conversation. Evelyn reached from one side of me to the other, but somehow, in my inebriated state, I fought her off. She was no match for me.

"Dear Mr. Lane..." I typed and read the text out loud. "What did you think of my date the other night?"

"What do you mean, your date?" Evelyn asked with confusion.

"I brought a date to Mr. Lane's first date with his perfect match," I responded as I air quoted 'perfect date,' and rolled my eyes.

Evelyn gasped. "Brielle! We have rules for that!"

"Y-ya, well, rules were meant to be broken." I snickered.

Evelyn urged with a hasty breath. "Just give me the damn phone. You are going to wake up in the morning and hate your existence."

"Too late because I already hit send." I smirked and looked over my shoulder at her.

Evelyn knew she had failed and backed off. I turned around, and she crossed her arms over her chest. Her head shook from side to side and she was unimpressed. But in my drunken stupor, I felt superior.

"You're going to regret this." Evelyn sighed.

Suddenly, my cell phone dinged with a notification, and excitement coursed through me. I really had no idea why, but the feeling was just there. I was the biggest genius on this planet.

Just for tonight.

"It's him!" I exclaimed and looked at his message.

Baxter Lane: 'Why do you ask, darling?'

'Because I thought Mr. Wade was a gentleman.'

Dots showed up, and I knew he had seen my text. Baxter was writing a reply, and I impatiently waited. I was hell bent on him knowing I had moved on. Mr. Baxter Lane was the furthest thing from me and I didn't care if he married little miss perfect.

My cell dinged with a new message.

Baxter Lane: 'And what did you think of my date, my darling Brielle?'

'She was too perfect.'

He wasted no time in responding.

Baxter Lane: 'Well, she should be, because you picked her for me.'

I loathed his words and let out a groan. I hated that I had to do this job. Someone could've taken on this task other than me.

Why did this assignment have to fall into my lap?

"What did he say?" Evelyn asked with curiosity, and peeked at our conversation.

"He just pointed out the obvious like he always does," I muttered with annoyance.

"Just don't respond." Evelyn shrugged.

"I'm not letting him off that easily," I sneered and repeated the words I typed out loud. "And Jack is perfect for me."

I felt pretty sure of my words until his response dinged through.

Baxter Lane: 'No one could be as perfect as you.'

My heart beat like a mad woman inside of my chest. The organ throbbed through my foggy haze and pounded loudly in my ears. My cheeks were already hot from the booze, but heated even more with his admission.

Why the hell did he need to do that?

Suddenly, my phone rang and wouldn't stop. Stunned, I looked at the device and knew it was Baxter. I knew I shouldn't answer, but my intoxicated state made me pick up the call.

"W-what the hell is wrong with you?" I asked, with an unwanted slur, "I-I'm trying to tell you I've moved on and you say I'm perfect."

"Well, you are, my darling," Baxter replied, and I envisioned his smirk on the other end of the phone line.

Evelyn yanked at my dress and I knew she wanted in on the conversation. She had tried to stop me, but had failed miserably. She invested and couldn't turn back.

So, I put the call on speakerphone.

"You are getting on my nerves," I informed him. "You and your little miss perfect."

"Well, that's unfortunate. The only thing I want you to get on is me," Baxter teased.

My cheeks burned brighter than they ever could, and Evelyn was stunned. Mr. Baxter Lane was in charge as usual and dominated the conversation with his sexual banter. He pressed all my buttons and refused to quit.

"That ship has sailed, Mr. Lane." I breathed with certainty. "Because you want me to find you a wife."

Baxter heaved a deep sigh. "Did you enjoy watching me with Beverly, Brielle?"

His question threw me off course. The mission I had set out to make was way off base. Baxter hit me with a curve ball and left me spiraling in the wind. He patiently waited on the other line for the response I didn't want to give, but in my intoxicated state, I couldn't lie. I had held the truth deep inside for far too long and the booze had loosened me up. I'd give him a true admission.

For tonight, at least.

"I hated seeing you enjoy another woman," I whispered.

The silence lasted a minute.

"Are you drinking, Brielle?" Baxter asked.

"I-I'm just enjoying some fine wine at a party," I admitted with a stammer, "Speaking of wine. I need more."

"I'm coming to get you," Baxter ordered. "Where are you, Brielle?"

"I'm not telling you where I am..." I mumbled.

But Evelyn answered, "She's in the city at a conference."

"S-sh, don't tell him that..." I shushed my friend.

"She'll be at the front entrance waiting for you," Evelyn added.

"What the hell, E-Evelyn?" I gasped with betrayal.

My best friend went on and gave Baxter Lane the exact address of my drunken whereabouts. I pushed off the wall to dismiss her directions and fell into her arms. Evelyn held me up as I leaned against her and everything spun.

Evelyn took my phone from my hand and disconnected the call before I could change Baxter's mind. She put the device back inside of my clutch and I wanted to pull away, but couldn't. I fired up inside and had nowhere to aim the blaze. I was too far gone for that.

Evelyn smiled at me and sighed. "You'll thank me later."

"Or maybe I won't..." I mumbled.

Evelyn guided me towards the foyer of the conference, and my mind was in overdrive. Baxter was on his way to come and get me. He dropped everything for me and would be here any minute.

The chill of the air greeted me as we stepped outside and I peered up into the midnight sky. There were two moons overhead, and I knew I was in trouble. The night was still young, and I was tipsy out of my mind.

I regretfully watched as a shiny black convertible pulled up to the curb and sapphire eyes met mine. Baxter Lane was dashingly handsome as always, and my heart went into my throat. He pushed the passenger side door open and Evelyn helped me inside. Everything about this had gone wrong, and I was about to find out how much worse the night could get.

TWENTY-THREE

Come For Me

"This isn't the way to my place," I mumbled from the passenger seat and looked around.

"I know," Baxter admitted and kept his eyes on the road.

"Where are you taking me?" I asked with confusion.

"Back to my place," Baxter said without a moment's hesitation.

"W-what? Why?" I asked with a scrunched-up face and reached for the steering wheel. "Turn the car around."

"No," he argued and grabbed my wrist.

"L-let go of me, Baxter," I stammered and tried to fight his powerful grasp, but it was no use. "What is wrong with you?"

I was in no shape to withstand him because of my intoxicated state. Any ounce of strength I thought I had meant nothing against him. Baxter was in full control, and even if I was sober, I couldn't fight him off.

The car came to an abrupt stop and Baxter's head snapped in my direction. His eyes blazed with control and I exhaled heavily from my struggle to win. The power inside of his eyes warned me not to push him, and he was the one with authority.

"You're everything that is wrong with me, Brielle. I'd give up everything to reach you. Especially in this inebriated state," Baxter expressed as his face turned to concern and his eyes studied my face.

"W-well, I'm perfectly fine and I don't need your help," I stuttered, with refusal to quit. "Take me home. Now."

Baxter's eyes burned into mine and his face went unreadable. He let go of my wrist and turned his attention back to the street ahead. The light changed to green, and he took off. But he wouldn't turn around.

"You are coming back to my office and the answer is final," Baxter said sternly, and he glanced at me. "I'm the boss, remember?"

I crossed my arms and huffed. "Well, it's after hours, Mr. Lane."

"Then I guess I'll have to pay you overtime," Baxter admitted with a smirk. "You can sober up with a clear head for the morning. I can't have you working for me in this condition."

Baxter was right, and I heaved out a frustrated breath. I'd tempt myself at home with a bottle of wine and pop the cork. I might not make it into work in the morning. The only problem was, Baxter had no idea he was the cause of all of this. I was sozzled because of him.

I added just for the hell of it. "Make it double."

"Done," Baxter agreed.

Evelyn better thank me for this one. I had to endure an entire night with Baxter Lane. Alone. At his office, but probably in his bedroom.

I was plastered, fired up, and in a playful mood. Those behaviors mixed were dangerous. I wouldn't be on my best behavior.

I grinned to myself as he pulled the car into a special parking garage at the side of Lane's Lingerie. The private parking spot was arranged just for him and a convenient need. One I could imagine Baxter ordered to be put in for himself.

Baxter exited the vehicle and came around to my side of the car when I didn't entertain him. He opened the door and peered down at me. His vibrant blue eyes were alive with need. He loomed over me with power as he leaned in and undid my seatbelt.

"Let me guess?" I taunted him with sarcasm. "You're going to carry me inside, too?"

Baxter shrugged his shoulders with approval and firmly said, "If you're going to be so damn defiant with me, darling, then yes, I will."

Baxter wasted no time, and he heaved me over his shoulder. I let out a cry of surprise and my belly fell flat against him with my ass up in the air. He closed the car door and swiftly carried me inside the company building. The strength of his arm pressed into the backside of my legs, and I couldn't even struggle. All I could do was create a fuss of refusal and hit my hands against his back. But the fight was no use, and I gave up in a matter of minutes.

"Are you absolutely out of your mind, Baxter?" I asked as the blood rushed to my head and I noticed we stepped onto the elevator.

"Only when it comes to you, Brielle," Baxter stated as the elevator climbed to the top floor and he stepped off.

"Well, I was more than capable of walking," I muttered with annoyance.

"Not with that attitude you weren't," Baxter groaned and gave my behind a light tap. "Now, be a good girl and stop being so fucking feisty."

Baxter put me down on my two feet, and the world wobbled. He held me until the dizziness stopped and let go of me. His playfully tap on my ass sent sensual sensations through me and I didn't need it. But that was what this man did to me. He caused me to stir with all sorts of commotion and pure havoc of the sexual kind.

Baxter's hand brushed my cheek, and he whispered, "I'm going to get you a glass of water."

"And what if I don't want any?" I asked with argument.

Baxter's eyes blazed with frustration, and his hand dropped from my cheek. I held his stare and wouldn't back off. He wasn't the only one who could bark commands every waking hour of the night.

"Then I will hold a straw up to your lips until you take a sip," Baxter said as he turned away from me and headed around the corner. "You can continue to be stubborn and sleep on the sofa or you can join me in my bed. The choice is yours."

Baxter went straight towards the bedroom and I already knew the layout. His last order had brought me there, but here I was again. Under my bosses every wish and command.

My mind screamed at me to stay put or run for the street, but my body refused. Every fiber of my being reached for Baxter and wanted to grant him his every desire. Plus, the wine didn't help me with my decision.

I followed in his footsteps and joined him in his bedroom. The room with his massive bed, a stripper's pole, and his strange fascination with a swing in his chamber. A weird request for someone as surprising as him, but the swing intrigued me.

Why was there a black cushioned swing in Mr. Baxter Lane's bedroom?

"I see you've come to your senses, my darling Brielle." Baxter breathed as he came towards me with a glass of water in his hands.

Every step Baxter took towards me made my head spin, or possibly it was the booze. He wore a white dress shirt with the sleeves rolled up to reveal his muscular forearms and bulging veins. The shirt was untucked, and he undid several buttons at the top. The scene gave me a clear view of his magnificent chest, and my mouth watered at the sight.

Images of his naked body played in my mind, and Baxter was a vision hard to forget. He was a dream I could recreate on repeat and never grow tired of. A creative form meant to be on the big screen and desired to the highest degree. But here, he was on show just for me.

Baxter stopped in front of me and brought the glass of water to my lips. I willingly took a sip because I was under his captivating spell. Lost in him like I usually found myself and unable to resist his charm. But this time, his need was to take care of me.

Once he had ascertained I had enough water, he placed the glass aside and looked down at me. Baxter's eyes searched my face, and I pondered every thought he had as he looked at me. I knew where my mind had gone and I wondered if he did the same. I questioned if his mind went back in time. Rewinding to the vacation, we ended up lost in together. The attraction we had given into and the desire we had experienced in paradise.

"Why am I really here, Baxter?" I asked.

Baxter's hand touched my braided hair over my shoulder. His fingertips traced along the zigzag of every twist and he lifted the piece into his hand. He leaned in close and closed his eyes as he ran his nose against my hair. He inhaled my scent and made my being tingle. The smell of me would linger within him and awaken a need we both knew he had.

Baxter groaned. "I couldn't bear the thought of you out there in this condition and someone taking advantage of you."

"I'm more than capable of taking care of myself." I breathed as his cologne surrounded me and made me highly aware of his nearness. "My whereabouts are not your concern."

His eyes darted open and locked on mine. "Everything about you is my concern."

"Why?" I asked with narrowed and confused eyes. "My job is simple—find you a wife. Not be the stand in until you find one."

I couldn't be certain, but I swear hurt danced through Baxter's beautiful blues. His demeanor changed and his eyes left mine. The emotion was gone as quickly as it came and he rested my braid back where it belonged.

Baxter cleared his throat. "You should get some rest."

My eyebrows knitted together with confusion at the abrupt switch within him. Something about the words I spoke held truth for him and caused Baxter to back off. But I couldn't sleep when my harsh truth created tension between us.

"I can't rest right now..." I sighed and changed the subject. "Not when there's a swing in your bedroom."

I walked away from him and towards the peculiar object I never would've guessed to be in here. Inside a billionaire bachelor's room. The swing reminded me of childhood, but if I knew Baxter Lane at all, there had to be some other explanation.

I touched the black rope hanging from a bar and secured the cushioned seat in place. A chain hung down from the ceiling and dangled the object in place. The only thing I found odd was the black padded stirrups.

"I see you're intrigued." Baxter breathed from behind me.

"Yes, I'm fascinated to know why there is a swing in here?" I asked, as I continue to admire the object in question.

I knew Baxter's eyes were on me as I contemplated his toy. His laser beam hold followed my hand as I touched the swing and caused a chill to run through my spine. He was intense, and I couldn't make sense of it. He had withdrawn himself from me only to make me his desired target.

"The harness is for fucking, Brielle," Baxter admitted with a husky tone.

"Really?" I flushed at the thought and his honesty threw me off balance.

"Yes, my darling. The sex swing is to fuck in," Baxter answered, and his hand touched my backside. "Do you want me to show you how it works?"

Baxter's caress danced down my back, and I quivered with desire for him. I shouldn't and knew this wasn't proper, but everything about the brush of passion felt right. Baxter Lane was my boss, and I worked for him.

"W-what?" I stammered as my heels swayed and I grabbed onto the swing.

Baxter leaned in close, and his breath tickled my ear. "Do you want me to fuck you in it, darling?"

The temperature in the room turned up to one hundred degrees and my breath hitched. The thought of Baxter screwing me in his sex swing took flight in my mind. My inexperience with the pleasurable play made me curious, and I wanted to take him up on his offer. But he was my client and completely off-limits.

I swallowed hard and said. "I think it would be highly inappropriate considering our business arrangement, Mr. Lane."

Baxter's hand dipped lower and laid on the small of my back. He contemplated my response and drew small circles against my back. The gentle touch ignited every desire within me, and I wanted nothing more than to turn around. I wanted Baxter Lane to kiss me and make me forget we had a professional agreement.

"I think we've crossed that fine line..." Baxter whispered as his lips brushed against my ear, "Don't you agree, Brielle?"

Baxter's words were crystal clear to me. I didn't speak a word as my eyes caught sight of his exotic pole and I moved away from the swing. I knew I shouldn't. My mind screamed at me to go to bed. But my body buzzed with mischief.

I seductively walked and glanced over my shoulder at Baxter. His blue hues sprung to life with curiosity, and he raised an eyebrow. My hand found the zipper at the side of my sequined dress and pulled the closure down. I caught sight of a slow grin spreading across his face and he moved towards his bed.

We both gave a slow dance to our desired positions, but our eyes never wavered. We never faltered from the vision we wanted to see, and it was the picture of us. A portrait of our passion we could never contain for one another. Our desire should be, but this night in time we didn't give a fuck.

We gave into temptation, and we did it together. The choice was ours and no one else. Not even a damn arrangement could stop us. Not tonight.

I was in a playful mood thanks to the alcohol in my system, and I let my dress fall to the floor. My heels kicked it aside, and I peered down at my very skimpy attire. A black push-up bra with a black lace thong to match. My hands brushed the black fabric at the top of my thighs and I admired my legs in stockings.

My eyes locked with his again as I grabbed onto the exotic pole and the stainless steel was warm in my hand. A flirtatious look came to life on my face, and I swung my body around the pole. But I imagined the pole was Baxter.

A stick full of desire I could bring to its knees. His rock-hard shaft I could dance around and give myself to. His stick would twitch with desire and I'd stroke him into ecstasy.

My brown eyes blazed with an invitation for him to join me, but Baxter remained on his bed. The bedsheet ruffled slightly from him being lost with his eyes on me. His gaze trapped on me and he was all mine.

His arms crossed behind his head and rested against the headboard in an upright position. His brilliant body relaxed and nothing about him was restless. Except for his blue eyes flaring with red-hot longing.

I wrapped my leg around the pole and tossed my head back. The steel spun around in a circle and my body followed. My braid whipped out behind me and my eyes caught him, but he was upside down. My hand hung onto the pole with a tight grip and I pulled my head back up. The leg I wrapped around the pole wove straight up, and my hand went up to grip the steel higher.

The strength within me pulled me higher and my other hand clenched the pole. I let my other leg suspend into the air and the pole whirled. My braid tossed to the side and my world took flight. The side spin variation was on point, but I was sure he was ready for a new position.

I put my form straight into a superman pose with the pole hugged between my thighs. My hand clung to the stainless steel, and my eyes found him. The pole slowed, and I saw him get more comfortable. He completely undid his white dress shirt and his teeth found his lower lip. I knew he sucked in a breath and the visual satisfaction of the seductive impulse made me on fire.

Baxter Lane desired me. Only me. Not his future wife or a new bride. He wanted me.

And I was on fire for him.

I let my foot slide down the pole towards the floor and hugged my other leg around the steel for support. My upper body flung backwards and my hair whipped back in a hasty movement. My arms were free, and I circled unbound. I closed my eyes for a moment and enjoyed the breeze against my face.

A chill ran up my spine as I let myself lower towards the floor when the exotic steel slowed. The sweat from me made the journey back to my feet as flawless as it could be. My eyes opened, and I caught sight of Baxter. He was no longer on the bed and headed straight for me.

His move was slow, and I let my back fall against the pole. With my limbs up in the air, I felt my body drop and the steel let me go. My hips swayed with allure and I pushed myself back up. My hand gestured towards him to 'come here' in a playful mood. I quickly changed it up and turned my backside to him. I held onto the pole and stuck out my ass for his enjoyment, but he never touched me.

I begged for his touch. I wanted his caress more than anything. The need for Baxter was insane, and my pussy purred with desire.

I soaked myself. Wet and horny. I had completely lost my mind, but I didn't care.

My plump behind swayed from side to side, and I waved it with a twerk. He groaned from behind me and a grin came to my face. Baxter relished in my master plan and fell right into the palm of my eager hand.

The twerk stopped, and I danced around the pole. The steel spun with me and I kept my eyes away from him. I didn't look at Baxter because I wasn't done with his pleasurable torture yet.

My leg hugged the pole, and I tossed my head back just for him. Baxter was close. So near I could reach out and touch him. The sexual tension hung thicker between us and I had a plan to make him break.

I lowered my leg and stopped myself from the never-ending spin. I held onto the pole with one hand and the exotic stick fell between my legs. My thighs hugged the steel in between me and my pussy lips rubbed against it. I worked my body sweetly up and down at a slow pace. The sensation of the warm stick against my clit made me shiver with an overwhelming need and I felt Baxter's eyes on me. He couldn't turn away and I didn't want him to. I craved him to be engrossed in me, wrapped up in me, and captivated by my seductive heat.

The excitement of the play seared from me, and I threw my head back with my eyes closed. My lips were agape and a seductive sigh escaped me. My hips turned in a slow and steady circle. Around and around, I fell into an intoxicated ecstasy. But then fingers traced my backside.

Up and down, Baxter's touch caressed me in a leisurely fashion. His contact with my body was torturous, and I wanted more. My head pulled upright as another sigh escaped me and my other hand reached back. My fingertips weaved through the strands of his dangerous dark hair and my head fell back onto his shoulder.

"Fuck, you are enchanting, my darling Brielle," Baxter whispered in my ear, "My cock is fascinated by you."

"That was the plan, Bax," I purred at him.

Baxter groaned. "Do you want to know the plan I have for you?"

Baxter placed both his hands on either side of me and they trailed in a tantalizing pace. His skilled hands moved lower down to the small of my back, but he didn't stop there. He kept on as his hands fell upon my ass and he tightly squeezed. His magnificent hands gripped my plump rear, and he moved the cheeks to his own rhythm.

"What's the plan?" I sighed with desire, and he tempted me to nibble his earlobe.

But he beat me to the case.

Baxter let out a throaty groan and flicked his tongue against my ear. The wetness from him left a chill as the sensation ran through me and made me want to pounce. He replaced the coolness with warmth as his teeth nipped at my earlobe and his aroused breath brought me closer to the edge.

"We're going back to paradise, darling," Baxter breathed as his tongue licked up my ear and he made my hips move.

"Oh, fuck yes..." I moaned as I held on and let him take over.

Baxter moved my ass cheeks faster, and my hips fell into his fast-paced speed. My clit rubbed against the steel stick, just like it would move against his dick. He not only made it swirl, he made it rock. Up and down, just like I would ride his cock.

The speed was on fire, and my pussy was ablaze. The vigorous rate made my heart race. My forehead was slick with sweet sweat and the heat of his arousal made the room feel like a blazing inferno.

Baxter made me get lost in him. Disoriented with each thrusted pace. Held prisoner in his temptation and I was about to explode.

"Oh, shit!" I whimpered as the peak came to light and my eyes saw stars.

Baxter followed my pace and thrust his hips right along with mine. The speed he created took over us, and I fell from grace. My climax erupted from deep within, and my juices flowed.

"Oh, Bax!" I cried out as I came and the waves of pure pleasure consumed me.

"Oh, my darling..." Baxter moaned in my ear and held up my spent shape. "So, sacred and all mine."

TWENTY-FOUR

Give Into Me

Baxter was my world. He was everything. And I just gave in to him.

I peered up at him as my orgasm faded and he looked down at me. My head still rested on his broad shoulder and his eyes were alive with a savage need. He wanted me and I couldn't tame him. He had sent me over the edge and I wanted him as obsessed with release as I once was.

Baxter's hot breath fanned my face, and my legs were weak. I no longer hugged the pole with my thighs and they were drained. But the flame deep within me still burned for him and I begged for more.

Hot flames of need swirled around in Baxter's eyes, and I knew he felt my call for him. He gave my ass one last squeeze as a low groan from deep within his depths escaped his parted mouth and his hands fell from me. His arms wrapped me up in him and he lifted me off the ground.

But his lips captured mine.

The kiss intoxicated me even more than the booze and my hands fell into his hair. I grabbed fistfuls of strands with a vicious, eager need and a moan escaped me. He captured the muffle with his tongue and my world swirled. His tongue lapped over mine with a hunger so fierce I thought I might never come back to earth.

Baxter carried me bridal style with a promise to ignite the planet I once knew into flames. His lips were a blaze I never wanted to burn out. The heat he gave me made my world soar, and he was about to blow my universe wide open.

A soft cushion met my backside as Baxter laid me down on it, and the world gently swayed. His lips left my mouth as he broke our fire and replaced it with feathered kisses down my skin. His teeth nipped at my flesh and a moan escaped my agape lips.

I peered down at Baxter, only to realize I was in his sex swing. I should've rejected and stopped this torturous play from my client, but I couldn't. He lit me ablaze, and I never wanted him to stop.

"Oh, Baxter..." I purred with passion. "What the fuck are you doing to me?"

Baxter halted his taunted tease and his ocean blues met mine. The vast blue spoke to me of the paradise he would cast me into. A utopia where I'd be his.

"I'm going to fuck you." Baxter breathed as his eyes cast a spell on me and a wicked smirk fell across his face. "Because you're mine. All mine, my fucking darling."

The arctic blue gaze held mine as his velvet lips touched my flesh. The soft caress was torment as Baxter's mouth worked over my navel and his tongue came out to play. He dipped his wetness into my belly button and goosebumps came to life in his wake. His tongue flicked out and trailed down my skin.

Baxter kept up the tease as he made his way down to where I needed him. The divine spot ached and wanted him again. My cunt knew of all his skills and craved him more than ever before.

"Yes, I'm all fucking yours, Bax..." I moaned, and the words flew out of me before I knew it.

The thrill Baxter gave me made me crazy. I couldn't think and had no time to process. All I saw was him.

Baxter Lane had me trapped. Lost in him. One hundred percent his.

Soft kisses landed on my mound, and my back arched. I wanted him to have full access to me. It was essential for him to have his way with me.

Baxter's hands worked down the sides of my body and his fingers trailed along my heated skin. The tips of his nails softly grazed and fell over my hips. Only to loop his fingers through the black elastic straps of my thong, and he pulled them back. He let the straps go with a snap against my flesh and a soft whimper escaped me. He continued his tease as I watched, and he took in each heavy breath of desire.

Baxter's teeth nipped at the front of my black thong. His hands squeezed my hips as I thrusted up towards him with a yearning so intense, I didn't know how much longer I could wait. His pleasurable torment was too much to take.

A finger trailed over my pussy and the thong piece over my entrance was pushed aside. A current rushed through me as his electric blue hues held mine and his warm breath fell over my opening. I welcomed him as a moan escaped my parted lips and I begged him to please me. I wanted him to amuse me. Enjoy me and fuck me.

Baxter flicked his clever tongue over my cunt. "My kitten is already wet and ripe for me."

Suddenly, but slowly, Baxter stood and left my need throbbing for him. I ached so badly my heartbeat matched the pace of my cunt as they throbbed in unison. The sound echoed in my ears as Baxter intensely peered down at me and he intended to savor every moment.

Baxter removed my heels one by one, their thumps reverberating in the air as they hit the floor. My escalated breath followed as he kissed each foot and placed each one into the black stirrups. He forced my legs to spread further, and they were just the way he wanted them.

I was open wide for him.

Baxter's hands fell to his belt, and my tongue immediately licked my lips. The anticipation was hard to take, and I quivered with need. He undid his belt with a flick of the leather strap and my teeth bit my lower lip.

My untamed ache for Baxter pulsated through me and my hands fisted the cushion below me. I needed to grab something or else I'd pounce on him. But Mr. Lane had a plan and I want to experience the vision he had in mind.

The belt pulled out of his pant loops, and Baxter pulled down his zipper. His pants came down with ease, along with his briefs, and his masterpiece eyed me. His massive cock was fully erect and glistened with his man juice on the tip of his dick. Baxter Lane was extremely aroused.

Very horny indeed.

My gaze roamed over Baxter's magnificent specimen as his shirt came off and he was bare in front of me. I wanted him so terribly. I needed him to fuck me till his thick head buried itself deep within me. Till he hit the hilt and made me want to explode all over again.

The belt remained within his grasp, and Baxter's powerful hands snapped the leather together. The sound was thick and aroused me even more than I thought possible. He leaned in close until his mouth was inches from mine. Our breath mingled, and the moment was feverish, but his lips never consumed mine. Instead, he looked up and placed my hands side by side. The belt looped around my wrists and bound them in place.

I let him place my leashed hands over my head with a jerk of the swing and I couldn't move. I didn't want to, even if I could. He had me transfixed on what he would do next. The thought of the unknown excited me to no end.

My breath met the air in shallowness and he peered down at me with a half grin. Baxter knew he had me right where he desired and he drank me in. His ice-blue eyes roamed over me and his massive dick nudged my entrance. He rubbed his shaft slowly against my pussy in sensual agony and a whimper of want escaped me.

The swing moved with each slow thrust and he breathed from above me. "I want to hear how much you want me. I want to hear just how much you fucking need me, darling."

I answered him with fevered anguish, "I want you so bad it hurts, Bax."

Baxter's dick slid down my opening and his mushroom head cock entered me. The thrust was slow, and a low growl escaped his wildness. He held back the beast inside, but he'd let the untamed savage out. I begged him to, with a slight push from me, and his firm length hit my very core.

"Oh, yes, my darling..." Baxter moaned with pleasure. "Your kitten is so fucking tight. So, damn wet wrapped around my dick."

"Oh, Bax..." I purred with desire.

My fingers crawled into my palms, and I formed fists. Baxter's fingers wrapped around my wrists as he couldn't hold back, and the barbaric beast came to life. His next thrust plunged into me and he wouldn't stop. The force of his blows made the swing rock at a rapid pace. My plump ass bounced off of his fit thighs with each pound. The swing swung in the opposite direction only to steer back towards him. Again and again, Baxter's rock-hard cock rammed into me.

"Fuck, yes, yes!" I cried out.

Baxter grunted from above me with a savage need as he pumped, and I held on for the ride. A red-hot sensation fueled through me and I bucked my hips. Each time he drove into me, the passion soared higher. Closer to him and everything he was.

Reality disappeared. We were the only ones to exist in paradise. A heaven we called our own. Except the promised land was on fire and we were both about to explode.

A hand cupped my breast and squeezed the soft flesh. The bra couldn't stop my nipples from growing against the fabric. Baxter had built an arousal so strong my buds had blossomed to life.

Suddenly, Baxter's length exited my pussy, and he rubbed his shaft against my clit. Up and down he stroked my nub with his firmness. My sweet juices made the sensation smooth, and I whimpered for more. My hands moved to guide him back inside, but he held me still. I found myself trapped and there wasn't a damn thing I could do about it.

"Not so fast, darling..." Baxter hissed with need. "I want this moment to last."

I wanted to protest, but his lips captured my mouth with a fierce need and my lips parted in a frenzy. His tongue danced inside and made my body buzz. We created a rhythm as his tongue swirled with mine and the swing moved to his own tempo. He gently caught my lower lip between his teeth and let it go with a flick. I returned the fiery need and added a luscious lick with the tease.

Baxter eased off and let go of my wrists, but didn't free them from his bind. I watched as he freed my feet from the stirrups and I shivered with longing. I needed him back. Desired him to be close to me. But I ached for him to fill me full.

He didn't waste any time and flipped me over. I ended up on my tied hands and knees. I had no idea what was to come, but the anticipation of the sensual situation thrilled me.

A wet sensation met my ass cheek and Baxter trailed his tongue over the plumpness. He slapped the other cheek, and I gasped with excitement. But his tongue immediately ran up the redness he'd created.

I heard Baxter groan from deep within himself, and the rumble filled the room. He bit his teeth into the flesh on my rear and claimed me. But the sexy sensation electrified me.

A fingertip ran over the lips of my pussy, and I'd take his finger over nothing. I moved my ass backwards to make him give in, but he wouldn't budge. His finger simply danced around my aching entrance and I'd take anything of his to fill my sweet hole.

"Fuck, darling, you're as sweet as honey..." Baxter moaned and tasted his finger. "But a beautiful sight."

Hands trailed up my backside, and goosebumps awakened. The hairs stood on end as his fingers passed and electrified to life. Baxter kept going and found my braided hair. He firmly grabbed the strands and wound the braid around his one hand.

"Fuck me, Bax..." I sighed with a feverish passion. "Please..."

"With pleasure, my darling," Baxter growled.

And he plowed inside.

The thrusts were harder than before and he yanked on my braid with each one. The pull of my hair and his hand on my hip forced Baxter deeper into the hilt of me. My pussy walls folded around his cock and he groaned from behind me. Each blow brought us closer to the edge. Close to the release that consumed our bodies and the very moment we both craved.

The finish line was just around the corner as Baxter drove faster, and the speed made the swing sway just the way we desired. He raced quicker and quicker. He was out of control, but I held on for the ride of my life.

My ass pounded against him, and the sound of our flesh smacked together. The tone of the noise made me quiver and brought me closer to climax. I cried out for him and he fucked me more.

Stars met my eyes, and I closed around him. I couldn't hold off much longer and he throbbed within me. Baxter was right there and his need was about to fill me.

"Look at me," Baxter heaved an order and pulled on my braid.

I turned my head, and my eyes locked with his lusty blues. Sweat glistened on his forehead and his dark hair had fallen into his face. But that didn't stop him from his thirsty need.

"Oh, yes..." I moaned from my agape mouth and my head jerked with each mind-blowing thrust.

Baxter growled, "Eyes on me, darling. I want to see you fall into ecstasy."

"Yes, Bax, yes!" I cried out my climax.

The stars shot and my release exploded. Bright light dashed and my cunt juice gushed. My pussy clenched around his cock and Baxter came right along with me.

"Oh, fuck!" Baxter cried out with release.

The seed from within Baxter flowed into me and his climax shook his body. He trembled behind me and tightly squeezed my ass within his grasp. I knew there would be a bruise, but I didn't care. The mark he left was for me to remember this moment and want it all over again.

I had drained my energy, and Baxter had spent all his strength. We were both sexually elated and our world's had collided into one. Our wild night of unexpected passion was over and a brand-new day awaited.

Baxter unbound me from his hold, and his arms surrounded me. I laid my head against his chest and didn't fight him. I was far too exhausted for an argument. Everything was weak as Baxter carried me to his bed and tucked me in close. He held me as the paradise we once created faded away and I fell into a slumber within his safe haven.

TWENTY-FIVE
Morning Blunder

An unfamiliar sound ticked in my ears and caused me to stir awake from sleep. My eyes blinked repeatedly and my hand touched my forehead. The pulse in my temple pounded and ached to the touch.

"Oh..." I winced in pain.

My head throbbed from the hangover, and my mind was in a fog about yesterday's events. Everything was a blur, and I blamed it on the wine. I wanted to only have one glass, but the alcoholic drink turned into several. One too many and I paid a hefty price.

But why did I drink so much?

Only one person came to mind. A very gorgeous man who was off-limits. But I broke that rule last night.

My eyes shot open as I pieced the puzzle together, and everything made sense. I got heavily intoxicated because of Baxter Lane. But he picked me up and...

Oh, no...

I sat upright in bed, but it wasn't my bed. The mattress was much too comfortable, and the sheets were far too expensive. But I was only in my bra, thong, and stockings.

My gaze frantically fell on the other side of the enormous bed and I was alone. A sigh of relief escaped me, but panic fell over me soon after. Baxter Lane left the other side of the bed unmade.

The side my boss slept in last night. After we had sex. Incredible, skillful and sweaty sex.

"Oh, my god..." I groaned as I threw myself back onto the pillow and wished the night away.

I had given myself to Baxter Lane once again. Only this time, we weren't on vacation. I knew who he was, and he knew me. I was his matchmaker hired by him to find his true love, not sleep with him. But Mr. Lane was my client, and I knew better.

I drank way too much and flirted too many times with a customer. I slept with my boss. But my god Baxter was a god in the sack.

I shook my head and mumbled to myself, "Snap out of it, Brielle."

Everything about this was highly unprofessional. Strictly inexcusable and far too risky. But Baxter had felt oh so good.

"He's my boss..." I whispered to myself as the palm of my hand tapped my forehead. "What was I thinking?"

Baxter Lane was too good to last, and this could never happen again. He was a business arrangement and a task I had to complete. My business was at stake, and I'd never forgive myself if I continued to jeopardize it.

I had to get out of here before Baxter came back. I had to flee the scene of my mistake and pick up the pieces afterwards. This bed had to be empty upon his return.

But my heart ached at the thought.

The image of me leaving Baxter and him discovering I had bailed tugged at my soul. I didn't want to disappoint him or make him question last night, but my behavior was inexcusable. I had no choice but to leave.

I hurriedly threw back the bedsheets and my head pounded, but I had a worse concern to worry about. My high heels were on my side of the bed and I picked them up. No time to waste as I grabbed my gold sequined dress and zipped it back up.

Baxter was nowhere in sight, and I tiptoed in my stockings towards the elevator. I had no clue where he was, but I wouldn't stick around to find out. I was out of there like nobody's business and got my heels on in the elevator.

I hadn't a clue what the time was or who I'd run into on the main floor of Lane's Lingerie. I simply didn't care. The only mission in mind was to get my ass as far away from Mr. Baxter Lane as possible and forget this night ever happened.

***

"How did your night go?" Evelyn asked as she eyed me with a raised eyebrow from behind the desk and rose out of her seat.

"I don't want to discuss the matter right now," I grumbled and kept my head high. "I have work to attend to."

"Oh, ya?" Evelyn pressed as she fell in step beside me and followed me into the office. "Like our client, Mr. Lane?"

The morning had been a disaster. I had walked down the busy city street and hailed a cab. Luckily, I had forgotten to lock the front door of my condo and could get inside. If not, I would've made a call to Mrs. Nosey over here to come and help me out.

The heavens were on my side. But as for the rest, I was sure the gate had opened up and sent me straight into the fiery depths of hell. Now, I had to face my maker and Evelyn wanted the scoop.

"No, actually..." I huffed and dropped my purse onto the desk. "I have to clean up all these files and get everything organized."

It was true.

I was behind on tasks because my primary focus had been on Mr. Lane. The rabbit hole had sucked me in and I had gotten lost in it. All the searching, arranging and giving into every one of Baxter's demanding needs. But that didn't include the sex.

Our intimate time together was on a personal level and not a matter of business. The hours we spent together off the clock were ours. But extremely inappropriate.

"You mean get your mind off of everything that happened last night?" Evelyn asked, as she leaned against my desk and crossed her arms. "It's okay to fall into the arms of another man, Brielle."

"Not into the arms of our client," I argued as I shot her a glare and wished she'd just drop the subject. "That would be highly unprofessional of me."

"So, did you?" Evelyn questioned me.

The air hung in silence. The moment was tense, and I wanted to crawl underneath the desk. Evelyn wanted the truth, and I wasn't ready to give her that. The cold hard fact was, I wasn't ready to admit to myself how good last night was.

Suddenly, the phone rang out a shrill from the front desk. Evelyn stood there for another moment as she stared at me and willed me to come clean. But my mouth remained sealed.

"Fine..." Evelyn mumbled and headed for the phone.

I blew out a sigh of relief and got back to the task I had set out to accomplish. My office required my full attention, and I set my mind on the chore for the day. Nothing could break me from the job I was determined to complete.

Evelyn walked back into the office and said, "There's a Mr. Wade on the phone for you?"

Or maybe Jack Wade would.

"What does he want?" I huffed in frustration.

"Something about a second date..." Evelyn answered with a slight smirk and curious eyes. "Could this be the date you failed to break the news to me about until yesterday evening?"

Last night still came back to me in bits and pieces. The conference had been a complete disaster and I might have let the fact slip that I had arranged a date. A very unprofessional step and I crossed the line. But now Evelyn was aware of my mistake.

"Tell him I'll call him later," I responded and ignored her interrogation.

"Mr. Wade sounds persistent, Brielle," Evelyn added. "Are you sure that's what you want me to tell him?"

"I'm dead sure," I responded without hesitation.

Jack Wade could wait.

"Okay." Evelyn sighed and turned on her heels to answer Mr. Wade.

I heard Evelyn give him the answer I had requested, and the call ended. I almost expected my cell phone to *ding* with a notification or ring with him on the other end, but it never happened. My eyes narrowed, and I shook my head.

I had better things to do other than worry about Jack Wade and another date. Match My Heart needed my full attention right now because who knew what tomorrow would bring. I didn't know what Mr. Baxter Lane would have in store for me next.

I knew Beverly had enjoyed her first date with our client. She loved Mr. Lane's company and his charm. She requested another date, and I'd be in charge of making the arrangements. Another task to complete on my checklist of to dos for the week.

But did I want to?

No.

I didn't want to watch Baxter enjoy another woman's company. To be put in agony again with his hands on someone other than me. I didn't want Beverly to fall in love with Baxter Lane. And I definitely didn't want Baxter to fall for her.

The second date meant one step closer to their first kiss. To them, holding hands wherever they went. And to the first time they make love.

I couldn't sit around and put myself through this torment. I had to do something for my sanity. There had to be a way to distract myself from the inevitable.

"Oh, screw it..." I breathed and grabbed my purse.

I retrieved my cell phone, and the screen lit up with a warm welcome. There were several messages from a certain someone and I must've missed them. Because I got caught up in another man's arms.

Baxter was behind me, and I had to move forward. I had to move on, and I knew the obvious fact from the moment I left Baxter in Hawaii. My finger pressed the call button, and I knew the answer was simple.

Mr. Jack Wade and our second date.

TWENTY-SIX

Mr. Jack Wade

"Mr. Wade is here for you, Brielle," Evelyn announced, with a knock on my office door.

"Perfect." I sighed with a smile and stood up from the desk chair. "How do I look?"

Evelyn smirked and crossed her arms in front of her chest. "Hot. Too bad Mr. Lane won't get to see it."

"I think he's seen enough..." I muttered underneath my breath and pressed my hands down the front of my outfit.

I chose a black front cutout one piece and a short mini skirt from the limited wardrobe I kept at the office. The fabric showed off my busty cleavage and tied together at the front. The thin cloth was tight enough, and I didn't bother with a bra. I had no fresh panties at the office and went with none. I felt sexy, chic, and adventurous.

Nothing could mess up this much-needed distraction. I wanted this date to cover up the mess stirring inside of me. This diversion had to go as planned.

I grabbed my black clutch and walked past a curious Evelyn. She knew I was up to something and I was, but this date was for the greater good. The romantic occasion would help keep my mind off Baxter Lane. The very man I had to arrange a second date for and keep our business afloat.

I strutted out of my office with a newfound confidence as my heels clicked along the floor, and Jack eyed my alluring attire. Mr. Wade wore a black tux with a tie and he was dashing as hell. Everything about him was sexy, and he was full of charm. But I pictured ocean blue eyes staring back at me.

I shook my head and held out my hand. "Shall we get going?"

"Yes, I believe we should." Jack agreed and took my hand. "You look incredible, Brielle."

"Thank you, Jack." I smiled with a nod of my head, and we made our way out of Match My Heart. "You don't look too bad yourself."

Jack chuckled. "Oh, it's nothing. This was just an outfit I had to model this morning."

"Really?" I asked with curiosity.

Jack opened the taxi door for me, and I took my seat. He closed the door and leaned his crossed forearms on the open window frame. A giant smirk spread across his face and he looked in at me like I was his delicious snack for the evening.

"Anything to impress you, beautiful." Jack breathed with certainty.

Mr. Wade left my side of the car and got into his side. He was confident about our date and his eyes danced with a lusty need. A desire to get laid. But I wasn't sure I was up for intimacy. At least, not with him.

"Have fun, you two!" Evelyn shouted from the open door of Match My Heart and gave me a quick wave.

I barely smiled as the taxi took off and towards the destination of our romantic evening. Jack had made the arrangements, so I had no clue where we were going. He had insisted since I planned our last date. But little did he know, I completely planned the date for another couple. I just snooped from the shadows.

"I hope you aren't afraid of heights." Jack admitted with a hint of what was to come.

"I don't think so, but maybe after this evening I will be," I joked, but was completely serious.

Jack Wade only laughed and reached out his hand. His touch met my bare knee and the pad of his thumb stroked me. I should have tingles ignite throughout me, but I was numb.

Instead, I craved another man's caress. Not this man who was extremely attracted to me. Jack Wade was handsome, but not tempting, unlike another man who should remain off-limits.

I bounced with each pothole in the city street, and Jack Wade admired my tits. I immediately wished I had chosen another outfit, but I wanted to keep up the appearance. The facade of wanting this date when I used Jack for my own selfish reason.

For a second time.

"We're here." Jack announced as the car halted out in front of a fancy hotel and he gave my thigh a squeeze. "Are you ready to be blown away, beautiful?"

I plastered on a fake smile. "As ready as I'll ever be."

Jack let go of me and paid the driver with a generous tip. He exited the vehicle and came around to my door as he helped me out of the car. My arm looped through his as he led me through the traffic jam and he zigzagged through the busy street.

Our journey on foot led us straight through the double doors and into a luxurious hotel. The space was vast, and I pondered where we were going. I knew we had dinner reservations, but I had no idea where. I never imagined we'd be at one of the most expensive hotels in the city, but this was Jack's plan.

Jack led straight for multiple elevators lined up in a row, but we didn't wait long to board one. I gazed around at many guests of the hotel who boarded with us, but not one of them stayed. They all left on different floors as the elevator climbed higher and never met our stop.

"Where are we going, Jack?" I asked with anxiety.

"To the top floor." Jack answered with a slick smirk.

Finally, the elevator dinged on the last floor and the doors opened with a slight breeze. The puff of air welcomed us to the peak of the hotel. The elaborate, but incredibly tasteful rooftop restaurant.

"You weren't kidding about the height reference, were you?" I gasped in awe.

"Not one bit," Jack said with confidence. "I'll do anything to entice you."

This easy distraction turned into a big deal. Jack went to great lengths to make this date special, and I felt extremely remorseful. I was here under false pretenses.

Jack Wade wanted me. He'd do anything to dazzle me. But I desired someone I couldn't have.

I almost let out a groan as Jack led me to a table right next to a beautiful view of the city. I cursed myself as he sweetly pulled out my chair and I took my seat. There was no way I could back out because Jack would be heartbroken.

So, I sat, and I'd try with all my willpower to enjoy this date. I created this mess, and I'd have to see it through. Mr. Wade deserved better.

I gave him my best smile. "The view is breathtakingly gorgeous."

My eyes turned to the city lights, and the beams sparkled from below. The different colors shimmered throughout the dimly lit evening as the sunset and everything about this moment was intimate. Everything except my doubtfulness.

"I thought of you when I reserved this place." Jack admitted as he poured two glasses of wine and took my hand in his. "Your beauty is as beautiful as the sunset."

My gaze left the view and locked on Jack's eyes. They glistened at me with admiration and danced with passionate lust. He spoke of promise and a future full of trust. But I couldn't guarantee the same with my heart drawn to another.

I picked up my wineglass and knew I'd need the liquor to sustain the night. Jack's thumb caressed my skin and I should be awestruck by him, but maybe I just required a drink to lighten the mood. I gave Jack a brief cheers and took a large gulp of the white booze. The liquid went down smoothly and I was thankful for the sweet taste.

Jack smiled at me and picked up his wine glass. I expected him to enjoy the alcoholic beverage, but his lips caressed my knuckles. He took his time on each one as his soft lips brushed with care. Jack was tender and everything about him was incredibly sweet, but I longed for more.

I craved the undeniable passion Baxter Lane consumed me with. The unforgettable desire within him as he lit me aflame and the blaze never burned out. Our persistent attraction never went away.

Suddenly, the table shook, and Jack's wine spilled from his glass onto his tux. I peered over with shock in the disturbance's direction and my eyes landed on an expensive watch. My gaze wandered up onto a black leather jacket and landed on the face of Baxter. A very jealous stricken man who was ready to flip our fancy dinner table.

"What the hell do you think you're doing?" I glared with outrage.

"Putting an end to this date," Baxter informed me as his icy blue eyes glared at my date and never wavered. "I think it's time for Mr. Wade to leave."

"You have no right being here and ordering me around," I argued with anger. "Are you stalking me now, too?"

"I went to your office because you left so abruptly this morning and Evelyn told me you were on a date," Baxter answered spitefully as he took in my date's hand woven with mine, and his jaw twitched. "I can see I showed up at the right time."

Goddamnit, Evelyn. She always has to be the voice of reason. The one to fuck with my flawless plan.

Jack let go of my hand and stood with his chest puffed out. He was ready to protect his territory and battle until the bitter end. A fight I was sure he'd lose to the likes of an envious man ready to stake his claim on me.

"If you'll excuse us, sir, we were just about to enjoy a glass of wine together." Jack expressed and tension sliced through the air.

I stood up and placed myself between both men before the situation got out of hand. This was my mess, and I wasn't about to let them fight over me. I faced Baxter, but he still locked his eyes on Jack with rage over my shoulder. His blue eyes were as cold as ice and his chest puffed with dominance. He wanted his competition to realize he stood no chance against him. Baxter was powerful, and he was sure. He was certain of his declaration to me.

"I may work for you, Baxter, but you don't own me." I voiced with irritation.

Baxter's eyes locked on mine, and he stated with certainty, "No, but I own this restaurant."

"You don't own this place," I argued with sarcasm. "What on earth are you talking about?"

"Yes, I own this place," Baxter said as his eyes left mine and locked on Jack. "I just bought it and Mr. Wade is no longer a reserved guest."

I huffed with anger and turned my attention to Jack. "Don't listen to him. My client has lost all hold on reality."

"No, listen to me, Jack," Baxter mocked my words from behind me. "Brielle is already spoken for."

Jack gazed down at me and back at Baxter. The jealous man who had crashed our date and was ready to take it over. The billionaire who had bought the place and was about to throw him out on his unfortunate ass.

"Is this true, Brielle?" Jack asked.

I couldn't answer Jack because I didn't understand the answer myself. Baxter couldn't be mine, and therefore, I couldn't be his. But most importantly, Baxter's gaze burned into my backside and waited for me to speak my truth.

I couldn't give him the satisfaction.

Jack could sense my uneasiness. My unwillingness to answer and his gentle eyes searched my face. He was a good man. Too damn trusting for me.

Jack took my hands in his and stared back at me with confusion. "I don't know what's going on here, but let's take this back to my place."

Jack Wade was the gentleman in all this. He was the knight in shining armour. Jack should draw me to him. I should want him. But I couldn't, with a fiery dragon breathing down my back.

Jack should be the one to slay Baxter, the monster. Jack should win the battle and I should walk out of here with him. Hand in hand, we should leave this place overtaken by Baxter, but something about his fiery need for me made me admit defeat.

"I should stay and deal with my overbearing client." I frowned with refusal. "I'm sorry about the mess."

I meant my words more than Jack could ever know. I had dragged him on this date and knew it could only end in disaster. Distraction from the inevitable was my only intention, but Baxter ruined the plan.

"Are you sure?" Jack asked with worry in his eyes, "This asshole doesn't deserve your time."

"This asshole pays for her time." Baxter breathed with resentment from behind me. "And the clock is ticking, darling."

I ignored Baxter's possessiveness and squeezed Jack's hands. "I can handle my boss."

Jack nodded his head and let go of my hands. "Call me when business doesn't require your attention. We can reschedule our date for another time."

"Don't count on it, Mr. Wade." Baxter breathed with confidence.

Jack left me with a smile and I was certain he stared down Baxter as he passed. They could cut the tension with a knife. The two men were at odds, but I had made my choice and I had to face off with the winner.

I spun around and my index finger pointed directly at Baxter's chest. "How dare you ruin my date!"

I was alone with Baxter, just the way he had intended. He used his money to force himself into a situation. The very circumstance I tried to use to be rid of the thought of him. The idea of Baxter with someone else. But he had to have his way and destroy it.

"You doomed your so-called 'date' from the very beginning," Baxter growled with annoyance and grabbed my wrist. "Because you're fucking mine, Brielle."

I pulled at his hold, but I was no match for his strength. Baxter tugged me in until our faces were mere inches apart. The separation of our mouths killed me and I wanted nothing more than his lips on mine. But I certainly wouldn't let him in on my sensual need.

"I'm not yours and I never will be," I snapped at him with frustration.

Baxter smirked at me and shot back, "Oh, but your sweet cunt was all mine last night, darling, when I fucked you until you screamed for me."

"Well, it's over, and you can bet it's never going to happen again, Baxter," I argued as our heated breath mingled and my eyes burned into his.

"I'll bet your tight kitten belongs to me." Baxter growled with power and his hand gripped the back of my neck. "No other man will bury himself within the depths I have claimed."

"Have you completely lost your mind?" I asked as my eyes caught his lips and they grew into a wicked smile.

"Only when it comes to you, my darling Brielle," Baxter admitted, and his eyes locked on my lips. "I don't want any man hitting on you, and I certainly won't have another man fucking what belongs to me."

Baxter's mouth took mine with a frenzied need and his lips claimed me. I couldn't protest and I couldn't deny him. My lips parted with ease and gave into his passion.

Our lips swirled, and my hands gripped the collar of his jacket. My fingernails bit into the black leather with a need so great the lust took over me. The tension we had built up only crashed down, and we replaced it with a fiery need. A necessity to fuck each other.

Baxter pulled back as his lips brushed mine and he huskily breathed. "Tell me I'm never going to lose you, Brielle."

"Why?" I asked with swollen red lips.

"Because I can't fucking stand a world without you in it," Baxter admitted with desperation.

Baxter's eyes shone with anguish at me. The truth he laid bare in front of me. His desperate need to keep me all for himself gave me a sight of Baxter Lane I had never seen before. A reckless side. A man who was unsure he could live without me.

Words wouldn't escape my mouth. Instead, I captured his lips because I wanted to show him. An explanation wasn't enough, but our deep, heated passion was. The undeniable chemistry could do all the talking.

Baxter growled with a fierce need and squeezed my ass cheeks. He lifted me up onto the table with a thud as the dishes clanked and a whimper escaped me. Baxter's new employees could watch if they desired as he immersed me in him. Wound up in his untamed claim on me, and I was ripe for the taking.

Baxter's hand fell between my legs, and his grin curved against my lips. "Soaked with no panties. My kitten is ready for me."

The hand holding my neck let go as Baxter's fingers trailed over the collarbone and down between my cleavage. He yanked the black tie at the front of my outfit and the fabric fell down on my shoulders. My tits were bare and exposed for him. He rubbed against my clit and my legs wrapped around my torso. My hands fell backwards onto the dinner table and his lips captured mine.

A soft whimper of pleasure escaped me, and he claimed my desire with his mouth. His thumb rubbed against my aching nub and he plunged two fingers between my pussy lips. The moist walls surrounded his fingers as he pumped in and out. His mouth concealed my muffled cries of passion as he built the fire inside my core.

"So, fucking beautiful and so very wet," Baxter groaned against my mouth. "My darling, you're all mine."

The sound of my pussy juice filled the air as Baxter repeatedly surged deep inside. The lube I produced made his journey smooth, and the warmth gushed from me. My hips thrust against his hand and my heart beat pounded in my ears. Blood rushed through me and built me for my release.

Baxter left my lips and made his way down my neck. The trip was slow and sensual as his tongue worked across my skin. His teeth nipped at my goosebumps and drove me wild.

"Bax..." I moaned as my hands found his hair and held onto the smoothness.

"Yes, my darling?" Baxter mumbled between my cleavage.

"Please, Bax, please..." I pleaded with him.

His tongue licked between the divide of each breast and he circled the wetness over towards one nipple. Baxter took the erect bud into his mouth as his tongue swirled around it and I tossed my head back. The passion inside of me exploded as he teased me with his teeth and latched on. His thumb rubbed at a rapid pace and his fingers pumped in union. But his mouth worked on my tits and sent me close to the edge.

"Oh, yes!" I cried out with excited desire.

I was right at the peak of my eruption. My core was about to implode. I was about to climax.

Suddenly, Baxter stopped. He tore his face from my aching breasts and his hand fell from between my legs. But my body was on fire.

"Bax, please, I need you..." I sighed in sensual agony.

Baxter locked eyes on me and, with a throaty groan, said, "Oh, I know you do. Your body yearns for me and I wish to give my darling all she desires. I just had to hear you speak the truth before I fuck you like the queen you are."

Baxter crashed his lips onto mine and made my world spin. Our bodies were flush against one another, with my tits flattened against his white shirt. The zipper of his leather jacket caressed either side of my heated body, and he lifted me from the table. His powerful form carried me over towards the glass railing. The only structure to protect us from falling over the edge.

Baxter kissed me with such passion I didn't fear the dangerous edge. I took a risk right along with him as my backside hit the clear glass railing and his rock-hard cock met my abdomen. He throbbed for me inside of his jeans and begged to be released.

My hands left his hair as I moaned into his mouth and our tongues danced. I trailed my fingers over his broad shoulders and down his muscular forearms. His hands rode up my thigh and underneath my skirt. Nails bit into my hips, but I didn't care. All I cared about was the untamable chemistry between us, and I wanted the flame to burn forever.

My hands found the zipper of his jeans and Baxter groaned as one hand rubbed him, but the other freed him. His raging dick sprang to life in my grasp and I stroked his thickness. But he tore his mouth from mine and spun me around.

"Oh!" I cried out in surprise and clung to the railing.

The breeze blew through my hair as the city laid out below me and the height should've frightened me. Instead, my adrenaline raced and my breath was rapid. The desire soared through me as the sunset hit the tall buildings and basked my bare chest in its light.

Baxter wanted me, and I belonged to him completely.

Baxter's cock peaked at my entrance, and he lifted my mini skirt. He was in charge, and his power loomed over the landscape. Baxter was the master, and I was his for the taking.

Baxter held my ass in his grasp and growled, "Now everyone can watch while I claim my queen."

And declared me Baxter did.

Baxter rammed his cock into me with a steady rhythm. He buried himself deep inside as my walls clung to him and I held on for the ride. My lips were agape as my moans filled the city skyline and my tits bounced to his beat. My plump breasts were over the railing and my erect nipples directed down the side of the skyscraper. Flesh smacked off of the clear glass and mixed with the sweet sound of his clap on my ass.

"Your sweet kitten is only mine to take." Baxter growled with command, and his hand bit into my red flesh. "You're fucking mine, Brielle, and only mine."

"Oh, fuck, yes..." I whimpered with pure pleasure.

Baxter screwed me faster to the point I wasn't sure he could give any more, but he proved me wrong. He grabbed onto my hips and hit me to the hilt. Faster and faster. Harder and harder.

"Say it, my darling queen..." Baxter growled, lost in desire, "Say you're all mine."

Baxter was a reckless man, and he staked his claim.

"I'm yours, Bax. All fucking yours!" I cried out for him, and each pleasurable call echoed throughout the night.

Baxter's name was the last word on my lips as the sunset faded and the stars came out in the nighttime sky. The twinkling light flashed before my eyes and I was right on the edge. But Baxter had fucked me till the sun didn't shine.

"Oh, shit, darling..." Baxter groaned as his climax hit and his seed filled me.

"Oh, yes, Bax!" I cried out with release as it resonated and filled the city canvas.

Baxter leaned his body flush up against me as we came down from our quick burst of passion. His cock still inside of me as it pulsated, and I leaned exhausted against the railing. He brushed the hair from the side of my face and tucked the strands behind my ear.

My eyes closed as he licked my earlobe and whispered a demand, "I don't want any man's hands on you, but mine. Understood?"

I opened my eyes to the night and knew I was solely his. My heart beat for Baxter. My body craved him and he sent my soul into flight. There was no one else but Baxter Lane, and he had made sure of it.

There was only one problem.

Baxter couldn't be mine.

"Yes, until I find you a wife." I breathed with heartbreak and the truth was a sting we both knew would come.

TWENTY-SEVEN
Undeniable Desire

The next morning, I arrived ahead of schedule at the office. Early on purpose to avoid Evelyn. Her multiple text messages throughout the night were a clear sign she wanted every detail. Right down to the risky sex I had with Baxter.

I regretted our quickie on the restaurant rooftop and the way I handled the situation afterwards. Baxter had invited me back to his place, but I refused. Our quick romp from the highest height of the city was enough for one day. The sexual activity between us had to stop, and I had to keep Baxter at a distance.

But today I couldn't.

This morning we had a scheduled appointment, and we had to go over the expectations for his second date with Beverly. Baxter's perfect love match and, quite possibly, his future wife. My attention had to be focused on their upcoming arrangement and the task I had to complete.

I didn't have time to think about our amazing sex.

His magnificent body I had become quite attached to. The way his grunt sounded just before he ejaculated inside of me, the way his body stiffened with each release and his constant need to please me. But I couldn't forget the way his ocean blue eyes begged me to be his.

Baxter had chosen me like I was his prized possession he could have whenever he wanted. That I was his and nobody else's. I couldn't help giving into him. Powerless when he requested me, but he was incorrect. I could never be fully his because he couldn't be mine.

I blew out a deep breath and laid my coffee mug on the desk. The laptop screen stared back at me with multiple tasks to complete before Baxter arrived. The process required my full attention.

Even though I had arrived early, I was happy with the outcome. I had gotten through half a day's work in only a few hours and the rest should come easy. Easier than my dreaded appointment with Baxter.

The front door chimed, and the sound signaled my best friend's arrival. Evelyn was right on time, as per usual. She was like clockwork and if she was ever late, there was a good reason for her absence.

"Well, someone is an early bird for her start of the day," Evelyn called out from the front room and her footsteps headed in my direction. "What has gotten into you, Brielle?"

And there it was.

The question I knew would come. The numerous notifications from her were a dead giveaway this conversation would happen. I knew the discussion would be the first topic out of her mouth on this fine morning. Evelyn was nosey with me, and she had every right to be. But her disruption to my date yesterday evening was uncalled for.

"You have gotten into me, Evelyn, you and the interruption you sent my way," I explained as I rose from my desk and prepared myself for a face-off.

"You mean our client, Mr. Lane?" Evelyn asked as she stepped towards me and crossed her arms.

I knew Evelyn wouldn't back down. She was determined to get answers. And she wanted them now.

"Oh, cut the crap, Evelyn..." I muttered with annoyance, "You had no right sending a client to my dinner date."

"And you have no right getting emotionally attached to our client, but you have," Evelyn snapped back. "Mr. Lane came here looking for you and he demanded I tell him where you were. I had no choice because he's the boss, remember?"

Evelyn was right. Baxter had me attached when I shouldn't be. He had created a work environment which had become chaotic. A place where he dropped a command, and I had to do as he pleased. Evelyn shouldn't be the one I was upset with.

That person should be Baxter Lane.

I blew out a breath and wrapped my arms around my best friend. "You're right and I'm sorry. Please forgive me?"

"I will forgive you for your bitchy attitude..." Evelyn muttered as she wrapped her arms around me and squeezed me tight. "But whatever has gotten into you, you need to sort it out. Our business is on the line."

I pulled back and looked into her eyes. "I know, but I never intended for everything to get so out of control. The job was simple—find Baxter Lane a wife, but he made the situation so much more complicated than that."

"How so?" Evelyn asked with curious eyes.

I let go of her and leaned back against my desk. "Remember when I had a meeting alone with him at his office?"

"Yes, I do," Evelyn replied with narrowed eyes. "What happened?"

"Well, he's the boss, and he wanted me to model for him," I responded with my eyes to the floor and I felt incredibly guilty.

"Model what exactly?" Evelyn asked.

"His lingerie," I answered.

"What?" Evelyn exclaimed with shock.

"I tried to refuse, but Baxter's the boss," I explained as the tip of my heel played with the floor in embarrassment. "And it only went downhill from there."

"Okay, that's completely unprofessional, but extremely hot," Evelyn admitted, as she grabbed my shoulders and met my eyes. "Did you sleep with him?"

"No..." I sighed.

"Oh, thank god because that would—" Evelyn breathed with relief.

"Not that time anyway," I interrupted her.

Evelyn let go of me and turned on her heels. She paced the floor from side to side and wouldn't look my way. Her index finger tapped her mouth, and I knew she processed everything we had discussed. I feared her response because she was not only my best friend, but my business partner. She devoted herself to me as a friend, but was obligated to the company we set up from scratch.

Her concern was valid on all fronts and she had every right to be completely pissed off at me. Hell, I was angry at myself. Furious to the point I had contemplated every decision I had made until this point. I knew that creating a personal relationship with a client was forbidden, but my body deceived me every time. I couldn't deny Baxter Lane, and he knew it.

Evelyn halted and turned towards me. I knew this could be the beginning of the end. This decision was a long time coming, and I was to blame. I wouldn't doubt if she wanted to take over Baxter Lane's profile.

I had no one else to blame.

"What you did was highly unlike you," Evelyn stated as she pointed at me with an unreadable expression and I got ready for her fiery. "A client is strictly off-limits and I should've been in charge once I knew you had a personal attachment to him."

"I know and you have every right—" I said.

"Let me finish," Evelyn interrupted.

My mouth clamped shut at her stern words. Evelyn meant business because this was about her company. Match My Heart was as much mine as it was hers.

"I'm as much to blame as you," Evelyn admitted as her eyes softened and she stepped towards me. "As your best friend, I've failed you and as your business partner, I trusted you. But I have one question for you from a professional standpoint."

"What is it?" I whispered, with tears in my eyes.

"Will you uphold your duty and find Mr. Baxter Lane a wife?" Evelyn asked.

The question hit me with full force. Baxter Lane required his perfect match. But I had become attached.

Could I still find Baxter a bride?

I looked Evelyn in the eyes and spoke the truth, "Yes."

There was a moment of silence as Evelyn took in my answer and the reels spun in her mind. She searched my face for further explanation, but there wasn't one. The answer was simple. I had a job to do and my company came first. Baxter Lane would find his match and I'd be the one to do it.

"Okay..." Evelyn breathed and smiled. "Now, from a friend's standpoint. I think Baxter is in love with you."

Baxter?

In love with me?

No way...

"What?" I gasped in shock and blinked repeatedly. "No, Baxter isn't in love with me. I'm supposed to find him the woman of his dreams. That's why he came here."

"But he's pursuing you, Brielle." Evelyn explained and tapped her head. "Think about it. He only wants you to work with him. He shows up here and demands to know where you are...."

"He buys a restaurant and kicks my date out..." I breathed as I pieced the puzzle together, but it didn't match up and I shook my head. "But there's only one problem. I'm his matchmaker."

"He what?" Evelyn gasped with surprise.

I nodded my head with certainty. "Ya, completely insane, right?"

"No, that's so romantic," Evelyn admitted, as she held a hand over her heart and swooned at Mr. Lane's gesture.

I shook her shoulders. "It doesn't matter because I have to find him his perfect fit."

"So?" Evelyn argued and shrugged her shoulders. "That doesn't mean he doesn't love you."

I dropped my hands from Evelyn's shoulders and sighed. "You're impossible and not helping."

"But what if it's true? What if Baxter Lane loves you?" Evelyn asked.

My heart pounded in my ears, and my head spun. The reality of Baxter falling in love with me was slim. He had come to Match My Heart with a clear intention in mind. Not to admit his undeniable love for me. Love with Baxter Lane was far out of my reach and never a possibility. He may love my body, but he certainly wasn't in love with me.

"Baxter should be here in an hour, and I've got work to do," I said as I ignored her question and the real answer hung in the air.

"Okay, I'll let you get back to it," Evelyn replied with worried eyes and backed off.

I listened to her heels click as she walked away and didn't push further. She knew the conversation was over and I refused to believe it. I couldn't imagine a world with billionaire Baxter Lane confusing his love for his matchmaker. The reality was a dream. One I wasn't sure I'd wish to come true.

***

An hour passed by and right on the dot, a knock sounded at my office door. "Mr. Lane is ready for his scheduled meeting."

I gazed up from my laptop screen and closed the device. I placed the laptop behind me on the windowsill and stood from behind my desk. My hands pressed down my pinstriped black and white dress. But my mind prepared for Baxter.

I needed to keep Mr. Lane at a distance and get through this without further issue. This meeting was about his next date with Beverly and had nothing to do with us. A nonsexual environment and I had to remind myself of that.

Baxter Lane's sexy way was prohibited.

Evelyn watched me as she moved aside and held the door open. She was concerned, but I held my composure and remained professional. I needed her to trust me and this process.

I could handle Mr. Baxter Lane.

"Thank you, Evelyn," Baxter said in a smooth, husky tone as he entered and walked straight towards my desk.

Baxter wore a grey suit with a black-collared shirt underneath. He took off his sunglasses and placed them in his pocket. His blue eyes found mine and shivers went down my spine. The sensation was all too familiar with him in my proximity, but I was to behave and Baxter would do the same.

"You may have a seat, Mr. Lane," Evelyn announced from behind him and looked at me. "If you need anything, I'll be at the front desk."

Evelyn closed the door to the office with a click and I knew she meant her word. She didn't just mean business wise; she meant emotionally. Evelyn was there for me and just a call away.

Baxter wouldn't break his eyes from me, and the intensity of his gaze did a number on me. His deep blues undressed me when I never invited him to. His mind dreamed of fucking me when I never gave him my consent. The air grew tense, and I found myself seated once again. I hid half of my heated body from his overbearing stare.

I grabbed some paperwork from in front of me and my hands shook. Baxter had me on edge, and the need to give myself to him was strong. My body wanted to just have him right here in my office, but my mind couldn't misbehave. I had to stay on course and resist temptation. Even though he peered at me from straight ahead.

Baxter found his seat and clasped his hands together on the desk. He appeared to mean business, but I knew him far better than that. I knew his hungry stare when I saw it. But if I was anyone other than me, I'd mistake him as a domineering boss.

"All right, shall we get down to business?" I asked skillfully and grabbed my pen.

"Yes." Baxter said with an eagerness about him.

"Good," I stated with a brief nod of my head. "We need to discuss where your second date will be with Beverly."

"Okay," Baxter said with a quick answer.

Something was off about him. Baxter Lane was far too quiet. He had to be up to something.

"Okay..." I breathed with puzzlement and gazed down at my papers. "We know Beverly is a seafood lover."

"Yes, she is," Baxter said.

I glanced at Baxter and breathed. "So, we should reserve a table for two at her favorite restaurant. Agreed?"

"If that's what you recommend, then I trust your judgement." Baxter nodded with agreement.

Good. This was off to a smooth start. No arguments and no touching. Baxter was at a distance, and there was nothing to worry about.

"Okay, next on the list is..." I said as I skimmed the paper with my eyes. "Flowers. What flowers should I order for your date?"

Baxter locked eyes with me and gestured his hand in my direction. "Well, what do you prefer?"

"Well, since it's a seafood restaurant, we could do an ocean theme with lilies or a lotus?" I replied with a shrug of my shoulders.

He chuckled. "No, I want to know your choice."

I responded with surprise. "Oh, well, in that case, I love a bouquet of red roses."

Baxter breathed with certainty. "Red roses it is."

Wait a minute...

Baxter just completely turned the conversation around and made the discussion about me. His behavior annoyed me and his delicious grin made me weak. Fragile enough to give in and he knew it. He couldn't mix business with pleasure and the subject of me was off the table. My earlier conversation with Evelyn and our forbidden sexual encounters reminded me of the fact.

His second date was with Beverly. Not me. I had to divert his request and turn back to the subject at hand.

"I'm not your date, but Beverly is," I stated in a professional tone. "Did Beverly mention what her favorite flower was on the first date?"

He gave a quick nod. "She did."

His quick response puzzled me again.

"And what is her favorite flower?" I asked with a raised eyebrow.

Suddenly, Baxter rose from his seat and my eyes followed his hands as he undid his buttoned suit jacket. The abrupt change of pace raced my heart and made my mouth water. I was not fond of the black-collared shirt being unbuttoned so low. The skin on his chest exposed itself and I knew all too well his sexy appearance underneath the shirt.

I didn't want him to come any closer, but my body betrayed me and I bit my lower lip. Baxter had me uncomfortable, but hot and bothered. The sensations sizzled through me and should be illegal. These feelings shouldn't all be allowed to mix together.

I wanted this meeting to go as planned. Smooth with no distraction. Strictly professional and not complicated. But from the expression on Baxter Lane's face, he was about to fuck the situation all up.

"What are you doing?" I asked as my voice trembled and my breath hitched.

Baxter left his side of the desk and headed straight for me. Time slowed down, and he moved in slow motion. His hand caught hair as it fell into his face, and he brushed the strands back in place. He took off his grey jacket and carelessly laid it on top of the desk. But his lusty blue eyes never left mine.

Baxter Lane was a man with a mission.

And his assignment was me.

"I want to know more about you, my darling Brielle. Like..." Baxter whispered as he stood by my side and sniffed my neck. "What's the name of the sweet-scented fragrance you wear?"

"Oh..." I swallowed hard and I lost myself in him.

My head slightly tilted to the side and gave him full exposure to my collarbone. A low groan escaped Baxter, and he took a lock of my hair in his hand. He slid the smooth blonde streaks along his skin and let a part of me caress him. But he couldn't get enough.

Baxter's nose smelled my hair, and he asked, "Or why does your hair smell just like honey?"

I wanted to answer Baxter, and my mouth opened to speak. No words came out and only my lips moved. I lost myself in his trance and one I knew shouldn't last. I had to gain control back before he took matters into his hands.

And I'd willingly let him.

I snapped out of his magic and replied, "Well, if you won't tell me Beverly's favorite flower, I will find out for myself."

I turned my head away from him, and my hair left his hand. My heels scurried from his side, and Baxter let out an agitated groan. He hated when I defied him, but the smart play was for our own good.

My attention turned to the filing cabinet over by the wall, where I classified every customer and all the online profiles. This was a pattern I used as a backup plan, and the idea had worked out to my benefit. My quick thinking saved us from another sexual disaster.

I knew exactly where I had put Beverly's file because I had made the folder recently. My hand pulled at the drawer and the cabinet opened with ease. I skimmed through the alphabetical order and found hers straight away. The folder effortlessly pulled out, and I closed the drawer.

"I found it and..." I breathed with relief and gazed down at her paperwork as I turned around. "Beverly likes..."

But I bumped right into Baxter.

He had followed me and I collided into his firm chest. The file folder crumpled against his solid exterior and he peered down at me. But the lust never left his eyes and remained darkened all for me.

"Forget about Beverly." Baxter growled as he grabbed the folder and dropped the file to the floor.

"But the file..." I whispered with surprise.

Baxter trapped me between himself and the filing cabinet as I backed away from him. My backside hit the cool metal cabinet, and I let out a gasp. His hand touched my neck and trailed down the arch. I licked my lips and Baxter's eyes caught sight of my tongue.

"Forget about the damn paperwork," Baxter growled with command and squeezed my breast. "No more talking. Instead, I want to hear my fucking darling moan."

Baxter's other hand gave my thigh a squeeze and worked upwards. His touch was everything, and his dominant order made my mind race. I couldn't win this sensual war that raged inside of me and gave in to him.

"Oh, Bax..." I gasped as his fingers found my clit and circled the fleshy nub.

Baxter let out a deep growl he had kept inside and his lips crashed onto mine. My body came alive and gave him everything he wanted. I moaned into his mouth as he parted my lips with his tongue and deepened the kiss. The passion from him was hot and heavy. Everything a pent-up beast could give and I was his darling queen.

Our tongues swirled, and his fingers circled my clit. My hips thrust against him and his cock dug into my hip bone. Baxter was fully erect and flush against the zipper. His cock throbbed to be let loose and buried deep inside me.

My hands gripped his neck and my fingernails bit into the soft flesh. Baxter groaned and pinched my nipple through my dress. Desire replaced the prickle of pain as his fingers worked on my nub and set the world on fire.

Our passion was too much. The moment was so fierce, the hunger for each other consumed us. But the thrilling pleasure needed to end.

My best friend was just on the other side of my office door. I had promised her this would end. I'd put a stop to our sexual bliss and be done with it. But here I was, giving myself to temptation, and Baxter had his way with me.

"No..." I whispered against his lips and pushed him away.

My quick shove of refusal surprised Baxter, and he peered at me with confusion. His lusty eyes burned into mine and I turned away from him. I couldn't bear the look of puzzlement as his eyes turned to hurt. Rejection didn't suit him and I knew I had pained him. The damage was done, but whatever this was, had to stop.

I had promised my best friend.

I walked back towards my desk and admitted, "No more. I gave my word to Evelyn and I can't break it."

"Don't you think your word means shit right now, Brielle?" Baxter roared from behind me, and I didn't dare look back. "Your kitten yearns for me the same way your swollen mouth craves me."

I got to the edge of my desk and said. "I think you should just go, Baxter."

"Go?" Baxter breathed with hurt in his voice. "I can't just go when my body aches all over for you. My mind can't think straight without you. My fucking heart beats only for you, my darling."

Tears burned my eyes, and my body trembled with pain. I, too, ached for Baxter, and I couldn't bear the idea of him in any agony because of me. This hurt me just as much as it hurt him, but we needed to distance ourselves.

This meeting was over.

"I can't do this..." I sighed in defeat. "We can't because my best friend is in the other room."

Suddenly, Baxter's quick footfalls sounded behind me, and he grabbed my wrist. My body spun around as a single tear fell from my eye and he saw I was just as pained by our situation as he was. He reached out and tenderly wiped the tear from my cheek.

Baxter tilted my chin, and I met his determined eyes. "I don't care who is there because all I want is you."

"But we can't. We..." I whispered, and he pressed a finger to my lips.

"Don't you get it, Brielle?" Baxter shushed me and pressed me up against the desk. "You are mine."

I moved his finger and argued, "But I'm not just some pawn you can use whenever you want."

Baxter growled at my refusal to quit. His dominance loomed over me and filled the room. He wasn't about to take no for an answer and was ready to have full control. Baxter was prepared to prove me wrong.

"I'm the boss, not you," Baxter ordered and sat me on the edge of the desk. "I will have you when I want and how I want."

Baxter reached up inside my dress and, with a grunt, ripped my thong from my skin. I gasped at his forcefulness and he squeezed my thighs within his powerful grip. My legs spread and he stood between them. Baxter Lane wanted me, and he wouldn't let me go easily.

"Now, you're right where I fucking want you, darling." Baxter growled as he yanked my hair and the air from his mouth fanned my neckline. "All wide open and one hundred percent mine."

Baxter reached behind me and cleared my desk with my belongings. I would've given my dispute, but his skill distracted me. I whimpered as he licked his tongue up my neck and laid kisses up to my ear.

"Oh, yes..." I sighed with desire.

"Now, you're going to show me you're mine," Baxter whispered in my ear with need and cupped my ass in his hands.

Suddenly, he lifted me, and my thighs hugged his hips. The world moved as we switched places and he sat down on the desk. The position forced my dress up and made me straddle his lap. His thick cock pulsated against my bare pussy.

Baxter's mouth sweetly kissed my lips, and I welcomed his tease. I should stop. I knew this would end with us giving in, but he was too close. He was far too tempting, and my body ached with desire. My cunt was on top of his thick manhood and I couldn't deny him. He was mine, and I was his. Just the way I needed.

"Yes, Bax..." I moaned into him. "Anything for you."

"I love your answer, but..." Baxter breathed as his lips brushed mine and he laid back on the desk. "I want you to sit on my face, my good little darling."

Baxter let go of me and gave me the option to run. To scurry away and leave his horny body behind. He gave me a choice and full control. His face awaited me, and his wicked grin taunted me. He wanted to eat me out, giving me complete power and my cunt would set the pace.

"But I... I..." I fumbled with embarrassment. "I've never done this before."

Baxter's hands ran up my thighs, and he breathed. "Well, I'll be your first, and you'll fucking love it."

"Why are you so sure of yourself?" I asked with tease.

"Because I fucking love your pussy," Baxter admitted without hesitation and grabbed my hips. "Now, give it to me. Let me taste your sweet honey and that's an order."

"Well, if it's what the boss wants..." I smirked down at him and brought my aching cunt to his eager mouth. "He gets."

Baxter's smirk faded as my pussy took over and I peered down at his darkened eyes. The ocean blue depths swam with desire and his need to please me. He wanted me to show him I was his, and he was determined to keep me.

"Yes..." I whimpered from agape lips.

Baxter's tongue lapped over my entrance and wet me with his warmth. I quivered above him as his hands held onto my hips and his tongue flicked. The quick movement back and forth caused a flurry deep inside my core. His tongue toyed with my pussy hole and worked upwards towards my clit. He ran the same flickering motion over the fleshy nub, but his teeth nipped it.

My hips moved, and I wanted more. I craved his tongue to be buried deep inside of me and my hands reached down for his hair. My own locks fell around my face as I peered down at him and he watched me. I envisioned his wild smirk and knew he'd do his worst. But in my case, this was for the highest amount of pleasure.

"Oh, fuck, yes..." I moaned from above and my hips picked up pace.

Baxter moaned along with me at the enjoyment my pleasure gave him, and his hands left my hips. He trailed his fingertips along my skin and his powerful grip cupped my ass cheeks. The plump flesh jiggled as he slapped one cheek and then the next. I gasped with desire and jerked my head up, but maintained eye contact. The thrill of his blue depths on me made me soar higher, and my climax wasn't far away.

Suddenly, his silky wetness dove inside of my entrance and his mouth covered my pussy. A squeal of delight escaped my mouth as his tongue worked inside my cunt's walls. Baxter flickered within the smooth flesh, his tongue swirled and pumped. The sensation rocked through me and I rode against his face. Tiny gasps left my agape mouth with each buck of my hips and I gave into the pleasure. The desire he gave me and the excitement was like no other. His hand left my ass and crawled up the front of me. Up towards my collarbone as I trembled under his trance and his fingers found my lips.

I rode him as he took me higher and higher. Right towards the edge, and he surprised me with suction. His mouth slurped me in, and I fell over the peak.

"Yes, yes, yes..." I cried out from above, and Baxter dove three fingers into my mouth to muffle my release. "Oh..."

My fingers fisted his hair and my hips rocked with urgency. I bit down on his fingers and I opened myself fully to him. My sweet like honey juices gushed from me and Baxter held on. He drank me in and let me ride till the very end.

My mouth released his fingers when the wave of climax stopped, and I breathed heavily from above. My hands let go of his hair and rested on either side of his head. I couldn't move as I closed my eyes and my entire being was fully exhausted.

Baxter was aware of my weakened state, and he gave my pussy one last lick. The softness of his caress made my hips buck, and I whimpered at the sensitivity lingering there. My pussy still ached for him and my body wanted him.

I could never get enough of Mr. Baxter Lane. He consumed me and my body refused to quit him. Baxter was a bad habit, but he felt oh so damn good.

I heard a zipper, and my eyes shot open. Baxter wasn't through, and I sensed his urgent need for me from below. His body begged to bury his cock deep within my walls of tight flesh and to fill me with his seed. Never to look back.

Baxter wandered his fingertips up my thighs and rested his hands on my hips. He moved my hips so my pussy no longer covered his face and licked his lips of my leftover come. A naughty grin crawled across his lips and his eyes swirled with wickedness.

Baxter moved my hips lower, and he breathed. "Now that you've ridden my face, I want you to ride my rock-hard thickness."

The tip of his dick brushed my ass and taunted my flesh. His length grazed me and he held me over top of him. My entrance was right over his erect cock.

"I don't know if I can..." I whispered with a struggle.

"I'll help you..." Baxter breathed hoarsely. "But only when you're ready to make me yours, my darling."

The words left Baxter's skilled mouth, and excitement coursed through me. I wasn't alone, and he was right here with me. He'd guide me and help me reach our peak of pleasured bliss together.

"I'm ready, Bax, and ready for you to fill me full." I sighed with desire.

Baxter lowered me slowly, and his tip entered me. "Oh, yes you are, my fucking darling."

"Oh, yes..." I whimpered from above.

And I let myself go.

The massiveness of him filled me and hit the hilt of my core. Baxter groaned from below as my hips moved at a slow pace and circled his dick. He helped move the slow pace and bucked below me. His cock dove deeper and my hips thrust up and down. The sensation was everything, and I wanted more.

I moaned and moved my hips faster as the desk rocked. The slight groan of the table excited me, mixed with Baxter's grunt of approval. He liked my sweet pace, but loved when I fucked him more.

"Yes, darling, ride my dick..." Baxter breathed hoarsely.

Baxter squeezed my hips and his nails bit into my flesh. The slight pain mixed with pleasure and my desire soared. I rode him faster and arched my back as my hair fell down my backside. I tossed my head back and whimpers escaped my agape lips.

I held onto his black dress shirt and controlled each wave of passion. The sensation coursed from my pussy all the way to my curled toes. I couldn't get enough and my legs took over to switch the cowgirl style up.

My knees firmly gripped onto the desk, and my legs worked. I fell onto his cock time and time again as my ass smacked against him. The ride had turned into a wild one and I bounced, but held on for dear life. Baxter was my untamed stallion, and I held the reins.

"Oh, fuck..." I sighed.

The sound of our sex filled the quietness, and the groan of the desk made me fierce. I thought the desk might break in half, but I didn't give a fuck. I rode him like I had never ridden another man in my life. Freedom overtook me, and Baxter was right there to catch me.

Baxter's cock twitched, and I knew his freedom was near. I wanted him to fill me full, and I wanted to be the one to make him lose all control. But he had other plans for me.

"Oh, darling..." Baxter breathed with need and sat up. "I'm not done with you yet."

I was no longer in control, and Baxter cupped my ass in his grasp. He moved my plumpness and my hips couldn't deny his sway. I thrusted right along with his eager need to take charge and his dick hit the back of me.

"Oh, yes, Bax..." I whimpered with need. "Yes, just like that..."

My hips rocked faster and faster to his rhythm. Baxter led the way, and I followed right along with him. The sensation was amazing and my clit rubbed against his pants. Back and forth I thrusted. Quicker and quicker, he made me ride.

Until Baxter rose off of the desk with his thick dick still inside of me and switched up the position one last time. I went right along with him as my hands clung to his shoulders and he lifted me with him. He turned around and my bare ass slapped onto the cool desk.

But he rammed into me.

"Oh, fuck, yes!" I cried out with surprise and he covered his hand over my mouth to muffle my pleasure.

Baxter barreled into me time and time again. His fast pace never stopped, and he never missed a beat. Pound after hard pound, he hit me to the hilt, and I tossed my head back. Each thrust he pummeled into me made my head jerk and the sex was out of this world.

Baxter's hand fell from my mouth, and he found my tits. They bounced within my dress, but one fell free from the black fabric. The nipple was erect, and he pinched it. The sensation drove me wild and my hips thrust to match his rhythm. I was a mad woman ready to explode at the hands of a man who drove me insane.

"Soak me, darling..." Baxter growled as he drove into me and he touched my clit. "Come all over my dick."

Baxter circled his thumb and did me in. Bright stars shone and flew me into oblivion. My second orgasm hit me in surprise.

"Bax!" I cried out as Baxter covered my mouth with his in an earth-shattering kiss and took me into his world.

Baxter hissed into my mouth, and I knew my name was on the only word of his lips. The need to keep quiet was top priority, and our intimacy had to stay hidden. We couldn't hide from our passion and bask in bliss.

"Oh, fuck..." He breathed heavily against my lips and his seed spilled inside of me.

Baxter filled me full as the tides of passion took us and he rode the climax until the last one. His dick throbbed inside of me and his lips left mine. But he kissed my forehead, the tip of my nose, and made me look into his deep blue eyes.

"You will always be mine, Brielle," Baxter whispered and touched my lower lip with his thumb. "Stop denying me and let me in."

Baxter gave my lips one last tender kiss, and he pulled himself out of me. My body was weak, and he zipped up his pants. I watched him find his jacket from the floor and pick up the belongings he had tossed to the ground. He put everything back where it was on the desk and flung his jacket over his shoulder as he backed up towards the office door. His eyes never left mine and burned deep into my soul.

With a turn of the doorknob, he left, and I was alone. Lost in thoughts of Baxter and what had just happened. Our meeting hadn't gone so well, but the sex had. He had ripped my panties in half and his come dripped from me. But there was one fact I couldn't deny.

I was Baxter Lane's.

And there wasn't a damn thing I could do about it.

TWENTY-EIGHT
Day Off

The next day had got off to a miserable start. I didn't even get to fix myself a morning brew, and I was behind schedule. Nothing was going as planned, and the day wasn't even close to over.

My fingers tapped on the keys of my laptop as the front door gave a sweet chime and I knew Evelyn was here. I had arrived late and expected her to be chipper at the front desk, but she wasn't. It wasn't like Evelyn to be behind schedule. She was like clockwork and I pondered what her explanation would be.

"You're late," I mumbled in Evelyn's direction as she strolled through the office door and I stopped working.

"Well, someone's in a grumpy mood." Evelyn acknowledged with a smile. "But I got something to turn that frown upside down."

Evelyn closed my laptop screen, and I exclaimed, "Hey! I was working!"

Evelyn threw clothes over the laptop and said, "That's the problem. We are always working."

I stared puzzled at the clothes and asked, "What is all this about? You don't work out."

"And neither do you, but today we are going to kick butt." Evelyn beamed as she grabbed some gear.

"What do you mean?" I asked.

"Just get dressed, Brielle," Evelyn ordered, and stripped down.

Evelyn placed her fancy dress on the chair and stood half naked. She had on a beige bra with matching panties and dressed in a rush. I had no idea what she was doing and contemplated she had lost her mind. I had work to do and didn't have time for this silly situation.

"Come on, Evelyn..." I groaned with refusal. "I'm not wearing that."

The color of hot pink highlighted my eyes, and I squinted at the brightness. Evelyn seemed out of character in a reflective pink sportswear outfit and a headband to match. She pulled her hair back in a ponytail and kept it out of her face.

"No silly. You will wear this one." Evelyn giggled and tossed clothes my way. "Now, no arguments. We're taking the day off to go for a run in the park because my best friend needs to clear her head."

I knew Evelyn meant business, and no one messed with her when she had a plan in mind. I wouldn't win this fight of the fittest and caved with a grumble. My hands grabbed the outfit without enthusiasm, and I pulled my dress over my head.

Evelyn had chosen a black activewear crop top with a drop armhole tank for over top. The fabric drooped down towards the grey leggings and they sculpted my perfect ass. The outfit was an exact fit, but I was out of place just as much as Evelyn was. I never jogged a day in my life, and neither did Evelyn. This could be an idea of dire consequences.

"Let's get this over with..." I grumbled and headed for the front door.

I tucked my cell phone into the pocket of the tank top while Evelyn locked the main entrance. Match My Heart was officially closed for the day, and my work was at a complete standstill. I could thank my best friend for the chaos tomorrow would bring.

"Taxi!" Evelyn called out as she hailed down a cab and we got inside.

"Shouldn't we actually be running?" I asked and made a confused face.

Evelyn giggled. "Are you kidding? There's no way we'd make it to the park."

The car took off through the busy city street. I knew the park was beautiful and had only gone there occasionally to enjoy a pleasant stroll. Other than that, the biggest park in the city wasn't my cup of tea. Work kept me occupied and paid the bills. My career came first before all else.

The sun beamed through the windows of the taxi and made my skin warm. Shadows flickered with each tall building we passed and vehicles honked in the streets. The day was gorgeous and maybe some fresh air would do me good.

The cab halted at our desired destination, and trees caught my eye. A mix of evergreens and maple trees as they swayed with the light breeze. An asphalt pathway led into the park and the entrance wasn't far from sight.

"Thank you and keep the tip," Evelyn said with a warm smile and she looked over at me. "Come on, let's go."

The driver accepted the cash as we exited his car, and Evelyn took my hand in hers. There was no need to watch for cars because the light was red and we ran straight for the park across the street. We laughed with an extra spunk to our step and our legs soon turned into a jog.

My cell phone dinged in my pocket, but I ignored the interruption. Evelyn had a plan, and I didn't want to mess with it. My best friend meant well, and this wasn't so bad after all.

We parted ways and Evelyn ran up ahead. We followed the path as joggers passed by with ease. The wind blew in my face and my ponytail swayed back and forth against my back. I labored my breath to keep up with Evelyn, and my legs picked up the pace. My arms worked at my sides and helped me run faster.

I knew my body was out of shape and felt the burn within ten minutes of running. The exhaustion took over me, but the atmosphere pushed me forward. The scenery encouraged me to get my out of shape ass back in business. But Evelyn's motivation meant everything.

"Isn't this great?" Evelyn shouted as she ran backwards and extended her arms out towards the sky. "We needed this! The fresh air in our lungs, the ground at our feet and a beautiful day!"

I smiled and nodded my head in agreement. My words failed me as my heavy breaths were my focus and kept me moving. I had to center in on my body because if I didn't, my legs would stop pumping. Conversation was not the main priority right now.

But a cyclist headed straight for Evelyn.

"Evelyn!" I hollered at her and signaled for her to move. "Lookout!"

Evelyn turned around and moved her legs back into my lane of the pathway. The bicycle moved past with a hasty speed and never slowed down. But Evelyn got out of harm's way just in the nick of time.

"Holy shit!" Evelyn shouted with sweat on her forehead. "That was close."

We were thankful the swift cyclist hadn't caused harm and realized this trail was also a bike path. The yellow line in the middle was a clear sign we had missed. We had to treat this pathway as a street and keep on our side.

"I'm feeling lucky!" Evelyn announced with an extra spring to her jog. "Let's race!"

"I'm really not up..." I muttered with staggered breaths.

But Evelyn didn't hear me over her excitement.

"Last one to get around the bend up ahead has to buy water!" Evelyn interrupted and took off.

"Hey! You got a head start!" I shouted with unfairness.

Now, I was determined. Hell bent on beating her cheating ass. I set myself on coming out on top.

My legs pumped faster than ever before. My runners hit the ground and my blood pumped with adrenaline. I flew past a shocked Evelyn and took the lead, but the bend was just up ahead. I knew I had her beat and turned around to see her face when I claimed victory.

I ran backwards and shouted with cockiness. "Thought you pulled a fast one on me, didn't you, Evelyn?"

"I almost had you!" Evelyn shouted as she smiled and the happiness turned into caution. "Behind you!"

I grinned and ignored her phoniness. "Ya, I'm not falling for that one!"

"No, really, Brielle!" Evelyn shouted with fright. "Lookout!"

I had gotten so lost in my success I had crossed over the yellow line. The sound of brakes filled my ears as I turned around and saw a cyclist headed straight for me. Right at the bend in the pathway and I panicked, but ran off the course.

"Oh!" I cried out as I hit the grass and tumbled down a hill.

The world spun out of control as I fell down the grassy slope and saw nothing but greenery. Everything continued to twirl even though my body stopped its downward spiral, and I laid on the grass. My head was dizzy, but nothing hurt.

I blew out a relieved breath and counted my lucky stars. The grass cushioned my fall, and I remained uninjured. Thank God only Evelyn caught my careless blunder.

"Oh, my god, Brielle!" Evelyn shouted from the top of the hill.

But a man came down the slope.

A very muscular and handsome man. His face was full of worry as he came closer. His electric blue eyes zinged over my body and back to my face. But I only stared at him in shock.

"Baxter?" I whispered.

"Brielle?" Baxter asked with concern, and his hands touched me. "Are you hurt?"

I blushed as embarrassment set in and answered, "Only my pride."

Baxter chuckled with relief. "Well, your cat-like reflexes came in handy."

"You were the cyclist?" I asked with puzzlement, "I didn't know you rode a bike?"

Baxter grinned down at me. "Well, there's a lot you don't know about me, darling."

To my surprise, Baxter scooped me up from the ground and wouldn't put me down. His feet worked back up the hill and I had no other choice but to let him. He was my knight in shining armour.

"I'm fine," I argued, to hide my amazement. "I don't need you to carry me."

Baxter's gaze caught mine, and he grinned. "But I never leave a damsel in distress."

My face reddened even more as he refused to put me down and took me back to the top of the hill. Baxter set me back on my feet, and the world was right again. But I missed the embrace of his protection.

Evelyn was shocked to find Baxter was the one to save me and carry me out of harm's way. "Mr. Lane?"

"Hello, Evelyn," Baxter said with a brief wave.

My eyes caught sight of the bike Baxter rode and almost collided with me. There was a black skid on the pavement from the brakes and his effort to miss me. But the bike had seen better days.

The bicycle laid on its side with the front wheel turned up like he had left it in a hurry. I scuffed the paint up and the damage didn't suit the expensive means of transportation. I cursed myself for being so careless, and I should've watched where I was going.

"I'm sorry about your bike," I muttered with awkwardness.

Baxter shrugged. "It's okay. Your safety is more important than the bike."

Baxter was a true gentleman, and his charm made me swoon. His need to protect made me flattered and a flustered puddle at his feet. I couldn't find any words on how to truly thank him for all he had done. Baxter Lane was a hero I never saw coming.

My cell phone dinged again in my pocket and pulled me from what had occurred. I pondered what was so urgent, but ignored the device. The phone could wait because I had a man in tight sport shorts and a muscle shirt in front of me.

The activewear hugged Baxter in all the right places. I admired his fit form and wanted nothing more than to touch his flexed muscles. Sweat glistened on his forehead from a good workout, and he tousled his hair on the side. He was out of character, but the appearance suited him. I could watch him in his element for hours and not grow tired of the sight.

My cell rang, and I sighed with annoyance. "Who is being so persistent?"

"You should get that." Baxter breathed and pointed towards my pocket. "Sounds like it's important."

I pulled the device from my pocket and flipped the phone over. The blue caller ID screen lit up in front of me and I read the name. James Lane.

I groaned and looked at Evelyn. "It's James."

"What the hell could that two-timing bastard want?" Evelyn asked with a frustrated breath.

James didn't deserve the wasted air. He hasn't earned a second of my time. And I wouldn't let him waste another moment.

I pressed the disconnect button and said, "I don't know, and I don't care."

"Good." Evelyn smiled. "We don't need him ruining our day off."

I looked over at Baxter and rolled my eyes. "That was just my soon-to-be ex-husband."

Baxter's eyes looked from my phone and up at my face. He searched my expression and his demeanor was unlike anything I had ever seen before. He had changed in the blink of an eye after the undesired phone call, and he wasn't himself.

The blues of his eyes heated with rage. "The man who left you at the airport is James Lane?"

I peered at Baxter with puzzlement. The missing piece to his odd behavior grew a concern within me I never knew I had for him. I reached out to touch his arm, but he stepped back from me.

"Yes..." I breathed in confusion. "Why?"

Baxter tore his eyes from me and ran his hands through his hair. His shoes paced the ground, and he mumbled words I couldn't make out. He made little sense and my worry grew for him. Whatever ate at him was eating him alive. One minute ago, he was himself and now he was losing his mind.

Evelyn touched my arm and whispered, "What the hell is wrong with Baxter, Brielle?"

I had almost forgotten my best friend by my side. She rarely called Baxter by his first name, and I knew she shared the same distress as me. But I couldn't answer her question.

Only Baxter Lane could.

I shook my head with wide eyes. "I have no fucking clue."

"Well, we better do something quick," Evelyn admitted with worry.

I had to do something. Evelyn couldn't. I was the only one who could get through his madness.

"What's wrong, Bax?" I asked.

Suddenly, Baxter halted on the spot. The nickname I gave him brought him back to me and his blue depths locked on me. His jaw twitched, and he clicked his tongue off of the roof of his mouth. Baxter's rage made him a ticking time bomb ready to explode.

Baxter walked straight towards me and breathed with hatred. "James Lane is my step-brother, Brielle."

TWENTY-NINE
Estranged Reality

Shocked was an understatement. The blow of the truth left me stunned and no words would form. Only air escaped out of my agape mouth.

"What?" Evelyn gasped, thrown off by the news. "You aren't serious... Are you?"

Baxter wouldn't turn away from me. His eyes fused with hatred, and he clenched his fists in anger. A pure loathing I had never seen from such a confident and affectionate man.

"I'm dead serious." Baxter breathed with certainty. "Your soon-to-be ex-husband is my step-brother."

I choked out in disbelief. "But how? James never once mentioned you. This is absurd."

"As absurd as this may be, I am related to James through marriage."

Baxter admitted, with truth written all over his face.

Not for one second would I even believe this to be true. I didn't want any of this to be real. This was some cruel joke life continued to play on me. I caught myself in a nightmare and I was right in the middle of everything.

Because I slept with my husband's step-brother.

My family.

"I think I'm going to be sick..." I sighed as my hands fell to my knees and I bent forward.

The world spun, and a dark cloud loomed over my head. Dizziness took over me as Baxter rushed to my aid and touched my backside. His caress circled my back and soothed me. I knew he shouldn't because he was not only my boss, but my brother-in-law through marriage.

How the hell could this happen?

James never once mentioned any siblings. Not blood, half or step. We had a wedding and Mr. Baxter Lane wasn't there. James never spoke a word of this, and nothing made sense.

I thought I knew everything there was to know about James, but I was dead wrong. James was not only a two-timing loser, but a liar with a past. He had skeletons in his closet and he left me in the dark.

Marriage was a shared pact, and he had completely blown that. I clearly knew nothing about a man who once meant so much to me. But from the expression on Baxter's face, there was much more to learn.

"James never once mentioned you..." I breathed through the hurt and my mind raced. "How could he do this to me, Bax?"

"Because he's a selfish man, my darling, and I'm sorry he's taken that side of himself out on you," Baxter whispered, and he was right by my side.

I couldn't catch my breath and Baxter knew it. He tilted my face up towards him and took a deep breath. In through his nose and out through his mouth. I repeated his pattern as our eyes remained locked on each other and the world calmed down.

Baxter was the voice of reason and my escape from the madness. Even though he was part of the source of this mess, he wasn't the reason. James was at his worst yet again, but this time, I wasn't alone. Baxter caught himself in this chaotic situation too, and he helped guide me through.

We'd get through this together.

I withdrew my hands from my knees, and my world stopped its spiral. I stood up straight and my brain processed everything. The version of what was once my life was gone, and this realization was my new existence.

I had to learn how to adapt to this newfound truth and live with what I couldn't change. My relationship with Baxter. A man who was technically my family. But not for much longer.

I looked deep into my brother-in-law's eyes and asked, "Why did he keep this from me?"

"Because he hates me." Baxter answered with a hint of hurt. "James and I are estranged. We haven't spoken in years."

The words he spoke made sense, but didn't make the harsh truth any more livable. Baxter was so different compared to James. Complete opposites in almost everything. Except their bond as family.

"I think it's best I give you two some privacy," Evelyn announced from the sideline and I had forgotten she was there.

"No, Evelyn, you—" I sighed and turned my attention to her.

"Yes, Brielle, you both need some time to talk," Evelyn interrupted as she squeezed my shoulders and stared into my eyes with compassion. "And you need to do this together."

Together.

Evelyn understood the depth of this circumstance. She knew everything and how deep the hole had been dug. She acknowledged we needed to live through this together. Just Baxter and me.

"Thank you, Evelyn," Baxter said with a brief nod.

"You're welcome, Baxter." Evelyn said with a slight smile. "But you better take care of my girl. She can't afford a breakdown because she has to find you a wife."

"Right..." Baxter sighed, as his eyes met mine with uncertainty. "A wife."

The footsteps of Evelyn's departure were the only thing I heard because my attention zoned in on Baxter. He held a look in his eyes of doubt. An unresolved focus of the unknown and where we went from here.

The swirl in his blue hues frightened me. Baxter was always the sure one. He was always in charge, dominant, and full of confidence. This side of Baxter Lane scared me. He was angry, unfocused and vulnerable.

"Maybe I should go..." I admitted in a soft voice.

"No, stay..." Baxter breathed as his hands grabbed mine and his thumbs caressed my skin. "Evelyn is right. We need to be together. I need to tell you the truth because my step-brother couldn't."

Baxter had a step-brother. The truth was raw. But the fact still hit me like a slap in the face.

"O-okay..." I choked out.

My world broke into pieces from this brutal reality. A place I scrambled around to find them to build back together. But Baxter would be the one to help me.

"But I don't want to do this here," Baxter admitted, as he squeezed my hands and gave me a hesitant look. "Could we go back to my office?"

I could tell Baxter needed this. He wanted to get his past off his chest. Old wounds demanded to come clean. But I feared how deep the scars buried themselves.

"Yes," I simply said.

"Good," Baxter sighed with relief. "Because I could use a drink."

A quick laugh escaped me, and I sighed. "I could too."

Baxter chuckled through the chaos and let go of my hands. He retrieved his bike from the ground and walked it to my side. His rear end sat on the seat, but he patted the handle bars.

"Want a lift?" Baxter asked with a grin. "You can ride back with me."

"I don't know if that's a good idea..." I hesitated with reluctance.

"Why not?" Baxter asked with a shrug of his shoulders.

"Because it's unsafe," I admitted.

But left out the part where I'd be too close to my brother-in-law.

"I could never be careless with you." Baxter breathed with sincerity. "You can trust me, Brielle."

I knew I could. I always had confidence in Baxter. That was the problem. Especially now with him as part of my family.

"I know I can, Bax," I breathed.

"Good," Baxter said with a gorgeous smile. "Let's get out of here."

I smiled and placed my foot on the front tire. My butt hit the handlebars as Baxter held the bike steady and I climbed aboard. My hands gripped beside his and my legs floated in the air. He leaned forward so my back could angle against him and I could relax.

"Are you ready, darling?" Baxter whispered the question in my ear.

"As ready as I'll ever be," I responded playfully.

"Okay, here we go," Baxter said from over my shoulder.

"Ah!" I giggled with excitement.

Baxter chuckled from behind me, and the vibration of his laughter lit my heart on fire. The cool breeze blew against my face and steadied my flaming heart. But the small child in both of us came out to play.

The bicycle went faster as Baxter peddled along the path and the paved walkway soon turned into a busy city street. We zoomed past pedestrians and vehicles caught in traffic. Horns honked, and we laughed at the freedom we caught ourselves up in. Together, we flew away.

Soon the ride ended as Baxter pulled up to Lane's Lingerie and we bounced over the curb. He steered the bike up towards the front doors and security opened them with welcomed arms. Baxter exchanged a brief word as we biked on past and right into the main foyer.

A giggle escaped me as Baxter didn't stop there and continued through the small crowd. The tires turned, and we zig zagged past guests at his business. But this newfound lively side of Baxter Lane was one I enjoyed.

A little too much.

Baxter rode past the elevators, and we came to a stop. "Your stop awaits, my darling."

I giggled uncontrollably and was sure we created a scene, but we didn't care. Baxter chuckled along with me as he held the bike steady one final time, and I hopped down. But a man came out to greet us and Baxter switched gears.

"Please donate this bike to a well-known charity for a noble cause." Baxter instructed as he handed the bike over and smiled. "I won't be needing it any longer."

"But, sir, this is your favorite bike?" the man questioned in disagreement. "You use this one every day."

"I have plenty more to use..." Baxter admitted as he looked at me and grinned. "But I think I'll take up jogging as a new workout routine. You never know who you might run into."

My heart skipped a beat at the sure word of Baxter. His eyes playfully blazed at me and he threw me for a loop by his generosity. He could've simply tossed the bike out for scrap. Instead, he donated the bicycle to someone in need.

"Very well then, sir," the man said as he took the bike away and left our side.

"Well, I didn't take you as the generous type, Baxter Lane," I joked with a smile.

Baxter playfully winked at me and boarded an elevator. "There's still much more to learn, my darling Brielle."

Baxter was right. There really was. But as I joined him and the doors closed, I remembered the latest development.

And our new existence was a hard pill to swallow.

THIRTY
Truth Be Told

The elevator ride was silent as we rode to the top floor and stepped out into his office. Baxter didn't wait for me and went straight to mix himself a drink. I slowly wandered into the room with my mind lost in random thought. But only one question seemed to pop into my head repeatedly.

What was next?

"Do you want a drink?" Baxter asked over his shoulder as he poured a drink and his hand lingered on another glass.

The last time I drank, we ended up lost in desire and we both couldn't afford that. I needed to hear everything. I had to learn the truth behind this secret kept from me for far too long. But in all honesty, a drink would ease the pain.

"Yes." I answered and strolled over to Baxter. "But make mine a double."

"Good thinking," Baxter agreed as he raised the whiskey bottle and poured himself another shot.

Baxter fixed my drink and handed me the glass. Our fingers brushed and his eyes locked with mine. Tingles ignited from our touch and the old flame lit. The fire flickered and burned hot between us, but we knew better than to give in to the flame. We had a newfound unresolved conversation to finish and there was no time for interruption.

"My father met a woman who took his breath away. She was everything to him and he'd do anything to make her his." Baxter breathed as he fell back in time and remembered the tale. "Love was an understatement when it came to her. My father grew obsessed with the very thing he couldn't have."

"James's mother." I breathed with realization.

James mentioned his mother on rare occasions, but the memories were brief. I knew she was a beautiful woman and a model who captivated any man in her sights. And she must've captured Baxter's father.

"Yes, Rebecca was extraordinary. She was a talented model on my father's radar. His admiration for her was out of this world and he did everything to make her happy," Baxter explained with a sigh and spun the whiskey around in his glass. "But I'm unsure she ever loved him."

"What do you mean?" I asked with curiosity.

Baxter leaned back against his desk. "Once she knew she had my father wrapped around her finger, he gave in to her every whim. Whatever Rebecca wanted, she got. She was pure beauty, but something broke inside of her."

I took a gulp of my drink right along with Baxter, and he gazed down into his glass. His demeanor hardened and his face was full of regret. But that didn't stop me from him.

I sat on the desk beside him and asked. "What happened to them, Bax?"

"They got married and James became family. Everything changed, but she didn't. As soon as she got what she wanted after stringing my father along for years, she became distant," Baxter explained as he stared straight ahead and was emotionless. "I never had an actual mother. She died giving birth to me. I never knew what it was like and when Rebecca became my mother, I thought this was it. But she never wanted another kid. She only wanted everything my father had."

I reached out and touched his hand. "I'm so sorry, Baxter."

Baxter looked down at my gesture and blew out a long breath. A shiver ran through me and he drew me to him. Sadness sank in, and I had a hard time grasping Baxter Lane without a real mother. He needed a woman to show him the way with a kind, motherly touch. A birth mother to hold him when he required affection. A mother to be there by his side. But Baxter Lane missed out on one of the most important relationships a boy could have.

A mom.

"James lost his father when he was young, and I thought we could relate. We could bond over our loss together. Be a family and I knew my father wanted that for us, too. He tried so hard to make the marriage work." Baxter breathed and his hand clenched the edge of the desk. "But Rebecca had other plans."

I watched Baxter as he took another swig from his glass and the alcohol must've bitten on the way down. His jaw clenched and everything about him became cold. He was right back there in the past. An adolescent about to become a young man with a harsh reality ready to hit.

"Rebecca was screwing around behind my father's back and he caught her in the act. She threatened to take everything from him, and he was heartbroken. She wanted his company. Everything. But my dad wouldn't let her and he fought back." Baxter breathed with hatred. "Rebecca wanted James to have what belonged to me. My birthright. Until..."

"Until what, Bax?" I asked as I squeezed his hand and urged him to go on.

"Until one day she was dead." Baxter breathed. "She drove her car into a hydro pole and killed herself instantly."

"What?" I gasped with shock.

"She was dead and all our problems appeared to go away," Baxter explained with bitterness. "But James never got over his mother's death. He was her world, and she was his. When his mother died, something inside James broke."

Baxter stood up straight and finished his drink. My hand fell from his and I drank the rest of mine, but the liquid burned. The same way this story went up in smoke, but the tale was Baxter's reality. This fate was his.

"You want another drink, darling?" Baxter asked as he poured himself another glass and reached out for mine.

"Yes." I replied with simplicity.

But nothing was easy about this.

Baxter never had a mother. James never could be honest with me. Step-brothers who were estranged. And I found myself caught right in the middle.

"My father could never love again. His primary focus was me and James, but James couldn't accept his new life," Baxter explained as he finished our drinks and handed me mine. "Without his mother, nothing was ever the same for him. My father realized he was in distress."

"I knew his mother had died, but he would never tell me how." I sighed with regret. "If he would've just let me in, if he..."

"James never could, darling. It was never in him." Baxter breathed with certainty. "My father gave him all he could, but James wanted the company."

"But he never got it and you did." I breathed. "And James hated you for it, didn't he?"

Baxter slowly nodded his head. "Yes. My father died, and he passed down the company to his birthright. Me."

"And that's how James became a selfish bastard." I sighed with understanding and chugged my drink.

The alcohol hit me hard, and the world spun. I held my composure, but I felt lost in the newfound world. A place where a man became cold and hid his true self from me. A life I never knew because he would never let me in. But his step-brother did.

"Thank you, Bax." I breathed as my hand landed on his chest and I stumbled into his arms.

Baxter caught me and held me in his protective hold. The embrace I had grown to love more than I should have. The undeniable temptation of my brother-in-law.

"For what?" Baxter asked as he peered down at me with a glimmer of want in his handsome blue eyes and lit my world on fire.

"For being you, for being honest." I sighed as my eyes searched his face and he captured me.

But Baxter caught himself up in me.

Baxter caressed my cheek with the back of his fingertips, and I closed my eyes. His touch meant so much and I could never get enough. My lips parted and my pulse rushed. He was everything, and I longed for more.

"Darling, I could never withhold the truth from you and it was bound to come out." Baxter breathed with his warmth against my lips. "It's something my father always taught me. Honesty makes a man, and without it, you have nothing."

My eyes shot open, and I whispered, "Then you must have everything."

"No..." Baxter breathed, as his lips were inches from mine. "Not yet."

The honest answer from Baxter threw me off, and I realized we were far too close. His delicious mouth was mere seconds away from a collision we both knew wouldn't be an accident. The desire was there, but our worlds had already collided.

We were family. Baxter Lane was my soon-to-be ex-husband's estranged step-brother. This was all too much, and the alcohol was a mistake.

"I think I need to lie down." I breathed rapidly and touched my forehead.

Baxter lifted me into his arms with full understanding and said, "You can lie down in my bed."

"I-I don't think that's such a good idea," I mumbled with uncertainty.

Baxter didn't listen and followed through with his plan. He brought me from his office and into his bedroom. The lights were out, and he didn't bother to turn them on. He threw back the bedsheets and laid me down to rest.

"It's a brilliant plan and you know it, darling." Baxter said from above me.

I did. Baxter was right. His arms felt right and his bed welcomed me. But I panicked in the darkness.

"Please, don't leave me..." I sighed with urgency.

I knew I should never speak those words, but after everything, I needed Baxter. I couldn't lay in his bed without him by my side. After he exposed his deepest reality with me, I didn't want to be alone.

"I wouldn't dream of it, Brielle." Baxter breathed as he kissed my forehead and left my side.

My eyes searched in the darkness for Baxter until they adjusted to the dimness. The shadow of his silhouette caught my eye, and I watched him on the other side of the bed. His muscles flexed as he took off his shirt and climbed into bed.

Baxter moved over to my side, and his hands worked at my ponytail. He freed my strands and laid them out across the pillow. His arms wrapped around me and he took me into his embrace. The warmth of Baxter cocooned around me like a solid shell and promised to never let go. He held me within his tenderness, caressed my hair, and left kisses along my hairline.

Baxter spoke no words as his heart beat against my hand and the sound of his steady breath filled my ears. We welcomed the quietness and fell into one another. Into a world where we were together and bound to dream of each other. A vision of us alone and nothing stood in our way. No promise of me finding him a wife and no step-brother in sight. Just us and only us.

And we drifted off to sleep.

***

My ears buzzed with the sound of silence, and my hair tickled my neck. The sound of nothingness was overwhelming until I heard something. The sound of a stern voice broke the silence. One I recognized, and the tone pulled me from my sound sleep.

"You heard me." Baxter snapped with harshness.

I barely acknowledged the person who spoke was Baxter. He sounded bitter and far away. His voice was low and full of hatred.

My eyes blinked, and I tried to focus in the dimly lit room. I remembered where I was and everything came back to me. Baxter at the park. His confession of his relationship with my husband. Step-brothers. Baxter Lane was my brother-in-law through marriage. Everything happened within hours and I fell asleep in his arms.

But Baxter was no longer on his side of the bed.

He rumpled the sheets and tossed them to the side. My eyes adjusted to the darkness, and I heard movement from the other side of the room. Feet as they paced the floor and tried to keep quiet.

But Baxter's voice filled the stillness.

"Don't even breathe her name," Baxter threatened. "Talk to her ever again and I will make your life hell."

Her?

Baxter was talking about a woman. Not me or Beverly. So, who the hell was she?

I always knew whatever this was between us couldn't last, but to hear Baxter want to protect someone else stung. He wanted to keep harm away from another woman other than me. I couldn't stand the thought and I saw red.

I didn't want to hear anymore. I had been through enough. Baxter expected me to provide him with a wife, but he had someone else on the sideline. Our secret sexual encounters weren't enough, and he had to seek more. I had been down this road with James and I wouldn't go down it again. Whatever side chick Baxter Lane had ended now.

Whoever she was, she must enjoy sloppy seconds. I certainly wouldn't let anyone make a fool of me. Baxter Lane had another thing coming and he wouldn't cheat on me.

I tossed back the bedsheets and sat up in bed. "Who was on the phone?"

Baxter turned on the bedside lamp, and the bright light made me squint. The back of my hand shielded my eyes, but his brawny chest came into view. He was no longer on his cell phone and held the device in his hand. The sighting of the phone made his conversation with someone else even more true. The harsh discussion about another woman was real and not all in my head.

Baxter placed his cell phone on the bedside table and got back into bed. He pulled the sheets over his body and laid on his side. His elbow was bent against the pillow and his hand held his head up. A gorgeous smile spread across his face, and he was as handsome as ever.

"Forget about it." Baxter replied.

Baxter opened his arms to me and motioned for me to come back to him. To be by his side and cuddle me close. He wanted us to forget about the world, but I couldn't. Not when he talked about another woman to someone else.

I raised up my hand and gave Baxter the silent treatment. His blue eyes narrowed, and he gave me a confused face. His whiskers were all out of place from slumber, and his dashingly handsome morning look suited him. But I wasn't in the mood for any bullshit.

"Tell me who was on the damn phone," I snapped and clearly had woken up on the wrong side of everything.

Baxter shot back, "Who do you think it was?"

I peered down at Baxter with an icy look and breathed with jealousy. "It seems like you're having a serious relationship with someone new I don't know about."

Baxter chuckled. He tossed his head back on the pillow and laughed at me. But his behavior only irritated me.

"What the hell is so funny?" I asked in frustration.

Baxter turned his back to me and leaned towards the far side of his bed. He grabbed something from the bedside table and turned back onto his back. His cellphone was in his hands and the screen shone in his face.

Seriously?

The audacity of Baxter Lane. He would choose to ignore me and scroll through his phone. Right when we were about to have a serious conversation.

Oh, hell no...

I was about to reach over and smack Baxter's device away, but he tossed it to me. I caught the phone by surprise and looked from him towards his cell phone. His personal phone with everything on it. All the private conversations and calls were all within my reach.

"It's funny how jealous you are when you're only supposed to be my matchmaker." Baxter breathed from beside me. "Do you have a thing for me, darling?"

I turned his cell phone over and the screen shone back at me. A picture of me greeted my eyes, and I was sound asleep in Baxter's bed with my hair laid out on his pillow. But a single text caught my eye.

Baxter: 'She's mine.'

And Baxter sent the powerful message straight to his step-brother.

My soon-to-be ex-husband.

Heat rose to my cheeks and embarrassment spread through me. I had jumped the gun and assumed the worst of Baxter when all he had done was stake his claim. He knew the truth and wanted his step-brother to know. Baxter Lane was simply being his protective self.

"I... I..." I muttered with shock.

I couldn't find the right words. I couldn't believe how jealous I had become over a man who was my boss. He was family, for fuck sakes.

Now, Baxter saw right through me. He knew the truth. He saw the reality of our situation and neither one of us wanted to admit it.

We were more than a work relationship mixed with pleasure. This wasn't some random hookup whenever the opportunity struck. I had a thing for Baxter Lane and he had made his claim on me.

"It's okay. We don't have to talk about it. Instead..." Baxter breathed and crawled his fingers across the bed. "You can call out my name when my head is between your thighs, my darling."

Baxter brought his hand to my pussy and pressed four fingers against my clit. He rotated them in a slow circle and the embarrassment faded. Replaced by a searing, passionate need to have him. To let him do as he pleased and fall into ecstasy.

I needed a place to forget all these feelings. All these thoughts and emotions that had stirred to the surface within the last twenty-four hours. I wanted our personal relationship to go away.

Baxter will give me that. We needed desire. He craved pleasure just as much as me.

"Baxter... I..." I said, but his other hand cupped my tit. "Oh, god..."

"Lie back, darling..." Baxter breathed, as his thumb caressed my erect nipple through the fabric. "Let me be your escape and bring you to bliss."

I listened to his every word. My body fell back and my head hit the pillow with a gasp. Lost in Baxter as his fingers played and toyed with me. My back arched to welcome his eager touch and a soft moan escaped my agape lips.

Baxter pinched my nipple and reached down to lift my workout shirt. He raised the cloth high above my breasts and his mouth devoured my tits. His tongue lapped over each nipple and he sucked each one into his mouth. A slow and intoxicating rhythm with his fingers still rotating on my nub.

"I could never be with anyone else, but you..." Baxter admitted against my skin as he brushed kisses between my cleavage and drove me wild. "You are my world and I told you. You're all fucking mine, my darling."

Baxter's fingers stopped rubbing and left my clit. His hands pulled down my leggings, and I lifted my ass off the bed to help him. He kissed down my belly, travelled further with his lips against my skin and down my legs. Each leg pulled out of my leggings and my socks flew off with them.

Next, Baxter worked on my panties and dragged them down my legs as I watched him. I drew my lower lip into my mouth and moaned in sexual agony. But he only kissed my feet as he freed each leg of my panties.

"Baxter, please..." I begged with heated desire.

Baxter only gave me a wicked grin as he tossed my wet panties aside and ran his hands up each leg. He had me cast in his spellbound world and I spiraled out of control. I wanted to grab his head and put his face right between my legs. I couldn't take his torturous play any longer. My body cried out for him and my pussy already dripped with wetness.

Baxter spread my thighs wide open and kissed his way along my flesh. "Relax, my darling Brielle. All good things come with time."

Slow. Agonizing. Time.

But I couldn't wait anymore.

I pushed up my upper body and grabbed Baxter's hair. Fistful strands of his smooth locks glided smoothly between my fingers and I yanked his head towards my aching cunt. Blue arctic eyes widened above my bare pussy.

Baxter growled against my soaked lips. "Or we can skip to the juicy part, darling."

"Oh, fuck, yes..." I moaned from above as my head fell back against the pillow and he devoured me like a delicious late-night snack.

Baxter dove right inside of me, and his eager tongue circled between my pussy walls. A need built inside of me and the sensation coursed over my skin. He was the only thought on my mind. Him and his skillful mouth as he caressed me with intent, longing all for me.

My cunt cried out for him as I held his hair and pulled him in deeper. His groans muffled against my sex and my legs wrapped around his neck. His broad shoulders held me and everything about him was powerful as I moved against his face. But his eyes never left me and watched me give in to my hungry need.

Hands met my rear, and he gripped my ass cheeks. Fingernails bit into the plump flesh and he squeezed my behind with a fierce need. His tongue continued to work, but his movement cast in and out of me. A fast-paced rhythm as my hips thrusted, and I moaned my approval. One pleasureful gasp after the other with each buck of my backside.

"Oh, yes, Bax, yes!" I cried out as my head bent back and bit my lip with desire.

My hands let go of his hair and one clutched the bedsheet. The other found my nub and gave into the bliss he feasted upon me. I wanted to let everything go. Forget our newfound reality and only be with Baxter. Lost in him, caught up in him and all his.

"Oh, yes, my fucking darling..." Baxter breathed rapidly against my pussy. "Touch yourself."

"Oh, fuck..." I gasped as my fingers circled my clit and I gave into temptation.

Baxter flicked his tongue against my pussy lips as I worked on my fleshy nub and fell further into desire. Into the pleasure he started, but I couldn't deny it. He knew what I needed and gave me everything I required. No wasn't an option, and he was more than willing to give me everything.

My hips thrust to the beat of my gasps, and his tongue was back inside of me. Buried within me as my body soared higher and my climax wasn't far off. My hand clenched his hair and pressed him in further. I couldn't get enough.

Finally, my hips bucked, and my back arched, but he never stopped. His tongue swirled as my sweet juices gushed from the core of me and greeted his mouth. My scream of release echoed throughout his room and filled my ears.

"Bax! Oh, yes!" I cried out with pure pleasured bliss.

Stars shoot behind my eyelids, and bright lines dazzled in the blackness. My heavy breath filled the air and mixed with the muffled sound of his groan. Baxter was right there with me for my climax, and he enjoyed my release just as much as I had. He needed this just as much as me.

Baxter licked up the last of my sweet juice, and my body quivered below him. His satisfied indigo eyes locked on mine and he never wavered as he kissed each thigh. But right after, he gave each one a quick nip with his teeth and a giggle escaped me.

Baxter gave my ass one last squeeze, and I let go of his hair. He came to my side and gathered me close within his embrace. His body heat surrounded me and his cock throbbed against my plump rear, but he didn't make a move. Instead, he held me with the beat of his heart against my back.

And whispered in my ear, "I've got a thing for you too, darling."

THIRTY-ONE
Unwell

I'm sick.

Again.

I was unwell for days leading up to this, but today I had to call into work. This was the worst day out of them all. But I knew why.

Baxter went on his second date with Beverly yesterday. My stomach was not only in knots about the entire situation, but my head spun. So much I couldn't scope out their date and Evelyn had taken my place. The thought of them together literally caused me to be ill.

I had no idea how the evening went, and my stomach turned at the very thought of another woman with Baxter. Them together as they held hands over a candlelit dinner I had planned for them. I had ordered excellent flowers and Baxter would impress Beverly with them. Her lips locked with his in a passionate first kiss.

I just prayed Baxter had the decency not to take their budding relationship to the next level, and he kept his cock in his pants. I knew we weren't anything, and I had no claim to him. We had an understanding, and I knew he needed a wife. But that didn't mean I had to like any of this.

Beverly could only hold out for so long with Baxter Lane's charm, and I knew that. Baxter knew how to turn on a woman, but I didn't want it to be anyone other than me.

Beverly, becoming intimate with Baxter, was just around the corner, and the very notion made me want to hurl.

"Oh, no..." I mumbled with agony as my hand covered my mouth and I ran for the bathroom. "Not again."

My legs rushed to the toilet, but I couldn't make it in time. Instead, I grabbed the wastebasket and threw up all the contents of my last meal. But there wasn't much left.

Today was horrible.

I couldn't stop the nausea, no matter what I had done. The vomiting was endless and this dreadful sickness must be a stomach bug. A terrible one I had caught from someone and the bug wanted to last for days.

But I was worried.

I knew I was under a fair amount of stress. Baxter was demanding and wanted a wife. Work was hard with the threat of losing everything because I had mixed business with pleasure. I had become attached when I knew better and my mental health could be at risk.

I should see a doctor straight away.

My body was weak and hunched over as I made my way towards my cell phone. An appointment had to be scheduled for today. I couldn't go on like this for fear something could be horribly wrong.

I was never like this. Me being sick was completely out of the ordinary. I rarely called in sick, but I couldn't take it.

Even Evelyn was concerned, and I heard the distress in her voice when I called into work. She knew me better than anyone. I wasn't a frail and unwell person. This wasn't like me.

I collapsed on the couch and dialed in a call to the doctor. The secretary answered on the second ring and I explained my dire situation. The urgency to see the doctor today.

"I can squeeze you in an hour from now," the secretary said, "Can you make it to the appointment in time?"

"Yes, I can, thank you." I sighed with relief and confirmed the spot.

I hung up and knew I needed to get out of these clothes. They were the same outfit I had worn yesterday because I didn't have the energy to get changed. But today, I had no choice.

I had to appear in public and couldn't go out looking like a tornado had torn through. My hair was a disaster, but there was no time to fix the mess. A simple bun would do for the trip.

All I needed was an answer. One simple reason for this illness and how I could get better. But deep down in the pit of my sore stomach, I held an uneasiness.

And the explanation with consequences.

***

The clock ticked by on the wall in the waiting room. My hands rested in my lap and my stomach swirled. I willed myself not to be sick here. Any place other than here. I needed to get through this with a level head, not a nauseated one.

I hadn't been waiting long, and another patient came through the door. The older woman's face was unreadable, and I became nervous. I hadn't been to the doctor in quite some time. I hated this place and avoided it like the plague. But this was an emergency and I couldn't go another day without a solution.

The door swung open, and the secretary held it in place with her foot. "Brielle? The doctor will see you now."

I gave a slight nod and followed the secretary's lead. I clenched my purse in my hands and my being quaked with unease. The little handbag was the only thing stopping the shake from taking over my body.

She led me into a tiny room with an examination table, desk, and chair. There were other instruments the doctor would acquire within the room, but I hoped none of them were for me. Not for this visit. I just wanted to get back home and crawl into bed.

My stomach agreed as the knot grew tighter and threatened to come loose. I held the urge back and sat down on the exam table while the secretary left. She told me the doctor would be right in and I couldn't wait.

I laid my purse beside me and held the cool table by the edges. Flimsy paper crinkled as I sat on it and I struggled to concentrate on anything other than my queasy stomach. The computer screen played out a beautiful beach scene and reminded me of my latest vacation. The time I had spent in the sun and in Baxter's arms.

The thought of Baxter made me wish everything was different. I longed to never have him as a client. I'd prefer the person to save Match My Heart to be someone else. Anyone. But then I'd never see Baxter again.

Suddenly, the door opened to a stern older man with glasses. He walked with a slight limp into the room and this doctor wasn't familiar at all. He also appeared to be on the grumpier side.

"I'm filling in for your regular doctor today. My name is Dr. Ross," he announced briefly. "What brings you in on such short notice, dear?"

Dr. Ross was grouchy, all right. He seemed like he woke up on the wrong side of the bed. Possibly the opposite side of life.

"Well, I haven't been feeling well for days now and..." I explained.

"Hm, I see, and what are your symptoms?" Dr. Ross asked as he cut in and tilted his glasses down to the edge of his nose.

The rude, elderly man made me nervous. Dr. Ross looked like he should retire. His slight hobble confirmed this statement. But he must be capable.

His attitude certainly wasn't.

"I've had nausea, dizziness, tender breasts, but I get really hungry." I expressed with worry. "I think I picked up some horrid stomach bug, but I came here to be sure."

"Have you been sexually active recently, dear?" Dr. Ross asked as he came over and pressed his stethoscope against my chest.

The mention of sex brought Baxter straight back to mind. All the secret encounters. The way he grunted with each hard thrust. My moan for him and his never-ending need to keep me as his secret obsession.

"Yes. Multiple times actually..." I admitted and realized how slutty the admission sounded. "With the same man, of course."

Dr. Ross looked down at my hand and asked, "Boyfriend?"

"Oh, no, he's definitely not my boyfriend," I confessed with a nervous laugh.

"Are you on birth control?" he asked with a raised eyebrow.

Dr. Ross was a nosy old bugger.

"No." I sighed with confusion.

"Well, dear, you may have more to worry about than just a stomach bug," Dr. Ross expressed as he passed me a plastic cup with a lid. "I need to collect a urine culture from you."

The doctor pointed towards the washroom door and wanted me to pee into the cup. I figured this was routine and part of his process. I followed his direction and Dr. Ross sat down at his desk to take some notes.

My mind reeled, and I wanted to see the memo he typed about me. I was certain this had to be some wicked bug or the dreaded flu. There couldn't possibly be any other explanation, and I just needed the doctor to confirm my theory. Then I could go home and rest easy in the comfort of my bed. Not sit here on an uncomfortable examination table.

The door clicked closed behind me and I went over towards the toilet. I had done this before and knew the process was standard protocol. Pee in a cup and I always received a clear result.

I was certain of this as I pulled down my pants and my underwear followed. The cup filled up within seconds because I had been peeing more than normal. But the issue wasn't a cause for concern. I was sure of it.

Now to get this test over with so I could be one step closer to an answer. A solution to all my latest symptoms. And to figure out when I could get back to normal.

I stepped out of the bathroom with a smile. "There. The test should come back clean, like always."

I was positive.

I handed Dr. Ross the urine sample, and he took the cup with a grunt. The bitter sound followed him as he left the room and I fell into silence. The grumble was rather rude and uncalled for, but I brushed off his sour behavior. Once I had an explanation, I was out of there.

Goodbye, Dr. Grumpy old man.

Time passed, but I was unsure how much. There wasn't a clock in the room and I was afraid to check the hour on my cell phone. The more time ticked by, the more I was worried there was a problem. An issue with my test result.

My anxiety was at its peak, and I grabbed my purse for comfort. The leather clenched in my hands to steady the unwanted quake from inside of me. A shockwave ready to breakaway and escape from somewhere deep inside. I was a mess and just wanted this entire situation to be over with.

Suddenly, the door opened and Dr. Ross appeared. He made sure the door was closed behind him before he grabbed his chair and wheeled the seat in front of me. He removed his glasses and rubbed his forehead before he took a seat.

Dr. Ross changed his demeanor from a grouchy man to a softer side. The drastic change of character surprised me and threw me for a loop. But my nerves picked up and my knuckles turned white as my hands gripped my purse.

Something was wrong.

I could sense the tension from this once cold and bitter man. Dr. Ross was a complete stranger to me, but I felt the shift in him. I didn't need to know him personally to know something was extremely off.

Dr. Ross let out a sigh. "Your urine culture didn't come back clear this time, dear."

"What?" I gasped with shock. "There must be some mistake."

"There's no mistake," Dr. Ross explained with certainty. "When was your last cycle?"

"Um, I don't know... It couldn't have been long ago..." I stammered with unease and thought hard about his question. "There's been a lot going on at my job."

Work. Baxter. Lots of sex.

"How long ago?" Dr. Ross urged as the question echoed in my ears and I couldn't think straight.

"A few weeks maybe. Maybe sometime last month..." I contemplated, but the answer shouted loudly in my head. "Oh, my god. I'm late."

I had forgotten. Lost in all the chaos of my new life. A vacation turned upside down and a divorce in my foreseeable future. My business was in shambles and on the brink of foreclosure. But Baxter Lane I never saw coming.

"Yes, you are late for your period and that's why I ran the test," Dr. Ross admitted as he looked down at my stomach and my gaze followed his.

My lips parted, and my hands touched my tender belly. A tenderness I hadn't noticed before and brushed everything off as a sudden sickness. An illness sure to go away any day now. But I had only been kidding myself.

I knew the answer before Dr. Ross even spoke of my new reality. Everything was clear and my heartbeat wildly in my ears. I still needed confirmation from him, but I was afraid. Scared of the truth.

I swallowed hard and gazed up at the doctor. "Well, Dr. Ross, am I pregnant?"

The doctor pried my hands from my purse and took them into his own. Tears stung my eyes, and I knew my entire world was about to change. The seriousness in his now gentle eyes told me so.

"Yes, Brielle, you are expecting a baby," Dr. Ross confirmed, and the result was one hundred percent accurate.

I was pregnant with my client's baby. My brother-in-law through wedding vows. Baxter Lane was the father of the baby growing inside of me.

"I'm going to hurl." I heaved with urgency, and I threw up in the nearest garbage can.

THIRTY-TWO
Broken Heart

The doctor's appointment didn't go according to plan. Nothing about this appointment was typical. The visit changed my life.

I was pregnant with a surprise baby and I didn't even know what was to come. I couldn't even comprehend how drastically my world would shift. But Dr. Ross was a lifesaver.

The doctor might, in fact, be grumpy, but he was extremely informative. After I threw up in his examination room, he answered every question I had. He explained what came next and how to take care of myself, along with the baby I carried. I had to get some routine bloodwork done to ensure the baby was healthy and figure out how far along I was. He'd be the doctor in charge until my original one returned. But I was grateful for him.

Dr. Ross wasn't an ill-tempered old man like I thought he was. He had his moments, but he meant well in the end. He was just the doctor I needed for a morning like today.

A day that altered my entire universe forever.

But I needed to tell the father straight away.

I left the doctor's office in a rush with my purse over my shoulder and didn't stop. I couldn't because I had important news, and the result was dire. This would change everything. Our work relationship, my company and his need for a wife. A child grew inside of me, and Baxter deserved to know the truth.

I headed straight for my convertible, and the car chirped at the press of my key fob. The top was up and I had no desire to put the roof down. Not on a day like today.

I was a woman with an urgent matter, and I needed to focus. My morning sickness also won, and I was nauseous as hell. The wind in my face would only make the situation worse.

The driver's seat called my name, and I took the wheel. I flew out of the parking lot and hoped I beat the upcoming afternoon traffic jam. The need for everyone to be out for their lunch break after a hard morning's work. A place I wished I was. Anything other than this position I had placed myself in.

There was no doubt this baby was my bosses. I should've been more careful and we should've used protection. But Baxter Lane was undeniable in every way.

I had no clue when we conceived our baby. We were intimate so many times I couldn't even count them on one hand. My egg had met Mr. Lane's sperm sometime between the vacation or after I found out Baxter was my client. The fact of the matter didn't matter at all and would remain a mystery. I was pregnant and there was no going back.

All I could do was move forward and head straight for billionaire Baxter Lane's office. The place where I intended to reveal our new reality. A pregnancy we both never saw coming.

Lane's Lingerie wasn't far from the doctor's office. The traffic held off like I hoped, and I was there in no time. But the adrenaline had worn off and panic took over.

I sat parked across the street from the building Baxter owned. My hands gripped the steering wheel, and I peered straight ahead. My knuckles were white and my breath was not at all calm. Anxiety took over me, and a million questions swirled throughout my head. But only one was important.

What if Baxter didn't want this baby?

The pregnancy was a complete surprise. Never intended and not even on the radar. Our undeniable need for each other was the only thought. But fate had another plan.

A child.

Baxter could deny our baby and want nothing to do with me. Toss us aside and carry on with his plan to find a woman suitable for him. Not his matchmaker and a woman who got knocked up with his kid. Baxter was a playboy before all of this. He could give us the cold shoulder and send me on my way.

No.

My thoughts were driving me crazy. My second guesses of the situation took over and would drive me straight into madness. There was only one way to find out how he would react to our surprise pregnancy. I had to tell Baxter the truth. He was the father, and he had every right to know I carried his child. A son or daughter who could very well be the birthright to the company I sat and stared at. Contemplated every upcoming decision when I didn't know how this would end.

Until I got out of this car.

I inhaled a deep breath and blew the air clear out of my lungs. My hands let go of the steering wheel and I gave them a shake. The rush spiked back up inside to do the right thing and tell Baxter Lane he was going to be a father.

"Here goes nothing..." I whispered to myself and opened the car door.

My mind was in complete focus on the journey ahead of me and I neglected to lock up my car. I didn't even grab my purse or watch for traffic as I crossed the street and cars honked at me. Only one verse repeated inside my head and nothing could stop me.

"Baxter, I'm pregnant," I repeated the words to myself and willed myself ahead.

I went through the main doors of Lane's Lingerie and knew exactly where to go. I hoped Baxter would be in his office, busy with his workday and shocked by my unexpected visit. An unanticipated drop in soon to change both of our lives forever.

My running shoes rushed along the floor, and the crowd bustled around me. Lane's Lingerie was busy in the early afternoon and I headed straight for the elevators. But something caught my eye in front of Baxter Lane's lingerie store.

A woman who looked just like a profile match at my company. She was beautiful and her hand touched a gentleman's chest as she gazed up into his eyes. His shimmering blue eyes and handsome features.

But the man was Baxter.

I panicked and hid behind the nearest pillar to keep out of eyesight. Beverly and Baxter couldn't see me, but I was too close. So near, I could hear every word of their intimate discussion.

"Our time together has meant so much to me." Beverly sighed.

I peeked around the pillar, only to find Baxter had placed his hand over hers. The sweet gesture struck me right through the heart. But when he brought her hand to his lips, the caress tore me apart.

Baxter kissed his hand and said, "I've enjoyed it too. You're an amazing woman, Beverly."

Baxter had done the same with me. His eyes shimmered down at Beverly with admiration, and the couple broke my heart. I should be happy he had found his match because my job was done. Beverly was his perfect match. I was successful and had found him his bride to be. Beverly would be the mother of his children and help carry on his family legacy.

Not me.

And not our baby.

Tears stung my eyes and the new happy couple went blurry. I tore my gaze away from them and looked down at my swollen belly. The tears let go and fell down onto my hand as it rested on my stomach. This baby was everything now, and Baxter was the past.

I softly cried in heartbroken anguish as I ran back to my car and didn't dare look back. I couldn't stand peering back at the man I had fallen for. All I had to do was lose Baxter to realize my heart belonged to him.

Baxter was with someone else, and I had to learn to live with it. Our child together would grow up without a father in its life. I had no choice. This baby would remain a secret and my love locked away in my heart forever.

THIRTY-THREE

Charity Event

I walked into the auction with Evelyn by my side. She was glamorous in a purple knee-length dress and the fabric hugged her ass. The breeze swept strands of her hair as we stepped into the lobby. A slight chill ran up my bare legs because I was wearing a dress made of silver and black shimmery fabric. The fabulous piece I chose cut off at my thighs and concealed my secret.

The baby growing inside of me.

My eyes watched Evelyn, who had no clue my belly grew. The secret was too much to share and my best friend would remain in the dark. I had no choice because everything was at stake. Too much was at risk to even mention a peep. The less Evelyn knew, the better.

The news of my upcoming newborn should be a happy one, but it wasn't. I was alone, pregnant with a man's baby and he was with someone else. There was no hope in an everlasting family. No dream of a white picket fence. Not even a promise of love.

I would keep this child unrevealed.

The notion was lonely, but I'd have my baby. A little one who would learn solely from me. And remind me every single day of the man I lost.

But I was strong.

I could do this. I had been through much worse and came out on the other side. The strength inside of me would pull me through.

I blew out a deep breath and stepped into the lavish event. Crystal glistened all around with chandeliers from above and sparkling glass from all around. The lighting was bright and bounced off of the objects.

The sight created an essence of an alluring life of pure beauty. Full of diamonds and expensive belongings. A lifestyle that wasn't mine, but I could imagine it was for the evening. Because after tonight I'd be gone.

My reality had changed in the blink of an eye. I had to transform with it. I had to move on.

But first, this charity auction required my full attention.

Companies from all over the city would be here, but we didn't know which ones. Everyone who represented the businesses would be there and the crowd would include us. Match My Heart had made the invitation list, and it was an honor to be here.

My eyes gazed over the guests in the near distance, and I scanned the crowd. Men dressed in handsome tuxedos and women decked out in glamour. Flashy rings on fingers and necklaces hung from their necks. Each person showed off their expensive taste and the money they made. Everyone was eager to bid on the prizes to come and support a good cause.

Someone handed me a bidding number, but was sure I wouldn't be able to use it. Match My Heart held on by a thread and without Baxter's income, we didn't stand a chance. We were lucky to make the cut this year, but had a few dollars to spend. Not like some others here who could toss bills without a care.

"I still don't understand why we came," Evelyn admitted from beside me.

"They invited us and it would be an insult not to show," I said just for her to hear. "Match My Heart has a status to maintain."

"Well, at least they have excellent wine." Evelyn shrugged as she grabbed a glass of red wine and held up a glass for me. "You want some?"

Nope, not good for the baby.

"No, thanks," I mumbled before I could realize my mistake.

"Since when do you turn down alcohol?" Evelyn asked with a raised eyebrow.

I had really screwed up. This was harder than I thought. I had to conceal the truth.

And fast.

"Since the last event we attended, and I made a complete fool out of myself," I lied and hoped she bought the fib.

"Fair enough." Evelyn breathed with a shrug. "More for me."

A giggle escaped me as we wandered into the auction area and skimmed over the items to bid on. Evelyn enjoyed herself and sipped her wine. I wished I could do the same and forget everything. Get lost in a place where Baxter didn't exist and I hadn't made the biggest mistake of my life.

I was still in limbo. Still hoping I'd wake up from this dream and not be pregnant. Not alone to raise a child on my own. My new reality was hard to grasp, but I'd get there. This pregnancy wouldn't remain a regret forever.

Mothers from all around the world gave birth every day. They learn to cope and transform their lives to raise a child. I could be a single mother and get through this just like them. I just needed time to accept my new truth.

The crowd grew bigger, and I sought through the guests to see who was in attendance. I recognized a few from advertisements and some from past events. Everyone mingled and got lost in the luxury. Wine glasses clinked and laughter filled the air. Blonde hair tossed with the flick of a hand and...

Someone caught my eye.

Her blonde hair flowed down her shoulders as she tossed her head back in laughter and rested her hand on a man at her side. Her perfectly manicured hand with lots of bling to show off her man's expensive taste. Money he'd rather spend on her and not me.

My heart hammered in my chest and rose into my throat. My anger grew and my face flushed. I was sure my cheeks were beat red. Rage fired through me and I couldn't hold the spark at bay.

My fake ex-friend was here.

But so was James.

The two timer and his whore. The cunt who stole my husband from me. Abbey.

Luck wasn't on my side.

James cheated on me. I fell in love with my brother-in-law, who I could never have. And I was pregnant with his child.

What's next?

"What the fuck is he doing here?" I glared as my nostrils flared and clenched my hands at my sides. "With his bawd."

"What are you talking about?" Evelyn asked as she followed my gaze and her eyes went wide. "Oh, shit..."

Abbey looped her arm through James's and he held her like a gentleman. His hand covered hers and her radiant smile was bright. But their entire relationship was fake as fuck.

We didn't even finalize our divorce, and he had the nerve to bring his mistress here. To an auction for a good cause, but there was nothing proper about his scandalous relationship with her. James cared about no one but himself, and Abbey was just a flashy prize on his arm. She caught herself up in the honeymoon phase too much to get it.

James was nothing but a cheater with a crooked cock. His dick was a deformity he couldn't help and served his personality. James Lane was a crooked asshole, and I had put up with him for too long. Him and his terrible moves in the sack.

I shook my head in anger and breathed through clenched teeth. "James has some nerve bringing Abbey here. What the fuck is he thinking?"

James clearly wasn't. He had other things on his mind. This wasn't the way he should represent his business, but he simply saw nothing wrong with it.

"How James always does," Evelyn snarled, as she turned to face me and grabbed my arm. "Come on, forget them, and let's go find our seats."

But I couldn't.

I couldn't look away as James let go of Abbey's arm and took his stance in front of her. Her eyes twinkled at him as he took her hands in his own and knelt down on one knee. Her well-groomed nails caught the light as he held her hand and reached into his pocket.

My eyes grew wide with shock as a diamond ring glistened between them and James spoke words of love to her. The same words he once spoke to me and I fell for every verse. Abbey's tearful eyes watched him and beamed with surprise. But that son of a bitch carried on and asked her to be his wife.

"Brielle, come on, don't let him..." Evelyn breathed as she turned around and looked towards James's proposal. "You've got to be kidding me?"

Evelyn was just as infuriated as me. The couple astonished everyone else and stole the show. This epic stunt had James written all over it, and I couldn't stand it one moment longer.

Abbey accepted his proposal, and James placed the engagement ring on her finger. Delighted cheers filled the room, and I saw red. He not only had the nerve to cheat on me with a woman who was supposed to be my friend, but propose to her. James Lane had it coming, and he had for a long time now.

I walked past a bitter Evelyn and headed straight for the newly engaged couple. Anger flashed in my eyes, dead set on them like a bull ready to strike. A furious one bound to steal the crowd and toss the happy couple with horns.

But a hand grabbed me.

The rage turned to shock as I peered into Baxter's sure eyes. His blue hues swirled with an understanding and he squeezed my arm. Baxter was here. By my side.

But why?

I looked back at the thrilled couple, and the rage returned. My chest rose and fell with a heated fury I couldn't contain. They both deserved to be punished.

"How dare you stop me!" I snapped with bitterness.

Baxter let go of my arm and held a bottle of wine in his hand. He popped the cork and peered straight into my eyes. He was powerful, certain, and determined.

"No, my darling Brielle, I'm not here to stop you." Baxter breathed with a smirk and passed me the bottle of bright red wine. "I'll stand by your side as you pour red wine all over him and make him reap what he sowed."

I took the bottle and blinked several times at the expensive wine. The red liquid inside was ready for me to destroy the very man who disrespected me. A man who never understood my worth, but his step-brother had. And Baxter handed me the torch to set my soon-to-be ex-husband's world into flames.

I returned his smirk and locked eyes on my target. Time slowed down as we stalked forward towards our sweet revenge, and I wasn't alone. Emotions swirled through me as we pushed our way through the crowd and the engaged couple stood within reach.

James's shocked eyes locked on me, along with Baxter. "Brielle? What are you doing here? What is he..."

I didn't let James waste his heartless breath and held the open bottle over his head. Bright wine poured all over James and I watched on with satisfaction. The asshole deserved every last drop.

I glared at Abbey, who stood in shock beside James and said, "Congratulations on your upcoming marriage to a two-timing bastard, home wrecker."

I shook the bottle until the final drop of wine touched his red soaked face and handed the empty bottle back to Baxter. He accepted it and we stared at a wine-stained James. His face flashed with anger from my revenge and he wanted to lunge at me. But Baxter stepped in between us.

"Don't even think about it," Baxter hissed as he held his ground and would budge. "You shouldn't cause a scene more than you already have, dear step-brother."

James shook with rage as he glared at Baxter, and his angry eyes caught mine over his shoulder. His gaze once admired me with what I thought was love, but now viewed me with nothing but madness. The heat from him flamed, but nothing could outweigh my vengeance.

James clucked his tongue off of the roof of his mouth. "Abbey, let's go."

Abbey looked at James in surprise. "But..."

"Now, Abbey..." James hissed his command.

Abbey clamped her mouth shut while James straightened his tuxedo jacket. Red wine flung and hit her white dress as she gasped in protest. James took off, and Abbey followed at his feet. A relationship I was glad she had to tolerate, and I no longer did. Our marriage was over and theirs was off to a rocky start.

Better them than me.

I smiled with relief at my newfound freedom, but the emotion was short-lived when Baxter turned to face me. He trapped me. Lost in my love for a man who couldn't be with me.

"I never knew how much I needed to see that until now," Baxter admitted with a slight smile and reached for me. "How does it feel to be free?"

I pulled back and touched my stomach. Baxter narrowed his eyes and peered down at me with confusion. The hair had fallen into his eyes and I wanted so badly to brush the strands aside. For him to take me into his arms and I could tell him the truth.

But fate didn't want us together.

Baxter's gesture of retribution changes nothing. He was with Beverly and I ached all over from the brutal fact. I had witnessed their devotion with my very eyes and couldn't ever forget. The doting couple had broken my heart and left my child without a father.

Baxter would propose to Beverly, and they would start a family. A child to carry forth Baxter Lane's legacy. They would get their happily ever after and I'd have his secret love child without Baxter having a clue.

Baxter reached for me again, and his hand fell over mine on my stomach. He knew something was wrong and worry swirled through his ocean blues. He wouldn't back down and I knew I had to get out of here.

"Are you alright?" Baxter asked with concern.

"I... I have to go..." I replied in panic and turned away from him.

"Brielle?" Baxter breathed from behind me.

My heart shattered all over again, and tears burned my eyes. My heels clicked as my legs took off and I didn't look back. Baxter wanted an explanation and one I couldn't give him. But his call for me faded, and I kept on.

"Brielle! Wait!" Baxter shouted as his voice echoed in my ears and stung my soul.

Evelyn caught my eye, and she quickly followed behind me without one word. My best friend knew something was wrong and never questioned me for one second. But I knew they were bound to come.

I had to be ready to conceal the truth. Everything about this was wrong, but I had no other option. This baby was my world, and I had to adapt to the change.

Alone.

The wind whipped my face and chilled the tears as they fell down my face. I sobbed into the night as my legs picked up pace and I ran out into the night. Far away from Baxter Lane and one step closer to my bigger plan.

Leaving the city for good.

THIRTY-FOUR

This Isn't Goodbye

The days following the charity event had been difficult. Work had been unorganized and Baxter was relentless. He wouldn't stop calling, texting, or showing up with his unexpected visits. But Evelyn had kept him away.

She made up every excuse there was for him not to see me. Every distraction led him away and so far, the plan had worked. But I ached all over for him, even when I knew I shouldn't.

This was just a drawn-out reminder of why I needed to leave. I had to say goodbye, even though it was hard to leave. Baxter wouldn't give up his need for me when he had clearly made his choice.

There was no further discussion. No explanation was required because my job was simple. I found Baxter Lane a wife. He got his wish, and I got too close.

I couldn't stay here. I can't watch the man I love be with someone else. A perfect woman I had chosen for Baxter.

There was no other alternative. I had to leave. But I had to go sooner rather than later. My heart couldn't take much more.

So, I put my condo up for sale and packed up everything I could. The hasty decision came together and before I knew it, movers were at my door. Today was a big day. My time to leave the city.

"Are you sure about this, Brielle?" Evelyn asked as she watched me pack up my belongings and get ready to leave my office.

I wasn't sure about anything. Everything inside of me screamed to stay and live through the heartbreak. To risk my business, my heart, and put everything on the line. My soul begged me to come clean and reveal the truth to everyone, but I couldn't. I couldn't put myself or my baby through any of this turmoil.

"Yes. This is the way it has to be," I lied through my teeth and packed a box full of files.

"Maybe everything could be different if you just told Baxter the truth?" Evelyn expressed as she gestured with her hands and she had concern written all over her face. "Maybe he would..."

Her voice faded, and Evelyn's question hung in my mind. She was right. Maybe everything could be different. But she doesn't know the entire truth either.

All Evelyn knew was I had chosen to move out of the city. I wanted to work remotely from my new home. She knew I had fallen for our boss. A billionaire man who was strictly off-limits, but my heart had other plans.

Evelyn knew of the love I had for Baxter Lane, and he had not one clue. She knew I kept the truth from him because I had seen Baxter's intimate encounter with Beverly. One I knew would come, but my undeniable attraction blinded me to a man I could never have. Because I had to find him his perfect match.

This was the half-truth I fed my best friend to make Evelyn take over my position at Match My Heart until further notice. All the other work had to be done remotely, since that was the only choice. I had to keep this pregnancy concealed. I couldn't risk anyone discovering the baby I had conceived with my boss because the news would be bad for business. My job was to create a happy ending for my clients. Not sleep with them.

Match My Heart made a comeback because of Baxter Lane. I couldn't stand the thought of being the one to ruin everything because I couldn't stay away. I had fallen so hard for him and I had to leave. Now was the time to mend my crushed heart.

"Brielle? Brielle? Did you hear me?" Evelyn asked as her presence brought me back to my harsh reality and I wanted to fade from existence.

"I'm sorry, Evelyn, but I've decided," I admitted as I lifted the last box and headed for my car.

"But Brielle, everything could change if you're honest with him," Evelyn urged as she held the door for me and followed close behind. "Maybe you are the one for him. Maybe he doesn't belong with Beverly and you are his soulmate."

"Or maybe I'm not." I breathed with remorse.

I walked towards my convertible and envisioned a car seat in the back. The infant seat was one I never had on my mind before this surprise pregnancy and now everything was real. My world had changed, and I was solo for the drive out of here. Except for the baby I carried inside.

I lifted the trunk of my car, but Evelyn slammed the lid shut. The car rocked, and I looked at her with shock. But she stood her ground, and I loved her for it.

I was lucky to have a friend who cared this much for me. Who watched out for me through all the good and the bad. She never once doubted my abilities and had always stood by my side. But I was about to leave hers and I was beside myself.

Evelyn huffed with determination. "Okay, listen. You're always finding others their perfect match. Don't you think you owe it to yourself to have the man of your dreams?"

"Baxter Lane may be the man of my dreams, but I'm not the woman in his." I admitted with sadness.

"How can you be so certain?" Evelyn asked and smacked her hand off my car. "Baxter's been trying to get ahold of you, and you won't hear what he has to say."

"Don't you get it, Evelyn?" I cried out with tears in my eyes. "I can't stand the thought of him telling me he's found the one!"

Evelyn cupped my face in her hands and breathed. "But the one could be you, Brielle."

I closed my eyes as tears fell down my face and I wished Evelyn was right. I badly needed her words to be true. But I saw with my eyes Baxter had made his decision.

"I'm not Baxter Lane's fate," I whispered in a shaky voice. "He can never know the truth because my heart can't handle the rejection."

Evelyn sighed in defeat and knew I had made my mind up. She dropped her hands, and I opened my eyes as raindrops fell onto my face. The sky had opened up a storm, and the rain washed away my tears.

"Fine. Your secret will stay with me," Evelyn said as she backed off and opened the trunk for me. "But promise to call me as soon as you get there?"

"I promise." I responded as I set the last box inside of my car and closed the lid.

"I wish you'd tell me where you're going..." Evelyn admitted as she came closer and pouted at me.

"I will in the coming days." I breathed and hugged my friend tightly.

"I'm going to miss you so damn much." Evelyn breathed with sadness. "You could pack me up and take me with you?"

I giggled, looked at Evelyn, and tucked a wet strand of hair behind her ear. "You, my dear friend, have to stay here and continue on with what we started."

"I know, but I hate this." Evelyn frowned. "I'm going to worry about you every second."

"You don't have to because I'll be just fine." I breathed with reassurance and squeezed her arms. "This isn't a goodbye. It's an I'll see you later."

Evelyn pulled me close one last time before she released me and let me go. I hated every second and wanted nothing more than to take everything back. But this choice wasn't just about me anymore.

I got into my car with my solution to the problem weighing heavily on my mind. My foot touched the gas pedal, and I looked back at my best friend all alone in the pouring rain. The distance grew between us and my hand rested on my stomach.

No matter how much this hurt, I made this move for everyone. Especially the child growing inside of me. Baxter Lane's baby.

THIRTY-FIVE
Months Gone By

Months flew by in the blink of an eye. I pulled out my keys to the apartment that became a place to stay. I climbed the stairs leading to the red brick apartment and looked over at the interlocked one beside mine. The neighbors were quiet and never bothered me. I liked the peacefulness of a small-town life and the calm differed from the busy city.

But I missed home.

I longed to be with my best friend and see her smile. I missed the city streets and the chaos each day. The mad dash to cross the street and make it to the other side in the nick of time. But most of all, I missed my job.

The active lifestyle I had created. The thrill I received from a job well-done. But the pride I gained from two hearts becoming one was the greatest gift of all.

Now everything has changed.

I sighed a long breath and saw a bird fly into the garden bed below. Pecking at the wet soil between the leaves, the robin drew out a worm. The wings of the bird moved and brought the animal onto the black iron rail. The railing surrounded the garden and gave the property a pleasant touch.

I watched as the bird ate the worm, and the insect never stood a chance. The wings of the robin flapped, and it ruffled its feathers. But soon after, the beautiful bird took flight into the morning sky.

The door to my apartment opened with ease and I waddled my very pregnant body inside. My eight-month belly, to be exact, and I was on the rounder side. I couldn't fit into my normal clothes after I moved in and bigger sizes did the trick. But I had maternity clothes tucked away somewhere.

I gazed around at my place, which was on the smaller side. The apartment contained two bedrooms, one bathroom, and the landlord combined the living area with the kitchen. Good enough for my baby and me. My new residence wasn't at all luxurious and more on the comfortable side. The place would do for now until I figured out a more permanent plan.

I had become more focused on the pregnancy after I left the city and my morning sickness calmed down. The dreaded queasiness tapered off months ago, and the change was a much-needed relief. Hunger had set in and the energy I needed to support this pregnancy increased. Meals now came in bigger portions, and my cupboards were always full of snacks.

Doctors' appointments became a routine, and I never missed a single one. I wanted to ensure my baby was healthy and I couldn't wait until I met him or her. The sex of the baby was never revealed because I could use a nice surprise.

My birth plan would be alone and the gift of the baby's gender was a pleasant present to me. But the greatest gift of all would be my child, safe in my arms.

I walked through my clean apartment and past the packed boxes in the corner. My energy level had lessened as each day passed and I hadn't brought myself to unpack anymore. The rest would stay in boxes until I found a permanent place. This place was just a means for now.

The nursery wasn't everything I had envisioned for my first child. Nothing about this situation was anything I had hoped for. I had wanted to be married to a husband devoted to me. A man who adored his child and wanted more kids soon. A growing family we could call our own. Instead, I had to become a single parent. A mother who did everything on my own with no help.

I gazed over at the crib I had struggled to put together by myself. The dresser I had moved around until I found the right spot for the heavy thing. The change table had been the easiest piece of furniture to maneuver because of the wheels.

The small nursery had no theme and no coat of fresh paint. The extra touch was too much work, and I didn't want to harm the baby with paint fumes. This wasn't enough for my first experience as a mother and I had wanted more for my baby, but life had other plans for us.

But I couldn't let this situation get me down.

I had to maintain faith. Everything would work out the way fate had intended. Our reality had changed, but we couldn't let it get us down. My child deserved a confident parent. One who could pull us through and we could come out together on the other side. Single moms do this all the time and I could too. I'd be a single parent with a successful business.

I smoothly ran Match My Heart from home, and Evelyn still had no clue I was expecting. We constantly video called about work and I had kept my enormous belly out of sight. I was one of the lucky pregnant women who had all the extra pounds go straight to the expanding belly. I had maintained the shape of my face, but the hair loss was another story.

Evelyn had bugged about visiting, and I created every excuse in the book. I started with the need to unpack and get everything in order. Which soon turned into the place was a mess and along came those dreadful sicknesses. I couldn't stand it if she were to catch anything. I even lied and placed the blame on Baxter. The need to move on from him and I had random men over to spend the night.

But the overdone sexual escapades made for humorous conversation.

Evelyn thought Mr. Baxter Lane had turned me into some wild woman. A sexual deviant who had intercourse on the brain. When, in fact, I was hornier than ever and there was no man to satisfy my needs.

This pregnancy made my hormones crazy. They were all over the place, and I had entered the stage of being turned-on by everything. I was ready to resort to the shower head in the bathroom for a quick release.

I missed sex. Craved the comfort of a man. But not just any man.

Baxter.

I missed him.

My eyes landed on the tiny clothes hanging in the closet with no doors. The cute outfits I had purchased for the baby. All gender neutral colors because the sex was yet to be revealed.

Suddenly, my cell phone rang from inside my pocket. I pondered who'd be on the other line and reached inside. But when I read the caller ID, my heart raced.

It was Baxter.

He had been persistent in his need to reach me and I hadn't answered. I hadn't spoken to him because I simply couldn't. I couldn't stand to hear about his relationship with Beverly.

I thought of changing my number, but I would lose all contact with Baxter. I wasn't ready for no connection to him. A world without the man I loved was hard to conceive.

I had moved away and I should cut all ties with Baxter, but he still had a hold on me. My heart still beats for him and only him. But maybe today was the day the vessel should stop.

I answered on the fifth ring. "Mr. Lane, you need to stop calling me."

"Finally, you pick up..." Baxter sighed through the line, and the sound of his voice made me swoon. "Darling, I miss you."

"Please don't call me that." I sighed with hurt.

I wasn't his darling any longer. Baxter needed to stop this obsession with me and focus on the future. He had made his choice, and I had made mine.

"I won't ever stop, my darling Brielle, because you're mine." Baxter breathed with certainty. "Where are you?"

"My whereabouts don't concern you, Mr. Lane." I huffed with annoyance at his reluctance to listen. "I don't work for you anymore."

"Forget about being a fucking matchmaker for just one second and listen to me—" Baxter snapped with frustration.

I envisioned his hands running through his messy hair, and Baxter disliked my need to not give in. His breath was heavy on the other end and I knew he paced the floor of his office. Stuck within those dark walls as his new bride waited for him in his bed and I longed to be the one in it. But I couldn't be because Baxter never chose me.

Baxter Lane had chosen Beverly.

I interrupted Baxter, "If you have anything further to discuss, you can take matters up with Evelyn. She is in charge now."

"But I want to talk to you, Brielle," Baxter insisted, and I heard a sharp intake of breath. "I want to know why you left me."

Everything hurts inside of me. Crushed me to my very core at the sound of Baxter's agony. The same torture I went through since I saw him with Beverly on that heartbreaking day. A day full of promise for a future between us, but shattered by the new beginning of a perfect match. One I had created just for him.

I breathed bitterly. "I never left you because I wasn't yours to begin with."

"You don't mean that," Baxter hissed.

I ignored his words and said in a professional tone. "I'm going to change my number after this call ends, Mr. Lane."

Baxter huffed with annoyance. "This has nothing to do with business and you fucking know it. I need to see you, my darling. I need to tell you something."

"Mr. Lane, your concerns are no longer my priority and Evelyn can help you." I breathed as tears clouded my vision and I knew I'd miss his voice. "Goodbye, Baxter."

The slip of Baxter's name was a force of habit. A slight mistake and one I wouldn't make ever again. This was the last time I'd hear from Baxter Lane, and my world shattered all over again.

The phone dropped from my ear as tears fell down my face and I heard his last plea to me. "Brielle, goddamnit, wait..."

But I hung up and Baxter was gone forever.

THIRTY-SIX
Friendly Reveal

The afternoon sunshine beamed through the kitchen window and I got everything set up for my scheduled business video call with Evelyn. The dishes were done, and the kitchen cleaned up from lunch. My stomach was full of a hearty salad and pasta just for the baby. I settled for bottled water to drink and I hadn't had a coffee since I found out I was pregnant. I missed the usual brew and even dreamed about it.

I set my laptop up at the table with my pen and paper for quick notes. The files we needed to discuss were ready and waited to be opened. Match My Heart was thriving, but was a tremendous relief.

Summer season brought more customers ready to find love in the sunshine. Those dates outdoors were in full swing and we were ready for them. Baxter had been our saving grace, but he had left the company months ago. Business came to a full halt with him after I had left the city. He gave no explanation, and he didn't ask for a red cent back.

I hadn't heard a word about Beverly and their relationship, but I assumed they were engaged by now. Baxter was a man of his word and he had wanted me to find him a wife. I had found him his perfect fit, and he was bound to be happy. But this situation was best left unknown.

For me, at least.

All this new business made Match My Heart develop into the company we had always dreamed of. We had to continue down this successful path and we couldn't let anything get in the way. Not even the child growing inside of me. My secret love child with a client had to remain unrevealed because our business couldn't afford a hit. We'd lose everything.

The laptop screen lit up and Evelyn came on the screen. "Hey, Brielle! Hold on for one second. I have to grab something."

"Okay," I said and adjusted my seat.

In the background was my old office. I missed my workplace so much. Evelyn had moved everything around in my absence, and the new look was great. An agreeable change she needed without me there. But I missed my job.

I wanted to be back home doing what I did best. All the chaos seemed so long ago, and I'd give anything to have the craziness all back. I was a matchmaker. I was born to bring couples together, not sit at home and work. But this baby had other plans for me.

My child was my number one priority.

"Sorry about that..." Evelyn breathed as she smiled at the camera and rubbed her forehead. "It's been a long day, and it's not even over yet."

"Why?" I asked with curiosity. "What's going on?"

"Well, our one client, Roger..." Evelyn huffed with annoyance. "He went rogue and found himself a date."

"Roger... Roger..." I mumbled as I looked through the files and found his name. "Ah ha, found you."

I opened his file and first saw his picture. Roger Adams was a handsome thirty-two-year-old man searching for his forever match. He had a successful job and a tight-knit family, but he wasn't close to them. He was a confident and skillful person, but he didn't like to listen. The bull-headed clients were the toughest to deal with, and Evelyn had her work cut out for her.

"Yes, that Roger..." Evelyn mumbled with frustration. "But his date is way out of his league."

"Let me guess?" I sighed as I tapped my nose and peered through his file. "Tall, blonde and beautiful, but the brains aren't there?"

"Exactly," Evelyn said as she pointed at the screen and brought her face closer. "But you know Roger. He won't listen to reason and the date will be a complete disaster. Just like all his other failed attempts."

"Yep. And that's why he came to us," I agreed and put down his file. "Did you remind Mr. Adams of this?"

"I did, but he's too stubborn to listen to me," Evelyn admitted with a shrug. "Maybe you could talk some sense into him, Brielle?"

"Give me his number and I will add the task to my list," I instructed, as I grabbed my pen and jotted down the number. "Perfect. I'll give him a shout this evening."

But a sudden discomfort threw me off.

My stomach stung, and I winced with discomfort as Evelyn talked. She went over the latest couples and their upcoming dates she had arranged for my approval. I knew she wanted the reassurance she had done each one justice, but my belly had other plans. The pressure grew more intense with each minute as the clock ticked by and I tried to ignore the ache.

"Brielle? Did you hear me about the flowers?" Evelyn asked as I caught sight of her concerned eyes and she tapped her screen. "Hold on, maybe something is wrong with my mic?"

"No, no, I did..." I mumbled through clenched teeth. "Just go on."

The pressure grew into an intense pain, and the sensation radiated throughout my belly. The sting of agony went down into my lower back and everything hurt. I clenched the table and tried to hide my face. But the pain was far too great and I couldn't take it anymore.

I rose to my feet to make the extreme throb go away, and the move didn't work. Instinct had kicked in, but I had screwed myself. The table no longer hid my belly and the roundness of me came into view on the screen.

"Oh, my god, Brielle!" Evelyn gasped with her mouth agape. "You're pregnant?"

Evelyn locked eyes with my very pregnant belly, and I was in full view for the camera to capture. Our conversation had taken a turn for the worst and I had slipped up. I had fucked up really bad and Evelyn knew my secret.

"Shit..." I winced in pain mixed with panic.

I did the only thing I knew to do and slammed the laptop screen shut. I was in full-blown terror and thought of every excuse there could be, but came up with none. Because there wasn't any when the truth was right in front of her face.

The pain intensified, and I clenched my stomach. Something wasn't right. This recent development was far too much to ignore. Something was wrong with the baby.

And now Evelyn knew the truth.

"Oh, god..." I cried out as the next wave of agony hit me and grabbed the table.

I bent over as the stab of pain pierced through my belly and my breath came out labored. The quick puff of air blew into my hair and sucked the strands back into my mouth. I couldn't think straight, let alone get myself help. I was alone, pregnant, and in desperate need of assistance.

Suddenly, my cell phone chimed on the table. The phone was within reach and I knew exactly who was on the other line. Evelyn certainly wasted no time.

"E-Evelyn?" I breathed with staggered puffs of air.

"Don't hang up! I'm in the car and headed straight for your place," Evelyn said with urgency.

"Evelyn, you don't need to do that. I'm... Ah!" I cried out in pain.

My hand gripped the edge of the table, and my knuckles turned white. The wave of distress tore through me and I couldn't even finish my sentence. Instead, a grunt of agony came out and I couldn't handle much more.

"Jesus, Brielle, you aren't fine," Evelyn answered with an argument and her worry filled the phone line. "Nothing about this is okay, and I'm on my way right now."

I breathed through clenched teeth. "No, please, Evelyn."

Evelyn replied with determination. "Yes. I'm coming and we're taking you to the hospital."

***

The drive to the emergency department had been excruciating. Every bump had been unbearable, but every minute of pain seemed to last forever. Evelyn rushed me to the hospital as fast as her car would allow, and she even cut through some red lights.

The hospital in the city wasn't far from my residence, and the emergency department took me right in. An extremely pregnant woman with a high level of pain was a top priority, and I was thankful. The pain was to the point I thought I might pass out if I didn't get to lie down.

But all my worries had been for nothing.

Turns out there was such a thing as false labor. I had a case of Braxton Hicks. My body got ready to give birth and the waves of pain were contractions. The over-the-top sensation would be my experience come time to deliver my beautiful baby.

"Your baby will be here before you know it," the doctor said as he hung his stethoscope behind the back of his neck and touched Evelyn's shoulder. "You did the right thing bringing your friend in."

"Thank you." Evelyn blushed with a flustered look upon her bright red face.

"I'm just going to get your discharge paperwork ready and you can go home, Brielle," the doctor declared as he turned and left the room.

"So, your baby is almost here and I feel completely out of the loop," Evelyn admitted with a nervous laugh.

"Well, so do I..." I breathed anxiously and looked up at Evelyn. "I've felt so alone and unprepared for everything."

Evelyn sat on the side of my hospital and sighed. "Why didn't you tell me, Brielle?"

"I couldn't risk our company. Everything was at stake and the repercussions of a matchmaker sleeping with a client would be damage we could never come back from," I explained with mixed emotions. "But a child conceived with the boss would destroy everything we've worked so hard for. I had no choice."

"So, you figured moving away and doing this all by yourself was the best option?" Evelyn asked with narrowed eyes, "What were you going to do once the baby was here? Hide a crying baby in the nursery for each business call?"

I shrugged my shoulders. "I didn't have time to plan that far ahead."

But it was too late to find out.

Evelyn knew the whole truth and the end of my pregnancy in sight. My best friend knew exactly who the father was and panic set in all over again. Evelyn couldn't go to Baxter and tell him the truth. I had to be sure of it.

I grabbed Evelyn's shoulders and looked her straight in the eyes. "Swear to me, this baby stays between us."

Evelyn searched my face as my wide eyes pleaded with her to understand. She didn't speak a word, and her silence slowly killed me inside. I needed this secret to remain hidden, and my best friend had to be on my side.

"I don't know..." Evelyn mumbled.

"Listen to me." I shook Evelyn and whispered with urgency, "Baxter can never find out. He can never know he's the father of my child."

"But why?" Evelyn asked with question. "Baxter would be a wonderful father and he..."

"And that's the problem, Evelyn," I whispered with necessity and tried to make her see. "Baxter would be a devoted dad, but we could never be a family."

Evelyn frowned. "Yes, you could—"

I interrupted, "No, we couldn't. He's made his choice and Baxter chose Beverly."

My best friend remained silent, and tears stung my eyes. The remembrance of Baxter with Beverly on that heartbreaking day tore me up inside all over again. I tucked a strand of hair behind Evelyn's ear as a single tear fell down my cheek and she brushed the wetness away.

"Please, Evelyn, please promise me you won't tell a soul this baby is Baxter Lane's?" I pleaded with her.

Evelyn sighed. "All right, I promise, but I don't have a good feeling about this."

THIRTY-SEVEN
Our Final Truth

Evelyn drove me home. Back to the place I didn't want to be, but had to be. And I showed her around my apartment.

My tiny apartment was a tremendous change from my condo, but Evelyn understood the circumstances. This was a perfect fit for me and my child. We required nothing fancy and huge. This apartment would do.

I explained to her this wasn't a permanent plan and just for the time being. Evelyn was over the moon with excitement for me and my soon-_to-_be motherhood. She loved the nursery and promised to come with gifts for the baby the next time she visited. This, after all, was an unexpected one. No thanks to me.

I withheld the truth from my best friend and I saw the error of my ways. Evelyn should've been the first person I went to with the news. She would've helped me through this life-changing situation, but I couldn't turn back time. I made my choice and left the city to start a new life. For me and my child.

But Evelyn would be right by my side.

My best friend promised to be there for the big day. The moment I gave birth to my baby, I'd no longer be alone. She'd be by my bedside and hold my hand. Breathe with me through each contraction and encourage me to push when the baby's head crowned. She could even cut the cord and she wanted to be there to place my newborn safely in my arms.

All these promises Evelyn made should come from the baby's father. The reassurance should come from Baxter, but never could be. Especially when he had no idea he was the father of my child.

I wandered into the nursery and lost myself in my thoughts when I spotted a scarf. The red fabric was out of place as the light cashmere scarf draped over the crib rail. I remembered the cloth piece hanging from Evelyn's neck and she must've forgotten it. She had left the scarf behind and this was just like her to misplace something. Her disorganization made me giggle, and I grabbed the fabric in my hands. I could envision the look on Evelyn's face when I spoke of her forgetfulness. I'd be sure to get this back to her when I saw her next.

Suddenly, there was a knock at the front door and the noise brought a smile to my face. Evelyn must've realized and had returned for her scarf. We'd have a good laugh about this and I'd remind her organization was key.

I headed straight for the front door with the scarf in my hand and waddled with each step. A knock sounded again just as I got to the door and placed my hand on the knob. I didn't need to look through my peephole to know Evelyn stood on the other side. She had just left and had come back for something she had misplaced.

"Hold on, Evelyn, I know you forgot your..." I breathed with an eye roll as I opened the front door to my apartment and the slight breeze blew through my hair. "Scarf."

But my world turned upside down.

Baxter stood on my doorstep and his ocean blue eyes stared into mine. The scarf fell from my grasp as shock took over and I was at a loss for words. He looked amazing in a suit and tie with the same appearance as always. His scent surrounded me and it lost me in him. Caught up in the man I loved with all my soul and he was here at my door.

Baxter caught sight of my very swollen belly and he breathed, "You're pregnant?"

Reality set back in and my hands fell over my round stomach. The baby kicked in the presence of its father and a wave of heat crept over me. Baxter was here. But he had caught sight of my secret.

"I... I..." I fumbled for words, but no explanation would come.

"I can't believe you're pregnant, Brielle..." Baxter breathed with disbelief as his hands ran through his hair and his eyes never left my belly. "Jesus... I tracked our last call, but I never expected to find you like this."

My hidden reality was out, and the walls caved in around me. Compressed me to the point I had nowhere to run and no way out. I had no clue what to do.

Dizziness soon fell over me and I saw two of Baxter. My world spun, and I went weak in the knees. The shock of his unexpected arrival had turned into utter regret. Shame for keeping the truth hidden from him. Remorse for him missing so much of my pregnancy. But most of all, pure guilt.

This was all my fault.

"I'm sorry... I..." I mumbled and grabbed the doorframe. "I think I need to lie down..."

But I fell forward.

Straight into Baxter Lane's arms.

"Woah... Easy now..." Baxter gasped in surprise.

Baxter wasted no time and caught me. He picked me up off the ground and into his safe embrace. If he hadn't, I would've fallen straight down the stairs.

Baxter didn't stop there and carried me straight into my apartment. He brought me to the only couch I had in my living area and laid me down. My backside sunk into the cushions, and he knelt beside me as my vision spun. My heart raced until he smoothed my hair back from my forehead and spoke sweet words of reassurance. Comfort that everything would be okay and I was safe. But nothing about this situation was fine, and this was all my fault.

"I'm so sorry, Bax... I'm so sorry..." I muttered repeatedly and slowly shook my head back and forth.

I felt the regret of what I had done deep within the depth of me. The agony of my secret hit me full force, and I ached all over. This was a kind of pain I had never gone through before. The torment of hurting someone I loved. I hated myself, and Baxter had every right to resent me. But I couldn't stand the thought of him despising our child because of me.

The off-balance of my world subsided and the guilt of what I had done set in. I reached for his hand and he took mine within his. Everything rushed back and the shame only grew.

Baxter's blue hues looked at me, and he asked, "How far along are you, Brielle?"

I answered with the truth. "Eight months."

"Christ..." Baxter breathed with anguish. "Why didn't you tell me, darling? I could've been there for you. I could've..."

"I wanted to, Baxter..." I admitted as the strength came back and I sat up. "But I couldn't because—"

"It doesn't matter, darling. None of this matters as long as I have you," Baxter interrupted and took both my hands in his. "I don't care if my step-brother is the father, because I fucking want it all. I want you and all of you."

"But wait, I..." I said and shook my head.

"No, Brielle, please hear me out." Baxter breathed as he got up from the floor and I stood in front of him. "I'll be there for you and my step-brother's baby. I will step up not only as this child's uncle, but as a father figure, too. A man for him or her to look up to in life."

The tender moment touched my heart. The kindness of Baxter's words pierced through me and collided with my soul. His devotion to me and this baby was clear. Not even his step-brother would stand in his way. But James wasn't this child's father. Baxter was.

"Baxter, please, I..." I sighed.

"No, my darling Brielle, I already lost you and I never want it to happen again." Baxter breathed with certainty and he rested our hands on my pregnant belly. "I vow to you from this day forward I will be here for you and this child. Even though the baby isn't mine."

Baxter was certain. He was sure. He wanted me and this baby, regardless of its paternity.

I could continue on with a lie. Baxter had presented me with an out and a way to conceal the truth from everyone.

Including him. But I love him and can't continue on like this. My life was a lie. Everything had fallen apart right in front of my eyes and I never wanted to go through this again. Baxter was the father of this baby, and he deserved to know the truth. Now was the time to come clean.

I couldn't risk this anymore. Evelyn knew the truth, and it was only a matter of time before Baxter did. I knew he'd go to his step-brother. He wouldn't be able to keep quiet and I couldn't ask him to lie. It was only a matter of time before Baxter spilled the beans to James, and my world fell apart all over again.

I stared up into the eyes of the man I loved with all my heart and soul. Blue tones of assurance swirled in Baxter's eyes and I melted for him even more. I feared the truth because of his reaction, but the time had come, to be honest.

"But Baxter, this baby is yours." I breathed and squeezed his hands. "This little one we created together, and it's not James's child."

Baxter opened his mouth and clamped it shut again. He let go of me and withdrew himself. My heart hurt and I knew this could be a likely reaction, but nothing had prepared me for heartbreak. Gut wrenching pain because I had hurt him so deeply. Everything was my fault.

"I'm sorry..." I cried through tears and reached out for Baxter. "Please, Baxter, I'm so sorry for keeping this pregnancy from you."

Baxter turned away from me and asked with hurt, "Not just the pregnancy, Brielle, but you were willing to keep my child from me."

"I know and I was wrong, but I'm so goddamn sorry, Baxter..." I pleaded with him for forgiveness. "Please. Please believe me because I couldn't stand you hating me."

My words stopped Baxter in his tracks, and he slowly turned around to face me. He became worn out and tired from the latest news. Hurt from my refusal to reveal the truth and keep his child from him.

"How could you keep this from me?" Baxter asked, as his voice was unrecognizable and full of despair.

"I never wanted to and as soon as I found out I went to your office..." I explained as the wet tears on my face clung to my cheeks and a chill ran through me. "But before I could get there, I found you with Beverly. Down in the lobby. You clearly appeared to be an item and when you kissed her hands..."

"You thought we were an official couple." Baxter sighed with understanding and stepped towards me with his face full of regret.

"Yes. I couldn't bear it and I left." I breathed with hurt from the awful day I wanted to forget.

Baxter touched my cheek and whispered, "Beverly was never the one, my darling Brielle. Because my heart belongs to someone else."

Baxter traced his fingers down my cheek and over my lips. "Who, Baxter?"

"You," Baxter whispered with certainty. "And you walked in on me, breaking things off with Beverly because I couldn't carry on with this any longer."

Baxter's omission of the truth shocked me. He had chosen me and wanted to be with me. He didn't want Beverly or anyone else.

But there was still one missing piece to our love story.

"Wait?" I breathed with question. "You couldn't carry on with what any longer?"

Baxter let his hand drop from my face and he placed his hands in the pockets of his suit jacket. His gaze never wavered from mine and I could tell something was wrong. Baxter was about to reveal his own truth, and I braced myself for impact.

"I needed to obtain a wife for business purposes, but I failed to tell you the true reason I came to Match My Heart," Baxter explained and his hair fell in front of his gorgeous eyes. "After I met you, darling, you were my breath of fresh air. The wind I never knew I needed, and you were it for me. When we first met, you captivated me, and it was love at first sight. But you left me alone with an empty bed in Hawaii and I was determined to see you again."

I couldn't believe this. Baxter had fallen for me first. He had known and kept the truth from me. Everything made sense. All the missing pieces fell into place, and I held my breath for more.

"I paid top dollar to find you and the odds you owned a dating agency blew me away. I required a wife because I needed someone to bear my children," Baxter explained as he gazed down at my swollen belly and he took his hands out of his pockets. "I had the perfect excuse to get close to you and make you see we are the perfect match. I loved you first, my darling Brielle, and I just needed to make you see you loved me, too."

"I can't believe this..." I breathed in disbelief.

Baxter took my hands in his and tenderly kissed my knuckles. His tender caress lit me aflame, and I craved him more than ever before. Baxter loved me and he had this entire time.

Baxter breathed against my hand, and his sure eyes peered into my soul. "I needed you to be mine, my darling. I want you to be my wife."

But I pulled away from Baxter.

Baxter hid his true feelings for me. He had played me along until I caved. Sure, I was stubborn and wanted to save my business. But he had kept this a secret and led me under false pretenses.

I truly thought Baxter wanted me to find him his perfect woman. I didn't know he believed he had already found that in me. His desire to make me his during every secret encounter. The jealousy he oozed when I went on a date with Jack. His constant need to do business alone with me and get to know me. Everything made sense, and the puzzle was complete.

None of this made Baxter or my choices right. We had deceived the very person we claimed to love. And that was each other.

"How could you toy with my emotions like this, Baxter?" I asked with hurt and pulled my hands away from him.

"I know, I fucked up, Brielle, but you did too when you kept my child from me," Baxter replied with pure honesty.

Baxter pointed towards our baby growing inside of me and I knew he was right. I should've been honest. We had both really fucked up and our baby didn't deserve to come into the world like this. Our child needed better from both of us.

"You're right. I fucked up, but none of this would've happened if you just told me the truth, Baxter." I expressed.

Baxter paced the floor in front of me. His hands raked through his hair in agony at the decision he had made. Because we both lived with the consequences of our actions. But he suffered the most.

"I know and I've missed out on so much..." Baxter admitted, and stopped to look at me. "But I can move past this. We can move on from this together."

No matter how much I wanted to take Baxter into my arms and forget all the lies from the past, I couldn't. My business was still at risk. I didn't know if I was ready to risk everything for a life with Baxter Lane. A forever created on twisted secrets. A pregnancy I had kept from him and his love he withheld from me. Our ultimate, unforgivable betrayal towards one another.

"I don't know how we move on from this." I breathed with sadness and hated to think this was our end.

A love story that was ending when it should just be starting. The start of a promise to be together until death do us part. The vow to be a family. A dream we both could have with each other.

Baxter dropped to his knees in front of me and groveled, "Nothing else matters now, my darling Brielle. My child is inside of you and you're carrying my legacy. Our future we created together. It has always been you and you mean everything to me. Please forgive me. Please forgive the biggest mistake I've ever made in my life. Because I had forgiven you the second I knew you loved me, too."

I peered down into Baxter's sure eyes and breathed. "But my company... How can we be together and I still run my business? I've worked my entire career to build Match My Heart and you can't expect me to just give it up?"

Baxter reached out and touched my belly. He stroked my skin the same way he touched our baby. With tenderness and unbreakable love.

"I would never ask you to give up something you love," Baxter said with love. "I'll buy Match My Heart in a heartbeat if it means being with you. My money means nothing if you aren't mine. Please, my darling, please forgive me and let me make it up to you for the rest of our lives?"

Tears clouded my vision, and I gazed down into his ocean blue eyes. The same stare I tried to deny countless times and never could let him go. His blue depths had stolen my heart and captured my broken soul. Baxter Lane had made me whole again after James left me at the airport and Baxter walked into my life. He had changed everything, and he begged me to be his.

Forever.

I got down on my knees in front of him and took his hands in mine. My lips placed kisses of promise on each one. Our child wiggled inside of me and I covered my hands over his on top of the one thing we did right together. Our beautiful baby.

I stared straight into his vibrant blue hues as they promised me a lifetime of love and whispered, "When do we start?"

Fate stepped in one last time, and our baby kicked. Baxter looked down at my round belly and he fell in love all over again. Not just with me, but with pure devotion for our family.

The End

Bonus Epilogue
Pleasure in Paradise

Warm beads of water trickled down my skin. My hands ran down my body and over my flat stomach. The slight stretch marks were still there from pregnancy, but slightly faded after giving birth. The smell of suntan lotion mixed with sweat filled my nostrils, and the water worked at washing the aroma away.

The Hawaiian sunshine had been a relaxing calm I had needed while Baxter took care of our newborn. The image of him in his full glory with our child brought a smile to my face. Baxter Lane was fit to be a father, and he was sexy as ever while doing it.

"God, you're so fucking beautiful." Baxter said from behind me.

I peered over my shoulder at him with a wicked grin. "I got the all clear from the doctor before we left the city."

Baxter was shirtless. His chest muscles flexed as he pulled down his swimwear and his massive cock sprang free. My eyes darted straight towards his nine-inch thickness and my pussy throbbed.

For far too long, my cunt has gone without attention. After birth was a real treat, but the gift was worth everything in this world. My baby.

But mommy wanted daddy something terrible.

My hormones raged as Baxter's eyes roamed over my naked form and he took everything in. My sun kissed lips, my swollen tits full of milk for our child, the faded stretch marks of my journey to motherhood and my bare pussy that gave birth to his legacy. His eyes devoured every inch like I was the most sexiest woman alive. And I was because I had his child.

Baxter came through the steam glass door, and he looked glorious under the sunlit sky. The natural light streamed down on us from overhead as the water sprinkled down onto the black-tiled shower. But Baxter knelt down to his knees on the floor at my feet in front of me.

"Does this mean what I think it does?" Baxter asked as his ocean blue eyes swirled up at me with lust and he ran his hands down my legs.

I shivered and breathed with desire. "Yes."

But Baxter travelled his eyes down my body.

"I'm sorry for putting you through that." Baxter breathed.

Baxter had nothing to apologize for. My body provided a home for our baby. My anatomy was built for this. I was one of the lucky ones to be granted the greatest love of all. Motherhood.

I tenderly touched his handsome face. "You don't have to apologize for giving me the most precious gift life can give."

Baxter peered up at me and touched my bare pussy. "No, darling, I need to apologize to my kitten."

Baxter trailed his fingers between my lips and touched my clit. He slowly circled my fleshy nub and a soft gasp escaped my parted lips. His eyes watched me with intensity and he brought his mouth to my navel. His tongue swirled inside and travelled down my abdomen. He nipped at my skin as he went and goosebumps came to life in his wake.

"Oh, yes, Bax..." I moaned from above.

My hands fell into his hair as he continued lower and my fingers curled into his strands. My diamond engagement ring sparkled with the light from overhead. The same twinkle that shone in his vibrant blue eyes on the day Baxter Lane proposed to me and wanted me to be his. Baxter had waited until James and I completed our divorce before he asked me to spend the rest of my life with him. James wasn't thrilled, but I didn't give a fuck.

Neither did Baxter because I was his and my heart had always belonged to him.

Baxter proved he claimed me as his mouth kissed me all the way down and he stopped over my bare mound. His fingers stopped the circular motion and my cunt ached for more. A mix of intense pleasure swirled inside of me and I needed only him.

"Spread your legs, darling," Baxter ordered with a growl.

I willingly followed his instructions and knew I was in for a real treat. My fiancé had skills like no other and I loved the practice I received from him. Every time was like the first and a sexy gift I only ever received. Because I was his and he was mine. *Forever.*

The wetness of his tongue grazed over my clit, and Baxter threw my left leg over his shoulder. He worked his muscle through my slit and I moaned from above. I was his goddess, and he was my god. He devoured me, wanted me, and taunted me. His tongue pushed deeper inside of me and I thrust my hips with each slip further.

"Oh, fuck..." I sighed with pleasure.

The play of Baxter's mouth had been long awaited, and the thrill of the sensation he gave to me was everything I craved. His tongue dove in and out. He flicked the wetness around and slurped on my sweet cunt. He dove right in and didn't waste a beat. My heartbeat went right along with each stroke and my mind went wild.

I was crazy about him. Out of my mind, intoxicated. Drunk on undeniable love.

Baxter brought his hands to my ass, and he slapped my wet cheeks. The sound echoed within the steamy shower and the temperature rose to the bright Hawaiian sky. I tossed my head back and my eyes flickered with beams of bright white light. The luminous sky mixed with the brilliance and my pussy walls contracted around his tongue. My glorious release hit me full force and the pure ecstasy was everything I had waited for.

"Bax! Yes!" I cried out my climactic pleasure.

Baxter rode out my orgasm as his tongue flickered inside of me with his face buried in my pussy. My juices gushed and creamed his mouth, but he ate me up like I was his delicious treat. But his eyes locked on me like he was ready to consume a full meal.

I released his hair from my grasp and watched as he licked his lips of my creamy delight. My knees were weak, and he released my leg, but balanced me against his rock-hard form. Baxter stood up from where he had once knelt and continued to treat me like his queen.

Baxter lapped his tongue up over my flesh and kissed me with tenderness. Up my belly, between my cleavage, higher up the nape of my neck, and he pulled away at my face. His passionate glare took in my satisfied state and his fingers brushed my wet strands behind my ears.

Until Baxter cupped my face and his lips crashed down onto mine. He kissed me like I was his oxygen and he couldn't get enough air. My breath mixed with his and gave him life. The same way he had just made me come alive with his skilled mouth.

My backside hit the tiled wall of the shower as the warm beads of water fell over us and it lost us in each other. Completely intoxicated, loved and cherished. We were in a frenzy as our tongues swirled, teeth nipped and mouths sucked. The moment was hot and full of need.

"My darling, you're everything to me." Baxter breathed as his lips brushed mine and his mouth travelled down my neck. "Mine to cherish for the rest of my life."

"Yes, Bax, I'm all yours..." I sighed through agape lips and my hands worked up his sculpted body.

The head of Baxter's cock pulsated against my thigh and made me want him. I was crazy for this man and needed sex from him like he was a drug. An addiction I couldn't quit and I was about to relapse.

Baxter pulled his mouth away from my skin and his eyes locked on my swollen breasts. He drank in the sight of my round tits that were bigger from the milk I provided for our beautiful baby. He squeezed my plump boobs in his grasp and his thumbs stroked over my erect nipples. My heart raced in my chest and I panted heavily within his hold. But my buds leaked breast milk, and he continued his play mixed with the warm flow of water.

Baxter looked from my bulged breasts and into my turned-on eyes. "My darling is full and needs to be expressed."

"No, Baxter, I just need you..." I sighed with protest.

But Baxter wouldn't give into my objection.

"And you'll have me, but first..." Baxter growled with determination and his tongue licked my leaking nipple. "I want to suckle from the sweetness you supply for our baby."

And Baxter captured my breast with his mouth.

"Oh, fuck, Bax... Yes..." I sighed with desire.

Pleasure soared for the father of my child, and he gave me more than I had ever felt before. Baxter wasn't tame, and he devoured my tits one by one. Unafraid of my milk, and drank from me like he couldn't get enough. Each suckle from his mouth sent me higher, and the sensation was unlike any other. His hand ran down the side of my body and he slapped my clit for added intensity.

"Oh, Bax..." I sighed a raspy breath and my fingers bit into his broad shoulders. "Fuck..."

My nails dug into his blades and scratched down over his chest. Baxter's dominance loomed over me and his power on me was everything. He was in charge and took what he wanted.

One finger circled my clit, and he pumped two fingers between my slit. The back of my head hit the wall, and a gasp flowed from my mouth. Pleasure climbed higher and my hips thrust to his rhythm. Baxter finger banged my pussy like there was no tomorrow.

He swirled his tongue around one nipple and jumped to the next. Baxter repeated this thrill of pleasure, and my buds couldn't stop their constant leak. He wanted more, and my lactating tits supplied him with all he craved. He lapped his tongue over my milk and drank from me until he was ready to stuff me full.

Baxter breathed against my tit. "My darling, you're so fucking sweet, but your milk is delectable like honey."

And Baxter continued his feast on my swollen boobs.

He couldn't get enough of me, and I couldn't escape Baxter. I didn't want to and not ever. I had waited for this moment for weeks and he gave me more than I ever expected. Baxter loved everything about me. Even my milky tits.

I was wet and ready for my future husband. His soon-to-be wife was ripe for him. Baxter was bound to dive deep into me, and the thrill of his incoming sex quivered through me.

Baxter pulled his fingers from me and gave my clit a flick. I moaned and dug my nails into his firm chest. He looped my left leg over his forearm and squeezed my hip. The tip of his mushroom head cock stood at my entrance and my pussy ached to welcome him inside. Baxter's dick was ready to plunge in deep and fill me like he never had before.

Baxter brushed his lips against mine, and I tasted my sweet milk in his mouth. He dove his tongue inside and gave me one magnificent swirl. But he left my mouth and had me craving more.

"Please, Bax, please stuff me full," I whimpered.

He growled with need. "I'm going to fill you full with another baby."

And the tip of him entered me.

"Oh, fuck..." I gasped.

"Are you okay?" Baxter asked with concern.

"Yes..." I sighed as his cock went deeper with a slow pace and I held on tight.

"Good..." Baxter groaned with desire and filled me. "Because I want my legacy to continue."

"Oh, fuck, yes..." I sighed with absolute pleasure.

"Do you want that too, darling?" Baxter asked with intensity as he peered down into my depths and wanted me to be sure. "Can I fill you with another child?"

I stared with certainty into his ocean eyes and sighed. "Yes, I've never been surer of anything in my entire life."

"Neither have I..." Baxter groaned as he picked up pace and licked my nipple. "Oh, you're so fucking sweet, my future wife to be."

My gasp echoed through the bathroom with each thrust. Every pump was harder as Baxter went faster and my fingers wove into the strands of his hair. My hands formed fists, and I held onto him for dear life. He rammed into me and my swollen tits bounced as he sought each nipple for more milk. They jiggled in his face, and he grabbed a nipple between his teeth. His mouth covered the bud as he suckled from me, and I cried out with desire.

My hips rocked with each of his thrusts and I couldn't hold back. The lust grew higher and higher until I was ready to explode. My sweet juices were ready to gush and greet his seed. I was eager for Baxter to fill me full and a race for the finish to start within me. A single seed to find my ripe egg and give us our second child.

Stars burst for the second time, and I was about to come. Baxter hit me to the hilt, and my world spun out of control.

The ultimate release I had waited for was here and not a moment too soon.

"Yes, Bax, yes!" I cried out my climax.

The pumps never stopped, and he throbbed from inside of my contracted walls. My pussy clamped down on Baxter's cock and he drove into me until his own world collided with mine. And his dick erupted his seed.

"Fuck, my darling..." Baxter groaned, and he grunted out each word, "You... Are... All... Mine."

Baxter ejaculated deep inside of me with one final plunge. He spilled everything he had and filled me full, just like he had promised. He mixed with my creamy juice and the journey began again. A second child would soon be on the way and our family would grow even bigger.

Suddenly, our baby cried from the other room. Baxter pulled out of me and his seed ran down my thigh. Baxter claimed my mouth, and I knew his hunger still ran deep. He wanted me just as much as I wanted him. But our lovemaking would have to wait because our beautiful baby needed his mommy and daddy.

I cleaned up and threw on one of Baxter's dress shirts. The white buttoned up shirt hung open and my breasts were ready to feed my little one who looked just like his father. A full head of dark hair and eyes just as blue as the ocean waves.

Baxter had left the bathroom before me to tend to our baby, who needed attention. He required our love and a bond only we could give him for the rest of our lives. The long-lasting promise of a loving family.

I walked out with a smile on my face and into our suite's bedroom. The same room Baxter and I shared all those months ago. The very one that began our love story lost in paradise and brought us to this moment.

Baxter held our son in his arms and sweetly said, "Mommy is mine and always will be. But you, my son, have claimed our hearts forever."

Join and Follow the Author

Come join Breanne's Blazing Beauties readers group on Facebook! It's a place where you can talk about Breanne Bergie's books, get exclusive book teasers of upcoming releases and more! Don't miss out and send a request to join today!

Breanne's Blazing Beauties Readers Group[1]

Stay up to date and receive a free short story by author Breanne Bergie.

Please subscribe by going to Mrs.BreWrites Website[2]

Follow me at:

Facebook[3]

Instagram[4]

Twitter[5]

1. https://www.facebook.com/groups/1238819146535136
2. **http://mrsbrewrites.wixsite.com/mysite**
3. **http://facebook.com/MrsBreWrites**
4. **https://www.instagram.com/mrs.bre_writes/**
5. **https://twitter.com/MrsBre_Writes**

Printed in Great Britain
by Amazon

63022110R00228